CW01667887

Praise for Blood and Feathers

"A hell of a ride, but heaven to read: eerie, compelling and very funny."
Michael Marshall Smith

"Dark, surreal and wickedly funny, Lou Morgan's reimagining of the war between Heaven and Hell mixes angels, alcohol and ammunition to serve up a joy of a read."
Tom Pollock

"It's a challenge to take concepts older than the calendar and make them seem new. Louise Morgan has done just that. How to describe this, her debut novel? Bloody Heavenly!"
Guy Adams

"Dark, enticing and so sharp the pages could cut you, Blood and Feathers *is a must-read for any fan of the genre."*
Sarah Pinborough

"A storming debut! Lou Morgan writes with confidence, style and verve. Who would have thought that going to Hell could be so much fun? A must-read."
Mike Shevdon

SOLARIS

BLOOD AND FEATHERS

REBELLION

LOU MORGAN

First published 2013 by Solaris
an imprint of Rebellion Publishing Ltd,
Riverside House, Osney Mead,
Oxford, OX2 0ES, UK

www.solarisbooks.com

ISBN: 978 1 78108 122 8

Copyright © Lou Morgan 2013

The right of the author to be identified as the author of this work has been asserted in accordance with the Copyright, Designs and Patents Act 1988.

All rights reserved. No part of this publication may be reproduced, stored in a retrieval system, or transmitted, in any form or by any means, electronic, mechanical, photocopying, recording or otherwise, without the prior permission of the copyright owners.

10 9 8 7 6 5 4 3 2 1

A CIP catalogue record for this book is available from the British Library.

Designed & typeset by Rebellion Publishing

Printed at Nørhaven, Denmark

To Jon.
For believing.

Presume not that I am the thing I was.
– Shakespeare, Henry IV.2

CHAPTER ONE

Fire in the Hole

THE BRICK SAILED through the air, spinning end over end. It was almost graceful... until it smashed through the storefront. On the street outside, a shout went up as three men shoved their way to the front of the crowd, kicked out the remains of the window and stepped through the frame, raising their fists in triumph. There was another cheer, and one of them clambered onto the counter to wrench a television screen off the wall.

The pavements were littered with glass: broken windows, broken bottles, broken everything. People had gathered on the road in the fading light; they stood in knots around the shattered shops, some clutching boxes tightly to themselves, some staring blankly around them as though unsure how they had come to be there. A burning bin smouldered, filling the air with acrid smoke as it melted into the pavement. Distant sirens sounded, but never seemed to get any closer. The mob rampaged up and down the road, tearing boards from windows and cheering its own triumphs as it went.

So intent were the crowd on tearing the street apart, they didn't notice the sudden chill in the May air. Few – if any – saw their breath curling up into the evening like clouds. Without knowing why, they paused, and parted... and a man stepped through the space.

He was dressed entirely in black: his boots, his jeans, his unseasonable coat were black. Even his hair was black... but around his wrist, clearly visible at the edge of his sleeve, was a bright white band, burned into his skin. The same mark was carried by the couple walking behind him: a young woman and a man with a burn-scarred face, laughing and nudging each other as they went.

The crowd broke apart, moving to let them pass, then reformed in their wake. They were like ghosts passing through, watching everyone and everything around them but watched by no-one. The man in the black coat smiled as he walked, and anyone on the street who *had* been watching would have seen that his smile was a little too wide; that he had too many teeth, and a look in his eyes that would cool blood.

But no-one was watching, and the Fallen moved through the riot leaving carnage in their wake.

They turned down a side-street, making their way to an open manhole. With only the briefest of glances behind them, one by one they clambered down the narrow ladder: the man in black first, then the man with the scarred face, and finally the woman. The sewer below was barely even damp: between the cold winter and the long dry spring, there was hardly enough water to wet the soles of their shoes. Stooping slightly in the confines of the tunnel, they walked in near-darkness, far beneath the chaos above.

The man in black came to a halt. There was someone else in the tunnel ahead: another man, leaning back against the curved wall with his arms folded across his chest. The white brand on his wrist shone in the gloom. "You took your time," he said.

"It's not like he's going anywhere, is it?" The man in black indicated a circular grate set into the wall, perhaps six feet in diameter, chained to which was an angel.

His wrists and ankles were outstretched, shackled to the bars. His wings were forced between the bars of the grate, the grey feathers torn and stained with blood. He was stripped to the waist, and jagged cuts criss-crossed his torso, carved into his flesh. His head lolled forward; the water pooling at his feet ran scarlet.

The man in black stepped past the guard and leaned closer to the captive angel, staring at the shackled wrist closest to him. In the darkness, the sigil emblazoned upon it shone like fire, a pattern of sharp angles and lines – its edges blurred by dirt and blood, but clear enough. Shaking his head, he reached forward and grabbed a handful of the prisoner's hair, cruelly twisting it; forcing his chin up. The angel's eyes were swollen almost shut, his face puffy and soft from the beating he'd taken – but he was still able to part his split lips enough to smile... and to spit full in his captor's face.

Disgusted – and not a little surprised – the man in black wrenched his hand away, letting his prisoner's head drop. Wiping his face on one sleeve, he pulled something out of his coat and fumbled with it in the dark. The angel raised his head, the muscles of his neck standing out like cords with the effort, and blinked. "He'll find you, Rimmon. You can run all you like, but he'll find you."

The man in black laughed. "We're counting on it." He gestured to the guard, who picked up a metal can, unscrewed the top and poured the contents over the captured angel's head. The smell of petrol filled the sewer. Still the angel watched as Rimmon held up his lighter, popping the lid open.

"Now. You're one of Michael's boys, so I'm willing to bet this wouldn't normally bother you. But you're Earthbound, and – let's face it – you're not at your best, are you? So..." He tailed off, taking a step back. "Tell them we're coming. If, of course, they find you in time..."

The lighter hit the floor and bounced.

The flint sparked... and suddenly fire was racing up the angel's legs, across his torso and through the feathers of his broken wings, lashing itself to him more tightly than his chains.

Rimmon turned and walked away, the others falling into step behind him. As the Earthbound began to scream, a smile crept across the Fallen's face...

CHAPTER TWO

New Girl

The Halfway to Heaven did not look like the most welcoming of places. To put it another way: from the outside, the Halfway to Heaven looked like a dive. Which it was. A dingy bar halfway down a street; a bar with gloomy windows and a rubbish-strewn alley alongside it, a swing board that hung, creaking, over the pavement, and a doorman with a black coat and an ID badge.

A doorman with a black coat and an ID badge, and wings.

The Halfway to Heaven was a dive, but it was the angels' dive. It was the haunt of the angels serving out their exile – the ones who had been barred from heaven (albeit temporarily) for any number of crimes and for any given length of time. The Halfway was where they drowned their sorrows and traded their war stories. It was their sanctuary: it was where they felt safe – and more importantly, it was where news and gossip were spread. An Earthbound angel is still an angel… and angels talk.

And there had been much to talk about. At first, it had been rumours. Rumours of a half-born, the daughter of a lost angel and a former priest; a half-born who burned. Rumours that she was being protected by none other than Mallory – the closest thing to a leader that the Earthbounds had, and one who was never less than an irritation to their Descended-angel superiors. Rumours that the half-born was being prepared for hell.

For once, the rumours had been true.

All of them.

The half-born, Mallory, the battle at the gates of hell itself – where most of the Halfway's regulars had joined the fight – and the final, triumphant capture of Lucifer's vacant body and the closure of hell. All of it was true.

Except… after a while, the triumphant capture of Lucifer's body didn't feel like such a triumph. After all, what good was his body without his mind? He was still free to hop from body to body, taking possession of his legion of Fallen angels as and when he pleased. Utterly unpredictable and completely unstoppable. And hell? Hell, it turned out, hadn't been so much a prison for the Fallen as their stronghold, and its gates were built not to keep them in but to keep the angels *out*. Nothing remained of it but ash… and the Fallen had scattered to the winds. They could be anywhere.

They were everywhere.

Cut loose, they crawled the cities looking for trouble – and if they didn't find any, they made it their business to start some. Anything to tip the balance ever further in their favour; to sway humanity towards them… and meanwhile, the angels' celebration toasts turned to drowning their despair.

Not that it bothered the woman sitting at the bar, eating stale peanuts out of a bowl. Her hair fell across her face as she picked at them, only occasionally looking up to reach for the glass of water in front of her.

"She doesn't belong here," said the Earthbound at the other end of the bar, speaking to no-one in particular. He had built a little wall out of empty shot glasses in front of him and his speech was slurred, although it was only half past four in the afternoon.

The barman shushed him loudly. "Don't you know who that is?"

"Half-born, slumming it with the Earthbounds?"

"It's *her*."

"Her?"

"Alice."

"Alice?"

"Alice. *That* Alice."

They turned to stare along the bar at her, one more fuzzily than the other. Alice glanced up from her peanuts and gave them a wave, and then went back to crunching her peanuts, as noisily as possible.

"*That* Alice? Fought-with-Lucifer Alice? Into-hell Alice?"

"That Alice."

"I thought she'd be taller. And a redhead."

There was an indignant snort from the other end of the bar; one the barman tried his best to ignore. Instead, he started to dismantle the wall of glasses. "Well, that's her. And she's good to drink in here as long as she wants. She's one of us."

"I don't drink," said Alice, sliding off her stool and brushing peanut skins from her hands. "And I'm not exactly one of you."

"Don't mind him, he's..."

"I get it. He's still adjusting – is that it? Not got used to having his wings clipped. I'm not the one he should be taking it out on, am I?" She smiled unhappily.

"It takes a while."

"I said I get it."

"I mean, *you*. You and Mallory and hell and Lucifer. If it wasn't for you, we wouldn't have Lucifer."

"*We* don't. Michael does. And what do you think he's going to do with him?"

"End it. End the war."

"Really?"

"You kill Lucifer, you end the war. Everyone knows that."

"Huh. Know Michael well, do you?"

"Sure. Well... no. Not personally..."

"Huh." Alice blinked at him. "I do." She slid a couple of coins across the top of the bar. "For the peanuts. And this." Her fingers closed around a slip of paper lying on the bar. Written untidily across it in green ink was a date.

A date, a time and a place... and the word "FALLEN."

* * *

IT HAD BEEN six months. Six months since the angels besieged hell; six months since Alice, along with her mentor Mallory and friend Vin, had climbed back up to the world – cold and exhausted, but victorious. *Moderately* victorious, at least. Six months since she had defied the Archangel Michael, and six months since she had seen Gwyn, Gabriel's favourite, stripped of his wings for betraying them all.

Six months since Michael had warned her that – sooner or later – he would come for her.

Six months since Mallory had left.

She still didn't know how she felt about *that*.

Mallory had, at long last, been able to go home. It was what he wanted – what he needed – and Alice knew she should be happy for him. *She wanted* to be happy for him... But.

However hard she tried, however much she wanted... a part of her still felt the same. Like he had left her; they had *all* left her: with Mallory's wings restored, he was able to go home, and Vin had wasted little time before disappearing back off to Hong Kong. And Alice had looked around at the ruins of her life and wondered what it had all been *for*, exactly. And every time she caught sight of the angelic sigil burned into her wrist, it reminded her of Michael, with his eyes full of spinning fire, and his warning that he *would* come, and she decided it might be best to just get on with things and keep her head down.

If they wanted her – any of them – they knew where to find her.

Her first problem had been finding somewhere to live. With Mallory gone, it seemed only logical that she should take over his home in the sacristy. It also seemed only logical that (given his somewhat laid-back approach to housekeeping) she should give it a thorough clean first. So she did. She scrubbed and polished and threw out a quite extraordinary number of empty bottles, which had been stashed everywhere from under the sink to inside the cold water tank. She washed the mould from the grout and shook the woodlice out of the sofa cushions – feeling only the faintest pang of guilt as she did so, given the number of times she'd woken up face to face with one of them – and she had a close encounter with a cockroach which made her entirely glad she was alone, because she screamed like a little girl. And flapped her hands. And screamed one more time before finally clamping an upturned bucket over the unfortunate creature and sitting on it, just for good measure.

But no matter how hard she scrubbed, she couldn't quite rid herself of the image of Lucifer's eyes, watching her from a face that was not his own.

It was on the Day of the Cockroach that there was a knock at the door; quiet but firm, and Alice ignored it at first. It came again, and she ignored it again. The third time, the knocking grew more insistent, and although she'd planned to ignore it just the same, the sky outside the tiny windows darkened and a pile of Mallory's old papers, stacked in a corner, rustled as though in a breeze. And while the sacristy was draughty, there were limits to what Alice was prepared to ignore.

"Alice," said a voice from the other side of the door. "I'm at the door. Whether you invite me or not, I am coming in – so don't you think we could start this on a more... *civil* footing?"

Alice opened the door.

On the other side was a neat man wearing a dark morning suit. His hair was cropped short and mottled with grey; his beard was clipped close to his chin. One hand was folded behind his back, while the other hung at his side, clutching the brim of a top hat.

"Going to a wedding?" Alice asked.

"Not exactly." He frowned at her, and Alice was startled to see that his eyes were black – as though pupil and iris had merged into one. Still, they twinkled at her.

"So," he said, turning the hat in his fingers, "will you invite me in, or must I invite myself?"

"I haven't decided yet. I have what you might call... *trust* issues. Of course, you could help by telling me who you are. And what you want."

"But of course – how rude of me. My name," he said, shaking out his black wings, "is Adriel. And I'm here to offer you a job."

Alice felt her jaw drop open and snapped it shut. "Adriel."

"Yes. You've heard of me, perhaps?"

"You could say that." She hadn't needed the name. Alice had spent enough time around angels to recognise him; the one who made them all twitchy. Black wings. Black eyes.

The Angel of Death.

"A job."

"A job. Yes."

"'Job' as in 'mission'?"

"No. 'Job' as in 'employment.' Paid employment."

"Why?"

"I'm sorry?" Adriel looked puzzled.

"You're offering me a job. Why? You don't know me."

"I don't need to. I was there, after all, in hell. I saw you, and what I saw impressed me."

"That was kind of a one-off."

"So I should hope. But you impressed me, and I find myself in need of a new member of staff. And I believe you are in need of a job, are you not?"

He wasn't wrong. Alice's own meagre funds hadn't exactly gone far – however careful with them she was – and she was rapidly depleting Mallory's emergency savings... which she had very nearly thrown away, hidden as they were inside an old pizza box. Along with a mummified slice of pizza. It was all well and good, this 'living below the radar' thing, but she still had to eat.

She sighed. Against her better judgement, she asked, "What kind of job?"

"One in a... *sympathetic* working environment."

"Working for you."

"Working for me." He nodded. "Somewhere you needn't worry about the... politics of your actions." He tapped the cuff of his sleeve, where every angel's sigil lay. He meant Michael, and his interest in her: of course he did. "So you know: anything you do while working for me will fall under my jurisdiction – not his."

Alice weighed her options. Or attempted to. She didn't *have* many options. She needed the money, and at least this way she didn't have to worry about explaining to her boss why things around her had a tendency to catch fire.

"And what is it, exactly, that you do?" she asked.

Adriel simply turned his hat over in his hands and smiled. "If you'll permit me, why don't I just show you?"

"No. Absolutely not." Alice folded her arms across her chest and stared at the wide shop frontage: a large window partly obscured by curtains, and a tasteful sign above it.

"Whyever not?" Adriel was a pace behind her. "You've been through hell. This should be easy."

"'Whyever not?' How about we start with the bloody obvious? That you're an *undertaker*?"

"People die, Alice."

"I'm well aware of that, thank you."

"...which means it's good business. We don't tend to experience much fluctuation in trade."

"But an *undertaker*. Seriously?"

"I fail to see your point."

"Of course you do." Alice shook her head. She'd seen enough. "You don't want me in there."

"I thought I'd already made it clear that I do."

"You don't. Not me. Trust me on this. The... my 'gift' as you lot like to call it? It gets triggered. It gets triggered by fear and grief and pain and – to put it bluntly – all those bad things that people feel when somebody dies. All of which they're going to be feeling when they walk through that door." She jabbed her finger at the shop to make her point. "What happens when some dead kid's mother comes in and I set fire to the curtains?"

"I don't think we need quite that level of hyperbole, but I understand your concern. If I thought it was going to be a problem, I wouldn't have made you this offer." He rested a hand on her shoulder and she fought the urge to shrug it off.

She needed the job.

"I'll need to think about it."

"No, you won't. I'll see you here on Monday morning. Wear something..."

"Black?"

"*Appropriate.*" He blinked at her with his black eyes. "Monday, Alice," he said as he moved towards the door. "I think you're going to like it here."

"Sure. Of course I will," she muttered as the door closed behind him. "It's not like I've got much of a choice."

DESPITE HAVING SPENT most of the weekend trying to argue herself out of it, Monday morning found her standing on the doorstep of Adriel's funeral parlour.

The door opened without a sound and as she stepped inside, her feet sank into thick, cream carpet. She hoped it wasn't going to be her job to vacuum it. She was in a waiting area: three comfortable-looking sofas arranged around a low coffee table, complete with a vase of lilies and a box of tissues. Across the room stood a small, dark wooden desk with an old-fashioned blotter and a leather desk diary. And another vase of lilies. Feeling her eyes start to water, Alice wrinkled her nose.

Further back, there were several doors which might have been offices, and another – half-hidden by a curtain – which was almost certainly not.

Unable to hold it back any longer, Alice sneezed. Loudly, and repeatedly. Fumbling in her pockets for a tissue, she sank into one of the sofas as she tried to get a grip on herself... or at least stop her eyes from streaming. Lilies. Of all the possible flowers, it had to be lilies. Eventually, she forced her eyes open to find Adriel sitting on the sofa beside her, watching her with interest.

"Good morning."

"Mordig," Alice said thickly, taking the handkerchief he offered her. "Sorry. Pollen. Can't..."

"I see." He folded his hands in his lap and watched as Alice dabbed at her eyes. What she really wanted to do was blow her nose, but she got the feeling that doing that in someone else's handkerchief was probably not a good idea. Maybe if you offered to wash it...?

"I'm pleased you came."

"But not surprised," she said with a sniff.

He smiled. "No. Not surprised."

"Uh-huh."

"Before we proceed, there are things you need to understand. Firstly, no-one here knows."

"About you, you mean." Alice sighed. Secrets were exhausting. She was learning this the hard way.

"About me. Or you."

"What happened to the 'sympathetic working environment'?"

"I think you'll find I can be very sympathetic. But the staff... they don't know, and that is how it must stay." He leaned forward as he spoke, lowering his voice.

"Never know. Got it." The handkerchief was still balled up in her hand. It felt decidedly soggy.

"Secondly, my name. My name, as far as everyone here is concerned, is Andrew. Andrew Langham. *Mister* Langham to you, especially in front of clients."

"Clients. Yes."

"Which brings me to my next point. You will sit there." He nodded to the desk across the room. "Your job is simply to meet clients as they come in, see that they're comfortable and then to inform either myself or my colleagues that they are here."

"You mean I'm the receptionist."

"If you like. Offer them tea, coffee..."

"I'm not being funny, Adr... *Mister* Langham, but a cup of tea? Really? Like that's going to fix their problems?"

"Alice, don't make the mistake of thinking yourself an expert on death simply because you have a little experience of it." He raised an eyebrow at her, and she wondered whether the sofa was big enough for her to hide under the cushions. But then he smiled, and continued. "You'll settle in soon enough. The staff here are... very human. You'll like them." He stood, and offered her his hand, helping her to her feet. With her free hand, she scrunched the soggy handkerchief into her pocket.

"Let me show you around."

And he led her towards the first of the doors.

Two of the doors opening off the reception led to near-identical rooms furnished with yet more sofas and low tables, all tastefully decorated in varying shades of beige. The third opened onto Adriel's office, with an enormous desk and shelves full of old ledgers. "Funeral records," he said, seeing her eyes settle on them. "We have a responsibility to keep them." He closed the door again before she could ask any more. The two chapels-of-rest, Alice decided to give as wide a berth as humanly – or inhumanly – possible, especially once he informed her that they were currently occupied. Instead, Adriel ushered her toward the curtain.

The door behind the curtain led to a gloomy corridor running out to the back of the building. There was a small staff kitchen, and a set of steel swing doors opening off the corridor to the left. Alice approached them, but Adriel placed a hand on her arm. "You don't need to go back there," was all he said, and she hoped the relief didn't show on her face – although it would have vanished when he continued, "but I do need to show you the barn." He opened another door.

Alice's hand flew to her mouth before she could stop it. The 'barn' was at least three times the size of the other rooms combined, and full of coffins. Coffins: leaning on their ends against the wall, or stacked on shelves, all neatly labelled according to height. Or length, depending on how you looked at it. A rack of shelves on one side of the space held what looked like rolls of fabric, and plastic-wrapped pieces of brass in baskets. Adriel brushed past her and beckoned her to follow, lifting something from a basket and handing it to her. It was a handle. A coffin handle.

Alice swallowed hard.

Adriel didn't seem to notice, and was instead pointing out the different items on the shelves. "Satin, for lining. And the staple-gun, for fixing it, as well as the staples. It jams sometimes: the screwdriver is kept over there." He pointed to a lower shelf and she nodded, wondering how she'd ended up here and whether she hadn't made a terrible mistake.

And then the door creaked open, and everything changed.

"ANDREW? IT'S MRS Jackson, I... Oh." The man who had stuck his head into the room stopped short when he saw Alice. There was a moment of silence, and Adriel looked from one to the other before clearing his throat.

"Alice, this is Toby: one of my assistants. Toby? Alice. She'll be joining us from today."

"Alice. It's nice to meet you," said Toby with a broad smile. A scar curved around the edge of his cheek, making his grin slightly uneven. "I'd shake your hand, but..." He waved a rubber-gloved hand at her. Much to Alice's surprise, she realised she couldn't reply. In fact, it was all she could do not to blush.

"Well," said Adriel. "Toby, I'll be with you momentarily."

Toby nodded, and with another glance at Alice, withdrew his head from the doorway. The door swung closed behind him.

Adriel turned to Alice. "They can't know, Alice. None of them." He held the door for her and ushered her through, back out into the hallway. "You'll meet the others later. If you'll excuse me, I have some business to attend to in the... with Toby." He nodded back towards the waiting area. "Perhaps you would like to familiarise yourself with the desk?"

"But what do I do? If someone comes...?"

"You'll know what to do, Alice. It's why you're here." And with a smile, he turned on his heel and walked towards the steel doors of the mortuary.

ALICE CONSIDERED THE sofas in the waiting room for a moment, then thought better of it and sank into the chair behind the desk. It wasn't nearly as uncomfortable as it looked – which was more than she could say for her shoes. Bearing in mind Adriel's comment to wear something 'appropriate,' she had forced herself to go and buy a pair of shoes Which Were Not Trainers, and as a result, she now felt as though a whole tribe of rats were gnawing at her toes – not to mention slightly resentful at having to chip into the last of her cash reserves. She told herself it was an investment. A back-aching, toe-killing investment. Groaning, she kicked them off under the desk and curled her sore toes into the thick carpet. A fly was making lazy circles over one of the flower arrangements – and although she couldn't hear it, there was something about it that annoyed her. A fly in a funeral parlour just seemed... *wrong*, somehow. She watched the fly for a moment as it spiralled around the flowers, then nodded in satisfaction as it burst into flames and disappeared in a little cloud of ash.

"Alice, was it?" The voice came from behind her, and made her jump out of the chair.

"What? Yes. Alice. Me. Right." She sounded flustered. She knew she sounded flustered. She tried not to.

"I just wanted to come and say hello properly," Toby said, stepping away from the wall where he'd been leaning. Had he seen the fly, she wondered? If he had, he didn't say anything. That would be a good start, wouldn't it: not even been in the place five minutes and giving the game away? Alice made a mental note to be more careful. The 'secret identity' side of this was clearly going to be harder than she'd expected. Alice thought she should probably be grateful that Adriel hadn't wanted her to be a spy.

Toby was holding out his hand to her – minus the glove, this time. He watched her staring at it. "I *did* wash them, if that's what you're thinking." He was grinning again, teasing her. She smiled, and took his hand. It was warm and soft, and his grip felt strong.

"Nice to meet you. Sorry. It's just that you startled me a bit. I was miles away."

"Wondering how the hell you ended up here, right?"

"Something like that, yes."

"Don't worry about it. It takes a bit of getting used to, you know? We're just like any other office, really, when you get down to it."

"Mmm. The difference being that here you've got dead people in the filing cabinets."

"I never thought about it like that," he laughed. Alice shrugged, and he continued. "We take care of people. That's all it is. The dead, the living; we take care of them. I... are you alright?" he tailed off, a look of concern on his face.

"What? Oh, yes. Fine." She wrinkled her nose and gestured to the floor beneath the desk. "My shoes. Now, those *are* going to take some getting used to."

"At least you don't have to wear the hat," he said, and Alice had to remind herself that Toby was entirely himself – and entirely what he seemed to be. Toby was human. Toby was *normal*. A normal person who knew nothing about angels, nothing about the Fallen. Just a *person*; a person who spent his time with other Just People. And Alice needed to be around people; to get on with her life. Or start having one, at least.

And in the meantime, she'd just try to overlook the fact the Angel of Death was her boss.

THE MORNING HAD not gone well. So far, Alice had knocked over a vase of lilies, spilled tea on the appointment book (and, while trying to mop it up, managed to smear the ink across today's page – which meant she would later have to tell Adriel that his three o'clock appointment was with a Mrs Hrrrddddgz) and had set off the smoke alarm in the kitchen. With the kettle.

No. The morning had not gone well. And it was only eleven o'clock.

SHE WAS STILL frantically trying to yank the battery out of the smoke alarm when Toby strolled into the kitchen, took one look at her and shook his head. Without a word, he opened one of the drawers and pulled out a wooden spoon, then reached up and whacked the side of the alarm casing with the spoon. Hard. The siren faltered... then picked up again, even louder. Toby pulled a face, and hit it again. It let out a final strangled squawk and stopped. The silence made Alice's ears ring.

"Thanks," she said weakly.

He grinned at her. "No problem. It's a bit touchy – next time, just give it a smack on the head."

"Is that how you solve all your problems?"

"Only the ones that don't shut up..."

Alice wasn't quite sure how to answer that, and Toby seemed to realise he'd said something off. "It was a joke, Alice."

"Whatever."

"Hey... did I say something wrong?"

"No, nothing. It's fine." She rubbed her forehead. "It's just... headache. Loud, you know?" He was watching her carefully, and he looked so serious that Alice felt suddenly awkward. He must have felt it too; he stepped back and started fiddling with the box of teabags on the counter.

"How'd you set it off, anyway?"

"I think the kettle... shorted. The fuse." Alice pointed to the blackened switch on the base of the kettle. "There was a sort of bang, and this big puff of smoke, and..." She shrugged. She wasn't about to tell him that she had managed to melt it, all because she wasn't paying enough attention to what she was doing.

The job wasn't exactly easy. Well. That wasn't strictly true: the job itself was fine. It mostly consisted of answering the phone, making notes in the day book, refilling the tissue boxes and making tea. A lot of tea. There were six of them there, not including Adriel. Besides Toby and Alice, there were the embalmer, the driver and two pallbearers – although the latter seemed to spend most of their time sitting in the kitchen and playing cards, looking for all the world like a couple of gorillas who'd been forced into suits.

So there were six of them, and Adriel, and they all rubbed along reasonably well. Alice kept her distance as best she could but somehow Toby always seemed to be around, asking whether she wanted a cup of tea, whether she was *making* a cup of tea, how she was doing, whether she had seen this film or that film... it just went on. And while it was nice; while it made her feel like a normal, real human being again – something she'd not felt in far too long – it was strange. To feel *normal* was... strange.

He had no idea that when the first clients on her first day had walked in through the door, Alice felt like she had been punched in the stomach. Everything about them shouted their loss out loud for the world to hear... but the only one who heard it was Alice. Alice heard it, and she felt it, and her heart broke. And it kept on happening. Every time the door opened, she felt it again and again and again. Over and over, until she couldn't take it any longer and she stumbled into Adriel's office and told him she had to go. He looked up from his paperwork and nodded at her, and she found her way home without remembering a step of the way; she locked the door to the sacristy behind her and she sat on the floor and she burned and she burned and she burned – and when the tears came, as she knew they would, they left tracks of fire down her cheeks.

Compared with that first day, melting the kettle was a definite improvement.

As she settled back down at the desk, a police car raced by with its siren howling. There had been more of them over the last few days, and if the papers were anything to go by, it was only going to get worse. The city was on edge. The riots were spreading, and however much everyone tried to ignore them and carry on as normal, it was getting harder. It had begun a few weeks ago: a simple scuffle between some teenagers on the far side of town, and from there it had spread until, every night, the streets became a battleground. Broken glass sparkled on the pavements in the mornings, and every day it seemed that another shop or office had had its windows smashed or its door kicked in... Oddly, though, no-one ever seemed to touch Langham Funerals, which remained an island of calm in the chaos. The others all said that it was down to respect for the dead. Alice suspected otherwise.

"Alice?"

"Mmph?" She hadn't realised Adriel had come out of his office.

"Are you alright?"

"Yes. Fine. I'm good. I'm fine."

"Alice..."

"I'm knackered." She slumped in her chair. "I'll replace the kettle."

"The kettle?" Adriel raised an eyebrow slightly, but otherwise his composure didn't change one bit.

"It's a thing. It's fine. I'm fine. I'm just... tired."

"You're finding this more of a challenge than you expected." It wasn't a question, and Alice snorted.

"No. I'm finding it exactly as much of a challenge as I expected, which is what I tried to explain to you."

"And yet, even though you've been here such a short time, I'm told what a difference you make."

"I... oh?" She had been about to make an excuse for whatever it was she'd done wrong... and then realised it wasn't a criticism. Not at all.

"I'm told you make the shop feel warmer."

"Yes, well," she muttered. "That's hardly a surprise, is it?"

"More alive." Adriel blinked at her. "I thought you should know. You're good at this, Alice."

And without another word, he turned and padded back to his office. Whether he would still think she was good at this (whatever *this* was) once she'd told him about Mrs Hrrrddddgz was another matter.

"You off?"

"Almost. I'm heading out in a minute. You?"

"More or less. I need to drop the suit off with the cleaner." He waved a plastic suit-hanger at her. "So. I was wondering."

"You were?"

"Alice, could you shut up for a sec, yeah? You're not half making this hard."

"Sorry." She did her best to look apologetic. "You were wondering."

"I was wondering..." He paused, as though he was expecting her to interrupt. She watched him expectantly; he took this as a sign and carried on. "I was wondering whether you might like to come out for a drink tonight? Later, you know?" Alice could feel his relief from the other side of the desk. At least it explained why he'd been so twitchy all day.

"Are you asking me out?"

"Do you want me to be?"

"Maybe. Although if you were, I'd hope you would be a little more definite about it."

"Then, yes. Yes, I am."

She was about to answer when she remembered. *Tonight.* She clapped a hand to her forehead. "Shit. Toby – I'm really sorry..."

His face fell. "No problem,"

"No, really – I am. I have to be somewhere tonight. Honestly, I do. God, I'm such an idiot: I should have said. Could we maybe do it another night?"

"Tomorrow?" He had started to perk up again.

"Tomorrow. Definitely." Alice nodded, praying that she could actually deliver on the promise.

"Alright, then. Tomorrow. After work." Toby was beaming now, shrugging his shoulders happily. It was funny the difference it made: he had seemed so unlike himself all day, and now everything was normal. She almost felt sorry for him...

"Sure. Look – I've got to go; how about we sort it out tomorrow?" She was waiting now, waiting for him to go, because she hadn't been making excuses. She had somewhere she needed to be this evening. And Toby, with all his normality, couldn't ever hope to understand why.

CHAPTER THREE

The Prisoner

FROM THE WINDOW, the Archangel Michael could see nothing but the sea. The air smelled of salt, of the open skies and of sunshine, and if he leaned out and looked down, he would see the tourists bustling about on the island below: humans with their maps and their cameras and their sunglasses. Small things in which he had no interest. Michael had more important things on his mind, which was precisely why he had come back to his fortress.

He rubbed a hand across his face as he tried to tune out Gabriel's whining. It wasn't easy: to say that Gabriel had not taken his punishment *well* would be an understatement. After all, as he was fond of pointing out – frequently – for an Archangel to have his wings clipped, to be sentenced to exile as an Earthbound, was unheard of. Until now.

Did Michael regret what he had done to Gabriel? Not for a moment.

Did he wish he had cut out Gabriel's tongue when he clipped his wings? Absolutely.

The battle for hell had not gone as Michael had hoped, something he blamed largely on Gabriel and his little favourite, Gwyn. Gwyn, he had taken care of; Gabriel was proving to be more problematic. Against his better judgement, Michael had offered him the chance to earn his wings back; he had initially jumped at the chance, but as the days passed, Gabriel grew more and more restless. Recently, he'd moved on from simply grumbling about his punishment to accusing Michael of tricking him, of giving him an impossible task and condemning him to an eternity of hopeless servitude. That little outburst had earned him a week in a windowless cell several floors below ground, giving him a chance to consider the exact meaning of 'eternity' and 'hopeless.' Needless to say, he had returned refreshed and reinvigorated. And quiet. It hadn't lasted…

Michael turned away from the window and back to the room. It was large and stone-built, with narrow windows on three sides giving views over the coast below, and a heavy table pushed against one wall, piled high with papers. Several wooden chairs with curved backs were lined up in front of it; the only other furnishing was an ornate seat carved from stone, set on a dais to one side of the room.

"And what is it you would have me do, Zak? Hmm?"

"I want you to be clear about the risks. Reuniting Lucifer, body and soul…" The angel sitting on the lower step of the dais shook his head and held up his hands. "But why would you listen to me?"

"Don't push your luck." Michael scowled, and Zadkiel eased himself to his feet and strode towards him. He had deep lines etched into his forehead and hooded eyes, but his face was round, and somehow soft. Zadkiel had been listening to Gabriel speak, rolling a coin across his knuckles thoughtfully, while Michael stared out of the window. Every now and again, he would roll his eyes and chime in, but mostly, he just listened – and because he listened, when he chose to speak, Michael tended to pay attention. Zadkiel was his unofficial lieutenant, the one soul he trusted, and the closest thing he had to a friend.

It was Zadkiel who had taken Michael to task over hell: over Alice, over Gwyn and Gabriel, and – above all – burning hell itself. "What the fuck, man? What. The. Fuck?" he had shouted, jabbing his fingers into Michael's shoulder with every word. And Michael had glared at him and spread his burning wings, and Zadkiel had looked him straight in the eye and simply said, "There was a line, back there, and you crossed it. I won't let you do it again." And with one more jab, he had walked away.

If it had been anyone else, they would have had to face the full, inescapable weight of Michael's wrath – but it was Zadkiel, and loyalty had its privileges. And he *was* loyal. It was Zadkiel who had hauled Lucifer's body, still imprisoned in its cage of ice, out of the lowest levels of hell. He had followed Michael to war in hell without a word of complaint, and when Michael refused to leave his prisoner in anyone else's hands, instead of going home, Zadkiel had followed him behind the thick stone walls he'd designed for precisely this purpose.

Which is how Michael found himself in the uppermost room of his earthly stronghold – a fortified priory on an island, linked to the mainland by only the narrowest of causeways, and its lower levels besieged by tourists – along with his closest ally, his greatest enemy (or at least, his enemy's body, in its cell of unthawing ice) and a recently-Earthbound Archangel having a tantrum.

Michael could think of places he would rather be.

Zadkiel stepped past Michael and leaned out of the window, his hands wrapped around the edges of the frame. He looked straight down at the people below. It was a running joke among the angels: the constant coming and going of the crowds had led some of them to nickname the place "No Man's Land," although they were careful never to say it too loudly around Michael. He was proud of his island, and had interfered in its construction until he was happy with it. "If they're going to name the place after me, I might as well have some say in it," he had said. And they did, and he had... and the final result was as defensible as it was beautiful, and they had called it Mont Saint-Michel. As for the visitors below, as far as they were concerned, this was somewhere to take photos and buy postcards; where the guided tours ran every thirty minutes in seven different languages. There were fewer of them lately, the tourists, far fewer, and those who did come seemed distracted. Quiet. Subdued. Desperate. It wouldn't be long before there were none at all, and the streets would stand empty.

When the world was as it should be, they came like a tide, sweeping through the steep streets below the priory – streets cluttered with restaurants and souvenir shops selling statues supposedly of Michael (which were a source of never-ending amusement for Zak) – and just like the sea they retreated soon enough, never questioning why a couple of hours in a place like that should leave them feeling so different... never knowing what hid in plain sight above and among them. He walked among them, sometimes, looking like any other man, with his hands in his pockets. He listened to their memories as they drifted past. He watched lovers walking hand-in-hand through the winding alleyways or along the walls, and if anyone should happen to see him, he would smile and nod, and turn away before they could see the sudden sadness in his eyes.

Whether there were many or few, Zadkiel walked among them, and he listened. Above all, he listened... and lately, he did not like what he had heard.

"Just how long are you willing to wait?" he asked.

"As long as it takes," said Michael.

"We might not *have* that long." Zadkiel pulled himself back inside, and sat on the windowsill, looking at Michael. "You may have his body, but his mind's still loose. The Twelve are still loose..."

"Not all of them."

"You're telling me he hasn't promoted? There's always Twelve, Michael. Always will be." He folded his arms across his chest. "And all the while they're out there, their influence is growing. I can *feel* it."

"Nonsense. You're starting to sound like Raphael..."

"Did it ever occur to you he might be right?"

"We've never been so close. Don't you understand, Zak? The war would be over. *Forever.*"

"And as I keep trying to tell you, look at what he's doing *without* his body: what do you think Lucifer could do if we force him back *into* it?"

"Without his mind, his body is of no use to me."

"And locked up, it's of no use to him. He's not stupid, Michael. How do you know he couldn't go right back in there if he saw any value in it?"

"No," Michael rubbed his chin, scuffing his foot against one of the steps. "He's cut himself free. He thinks he'll be safe. Thinks he can hide."

"He's not *hiding*. The things they're doing... the hold they've got..." Zadkiel frowned, closing his eyes, and the lines on his face deepened. "The things these people remember, Michael. The things they've *seen*. The Fallen aren't running. They're taunting us. The war's not over, it just escalated. I didn't even know that was *possible*! They're not content with the scraps any longer. They want it *all*. And we've made sure that they have absolutely nothing to lose."

"There's always something for them to lose."

"You sure about that?" Zadkiel glanced back over his shoulder and out of the window. "Because from where I'm sitting, it looks like the only ones with something to lose are us. And them." He jerked his head back at the window. "All I'm asking is that you consider how much you're prepared to sacrifice for the sake of being right."

Fire flared around the window, pouring out of the stonework and along the floor, as Michael finally lost his temper. But Zadkiel was already gone – slipping out through the open window and opening his wings.

* * *

"ARE YOU QUITE FINISHED?" Gabriel was still clutching a bundle of papers to his chest. Michael glared at him as the fire receded. He would deal with Zadkiel later.

"Fine," he snapped, waving Gabriel across the room. The other angel dropped the papers on the table, on top of the ones already there.

"I might have found something. In the archives..."

Since their arrival – complete with Lucifer's body and the majority of Michael's choir – Gabriel had spent his time working in the archives. Not the priory's archives, which were popular with scholars for their collection of early-medieval manuscripts ("pretty," Gabriel scoffed, "but pointless") but the *other* archives – the ones holding Michael's library, the history of the angels. This was to be Gabriel's punishment and his redemption: find the way to destroy Lucifer. "You wanted to be the one to end the war," said Michael as he had unlocked the door to Gabriel's cell. "Here's your chance."

Gabriel smoothed the roll of parchment out on the table, and pointed to a single line of looping text. "There."

"Is that all?" Michael snorted, peering over this shoulder. "This is nothing." The parchment began to blacken at the edges, curling up and in on itself. "Come and see me when you've uncovered something useful, Gabriel." And with that, the Archangel swept out of the room, leaving Gabriel shaking with fury.

On the street below, a young man stopped to take a photograph of his pretty new wife as she stood in one of the priory gardens. She smiled, and posed for the picture – then, as usual, demanded to see it so she could decide whether or not to delete it. And while she decided her appearance was satisfactory, she frowned at the camera screen – because although the day was bright and warm, and the sky was a bright cloudless blue, the tower at the back of the shot had a peculiar blue halo... almost as though it had been struck by lightning.

* * *

SOME TIME LATER, a door on the lowest level of Mont Saint-Michel opened in the dark. Far below the rooms Michael kept for himself, or the main body of the priory, or the tourists, lay the oldest part of the stronghold: the chapel. Abandoned soon after the main priory church, with its soaring roof and bright-stained glass, was built (under Michael's watchful eye, naturally), the chapel had been forgotten by all but the angels. Sea-water seeped through the masonry, and the only light came from candles scattered around the room. No-one ever lit them: should Michael walk in, they simply lit themselves and that was good enough for him. It didn't ever occur to him that they might not do the same for everyone... or if it did, he didn't really care. So when Gabriel crept into the chapel, it was dark – until he opened his arms. Electricity bounced across the walls and vaulted roof, arcing around him and filling the chamber with brilliant white light... which slowly collected itself around a single lightbulb left lying on a mildewed bench. The bulb glowed gently as Gabriel closed the door behind him.

"He thinks he can treat me like a child. Like a child!" White sparks spat from his hair as he paced the gloomy chapel. "I've been nothing but loyal – *nothing*. Haven't I done everything he ever asked? Haven't I done my utmost? Have..." He tailed off as he remembered that he was not alone.

In the corner, half-hidden from the light, stood a large block of ice. Sturdy-looking chains were wrapped around it, secured with a dozen padlocks the size of a man's hand. They were more for show than anything else: the ice showed no sign of melting, but knowing the chains were there made Michael's choir feel better. Because inside the ice, his eyes open and unseeing, his face set in a permanent sneer, was Lucifer.

CHAPTER FOUR

Controlled Drowning

THE DOOR WOULDN'T open, not even with a good kick. Not entirely surprised, Alice backed up a couple of steps and tried again, glad she had switched her work shoes for something a little more sensible. Still nothing. She sighed, and looked at the side of the building. There was a small window a little way down the alley, with a pile of rotten-looking crates underneath it, and shards of broken glass sticking out of the frame. It looked about the right size. She knocked the worst of the glass out of the frame and clambered through, dropping to the floor on the other side. A cloud of dust kicked up from beneath her feet as she landed, and somewhere a bird took off, startled by the intrusion, but other than that everything was still and quiet. It didn't seem like anyone had heard...

Except, of course, for the angels.

Huddled around the walls, they straightened up as she climbed inside. Earthbounds and half-borns; all different ages, all different choirs, all coming together for one reason.

To fight the Fallen.

It was always the Earthbounds: never the Descendeds. Never the ones who could make it an easy fight. They were all so busy hunting the *other* Fallen, Lucifer's generals – who were known as the Twelve to most, and as "a fucking nightmare" to Mallory – that these minor battles, these backyard skirmishes, always fell to the Earthbounds and whatever allies they could scrape together. Never mind that the small fights were the ones that did the most damage. Never mind that even the lowliest, weakest of the Fallen could do untold damage if they got the chance – and more importantly, *would*. Multiply it by a hundred, a thousand, a hundred thousand and the odds were not in the angels' favour.

Alice was not the only one who had realised what was happening. With nowhere to retreat to, the Fallen had decided to go for broke and throw everything they had at the world. No retreat, no surrender... and no mercy. The bruises from her own battles had barely faded when the first Earthbound had found her, just as Mallory had said they would.

"They'll come to you, and they'll want you to lead them. And they'll be right, because you'll lead them like no-one else could – because you *get* it. You know what's at stake, and you know the price. But this kind of thing... once you're in, you're in. No backing out."

Alice had restrained herself from telling him that, actually, she'd been in since the day he'd turned up on her doorstep. Since before then, even: since the day she was born. She'd known that this would only set him off on one of his rambles on 'choices,' and she just didn't have the energy.

Of course, he'd been right, and sure enough, the notes had started turning up at the Halfway, all of them exactly the same. A date, a time, a place and a fight. Yes, Mallory had been right. Like it or not, she was now so far in that she didn't think she'd ever be able to get out again.

Which left her clutching a tatty bit of paper in a dirty warehouse with broken glass on the floor, and a bunch of dishevelled Earthbounds waiting for her... just as they had been the time before, and the time before that, and all the other times. Because they *had* come, and she had gone with them. She had gone because she was needed. Or because she needed to *be* needed. She hadn't quite worked out which.

An Earthbound with untidy reddish-brown hair and a scattering of freckles across his nose, Zadkiel's sigil just visible at the edge of his sleeve, nodded at her as she brushed dust and glass from her sleeves; stepping closer, he tucked his wings tightly behind him. "They came in about four o'clock. Went straight up and we've not seen them since."

"You're sure they're still here?"

"Where else are they going to go?"

"Anywhere. They could go anywhere."

THE STAIRS WERE pressed metal, the treads rusted through in places, stretching up to the first floor in a straight line. The upper floor of the warehouse was entirely in darkness, and Alice raised her hands. Sparks drifted up from her palms, dancing and spinning away, tiny stars pricking the dark. Behind her, she could hear the rustling of feathers as the angels fell into line. Without a word, she put her foot on the lowest tread and fire raced up the handrails, blazing ahead of her as the angels followed.

The Fallen would know they were coming now: that was the point. It was too late for them to run, and even if they tried – which, in Alice's painful experience, they wouldn't – there were more Earthbounds outside, surrounding the building. Some of them had been in hell. Some of them had not. All of them were just as eager to fight... and Alice wanted the Fallen to know they were ready.

The upper floor was little more than a steel platform, wedged into the shell of the warehouse and supported by girders, but one corner was partitioned off behind a solid-looking slab of metal, resting on tracks set into the floor. A door. Fire streamed out and across it, making it tremble, until it buckled, one corner twisting away from the wall.

Alice watched as the huge door shook harder and harder... then ducked as it tore completely free with a horrible groan, flying over their heads and crashing onto the concrete floor below in a thick cloud of dust. As the dust cleared, Alice glanced up and ahead from her position on the stairs... and she saw them.

There were maybe a dozen of them, standing in a line just behind the door's runners, grinning at her with the blackened ruins of their wings extended. She recognised one or two of them, but it was the man in the middle who caught her eye. A tattoo covered the entire lower half of his face: twisting blue lines which seemed to writhe across his skin... and as she watched, one of the tattoos peeled away from his face, reaching towards her.

Too late to turn back now.

The tattooed Fallen threw back his head and let out a howl that sounded more animal than man, and the stand-off was broken. Alice took the last two stairs in a single step, racing towards the Fallen with the angels at her back. Some of the Fallen stepped forward to meet them; some dropped into a crouch with their hands out in front of them. Some even turned and dropped back into the room. Only their leader stood firm, his eyes on Alice, the ink lines on his face winding around his jaw and, one by one, pulling out and away from him.

Their eyes locked as she ran towards him, surprised – as always – by how calm she felt. She could feel the fear of the others around her, some of them angels, some of them Fallen, but none of it was hers. She was not afraid: the fire that burned around her wrists and in her hair and in her footsteps saw to that – stripping away the cold and the dark and everything else she felt inside, emptying her out. She did not feel afraid; she felt alive.

The first of the Fallen to reach her threw out his arms as though to catch her between them. Alice ducked smoothly and twisted away, leaving his hands to close on empty air. Pivoting on her heel, she kicked up and out with her other foot, slamming it into the middle of his chest. He flew back in a cloud of flame. To her left, one of the Earthbounds from Gabriel's choir had another of the Fallen pinned down, hand clamped over his mouth and a halo of lightning crackling around the Fallen's head as his eyes rolled back in their sockets.

The only light came from the sparks still hanging overhead, and it wasn't enough. It was too dark, and there were too many of the Fallen. A scream cut through the air – a man's voice, whether angel or Fallen, Alice couldn't tell... and she realised she had lost her opponent. He had been *right* there, right in front of her, but then she had been distracted by the other Fallen, and she could have kicked herself for being taken in so easily. Of course she'd been distracted: that's what he'd wanted. And she wasn't going to let him get away. Shutting out the chaos around her, Alice took a deep breath and closed her eyes... and the air above her erupted into boiling orange light. Flames scudded through the air and lapped at the walls.

Shadows crawled along the floor, twisted by the movement of the flames overhead; fingers reaching out to claw at Alice as she moved through the fight. The Earthbounds were proving as vicious as the Fallen, and several of the enemy were already down. Judging by the angles of their limbs, or the thick puddles around them, they wouldn't be getting up again.

At the far side of the floor, she saw an Earthbound in the grip of one of the Fallen, and with a sickening lurch in the pit of her stomach she realised it had to be another of the Twelve. He was half a head taller than anyone else there, and his fists were wrapped with what looked like barbed wire. Every blow he landed raked bloody holes in the helpless angel's skin, and Alice could do little more than watch in horror as he sank his teeth into the angel's neck. He tore out a mouthful of flesh, spitting it onto the floor with a laugh – and then his eyes met hers. His lips peeled back into a sharp smile, blood still dripping from his teeth. He dropped the body of the Earthbound and stepped over him, beckoning her... and was immediately thrown sideways by another of the Earthbounds, who hurled himself straight at the Fallen. Tangled together, they staggered backwards in a whirl of feathers and blood, crashing through the remains of a shattered window.

A Fallen with a bloodied nose stumbled into her from nowhere, and she shoved him away, knocking him to the floor, jumping clear of his hands as he reached for her. And across the room, the other was waiting.

The blue lines of his tattoos writhed around his jaw, almost completely covering the grin plastered across his face. Even at this distance she could hear him taunting her. "The half-breed! I thought you'd never come."

The burst of flame she sent his way caught him off guard, dropping him to the floor. He rolled, but picked himself up in an instant and, before she could react, hurled himself at her. And it was only as his body collided with hers that she realised the tattoos were not vines, as she had at first thought, but snakes. Actual, live snakes. And each of them was snapping at her with sharp silver fangs.

"What the...?" Horrified, she threw him off and pulled herself clear.

He crouched low, and as the snakes drew back around his face, preparing to strike, she saw him grin again. "Surprise!" He threw himself at her again, but this time she was ready, and curled her body away from his; his blow missed her throat and connected with her ribs. He staggered slightly, off balance, and Alice scrambled to her feet, pushing him away with all the force she could muster. He fell forwards, away from her, and the snakes all whipped their heads around and glared back at her, hissing and snapping their jaws. "That is *not* right," Alice muttered as she ducked an Earthbound flying overhead, his wings trailing smoke.

Glancing up, she realised she was handicapping them: not being an angel, it was easy to forget that one of the greatest advantages even the Earthbounds had over the Fallen was the use of their wings. They may not be able to fly far, but they could use them enough, and by slapping a great big burning ceiling on the room to give them light, she'd levelled the playing field for the Fallen. With a 'whoomp,' the plane of fire shot upwards, giving the Earthbounds room to operate. The only problem was that it was now directly beneath the roof... and the roof would burn.

A cold, stabbing pain in her shoulder snapped her attention back to the fight, where an inky-blue snake was sinking its fangs into her shoulder-blade, making her yelp in pain. Inwardly, she cursed herself for letting him get so close – then clamped her hand around the snake's head. It burst into flame, the head shrinking to ash and a ripple of fire chasing all the way back along its body to its tail. Which was tattooed onto its owner's face.

He threw his hands up over his cheeks as the fire ripped through his skin, burning out the tattooed snakes – and when he peeled his fingers away, there was nothing left but charred flesh, and a ragged hole in one side of his face. With a screech, he leapt at her. She tried to jump back, but lost her balance, her foot sliding on the slippery floor. She was already halfway down when he landed on her, rolling her onto her back and pinning her down, raining blows down on her as she tried to wrap her arms around her head to protect herself.

From far away, she heard a vaguely familiar voice: one of the Earthbounds, the one from Zadkiel's choir who had spoken to her earlier. She couldn't make out what he was saying – her ears were covered by her arms and everything was muffled – and this Fallen showed no sign of letting up. If she didn't stop him soon, he would simply beat her to death, but she couldn't do anything until she knew... and she couldn't know until she heard....

Bracing herself for the pain, she pulled one arm free and wrenched her head up, hard and fast, directly into his forehead. There was an awful crack of bone as skull met skull, but he was so shocked that she'd actually headbutted him, he hesitated. Just for a moment, but it was enough; through the ringing in her ears and the thick black curtain falling around her, she heard the voice again.

"Alice! Clear!"

They were clear. There was only her left... only her, and the remaining Fallen.

The snake-man had recovered himself enough to sneer down at her. "This was easier than I was expecting. You should know that."

"Funny," said Alice, gritting her teeth, "I was about to say the same to you."

She threw her arms around him, drawing him close and holding him to her as the room filled with fire.

The last thing he saw was Alice's eyes as she pulled him in, filled with triumph and spinning flames.

THE FIRE TOOK everything. Buried everything. It made her feel safe, wrapped in the flames. And then it died away, and there was only Alice. Only Alice, lying on the floor, surrounded by ash and scorch marks. Only Alice, bloodied and bruised and aching all over. Smoke curled from the rafters, and the floor glowed in places, the steel puckered from the heat.

Alice lay on her back in the middle of the floor, breathing the boiling air and wondering exactly how much it was going to hurt when she stood up, and then she heard feathers moving above her.

"Need a lift?" The Earthbound was hovering just above her, his wings beating lazily.

"Show-off," she groaned, easing herself upright.

He shrugged. "Floor's a bit... unstable, thanks to you." He pointed at a ragged hole in the floor just to Alice's left. Something unpleasantly liquid was bubbling around the edges.

"I'll be honest. I don't make a habit of accepting lifts from strange men..."

"You might want to make an exception. What with the floor about to fall apart." He held a hand out to her, and – wincing – she took it. "Name's Castor."

"Nice to meet you, Castor. I'm Alice." She allowed herself to be lifted clear, and carried across the floor. Castor gently set her down on the cooler steel of the stairs.

"I know. I was at the gate into hell."

"I missed that bit. I was... busy." It didn't quite cover it, but it sounded slightly better than *Actually, I was fighting with my dead mother, who was trying to kill me at the time. I won.*

"It was quite a show. Maybe not as big a stunt as the one you pulled: you burned hell, didn't you?"

"No." Her voice was sharper than she'd meant it to sound. "No. That was Michael. All Michael." There was a worrying creak from overhead, and Alice remembered the roof. "We need to go. It's not safe..."

As if to prove her point, a siren sounded somewhere nearby.

Half-running, half-stumbling down the stairs with her ribs and shoulders screaming, Alice felt a tug at her shoulder and Castor pressed something into her hand as he ran past her. It was small and curved, and cold. As she reached the ground, she stopped just long enough to open her fist and peer inside. A tooth. No... a fang. One of the tattoo-snake's fangs. It had stuck in there. She stared at it for a moment, more than a little shocked – and it was only the siren sounding directly outside the front of the warehouse that brought her back to herself. Balling her fist around the tooth again, she clambered out of the same broken window she had come in, and hurried away.

Toby had heard the siren, but there didn't seem to be any sign of a car or fire engine now. Not that it mattered; he was only being nosy, and could do with something to brighten up the walk home from the pub. It wasn't like sirens were a rarity these days, anyway. Not with the riots, and everything else that seemed to be going on. He'd left his friends watching the football; he wasn't in the mood. He must have been lousy company, because they didn't try to persuade him to stay. They weren't exactly great conversationalists themselves this evening, but he took the hint. Besides, an early night would do him good.

He turned up the collar of his jacket and stuck his hands in his pocket, whistling tunelessly as he walked – and then something caught his eye. He'd only seen it for a second, just as he passed the end of an alley, and when he looked again there was nothing there. But it was odd; he could have sworn, really *sworn* that he had just seen someone moving in the alley. And – just for a moment – it had looked like they were on fire.

Satisfied there was nothing there, that it had been a trick of the light, Toby went back to his whistling and carried on towards home.

Alice pressed herself deeper into the shadows and watched him go.

CHAPTER FIVE

Broken Wings

ADRIEL DID NOT look surprised when Alice knocked on his office door. He didn't look up at all – just gestured to the chair in front of his desk with one hand while he carried on writing with the other. It didn't even seem to bother him that it was almost midnight and she was covered in bruises.

She pointed this out to him as she sat down.

Adriel capped his pen and set it to one side, closing his notebook and folding his hands on top of it before fixing her with a stern gaze. "And what, precisely, would you like me to say?"

"Well... nothing. I was just –"

"My dear girl, do you really think you are the only creature to walk through that door in the middle of the night? Or, indeed, the strangest?" There was a rustling sound as he sat back in his chair.

"If you put it like that, then fine." Alice folded her arms, and winced. The pain in her ribs had decided to move right on up to the next level.

She didn't quite know why she'd come to the funeral parlour. It wasn't on her way home and she hadn't exactly expected Adriel to be sympathetic. It was just that she couldn't quite face going home to that empty room and trying to clean herself up. Now the adrenalin had faded, and the bruises were starting to ache, she just felt tired, and alone. Adriel might not be sympathetic, but at least he understood.

He may have been unimpressed by her appearance, but he was still watching her. "You would appear to have had an… *active* evening."

"You could say that." She leaned forward, ignoring the complaints from her ribs and her shoulders, and dropped the snake fang on his desk.

Looking surprised for the first time, he picked it up and turned it over in his fingers; first holding it up to the light, then – bizarrely – tapping it against one of his own teeth.

"It was in my shoulder. In. My. Shoulder. I don't even know where to start with that." She turned sideways in the chair, rolling her injured shoulder towards him. Two holes were clearly visible in the fabric of her jacket, and Adriel looked from the fang to Alice and back again.

"So it *was* you who had the run-in with Murmur. I had my suspicions. The fire, for one…" He sighed, and took a small box out of one of the drawers of his desk, dropping the tooth into it and tucking the whole thing back out of sight. "This is why I wanted you here, where I could keep an eye on you."

"Keep an eye on me? What's that supposed to mean?"

"Precisely what I said."

"No. No, no, no. You don't all get to treat me like I'm some barely housetrained puppy that someone's left with you for the weekend…"

"Puppy? I'm afraid I don't follow the analogy."

"It's just… it's like… Look, it sounded really good in my head, okay?" She slumped back in the chair.

"I'm sure it did." He stood up. "Come with me."

"Last time I listened to an angel who said that, I…" She tailed off when she saw the look he was giving her. The whole room darkened under his glare; shadows pooled in the corners and crept along the walls.

"It was not a request, Alice."

Of course it wasn't.

* * *

TRYING HER HARDEST to ignore her aching... well, *everything*, Alice followed him out of his office and towards the steel swing doors. The lights were off, and Alice could barely make out where his black wings stopped and the dark of the hallway began... but she knew where he was going.

The mortuary.

ALICE HAD YET to venture into the embalming suite. Not that she had any particular desire to go there, of course, but for Adriel to casually saunter through the door and tell her to follow him felt... odd. Particularly when she distinctly remembered him telling her she didn't have to go back there. She'd hoped that would be a permanent thing. Clearly not.

The lights flicked on automatically as Adriel walked in, and a shroud of cool air wrapped around them. It smelled like disinfectant: to be fair, she'd been expecting worse. The ceiling was higher than the rest of the office, and was punctuated by a variety of ducts, pipes and vents. Around the walls was an array of what looked suspiciously like kitchen cupboards, and a plastic skeleton dangling from a noose. Alice raised an eyebrow at it, but Adriel simply shook his head. "It takes a certain kind of man to live with the dead. It isn't your place to judge."

"Maybe not, but that's just all kinds of *wrong*."

"This coming from the woman who just burned a man alive?"

"Woah there. Hold on." She pointed a finger at him. "Firstly, that wasn't a man, that was a Fallen. And secondly, how the hell do you know that's what happened?"

"He died, yes?"

"Well, yes. But that... oh. Angel of Death. Got it."

"Indeed."

The centre of the room was dominated by an enormous steel table, draped in an extremely white sheet.

There was something underneath the sheet. Alice watched, feeling slightly queasy as Adriel pulled it aside, leaving the table and its contents exposed and horribly spotlit.

It was a pair of wings. A pair of wings which had been torn from the back of an angel.

They lay outstretched on the steel of the table, side by side, the feathers bedraggled and sad, and matted with blood. Those on the outer edges of the wings were slightly blackened, and Alice caught the smell of burning. Her stomach turned a quick somersault, but somehow, she couldn't stop herself from reaching out for them…

At the touch of her fingers, the wings burst into flame, but they did not burn. Instead, the flames settled, quietly scudding across the surface of the broken feathers. And Alice looked in horror at Adriel.

"This is one of Michael's choir."

"He was."

"What happened?"

"The Fallen."

"They did this?" Alice looked back at the wings spread out on the embalming table, the flames dying out as they fanned out over the feathers. She could see the bones, the muscles and sinews bunched beneath the flesh and feathers, and even she understood that this angel – whoever he was – had been tortured. The bones were broken; the muscles twisted… the wings ripped from his back.

"This is a message," Adriel said, pulling the sheet back over the broken wings. "Not a subtle one, either. They are coming. No – more than that: they are already *here*. And for all that you want to fight, Alice, you are too much a human for this."

"That's what Xaphan said. In hell. Just before he murdered my friend and made me watch. He said I was too human."

"Just because Xaphan is one of the Fallen doesn't mean he can't tell the truth when it suits him."

"He was wrong. Still is." She curled her fingers tightly in on her palms.

"I understand – but don't confuse the will to fight with the strength to do so. You are *like* them, but not *one of* them."

"How?" Alice held out her hands, and fire danced across her palms; spun around her wrists. "Tell me how. You look at me and tell me how..."

"Because you can die, Alice. All too easily, you can die."

Adriel smoothed the sheet over the wings and quietly walked away, the steel doors swinging shut behind him and the lights switching themselves off as he left. And Alice was alone in the darkness with only dead wings and fire for company.

She thought about it for a moment, and decided that it wasn't enough.

"No. You don't get to say that. You don't. You don't get to take away everything I had, and leave me with this and tell me that I'm not one of you." She stormed down the corridor after him, catching up with him as he sat back down in his chair. "He died, didn't he? That angel – whoever he was. He died."

"Yes, he did."

"So. You said it yourself: everyone dies. Even angels, right?"

Adriel simply blinked up at her. "What is this obsession of yours? This need to be one thing or another? Why can you not simply be what you are?"

"That's exactly what I'm trying to say."

"And it's precisely what makes you human." He steepled his fingers together and peered at her over the top of them. "Angels do not doubt what they are. Angels do not question their place. They simply *are*. But you? You want to be this so very, very much. You want it so badly that it burns you. Metaphorically speaking," he added, seeing Alice open her mouth to interrupt. "Be as you are and be content. Besides," he said, shuffling papers on his desk, "have you not understood what it is to be an angel? I would have thought Mallory could tell you that. Pain and war and little else."

"That's not what Mallory would say."

"Not what he'd say, perhaps, but isn't it what he thinks?"

"I wouldn't know. I haven't been able to ask him. He left."

"And so you try to fill the space he has left. Be careful, Alice. The footprints you follow are not meant for you." He blinked again, and it was clear that he had no interest in discussing the matter any further.

Alice was furious. More than furious. "I'm not afraid of the Fallen," she said quietly. It wasn't entirely true, but she said it anyway. Her shoulder was starting to throb.

"Neither are they. You must understand – the angels aren't afraid of the Fallen. They're afraid of death."

"Of you."

"In a manner of speaking, yes." He folded his hands neatly on the blotter on top of his desk. "You're quite right. Everything dies, Alice. But believe me when I tell you it takes considerably less to cause your death than it would, say, Mallory's. And angels have died for this war. Many of them. Does that not suggest that perhaps you *should* fear the Fallen? Have you seen what they do to your world?" He pointed at the door; at the looting, the violence... the madness that had come from nowhere and seemed to be building with every passing day. The streets outside were a carpet of broken glass. It was quiet out there now, but it wouldn't last.

"The Fallen have lost everything. They won't forgive that. And Lucifer, if I remember correctly, has a particular interest in *you*. So yes, you should fear the Fallen. And you should stop seeking to place yourself in harm's way. I have gone to considerable trouble to protect you from them, Alice, but I cannot protect you from yourself."

And with that, he waved his hand at her, and it was clear she was dismissed. She was still furious, but she was something else, too. Everything Adriel had said sounded suspiciously like the 'you've let yourself down' speech she'd heard too many times in the past. She had disappointed him, and it left her with a fresh ache in her chest: one that had nothing to do with the beating she'd taken. Was that it? All this, it wasn't just to keep an eye on her. It was to keep her safe. And she was just getting in the way.

She hadn't forgotten about Lucifer. He wasn't exactly easy to forget, speaking with her mother's voice, looking out of her mother's face; asking her to join him. She hadn't so much 'forgotten' that as 'chosen to ignore.' Plus, of course, there was the whole problem of the fact she'd managed to set two Archangels against each other and... it was all just such a *mess*. And where was Mallory? Gone.

She sighed, fury abating, and turned towards the door. As she reached it, Adriel called her name and she stopped, looking back at him.

"Alice? I think perhaps you should take a few days. Think of it as sick leave: I'm afraid it simply won't do to have you covered in bruises. It's bad for business, and people will ask questions. I don't enjoy questions, as I'm sure you can understand."

"Sorry. I didn't think." And she was sorry, she really was. She hadn't thought, had she? Because she was used to there being someone who could patch her up whenever she needed it. All traces of her anger were gone now, replaced utterly by regret. She hung her head, and was about to step out into the corridor when Adriel coughed quietly. Again, she stopped.

"One more thing," he said – this time, with what looked like a half-hidden smile on his face. "If you really must persist in getting into these running battles with the Fallen... at least stop letting them hit you, hmm?" He held her gaze for just long enough to make his point, and then nodded goodnight. She closed the door behind her.

ADRIEL SHUFFLED HIS papers again and sighed, listening to her footsteps heading down the corridor, and to the door banging as she let herself out.

"You not done with all that paperwork yet? You've been fiddling with it long enough," said a voice from the corner of the room.

Adriel glanced up. "I find paperwork soothing. Particularly when talking to Alice. She's… struggling."

"She's not."

"I beg to differ. That… *girl*" – Adriel paused – "is in free-fall."

"She's fine." The angel who had been standing unnoticed in the darkness stepped out into the room, his leather jacket creaking as he flopped into the chair across from Adriel and swung his boots up onto the desk. Adriel scowled at him pointedly, and he swung them back down again. "She needs to find her feet again. That's all."

"I'm not sure it's that simple."

"I didn't want her to know I was here, Adriel. It would defeat the point of all this."

"I understand. But…"

"It was for the best, but you're right. Things *have* changed, haven't they? And whether you believe it or not, I do appreciate you calling me. She's pissed off. I didn't think for a second that she wouldn't be. Frankly, if I didn't think she missed me, *I'd* be pissed off. I'm the kind of man you'd miss, don't you think?" He cracked a grin, burrowed down into the chair, and this time, when he swung his feet up onto the desk, Adriel simply rolled his eyes.

"Now. You got anything to drink around here?"

CHAPTER SIX

Dancing on Pins

"YOU CAN LET him go now, Zak."

Michael was pacing the floor. Behind him were a half-dozen angels, all standing to attention and blocking the doorway, and in the middle of the floor between them was Zadkiel, his boot firmly placed on the back of one of the Fallen, pinning his chest to the floor and his wrists to his spine.

"You sure? Because I'm good here."

"Zadkiel, let him up. He's clearly of no use to me." Michael snapped his fingers and a very small flame appeared on the floor, an inch in front of the unfortunate Fallen, whose eyes crossed and then widened as he tried to focus on it. "Unless, of course, he happens to remember something I want to know..."

"Wait!" The Fallen thrashed, trying to turn his head away from the rapidly growing flame. Michael snapped his fingers again, making the flame vanish, and dropped into a crouch directly in front of the Fallen. He tipped his head sideways to look at him.

"Yes?"

"That half-born! The one with the fire!"

"Yes?"

"She killed Murmur."

"Did she now?" Michael sat back on his heels and glanced up at Zadkiel – who shrugged, then took his weight off the Fallen's back and stepped away.

The Fallen sat up, slowly at first, and was obviously about to scuttle into a corner when he spotted the other angels, and thought better of it. He met Michael's calmly inquisitive gaze.

"So... what's your name?"

"Astorath."

"Astorath. You look familiar. Have we met?"

"I don't..."

"Frankly, I don't really care either way. And I don't have to tell you how this will go, do I? You'll tell me whatever it is you know, because *I* want to know it."

"And you'll let me go?"

"Yes, yes. Something like that." Michael waved a hand vaguely. "Now. Tell me about Murmur."

"He was... in a warehouse. The Earthbounds came. They had the half-born with them and she..."

"She burned him, I imagine. Well, well. Look who's all grown up. Murmur, you say?" He frowned, and looked up at Zadkiel, who made a looping motion with his finger across the lower half of his face. Michael got the message. "Ah, *him*. Mmm."

He rocked back on his heels and stood up, running his hands through his hair as he turned away. Behind Astorath, Zadkiel took a quiet – but exaggerated – step back.

"That's it? That's all you wanted to know?"

"Why? Do you know more?"

"No. No, no. I don't know anything."

"Well, then." Michael had stopped with his back to Astorath, and the Fallen clambered to his feet, one eye on the door.

"I told you what you wanted to know. I can go now, right? You said you'd let me go..."

Michael was back across the room, eyes blazing and wings unfurled, in a heartbeat. He swung one of his wings at the unfortunate Fallen and knocked him sprawling onto the floor. "Let you go? For what? To go snivelling back to your master? *Vermin*," he hissed, and suddenly his sword was in his hand. He raised it high... and then stopped. Astorath – who had curled into a ball and wrapped his arms around his head – peered out between his elbows. He watched as Michael lowered his sword, then smiled. When Michael winked, he drew his arms away from his head... and then burst into flames. Michael stood and watched as the Fallen burned away to nothing – not even ash – and he folded his wings behind him.

Zadkiel shook his head from his perch on the windowsill. "You're a mean old bastard, aren't you?"

Michael waved the other angels away, and as one, they turned and marched out of the room. As soon as they were gone, he scowled back at Zadkiel. "Would you care to elaborate on that?"

"Not really."

"He was looking for Lucifer."

"So that would be exactly what I said would happen, then, wouldn't it? I really don't care if you kill them, but there's no need to get their hopes up before you do it. And if it were up to me, I'd weigh Lucifer down and drop him into the ocean."

"It isn't that simple."

"You sure about that? Because from where I'm sitting it looks pretty fucking simple."

"And that is why you are not the leader of this army. You've made your point, Zak," Michael said, placing his sword on the floor alongside the throne. "Now, I suggest we move on."

"You want to talk about Alice. There's a surprise."

"She killed one of the Twelve."

"Funnily enough, I got that. Has it occurred to you that you should be thanking her for it? I mean, it's just a thought, but aren't we all supposed to be on the same side?"

"How can I keep order if she wilfully disobeys, and then does... this?"

"Aaand we're back to that." Zadkiel dropped his head into his hands; his fingers rubbing at the corner of his eyes. "*Again.*"

"She needs to be brought into line."

"Why? Let her run for a while. She scares the Fallen and, to be honest, that's what you need her to be doing. And, besides, don't you have other things to be worrying about?"

"There is nothing more important than..."

"... order, discipline, boring, boring, boring. Whatever. I'm telling you, Michael: if you don't act, before long there won't be a world to fight *for*. And then what good is your precious little half-born?"

He fell silent, and watched Michael pacing up and down. He'd said enough. Michael tolerated him speaking his mind, but he had limits. And being told he was wrong didn't put him in the *best* of moods.

"I've let her run long enough. It's time. The very fact she's taken on the Fallen – the Twelve, no less – by herself..."

"She wasn't by herself, though, was she? 'The Earthbounds came.'" Zak slid off the sill and leaned back against the wall as Michael finally gave up on pacing and sat on the steps of the dais. "That's what's really getting under your skin: that she won't do what she's told and now the other angels are turning to her instead of you." He didn't quite manage to hide the grin creeping across his face before Michael looked up at him. Clearing his throat loudly, he rubbed his chin, hoping he'd covered the worst of it...

"It's time that stopped."

"And what? She's got Adriel – *Adriel* – keeping an eye on her, and I seem to remember that last time you tried ordering her around, it didn't work out so well."

"You don't see, do you? The longer this continues... the Fallen might be frightened by her, yes, but it won't take them long to start seeing her as a weak point. And once they do, they will exploit that."

"And the only one who gets to exploit Alice is you, right?"

"Enough!" Michael's shout echoed around the room. Zadkiel wrinkled his nose in displeasure, but held his tongue.

"I know precisely how to deal with Alice," Michael said, his voice suddenly soft and calm again. "And you are going to help me to do it."

CHAPTER SEVEN

Wreckage

"So, what happened to you, then?" Toby leaned against the edge of the desk, trying to look nonchalant. Alice had been waiting for this, ever since she'd stepped through the door that morning. As soon as Adriel sent her home – bruised and beaten and generally pissed off with the world, her life and herself – she had remembered that she'd agreed to go out with Toby. And that she'd agreed to arrange it the next day, before promptly vanishing. Way to make a great impression.

It took almost a week for the bruises to fade, and she had rehearsed all her possible excuses on her way into work, but had stopped when she saw the state of the street. There was even more broken glass carpeting the pavement than she remembered, glittering like so many diamonds. A burned-out car slumped in the middle of the road, half-overturned and still smoking. Across from it, a police van stood abandoned, its doors open, creaking slightly in the breeze. All its windows had been smashed and the metal grilles (or parts of them) were scattered across the street. One appeared to be sticking out of a newsagent's window. There was rubbish everywhere: pages of damp newspapers, food wrappers, a brick... a discarded shoe. Just the *one* shoe; presumably, whoever had done this hopped home afterwards.

She stared around her. This was worse than she had seen it – and still the only window in the entire street which hadn't been smashed or cracked was Adriel's. Definitely not a coincidence.

Suddenly uneasy, she took a step forward, and into a puddle. It took a second for her to understand the rush of heat that swept through her, the flames erupting around her hands. She flapped ineffectually, trying to put them out. Nothing happened, and she jumped back, away from the puddle.

The puddle of blood.

The flames gradually died, leaving her breathless and aching and feeling like she'd been hit across the back of the head with a blunt instrument. It was while she was glaring at the brick on the floor that she spotted the newsagent across the road, broom in hand, staring at her. She smiled, and pointed to the air in front of her. "Wasp," she said loudly, hoping that was a good enough explanation for the mad hopping he'd just seen.

And now, here was Toby asking where she'd been.

Good question. *Good* question.

"Well, Toby. Here's the problem. I'm actually not quite what you think: I'm half angel, on my mother's side. And she was in hell, and the devil possessed her and it's a whole big *thing*. And then I came to work here – and did you know that your boss is actually the Angel of Death? – and I kind of got in a fight with a couple of Fallen angels and got seven hells kicked out of me, so the boss said I should take a couple of days. You know, just until the swelling went down. How're you doing?"

She *could* say that. But it probably wouldn't end well. So instead she mumbled something about a stomach bug, and went back to opening the post which had built up over the last few days. Adriel, it seemed, didn't *do* post.

"I thought we were, you know, going out or something?"

"We were. Are. Will. Promise."

"It's fine, really. I just thought if you wanted to change your mind or something..."

"I promise I did not take a couple of days' sick leave just to avoid you. There. Make you feel better?"

"Much. Cheers." Toby visibly relaxed and picked up a handful of envelopes, slicing them open one at a time with his finger and handing them to Alice.

"How is it where you live?"

"Huh?" She wasn't quite sure how to answer that, other than with 'messy.'

"The riots." He nodded towards the window. On the other side, a man with a dustcart and a broom was fighting a losing battle with the litter blowing around. It didn't look like he was even going to contemplate the rest of the debris.

"Oh. We seem to be okay. It's pretty quiet where I am. And I don't live right on the street, so..."

"Lucky. The shop below my mum's flat got firebombed or something."

"Is she okay?"

"Yeah, she's fine. Scary, though. What's the world coming to? It's like it's all going to hell."

"Mmm." Alice stared at a bill, and then concentrated very hard on dropping it into a filing tray. He was right: the world *was* going to hell. He just didn't understand how right he was. And that was the way it was going to stay.

Despite Toby's cheerful – and constant – chatter (particularly now he'd been reassured that no, she hadn't been avoiding him) the mood was oppressive. And for an undertaker's office, that was saying something. The usual calm and quiet of the office felt claustrophobic, itchy and unsettled. Outside, with the exception of the occasional policeman or pedestrian, the street stayed deserted. With the road closed, there was no traffic, and the garishly striped police tape wound between the lampposts kept most of the passers-by at bay. The sky overhead was a leaden grey, with clouds that hadn't seemed to move all day.

There were no clients that morning, and no phone-calls, but Alice had plenty of catching up to do anyway, filing and sorting and tidying paperwork that she was absolutely sure hadn't been in the desk drawers before she'd gone off. Apparently, it wasn't only post that Adriel didn't do.

She had just lifted another bundle of invoices and receipts out of the top drawer when her fingers brushed against something soft in the middle of the pile. Riffling through the papers, she slid the top half of the stack off to one side… and there, sitting on the paper, was a feather. It was almost as long as the sheets of paper it hid among, and it was white. This was no Earthbound's feather: it had come from the wings of a full-blown angel. A Descended, there was no doubt about it; but whose was it? And what was it doing in her desk?

As she was sitting, staring at it, she heard a polite cough from beside her, and looked up, startled. So engrossed had she been that she hadn't noticed Adriel appear alongside her.

"Alice? A word, if you would?"

"Hypotenuse."

"I'm sorry? I don't…"

"You said 'a word.' That's a word."

"Ah. Humour. Yes."

"Never mind. What's up?"

"I think, perhaps, it would be wise for you to go home."

"What? But I just…"

"I don't think you understand. This is not to do with you. It's to do with *them.*" He pointed to the door with a long, slender finger. "There's trouble coming."

"Fallen? They're coming? Here?"

"Why not? The riots are, broadly speaking, their doing. They have watched them build and build, and they have been there through them all. This one will be no different, and it will happen right outside the door. You shouldn't be here." He saw her open her mouth to reply and shook his head, raising his hand to stop her. "I said: this is not to do with you, per se. This is about my responsibility, on every level. You are part of my staff, and I am responsible for your safety. I made a promise..."

"A promise?"

"A promise which is none of your business, but which is a promise nevertheless."

"And if I don't want to go?"

He shrugged. "Of course, that would be your choice..."

"What about you?"

"Me?" He seemed genuinely taken aback by her interruption.

"You. Where will you go?"

"To work, Alice. To work."

Alice was still trying to decide what to do when she saw the first police van. It drove up the road slowly, trundling past the wreckage. It was another riot van, with black metal guards across the windows. "Well, that can't be a good sign," she said to no-one in particular. Should she go, she wondered? Adriel wanted the office empty, but on the other hand, he'd as good as said that the Fallen were coming. And if they were coming, then how could she run? He was trying to protect his staff: after all, he'd said they were all normal. Human. But she wasn't, was she? She stared out of the window at the van, watching as the doors swung open and a dozen police officers jumped out, already half in their riot gear. They held round perspex shields and black helmets. One of them – a tall blond – carried a baton, which he swung experimentally... almost hitting one of his colleagues in the process. "That *definitely* can't be good," she muttered.

"What've you seen?" Toby was walking down the corridor from the kitchen. He had changed out of his dark suit, and was now wearing jeans and a t-shirt with a pair of tatty white trainers. He leaned around her to peer out of the window, and she caught the smell of hair gel. That was the thing about people – they *smelled* like people. Angels smelled... different.

"Oh," he said when he spotted the van. "Yeah, that's not good." As they watched, another van ground to a halt behind the first... and another. "Not good at all." For the first time, it occurred to Alice that this was really happening.

She was relatively cavalier about the Fallen, but this was something else. The Fallen were other, somehow; set apart from the real world. The Fallen were hell and battles and the stuff of nightmares – and despite the fact she was working for Adriel, despite the fact she'd seen them on the streets herself, knowing they were coming *here*, and were in the day-to-day world and trying to bend it to their own will… it was wrong. It was frightening.

A sudden pressure on her hand made her look down. Without her realising it, her hand and Toby's had tangled together, their fingers intertwined. She was about to pull away when it dawned on her that he didn't seem to have noticed either. And if he hadn't noticed, it wasn't like he'd done it on purpose, was it? And he was as afraid as she was, more so, even. She could feel it. So they stood there, hand in hand, watching the police lines form right outside the window, amid the bricks and the glass and the wreckage.

And then they heard the shouting.

It came from somewhere out of sight: voices raised in rage and hate and nothing more. It wasn't a battle chant, it wasn't a cheer. It was a howl, empty and hollow and furious. And Alice had heard something like it once before, echoing through the lower levels of hell.

Toby's fingers tightened around hers.

There were footsteps then – Adriel, hurrying back out of the office with a stony expression, and looking as close to an angel as Alice had ever seen him; his wings barely concealed in a shadowy haze around his shoulders. But he looked through her, and spoke to Toby. "You need to leave. *Now.* Go." At the far end of the corridor, the back door swung open.

The voices got louder.

"Come on!" Toby tugged on Alice's hand, but found her utterly immovable.

"I… can't," she said, barely recognising the voice that passed her lips.

"What?" Toby turned and stared at her.

"I need to stay."

"You need to *what*?"

"I have to stay. I can't explain. I just... I have to."

"Are you crazy? I mean, really? You want to stay. Don't you know what's coming? Five minutes and it's going to be a fucking warzone out there."

"You should go."

"Without you? Not a chance."

"Toby!" Alice snapped. "Go. Just go. I'm not going to explain myself to you. I barely even know you, and you certainly don't know me. So whatever you think *this* is," she gestured to the space between them, "you can guess again. Now just leave me alone, alright?"

She saw the anger flash across his face before he could hide it, but she felt it all the same, boiling under her skin just as fiercely as it did under his. She had hurt him.

She felt his fingers slacken with horrible deliberation and pull away from hers. Adriel, framed in the doorway, watched but said nothing.

There was silence inside, rising chaos outside; shouting, the sound of running footsteps and the rhythmic beat of the police batons on shields.

Toby took a step back and looked her up and down. She felt his gaze travel every inch of her, and she hated it. He looked so coldly at her, this man who only a moment before had held her hand in his. Then he shook his head once and his lip curled into a half-sneer... and without another word he turned and was gone. The back door slammed behind him.

"Interesting approach," said Adriel.

Alice swallowed the lump that was building in her throat. "Worked, didn't it?"

"And you...?"

"I'm fine. And I'm not going anywhere."

"On your own head be it, Alice."

"I'm a big girl, thanks."

* * *

She turned back to the window and looked out – and there, on the far side of the street, half-hidden behind a shattered bus shelter and watching her, was a man with black hair and dark-ringed eyes and a white brand around his wrist.

Rimmon.

Adriel opened the door, and the sound of shouting and jeering grew louder. He sighed, and suddenly looked sad.

"You pushed Toby away to keep him safe," he said. "But at what cost? What cost to you, and what cost to him?"

"It doesn't matter."

"Of course it matters. All our choices… all *your* choices, they matter."

"I lost enough people I care about to the Fallen. I don't want to lose any more."

"'People you care about'?" The corner of Adriel's mouth twitched.

"You didn't hear me say that."

"My lips are sealed."

The sound of batons on shields was almost deafening now, and the street was suddenly full of people – running, walking, jumping – their faces covered with scarves and hoods. Adriel slipped out of the door.

A bottle smashed on the pavement outside: the burning rag stuffed into its mouth falling clear and smouldering harmlessly on the ground.

She had to go too, didn't she? It was where she belonged, after all – so much more there than in an office. Her eyes fixed on the crowd, Alice followed Adriel through the door, leaving it open behind her.

As she passed, the rag on the pavement burst into bright orange flames.

* * *

As she lost herself among the bodies, the office's back door opened and Toby ran in.

"I don't care, alright. It's mental out there and I'm not leaving y..." He tailed off, seeing the door swinging open, and Alice vanishing into the mob.

"Alice! *Alice!*" He ran to the front door, gripping the sides of the frame and screaming her name. She didn't stop: in fact, he could barely see her – only a flash of her jacket here, the top of her head. His voice was just one among many.

She didn't hear him. She didn't want him.

But he couldn't leave her.

Shaking his head and against his better judgement, Toby turned the collar of his jacket up and plunged into the riot after her.

A wave of noise swallowed Toby whole. The road had become a corridor of bodies: colliding with one another; dancing around one another, arms aloft, faces hidden behind black and white patterned scarves. A woman with long blonde hair had climbed onto the ruins of a car and was waving a child's doll, its blazing hair dripping molten plastic on the people below as its face twisted grotesquely. The woman laughed as she threw the burning doll into the crowd.

Someone nearby was screaming; as Toby staggered through the crush of bodies, he saw a man – a kid, really – lying on the ground. Blood was pouring out of a gash in his thigh, and his face was a pale shade of grey. There were dark hollows under his eyes. It was the young woman crouched beside him who was screaming, a brick in her hand.

Jeers from somewhere behind him made Toby look away. The crowd had parted around a man in a crumpled suit. He had a phone in his hand; he'd been filming the mob, and the mob had turned on him.

The first missile landed at the man's feet and shattered: a glass bottle. The second clipped his knee, forcing him to step back. The third hit him in the side of his face.

As he fell, the baying crowd reared back before collapsing in on him like a pack of animals.

In his mind's eye, Toby saw himself plunging through them, pulling them aside until he reached the poor bastard at the centre; hauling him to his feet and dragging him out... getting him to the police, to an ambulance, to safety, to *anywhere* but here.

But Toby didn't move. He stood right where he was. He heard the soft, sickening sound of flesh on flesh; of bricks and bones, of the mob laughing as they broke their prey... and he didn't move. He couldn't.

It was the *thud-thud-thud-thud-thud-thud* of batons on shields that pulled him out of his stupor.

Turning his back on the horror in front of him, Toby began frantically scanning the crowd for Alice. Jostled from every direction by the bodies crammed around him, he looked in vain for her face. He fought to stay upright, to not be swept along by the mob.

He was still searching as the first canister of tear-gas sailed over his head in a graceful arc and landed twenty feet behind him with a clatter and a whoosh.

Still the heartbeat of the riot sounded above the screams and the shouts and the chants and the shattering of windows.

And beneath his feet, beneath the feet of the world, unseen and unheard and unfelt... the balance tipped.

For the first time in forever, the Fallen were in control.

CHAPTER EIGHT

Ring of Steel

ALICE HAD PUSHED her way through the crowd early on – or rather, it had parted before her. Perhaps they looked at her and saw the faintest of heat-hazes about her shoulders. Perhaps they saw the tarmac of the road bubble beneath her feet, or the tiny sparks that spat from her fingertips.

Or perhaps they saw the look on her face and decided that it was best to get out of her way.

One – a teenage boy barely old enough to shave, scarf pulled up to his eyes – had tried to slow her down. He had held his ground and sniffed at her disdainfully, and pulled a knife out of his jacket pocket. He screamed as molten metal poured from between his fingers, and Alice moved on.

This wasn't just a riot. It was angry and it was chaotic and it was cold – much colder than it should have been. The temperature had dropped by several degrees in the last hour, and that could mean only one thing.

This was *them*.

This was the Fallen. Rimmon she'd already seen – and that was most likely part of his plan, if he had one – but it wasn't him she wanted. She was looking for Xaphan.

Memories flooded her mind, of a metal cage, a scarred face with a cruel smile, and a man strapped to a wheel, swallowed by hungry black fire. The leaves on a plane tree at the side of the road began to curl and shrivel.

"Get a grip," she muttered to herself as a tall man in a black jacket and hood barged into her, almost knocking her sideways – but recoiling when he saw the scorch mark on his coat. He screamed and lunged at her, but it was so little effort to dodge him that she almost laughed as he tumbled into a heap beside her. She grabbed his shoulder, half-hauling him to his feet; he swung at her again and she ducked, popping back up to yank his hood down. "Go home!" she shouted, looking into his startled eyes. All she saw there was fear.

The clouds overhead had thickened, bolstered by smoke, turning the afternoon to dusk. Against the chaos of the crowd stood the immovable police line, batons and shields raised, helmet visors down; a wall of armour and flesh and bone. But all walls can be broken, and Alice watched as the first brick smashed into a shield. There was a cheer as the officer behind it staggered slightly, then drew himself up again. She could feel it all around her: the fear, the pain, the hate. It was carried on the air like a sea breeze.

Another brick smacked into a shield and, as one, the police line took a step forward.

One more brick, and a cheer from the crowd as the riot police beat their batons against their shields. The cheer became a chant, and the sound of baton-on-shield became a drum, and the clouds overhead were growing thicker and thicker...

The lightning bolt hit with no warning. The chanting and the cheering and the jeering were cut short, replaced by a stunned silence.

The air smelled of ozone; of bleach and metal and blue glass. Alice knew what that meant.

She clambered onto the top of a litter bin. Slowly straightening up, she could see clear over everyone and into the centre of the road, where the lightning had struck. A large gap had formed in the crowd. All thoughts of rioting had evaporated as the crowd stared at the feathery lines radiating from the spot where the lightning had struck.

And at the man who stood at the centre of the shattered circle of tarmac.

The man who stood with his head bowed and his hands folded.

The man who, as the crowd watched in a combination of terror and awe and utter confusion, slowly opened his wide white wings.

"Shit," said Alice.

A Descended. Not even an Earthbound, but an actual *Descended*, an honest-to-goodness actual, full-fat, proper angel. Out in the open. And, judging by the entrance, one of Gabriel's.

He rolled his shoulders and faint white sparks jumped across his wings. He smoothed down the front of his t-shirt, apparently oblivious to the eyes on him.

Alice had noticed his clothes straight away: if he'd been in armour, she would have been really worried. But a t-shirt and jeans? That was slightly more encouraging. As were the bare feet.

And then she remembered that was exactly how the first angel from Michael's choir she had met – A'albiel – had been dressed when he almost tore the head off one of the Fallen in a car park. So maybe it wasn't so good. But still, it was only one Descended, right? It wasn't like there was an army of them, or…

Something moving at the far edge of the crowd caught her eye. For a single, sickening moment, it had almost looked like a wing. But it couldn't have been, could it?

Another flash of white – this time down the street to her right – and the queasy sensation crawled into her throat.

Behind the crowd, there were three angels, standing to attention. And they *were* in armour.

"*Shit*," she said, with a little more force this time, scrambling down from the top of the bin. The crush of bodies in front of her seemed to have miraculously thinned – at least, enough for Alice to see what was happening. The Descended in the t-shirt was still standing there, head bowed and wings outstretched.

No-one made a sound: it felt like the whole crowd, so intent on tearing itself apart only moments before, was holding its collective breath.

And then he raised his head and looked around. Bright blue eyes like searchlights skimmed the faces surrounding him – and magically, people began to find their voices. Some whimpered, some muttered prayers under their breaths. One or two laughed. More cried.

He looked straight through them all.

His gaze settled on her, and even through the now all-encompassing terror that surrounded her, Alice felt his surprise. He blinked at her, then nodded, and his eyes moved on. She heaved a sigh of relief: she didn't think she was exactly flavour of the month with Gabriel's choir at the moment... she couldn't be sure, but she got the feeling that they probably wouldn't look very kindly on her involvement in their general and Archangel becoming Earthbound, or his second-in-command being thrown to the Fallen... Of course, she could be wrong. But she doubted it.

At the moment, however, he didn't seem to be particularly interested in her; his ice-blue eyes kept on looking. *For what?* she thought, staring at the people around her.

More than once, Alice had wondered what would happen if the angels were to appear like this, to a crowd. She knew Descendeds popped up every now and again – but only to individuals and never so openly. She would also put good money on there being more than one Earthbound hidden in amongst the rioters... but, knowing most of the Earthbounds she'd met, she'd also put good odds on them being the ones throwing the bricks.

The spell was broken by a single scream. It rang out through the silence, then swelled as the rioters snapped out of their trance. Away from the angel, right at the front of the crowd, a police officer had taken advantage of the distraction, breaking the line and stepping forward. He was now standing over a prone man, whose hands flapped ineffectually at the blows raining down on him. Again and again the policeman brought the baton down, blood spattering the tarmac as the crowd swelled and turned in on itself, jostling to look, or to intervene, or to attack.

A burning bottle smashed in front of the police line, and they charged.

When the two lines of bodies met, there was an awful crunching sound that almost rivalled the shrieks and howls on both sides.

Alice could no longer see the man on the floor; he had been lost beneath trampling feet. She had to fight against the movement of the bodies around her just to stay in one place. Everyone in the crush turned against one another as they tried to reach the front of the mob, or to get away from the nightmare in their midst: the cold-eyed angel who dripped lightning from his fingers and was currently glaring at the Fallen he had plucked from the mayhem and pinned to the ground. Both of them appeared completely oblivious to the rising panic around them.

Remarkably, it looked as though the police charge was having some effect, although that could be the tear-gas, Alice thought, her eyes smarting. Ahead, another police line was forming, this one admittedly a little less solid than the last. She looked back over her shoulder and counted the angels. Five of them now. Five Descendeds. More than enough.

Trapped between the line of police shields and the angels – with who knew how many Fallen in the middle – Alice was rapidly running out of options.

CHAPTER NINE

Like Bringing a Spoon to a Knife Fight

Toby didn't understand what was happening. He was so far from even beginning to understand what was happening that he'd more or less given up. There had been a blinding flash of light and a tearing sound… and then silence. Silence and then – where he stood, at least – screaming. He couldn't see much: all around him, people shoved and crowded him, but it seemed like something big was happening and the riot stilled for a moment before erupting again.

Acrid smoke billowed across the street. It tasted of petrol and oil and soot. Toby held his arm across his face, trying to breathe through his sleeve. The sky overhead was getting darker and darker – still glowing that infernal shade of orange – and it could almost have been night.

He stumbled forward, then backward, turning this way and that until he no longer knew which way he was going; all he knew was that he couldn't leave Alice out here, in the middle of this.

Head down, he did his best to push past a group of teenage girls leaning against the side of a wrecked police van, looking for all the world like they were watching a carnival – apart from their hoods and the bottles of vodka, which they were swigging from and then hurling over the heads of the people in front. They laughed as one connected with the back of a man's head.

Finally getting past them, Toby found his way blocked. Eyes watering from the ever-thickening smoke and gas, he blinked, and looked up.

In front of him – and at least a head taller than him – was a man with short hair and hooded eyes, his forehead heavily creased. His arms were folded across his chest. And he was wearing armour.

Toby was about to tell him that he was taking this 'riot' business a little seriously when the man raised an eyebrow at him, nodded slightly and stepped aside to let him pass. Gratefully, Toby edged past, and it was only when he turned around to shout his thanks that he saw the wings.

They were huge, and the feathers were white. They weren't just white – they *glowed*.

Toby's mouth dropped open. His feet wouldn't move. His eyes widened as his mind tried to catch up with what he was seeing.

An angel.

Which was impossible. Right?

The angel must have sensed him staring, because he suddenly cocked his head to one side and turned round. There was a tattoo on his forearm: an unrecognisable squiggle, but just like his wings, it glowed.

And this time, as the angel met Toby's eyes, he looked almost amused. He opened his mouth as if to speak, but a sudden scream cut through the chaos around them, and he was gone, leaving Toby standing in the middle of the crowd.

Toby had the distinct feeling that he had just seen something; that something had just happened... but he couldn't quite seem to remember what it was. There was a hole there. He couldn't have forgotten, surely.

But the more he thought about it, the more unimportant it seemed. What mattered was finding Alice. Wherever the hell *she* was.

* * *

WHILE TOBY WAS trying to process his first meeting with an angel, Alice struggled to find her way through the thickening smoke towards one of the others. It was the smoke that bothered her most: more than the gas, more than the crowds. This smoke tasted like naphtha; a Fallen weapon if ever there was one. All of this felt like their handiwork – the way the people were turning on one another, the random *violence* of it. With one hand covering her mouth and nose, she peered through the gloom and headed for the faint glow of wings.

"Alice."

Was it really too much to ask for people to be in front of her if they wanted to talk to her? She turned around and found herself almost nose-to-nose with an Archangel.

She could tell he was one of the Archangels, just by looking at him. Something about the way he held his head; about the way he folded his arms across his chest – and looked utterly unfazed by everything happening around him. Admittedly, the sword hanging from his waist and the glowing sigil on his wrist helped.

The symbol was familiar, but even if that hadn't given him away, the scent that hung around him, cutting through the smoke, probably would have done. He smelled like cut grass and tomato leaves, like old books and poster paint, like tarmac baking in the sun. He smelled like the past, like childhood. Like memories.

She was standing in front of Zadkiel.

"You shouldn't be here," he shouted.

Alice stared pointedly at his wings. "Neither should you!"

"Things are changing. I'm... necessary. All this" – he waved his hand around him – "it has to be contained."

"Like Michael contained hell, you mean?" Alice snapped.

Zadkiel looked taken aback. "He told me you'd say something like that."

"Did he really? Well, let me assure you that whatever he says, Michael doesn't understand a thing about me. Or he wouldn't have sent you after me."

"You? I'm not here for you!" Zadkiel said with a shake of his head. "I'm here for this. We all are."

"All?"

"Look closer, Alice." He gestured to the crowd behind her, and she turned and looked.

The air shimmered – and suddenly she could see angels everywhere. Among the crowd. On the rooftops. Behind the police, *among* the police. In the air, beating their wings.

"But... why couldn't I see them? Before?"

"Because I didn't want you to. Not all of them." He patted her on the shoulder. "You take care of yourself, Alice. It was nice to meet you. Michael sends his regards." His fingers closed around the hilt of his sword as he stepped around her. "We could use a little help, you know." The creases at the corners of his eyes deepened, and Alice took the hint. Something told her it wasn't a great idea to get on the bad side of *another* Archangel.

"*He told me you'd say that,*" she mimicked, shaking her head. "Angels. Can't live with them... end of sentence."

It was as she was turning away that she spotted the back of a jacket. A horribly, horribly familiar jacket.

She only saw it for a second, and then the press of bodies closed in again, but she'd seen enough, and her heart sank.

Toby.

He was supposed to go home. That was the whole *point*... he was supposed to be safe, far away from all this. But there he was, right in the middle of it. Should she go to him? Would she be protecting him, or putting him in harm's way?

Torn, she tipped her head back, hoping to find some kind of answer. The angels were still there – although Alice had no idea whether everyone else could see them. Could Toby? What did that mean? Did they know what was happening here? Did he? They'd certainly all seen the Descended arrive: *he* had been hard to miss. But since then... she turned again and looked back to the centre of the crowd where he stood. No-one was staring, or shouting, or doing any of the things she would have expected them to be doing. Their eyes slid over him; they moved around him, but no-one seemed to notice him. And that had to be Zadkiel's doing. He could control memories, after all.

"Collateral damage, Alice. Collateral damage..." whispered a voice behind her, and as she whirled to find its source, she saw only red eyes glinting behind a heavy visor.

Lucifer.

He was here.

Stumbling back, she fought the urge to run. What good would it do, in the midst of the pandemonium? Even the angels had finally, typically, vanished.

Lucifer was taunting her. That was the point.

But Lucifer never wore his own body, and she had only ever seen him speak through the Fallen. That was part of the deal: that at any moment, he could invade their heads and make them his own.

And that meant the policeman, standing in front of her and swaddled in his heavy riot gear, was not what he seemed.

His shoulders began to smoke, and then to burn, small flames running down his arms, but he simply laughed, patting them out with his gloved hands. "Fireproof. Nice touch, don't you think? You'll have to try harder than that if you want to burn me, Alice."

...and then the red glow vanished.

As she watched, he dropped his shield, tossing it aside like a toy. It rolled along the pavement, where it was immediately snatched up by a woman who swung it straight at the head of the man pushing past her. It connected heavily and he fell to the ground.

Alice should run. She should; she *knew* she should. Suddenly her determination was fading, and was being replaced by something very like fear. She should do something, *anything*... but Lucifer had had the opportunity to sneak up on her and he had let her know he was there. Why? He could have hurt her, could have killed her, yet he hadn't. If he had a reason for leaving her unharmed, there was no way he would let another of the Fallen hurt her...

... she hoped.

The policeman tucked his baton into his belt and lifted the visor of the helmet, pulling the whole thing off his head and letting it fall to the ground. Everything except for his eyes was hidden behind black wool. He yanked his hands out of his gloves, throwing them away too, and grabbed the front of his balaclava, pulling it up and back until she could see him clearly.

Xaphan.

"You."

"Me." He flashed her a shark-like grin, and suddenly his hand was moving to his belt – and before Alice could blink, the baton smashed into the side of her head, sending her stumbling sideways. She hit the ground hard, and pain flared from her hip to her shoulder as she rolled, fire dancing across the tips of her fingers. She swallowed the pain down, held the fire back and sat up. Black stars burst behind her eyes and the world began to sound tinny and far away. A foot came down on the back of her hand as she tried to push herself up.

She tried again, but her legs felt weak. A knock to the side of her head added bright red suns to the black stars dancing in front of her. She blinked hard, shook her head.

And then, swimming into view, a scarred face and a too-wide smile leaning over her.

"You were looking for me, weren't you? Here I am." He tossed the baton aside.

Alice recoiled, but Xaphan simply grinned harder and clamped a hand around the back of her head, reaching out with his other to stroke her hair. "Now, now. You don't have to be like that. I thought we were friends. How do you like our party?" he asked, turning his head away from her and surveyed the crowd. "It's quite something, isn't it? And this... this is only the beginning."

Something slipped over Alice's head, around her neck, and pulled tight.

Alice gagged and swatted at Xaphan, but it was no use. Fire blazed up around her hands and throat, weaving through her hair like ribbons, but Xaphan just laughed.

"I thought we were past all this, Alice! You know me, and I know you. You'll always try and burn your way out of everything." He leaned closer, brushing her hair aside and whispering into her ear. "And I won't let you." She could feel his breath on her neck. He smelled of oil and soot, and something faintly metallic. "What is it that fire needs to burn? Oh, yes. *Air.*"

Everything was fading: the street, the world and the fire with it. The pain in Alice's throat had faded to a dull throb, and her lungs felt like they were full of water. Through the sound of her heart hammering in her ears, Alice was almost sure she heard Xaphan humming a tune.

The black stars were spreading across her field of vision, shutting out everything else. There was only darkness, and her pulse starting to slow, and the world was so very, very far away.

With a roaring sound, everything exploded into focus. Air rushed back into her lungs, forcing its way down her aching throat. Alice coughed and flames blazed across her skin.

Blinking as the world came back into focus, she saw Xaphan being thrown into the crowd by an Earthbound in riot gear, his grey, foreshortened wings twitching as he moved. Xaphan snarled, but the Earthbound simply pointed at him, glaring from behind his helmet. The Fallen scowled, spat in his direction and vanished into the crowd.

The Earthbound turned back to Alice and dropped to his knees beside her, pulling off his helmet and balaclava. It was Castor, the angel from the warehouse.

"We really need to stop meeting like this," he said with a grin.

"Nice outfit," Alice croaked. Her throat felt like someone had poured paint stripper down it. "Aren't you a little old for dress-up?"

"Who's dressing up? I'll have you know this is for real!" He stroked the front of his uniform, looking offended.

"You're a police officer. Seriously."

"What the fuck else am I going to do with myself?" he asked, holding out a hand. "Can you stand?"

"One way to find out." She let him help her up as the flames burned out, trying to decide which she wanted to recover first: her dignity or her balance. She went for balance. She wasn't sure dignity was an option. "Where did he go?"

"The Fallen? No idea."

"You know who that was, don't you?"

"Do I look like I was born yesterday? Right now, I've got bigger problems than Xaphan. I've got a full-scale riot, and three officers separated from the line. If we don't get them back, this lot'll tear them apart. You need to get out of here."

"People keep telling me that."

"Maybe once in a while you should listen, yeah?" Castor was already walking away from her, pulling the balaclava back over his face.

And she would have answered, except that when she turned around, Toby was standing directly behind her, his eyes wide. Their eyes met and he took a step back from her.

"I came looking for you. I came back for you."

"Toby."

"What was that? You... you were burning. But you're fine... Look at you. You're fine." He waved a hand at her, oblivious to everything else. "How's that even possible?"

"I can explain... well. Not explain, maybe, but..."

"I don't... What's happening? What *is* this? What's happening, Alice?"

She already knew she'd lost him. It didn't matter what she said or didn't say; he was looking at her like she was a monster or a miracle.

She didn't have time to plead with Toby, or to tell him to go. She didn't even have time to tell him that this wasn't – any of it – what he thought. But the look on his face told her: whatever she said, it would never be enough.

She didn't have time; as she opened her mouth to speak, the smell of incense filled the air, and a single gunshot rang out.

Alice's head whipped round.

Mallory.

ALICE NO LONGER heard or saw anything around her. The smoke and the gas were forgotten. The Fallen were brushed aside, and the memory of Toby faded from her mind until it was less than a shadow. All these things were nothing compared to the thought racing through her head.

Mallory's back.

She craned her neck, but all she saw was the remnants of the riot. The sound of the shot might as well have gone entirely unheard for all the reaction it got: it was as though no-one had heard it at all. Perhaps, she thought, remembering Zadkiel's presence, nobody had.

Nobody but her.

She turned on the spot, but there was no sign of him, and so absorbed was she in looking for Mallory that she didn't even notice Toby was gone.

From somewhere down the road, she caught the scent again; that smell of incense... and now she could feel him. Feel his anger at the chaos, feel his determination... and something else. Not fear, exactly; concern? He was nervous, certainly. Not afraid, but...

Slowly at first, and then with increasing confidence, Alice made her way down the street.

The crowd was less dense here; there was no attack, only retreat. Some were walking, some were running. Several were limping, bleeding heavily. One man had his arm slung around another's shoulder, leaning on him for support. Others jogged backwards, jeering and raising their middle fingers at the rest of the crowd, at the police. Alice passed a couple sitting on the edge of the kerb, their heads in their hands, sobbing. She sympathised. Keeping a lid on her gift, on the all-encompassing desire to burn out the pain and the confusion of the crowd, had left her exhausted. It was all she could do not to sit down beside them and sob with them.

None of these people knew what had really happened here, that they had been sucked into the front line of the fight between the angels and the Fallen. The Fallen had pushed their buttons, had manipulated and twisted them, and the angels had turned up to put a stop to it.

No wonder the people were dazed: they had seen a Descended manifest in their midst, and had had all memory of it wiped from their minds by Zadkiel and his choir. Alice understood, and – if she was honest – was relieved, but on the other hand, if Zadkiel could make a hundred, two hundred people all forget what they had seen, what else could he do?

A shiver ran down the length of her body – one which had nothing to do with the chilly air. Michael with his fire; Gabriel with his lightning, and Zadkiel, who could take away your mind on a whim. She wasn't sure who worried her more: the Fallen, or the Archangels.

An angel – a Descended – suddenly stepped into her path, blocking her way. He looked vaguely familiar, with sandy hair cropped close to his skull. He looked her up and down. "He said you'd come."

People really *did* seem to be making assumptions about her today.

He blinked at her, then stood aside.

And there, behind him, was Mallory.

He looked almost exactly as she had expected, down to his boots and torn jeans; his leather jacket was as ropey as ever. But there were more lines than she remembered around his brown eyes, and his dark hair was flecked with fresh grey. He was fiddling with his gun as the other angel stepped aside, so absorbed that he didn't notice her watching him. The tiredness came off him in waves.

She felt unexpectedly guilty. She had spent the last six months being angry at him for leaving her; where had he been to leave him so worn-down? What had he been doing?

He looked up, and their eyes met – and for what seemed like an age, they simply looked at each other.

And then he was smiling, and striding towards her and throwing his arms around her; lifting her off her feet in a bear-hug, and before she knew what she was doing, she was crying.

"What's this?" He pulled away from her, rubbing at her damp cheeks with his thumb. "If it's that bad seeing me, I'll go again..." He started to turn away, and she grabbed onto his arm.

"No. It's not! Really."

"I'm kidding, Alice. Stop being so bloody wet, would you?"

"Sorry." She scrubbed at her face. "It's been a bit of a trying day, you know?"

"Is that what you call it? Personally, I'd call it getting the shit kicked out of us. I think it's fair to say we lost this one." He safetied his gun and it disappeared into his jacket. "And you? How're you doing?" He put his hands on her shoulders and held her out at arm's length, ducking down slightly to peer at her. "You look like you've been in the wars."

"Something like."

"You've been getting into trouble, haven't you?"

"No..."

"That's not what I heard. I heard you've been causing quite a few problems for the Fallen. You and your little crew of Earthbounds."

"What else was I supposed to do? What would *you* have done?"

"I thought you'd have learned by now that the *last* thing you want to do is follow my example, kid." He grinned, and folded his arms across his chest. "But whatever it is you've been up to? It stops. Now."

"Now *you* get to tell me what to do, too?"

"Damn straight I do."

"You don't just get to..."

"Now you listen to me, Alice..." Mallory's voice was suddenly hard as he leaned closer to her. "You may think that you're indestructible. You are not. And I've lost enough to know better than to let you go throwing yourself into every scrappy little fight that comes your way. You're too..."

"Important?" she spat. "Yeah. Right. I remember." And she did. She remembered Michael telling her that she was a weapon – *his* weapon, to be used against the Fallen as he saw fit.

"Yes. Important." Mallory's voice softened, and his eyes looked sad. He sighed. "But this is neither the time nor the place. We need to go." He raised his voice, calling to the angel who had blocked her way. "Pollux! We're moving."

Alice glanced behind her and saw Pollux nod once. He really *did* look familiar, but she couldn't work out why. She pushed the thought away, simply relieved to have found Mallory again. Descendeds might make people feel better simply with their presence, but this was something else, more than that. This was Mallory; here, now, back again. And Alice felt better than she had in a long time.

CHAPTER TEN

Echoes and Ghosts

"WHAT TOOK YOU lot so long? You look like shit, by the way." There was a man sitting at Adriel's desk, leafing through one of the ledgers. A man who was most definitely not Adriel.

"I see you've yet to develop anything like manners. Or charm," Mallory replied, leaning against the door frame.

"Charm's overrated." The intruder leaned back in the chair and pulled a pair of sunglasses down from the top of his head, folding them up and stuffing them into the pocket of his jacket. "And speaking of people with neither charm nor manners, it's good to see you."

"Really? Did you miss me, Vin? I'm afraid I didn't miss you. Not once. Not even slightly." Mallory's scowl crumbled, and he grinned. Vin winked back at him.

Alice shook her head. Some things, apparently, never changed.

"Where'd you get the book?" she asked, pointing at the ledger the Earthbound had been reading.

He blinked back at her, then pointed over his shoulder. "On the shelves. I got bored waiting. Don't you guys keep some magazines in or something?"

"It's not a dentist's office, you know. How did you get in, anyway?" Alice leaned back out of Adriel's office doorway, and looked at the door swinging open on its hinges. The way she'd left it.

Whoops.

She glanced back at Vin, who looked innocent. "Someone forget to lock up, did they? I tell you what: you're lucky I didn't lock it with me inside and leave the lot of you out there. Have you *seen* it out there?"

"Still trotting out that 'I'm a lover, not a fighter' line, are we?" Mallory had leaned across the desk and spun the open ledger round, and was now flipping through it. "We *were* outside."

"And a fat lot of good I bet it's done you." Vin suddenly looked serious. "There are Fallen everywhere. In the open. Right there. You can say whatever you want about me, but I've paid my dues, and I've not complained – not once – but I'm not touching that mess. Not with a forty-foot pole. Screw it."

Alice frowned at him. There was something... off about him, somehow. Something she couldn't put her finger on.

She realised she wasn't just frowning, but staring. And, being Vin, he was staring back with an expectant look on his face.

"It's bothering you, isn't it?" he said.

"I couldn't tell you exactly what *it* is, but yes."

"It's the hair."

"Funny."

Mallory cleared his throat. "No, really," he said, "it's his hair."

Alice looked at Vin again – and now she saw it. The faint streak of grey that ran through his black hair and disappeared behind his ear.

Like Mallory, he had grey hair. *New* grey hair.

She looked from one to the other of them, and Mallory nodded. "I know. Later."

Vin spotted the change in his tone, and ran his fingers through his own hair. "I thought it made me look distinguished. Silver fox, right?"

He ducked as Mallory threw the ledger at him.

It landed with a thump and a ruffle of pages. The room darkened, and the air filled with whispers and echoes. Alice, Vin and Mallory turned to see Adriel silhouetted in the doorway, his wings folding behind him. As he came closer, the heavy book flew back up to the desk – narrowly missing Vin again on its way – and settled on the polished surface.

As soon as he stepped into the office, the shadows retreated; the voices faded, and framed in the door was a man with nothing more remarkable about his appearance than a pair of dusty patches on the knees of his suit. He surveyed the three of them and arched an eyebrow, and Alice wondered just how bad they looked: how bad *she* looked, covered in dust and dirt and shards of glass; her face stained with smoke and her eyes red from the tear gas.

After she had found Mallory, it became entirely apparent that there was no point in staying out on the street. The Fallen were there – no doubt about it – but they were too well camouflaged. There were too many people for them to hide among. And when the Descendeds and Zadkiel the Archangel disappeared, it was obvious that Lucifer had too. The angels had lost their prize, leaving only Mallory, Pollux and a handful of Earthbounds scattered through the chaos. And it *was* chaos. With the angels gone, the full weight of everything that had just happened began to sink into the crowd. They still didn't remember the angels, but they remembered everything else. The bottles. The batons. The bricks and the flying glass.

Clouds of smoke and gas drifted along the street and they began to understand what they had done.

And as they began to feel it, to *really* feel it, the inside of Alice's skin began to itch. It wasn't much – not at first – just a tiny prickle on the back of her hand. But it was spreading, and fast.

"Mallory?"

He didn't seem to hear her; he was staring down the street towards a man leaning against a lamppost.

"Mallory! I could really do with not being here, if you get my drift."

"Couldn't we all?" he muttered, stubbing at the bottom of a broken bottle with his toe. But he had seen the fire burning in her eyes, and he turned and whistled at Pollux. The other angel nodded.

"Where to?"

"The office." Alice ducked her head and wrapped her arms around her ribs, trying to keep herself from shaking. "It's just over there."

"I know where it is." Mallory put a hand on her shoulder and steered her through the ragged crowd. There were still knots of people, scarves pulled over their faces, jeering and chanting, and one man peeled off to rush at them as they walked. "You've got to be kidding me," muttered Mallory, raising his elbow and driving it sharply into the man's face. Their would-be attacker stumbled back with a stunned expression, blood pouring from his nose. Alice's face started to ache as Mallory shook his head in disbelief. "Some people."

The windows of the funeral parlour hadn't been quite so lucky this time around: one had been completely shattered, and a starburst of cracks glittered in the middle of the other. The door was, of course, open, and creaked as Mallory marched Alice through it. Pollux hung back, turning to face the street like a sentry and waiting for them.

Alice leaned against the desk, tipping her head back and swallowing deep breaths of quiet, calm air. Even with the window broken and the door hanging open, the office was serene compared with the world outside, as long as you ignored the glass all over the carpet. And the brick sitting in the middle of the sofa. And what looked like a firework sticking out of one of the flower vases. In here, away from everyone else, she could think. And she could burn it all away.

Spirals of fire sprang up around her wrists; wound through her hair and around her neck. It burned away the pain, the confusion and fear... everything from the crowd, everything from Lucifer, from Xaphan, from Zadkiel. All of them. As the fire died down, Alice was the only one left in her head, and everything she felt was hers alone. She felt better. She didn't even feel guilty about the carpet. Not much, anyway.

Mallory was perched on the back of the sofa, waiting. "Outside. All that... you kept it in. I'm impressed."

"I've had plenty of time to practice."

"Oh, no. I'm not getting into that conversation."

"Mallory..."

"I said no." His voice was still quiet, but it was firm. His absence was not up for discussion. "Besides, you've got company." He pointed to the door to Adriel's office, which was slightly ajar, and that was where they found Vin, hunched over Adriel's desk and completely absorbed in reading the ledger.

The ledger upon which Adriel now drummed his fingertips like a disappointed headmaster about to discipline a class. He looked from Alice's smoke-stained face to Mallory's boots to Vin's fingers, blackened by ink where he had touched the pages. "Open it," he said, tapping the closed cover. "Open it to any page."

He pushed the book towards Vin, who looked nervous but did as he was told.

Adriel nodded at the book. "A name."

"Err... Holland?"

"Thirteenth of July, nineteen twenty-three. Oak coffin. Another."

Vin ran his finger down the page. "Samson."

"Pauper burial, nineteen twenty-four. Shroud, no coffin. No family. Another."

"I think I get the picture..."

"I said *another*!"

"Fine." He rolled his eyes, and Alice saw Adriel's jaw set in a grim line. "Smith."

"Do you really think it's wise to tease me, Vhnori? If you had taken the time to count them, as I have, you would know that there are five hundred and thirty-two Smiths in that volume alone. But you wouldn't know this, because to you, that book is simply something to occupy your largely empty mind." He snatched the ledger from the desk, holding it close. "Every one of these names is a life. A life now lost. Some of these souls had none to mourn them, none to remember them. None but me. It is my privilege to do so, just as it was my privilege to care for them in death. These names matter. These ledgers matter. I will not see them taken lightly." He glowered at Vin, who stared at his shoes, looking suitably cowed.

"He didn't mean any harm," said Mallory, but Adriel shook his head and slid the book back onto its shelf.

"Perhaps not. But the result is the same, intentionally or no. The angels have grown careless; forgetful. They forget that humans are where the power lies. The Fallen have not been so foolish."

"Never thought I'd hear anyone saying that. Least of all you." Mallory did not sound surprised. Resigned, but not surprised.

Adriel opened his mouth to reply, but suddenly seemed to remember that Alice was in the room and closed it again. Instead, he looked her up and down and simply asked, "Are you alright?"

"I'm fine. I think."

"I should have been more specific, perhaps: are you hurt?"

"No. No, I'm not hurt." Her hand went to her throat. "Much. But..." Where should she start?

With Toby.

Adriel listened, his face a careful blank, as she told him what had happened. How she had been ambushed. How Castor had come to her rescue. How Toby had seen everything. Finally, he sighed and rubbed his hand across his forehead. "It could not be helped, Alice."

"I'm sorry. I am."

"One man is not the issue now, I fear. A street full of people, on the other hand, that *is* an issue, and one I imagine the Archangels will be most *eager* to discuss, Zadkiel or no Zadkiel. He does not take kindly to having his hand forced."

"Ah. Yes. Them." Alice had hoped that her meeting with Zadkiel might have covered that. With every word that came out of Adriel's mouth, it was sounding less and less likely.

"Indeed. And I presume that now the Archangels know where to find you."

"Yes."

"They've always known," Mallory snorted. "Michael's not stupid, and even if he was, all he's got to do is look inside her head to find out where she was. He's just too fixated on Lucifer to give a shit about anything else right now. I don't blame him, either: it's the Fallen I'm bothered about for the time being. At least we can count on the Archangels being on our side *some* of the time."

"Maybe. But what happened today..."

"What happened happened. We got sloppy. The Fallen punished us for it. It won't happen again."

"You sound very sure." Adriel stared at Mallory with his black eyes.

"I am sure. It won't happen again."

Vin interrupted them. "Well. This has all been lovely. And educational. I feel like I've grown as a person. But I'm starving, and I get cranky when I'm hungry. You don't want that. So can we, you know... go?"

"You're like a child, aren't you?" Mallory sounded more amused than he looked, and Vin shrugged.

"If that's meant as a compliment, yes. Yes, I am."

"You are. And it wasn't." He shook his head. "Adriel. A pleasure."

"Likewise, Mallory. Likewise." Adriel turned to Alice. "You will always be welcome here, Alice. You have a place here, a role to play. Know that."

"You say it like I'm not going to see you again for a while."

"Most people would find that a relief."

"I'm not most people." And before she could quite stop herself, Alice found that she was hugging him. Actually hugging Adriel, the Angel of Death. She mostly ignored Vin's raised eyebrow, only paying attention enough to pull a face at him over Adriel's shoulder. He pulled a face back, and Mallory muttered, "like a *child*," under his breath.

As Alice stepped back from Adriel, he straightened his tie. "I'm unaccustomed to this sort of behaviour."

"You mean no-one's hugged you in a while?"

"Or, indeed, ever. No."

"Well, now they have."

"They have. Look after yourself, Alice."

"Hungry, people. Hungry!" Vin was now pacing up and down. Alice grinned, and Mallory shook his head. "Five minutes. Five minutes, and already he's trying to kill me."

"Maybe if we feed him..."

"He'll shut up? Remind me: has that ever worked before?"

"There's a first time for everything, isn't there?"

But even though she was back with both Mallory and Vin; even though Adriel seemed to have given her his blessing to go (or sacked her, possibly) Alice couldn't quite shake the uneasy feeling she'd been carrying with her for days; the sensation that something wasn't quite right. As she reached the front door, she turned back to see Adriel outlined in the entrance of his office, his shadow ahead of him on the floor. He nodded, once, and was gone. One thing she did know, however, was that he and Mallory had said something to one another in that room – right in front of her. They had told each other something, something important, and she had absolutely no idea what it was.

CHAPTER ELEVEN

Just Because You're Done With the Past Doesn't Mean it's Done With You

"GET OFF MY bloody roof." Mallory had stopped midway along the path from the gate to the sacristy door.

Beside him, Alice cleared her throat. "*Your* roof?"

Mallory snorted. "My roof, your roof. I lived here first. When you've spent three sodding days up there with a hammer in a howling gale putting the slates back on, you can call it yours with my blessing." He turned his attention back to the roof. "Are you coming down, or am I going to have to come up there and fetch you?"

The angel on the roof stood up and stretched its clipped wings.

As they watched, the Earthbound shook out his feathers and jumped, gliding in a circle overhead before landing in front of them.

It was Castor, and Alice suddenly realised why Pollux looked so familiar; the similarity between them was obvious now, even down to the way they moved. They were brothers.

Castor walked towards them, his face breaking into a smile as he saw Alice.

"Well, well. Look at that. You made it out in one piece."

"I did. Thanks, by the way."

"Just doing my job. Both of them." He winked. "I meant it, though: you should try staying out of trouble once in a while. You might like it."

"I doubt it," Alice muttered, and caught the frown Mallory shot at her. "How about you?" she asked, hurriedly.

"Not so bad. Bit bruised after that little skirmish. One of the bastards blindsided me with a brick."

"Who was it?"

"Not Fallen. Human."

"Really?"

"Privilege of wearing the uniform, isn't it?" Castor gestured to the beautiful bruise beneath his left eye. "Mind you, I had it easy compared to some..." He tailed off, looking pointedly at her.

Mallory caught the look. "Oh? We obviously hadn't got to that yet, had we, Alice?"

"It's nothing."

"Nothing?" Castor chimed in. "Nothing? Sure." Alice gave him what she hoped was a stern glare – her sternest, in fact – and he smirked, but he also shut up. Eventually, he sighed. "Look. This is grand, really, but there is an actual point to my being here, as opposed to, you know, in the pub, which is where I would be if there was any justice in this world. Possibly with a bottle of Scotch." Seeing Mallory's eyes light up, he frowned. "I thought you'd given up?"

"Do I look like a quitter to you?"

Castor shook his head, then folded his arms across his chest. "Either way, you've got a visitor."

"Who has?" Alice asked. "Mallory, or me?"

"Well, I'm going to guess he's here for both of you: he was waiting, comforting as that is. I took the liberty: over here."

Castor trotted away from the path, leaving the others looking at each other in bemusement. "You heard the nice police officer," said Mallory with a shrug. Vin muttered something about a sandwich and kicked a stone, while Pollux said nothing, scowling. With more than a faint sensation of *deja vu*, Alice set off after them.

She had already met more than her share of the Fallen in the churchyard: the first she had encountered, Lilith, had been fairly quickly despatched by Mallory and Vin, but there had been others. Batarel. Goap. Jeqon. It was where Lucifer had spoken to her for the first time; where Mallory had shown her what he was capable of when he tied Rimmon to a tree and tortured him, to teach *her* a lesson.

Castor had stopped with his back to her, arms still folded across his chest. But she could already tell something was very wrong when Mallory's gun appeared in his hand, and that was without the look Vin shot her over his shoulder.

As she stepped between them and saw the Fallen leaning back against the tombstone, she understood why.

Xaphan was sitting on one of the newer graves, his legs crossed. The position looked slightly awkward, as he had had to arrange his limbs around the long metal spike which had been driven through one of his thighs, pinning it to the ground. Not that it seemed to bother him all that much; Alice could still hear him humming a tune under his breath. And he appeared to be making a daisy-chain.

He ignored them for a moment longer, then laid his hands in his lap and smiled up at them.

Flames rippled across the top of the headstone, spilling down the sides. The string of daisies in Xaphan's hands flared brightly, then collapsed into ash. The grass curled and blackened, forcing Vin to hop sideways in an attempt to get clear. It fell to Mallory to step closer to Alice and lay his hand on her arm.

"Alice?"

She ignored him, keeping her eyes fixed on Xaphan.

"Alice." Firmer this time, Mallory's fingers closed slightly around her elbow. He watched the flickering behind her eyes.

"Alice."

The fire died down, flames waning to nothing and leaving only a wide scorch mark in the grass around them.

And then Xaphan grinned at her and said, "How's the neck?" and the air caught fire.

* * *

MALLORY LEAPT BACK, pulling his hand away as the fire engulfed Alice with a roar; wrapping itself around every inch of her and spreading out across the ground like a flood. He shot a look first at Castor, then at Xaphan. Finally, he hauled Vin across to him and hissed in his ear. "Get her out of here. Calm her down. Whatever it takes."

"You serious?"

"What do you think?"

"Calm her down *how*?"

"Just get it done." And with that, he shoved Vin towards Alice.

Vin's voice drifted back to Mallory, "But *then* I get to eat, yeah?"

Mallory ignored him and turned his attention to Xaphan. Both Castor and Pollux had dropped back as Vin dragged Alice away, leaving them alone.

"Is this the part where you threaten me? Or are you going to just shoot me?" asked the Fallen.

"If I wanted to shoot you, you'd have been shot."

"No doubt. Perhaps you're planning to torture me first, *then* shoot me. I hear that's more your style." He tipped his head on one side and looked up at Mallory. "Of course, I'm forgetting. You're on a shorter leash these days, aren't you? Descendeds aren't supposed to get their hands dirty; at least, not as dirty as you like to. Earthbounds, on the other hand..." He gestured to the spike sticking out of his leg. "If I didn't know better, I'd think your boy rather enjoyed doing that. Well," he mused, "what do you expect from the police?"

Mallory struck him across the jaw, knocking his head violently enough to make the bones of his neck click. He crouched down in front of the Fallen and levelled the barrel of his Colt directly between Xaphan's eyes. "Now, I'm only going to ask you this once, so if I were you, I'd pay attention." The gun twitched as he spoke; Xaphan's eyes followed it. When Mallory leaned forward, his next words were little more than a whisper. "Where's your girlfriend?"

Xaphan smirked, and Mallory's finger tightened on the trigger.

"Stop. I'm here. I'm here, Mallory." The woman's voice came from thin air.

Satisfied, Mallory lowered the handgun and rocked back onto his heels. "Of course you are, Florence. Why don't you join us?"

A way off to his left, the air shimmered and a young woman appeared. Her hair was almost entirely white, except for a streak of black, although her face was young. There were dark circles beneath her eyes, and she looked tired and pale.

"Let him go. Please."

"Let him go? One wrong word and I'll get Alice back here before you can blink, and then you'll be begging me to shoot him in the face, never mind what she'll do to you, Florence." Alice had made it clear she would kill her if their paths crossed again. Kill her very, *very* slowly. It was Florence who had helped the Fallen get their foothold in the world; Florence who was largely responsible for them tracking Alice through hell, and Florence who had stood by as Alice was locked in a cage and forced to watch an old friend murdered by Xaphan. Alice had thought of Florence and her brother Jester, both half-borns like her, as friends... making Florence's betrayal even harder to take. And yet here she was, on Alice's doorstep, waiting for her. Why?

Florence took a step forward. "We... I... It's Jester. He needs your help."

ALICE WAS TOO angry to do anything other than let herself be led. Eventually, Vin decided he had got her far enough away from Xaphan and settled himself on the back of a gravestone. "You know," he said, "I read this book once. It had a line in it about someone getting 'incandescent with rage.' I thought it was a stupid line, but you've got pretty close to it, haven't you?"

"Only the one book, Vin?" The fire dimmed slightly.

"Yeah. It didn't have any pictures in it, kind of put me off." He shook his head, but kept half an eye on her all the same.

The fire fell away as Alice laughed. He looked so serious that there wasn't much else she could do, and she settled herself on the next grave along, belonging to 'L. Harris.' She didn't think they'd mind. Vin peered over his sunglasses at her.

"Holding up?"

"Not really."

"What did he do? Not... back there. Now. This time. Why the pyro?" He was edging around what had happened in hell. What had happened when Xaphan had locked her in that cage in his lab. She shook the memory away.

"He came to say hello earlier, out in the street. And he wasn't alone."

"Lucifer?"

"And a rope." She rubbed at her neck again.

"You alright?"

"Fine. It's nothing."

"Nothing. Sure. I wish I could say I was surprised, but these days, they just won't stay down. And you've not told Mallory yet. Why?"

"Because he doesn't need to know."

"Uh-huh."

"What? I can take care of myself!"

"Sure you can. The way I heard it, that's absolutely true."

"And what's that supposed to mean?"

"Oh, nothing. Except that I heard you'd got yourself beaten half to a pulp taking on Murmur."

"Won, didn't I?"

"Sometimes, Alice, it's not about the winning."

"Never thought I'd hear an angel saying that."

"Yeah, but I'm not just any old angel, am I?" He winked at her.

"So now I have to sit here with you until the grown-ups are finished?"

He looked wounded. "Don't make it sound like a chore."

"You could at least tell me what you've been doing for the last six months, seeing as you seem to know everything about my life. How's Sari?"

"Next subject." Vin's voice took on a hard edge, and he turned his head away.

That was a shock. The last she'd heard, Vin was besotted with Sari. For him to react to her name like that...

"You want to talk about it?"

"Let's just say 'no' and leave it at that, shall we?"

"If you change your mind..."

"Yeah. Thanks." And that was that.

Except it wasn't. She could feel it, even from here. He hurt. He hurt *so* very much. And even though he knew that she couldn't help but feel it, he was still trying to hide it. "I mean it."

"I know. Thanks." He relaxed and the cold edge melted from his voice. "But you don't want to hear about my love life. I, however, want to hear about yours..." He shot her a grin and waggled his eyebrows, and even though there was nothing to tell – even though he was obviously teasing – she felt her face flush. His grin widened.

"Oh. *Really*?"

"Shut up, Vin."

"No, go on."

"Shut *up*!"

He swiped at her shoulder, and she swiped back, and that was the exact point at which Mallory walked around the corner.

"Are you *kidding* me? I can't leave you two alone for a minute. It's like being a bloody teacher. Worse: a nanny. For fuck's sake." He was less angry than he was trying to sound, but something was definitely bothering him. "Inside. We need to talk," he said, "and you're not going to like this. Either of you."

CHAPTER TWELVE

Where Angels Fear to Tread

ALICE SHOULD HAVE known what was happening: from the way Castor stood just inside the door, from the way Pollux watched her as she stepped inside, from the way Mallory kept a hand resting on her back as he ushered her ahead of him. All this, and still she didn't see it coming. Not until she walked into the sacristy and saw the two of them sitting on the beaten-up old sofa in the middle of the room.

The world blurred. She felt herself lunge forward, but she suddenly had no control over her body. Someone else was at the wheel, foot to the floor, making her spin and spin as she hurled herself at Florence. There was a sound like an animal screaming: something roaring in pain, and it was only as she felt her arm connect with flesh and saw Castor stumble back that she realised it was her. It was all her.

The moment she had laid eyes on Florence, her mind emptied. Where there had been thoughts, feelings, something *rational* before, now there was only fury. No fire, no flames. Just hate. The implacable need to tear the woman in front of her to pieces.

She was wrenched back, away from her prey, and thrown to the ground. Mallory leaned over her, a hand on her chest, pinning her down. "Get a grip, Alice."

Alice couldn't do anything more than splutter at him. He was on *their* side? She stared up at him and he stared straight back. "Trust me."

She nodded mutely, which he took as a sign that he could let her up. As she brushed herself down, she caught sight of Vin, still in the doorway. He was watching Xaphan and Florence with a look of barely-disguised contempt, his fists curled into tight balls and clamped down by his sides.

Florence had the grace to look uncomfortable. How else could she look, sitting in the back room of a church and surrounded by people who wanted very little more than to see her dead? Xaphan was one of the Fallen – more than that, he was one of their generals, one of the Twelve – but Florence was a traitor to the angels. She had betrayed them all: her mentor, her friends. They had good reason to want her dead.

"Tell them what you told me," Mallory barked. "And quickly. I can't promise you they'll both control their tempers for long."

"I don't know what to..."

"Then choose. You want to burn to death, or you want to join the statues out there?" Mallory nodded first to Alice, then to Vin – neither of whom had taken their eyes off Florence. Xaphan muttered something under his breath, nursing the bloody wound on his thigh... and quick as a flash, Mallory was across the room again and in front of him, the barrel of his gun pressing into the ragged hole in his leg. Xaphan howled, but Mallory only pressed harder, twisting as the barrel dug deeper. "Did I ask for your opinion?" he snarled, then looked back up at Florence. "Spit it out, girl."

"We need your help. I do. He does..." She shook her head. "Jester. Jester does."

Hearing Jester's name, Vin twitched. "What did you do to him?"

"Me? No – I didn't!" Florence pressed herself back into the sofa as Vin took a step forward. Alice had never seen him look so angry.

"Where is he?"

"He... they... Michael. Michael took him."

"*What?*"

"Michael took him." Florence's face had gone from pale green to bone-white. "I need your help to get him back."

"FROM MICHAEL? WHAT the fuck would Michael want with him? He's not done anything –" Vin suddenly tailed off, whipping round and kicking out at the wall. "Idiot. I warned him."

"You warned him? About what?" Mallory had pulled his gun out of Xaphan's leg, and was wiping the blood off the barrel with what looked like Alice's favourite tea-towel. On any other day, she might have been annoyed.

Vin's mouth set in a line. "I heard that Michael was after Jester. I didn't believe it, but I told him to keep his head down. There's been nothing from him in a few days, so I thought he'd actually listened for once..."

Alice had just about got enough of a grip on herself to be able to concentrate on something other than not setting fire to the building. It was challenging – a little like trying to pat her head and hop on the spot at the same time – but she was reasonably confident she could do it. Reasonably. She wondered whether she'd replaced the fire extinguisher under the sink: she'd gone through the last three so quickly that she couldn't quite remember.

"Why did Michael want Jester?" she asked.

Vin rubbed a hand over his eyes. "Purson."

The name made Alice's fingers itch. Fire threatened to fight its way back out from inside her, but she swallowed it back down. Purson. She remembered *him* all too well: Lucifer's favourite torturer and executioner, he had vanished during the battle for hell. The angels had, for the most part, assumed he was dead, but judging by Vin's face, she wondered whether that was the truth. He looked... shifty. There was no other way of putting it.

"Vhnori," she said, using his full name and making him roll his eyes, "why did Michael want Jester?"

"We took Purson, alright?"

"You what?"

"We took him. We caught him, and we took him."

"To Hong Kong."

"Yes."

"And?"

"You don't want to know."

"I don't... oh, tell me you didn't? Please tell me you didn't."

Vin had fixed his gaze firmly on a spot on the far wall. "You weren't there, Alice."

"I wasn't there? Wasn't there when, exactly? I wasn't there when he executed someone in front of me? Or I wasn't there when he dropped you off the top of a building? Don't you *dare*."

"It doesn't matter." He hung his head.

"What doesn't matter? That you've tortured one of the Fallen?"

"Hey, I didn't see you judging anyone when Castor stuck a spike through Xaphan's leg. Or when Mallory just jammed his gun into an open wound."

"That's different."

"Yeah? Funny how that works, isn't it?"

"You know what he did."

"And like you said, you know what Purson did to me."

"I never thought you were the type to do it back." She shook her head. "So now I have to worry about Mallory *and* you doing it?"

"Oh, you can leave me out of this," Mallory said from the corner of the room. He wasn't watching them: he was watching Xaphan. None of this seemed to come as a surprise, and if Alice didn't know better, she would have assumed that Mallory already knew...

Her mouth dropped open." You knew about this?"

"About this?" He waved his gun at Xaphan and Florence. "Or about that?" He gestured at Vin. "Because *that* I knew about. You don't seriously think I wouldn't, do you?"

"Jesus. Next you'll be telling me you helped him..." Mallory sniffed and refused to look her in the eye. "Oh, come *on*."

"Can you perhaps concentrate on the matter in hand, Alice? You're perfectly free to tell me how disappointed in me you are, but now isn't the best time."

"I can't even..." Alice held up her hands and shot Vin a dirty look. "What happened to you?" she hissed at him, but he shook his head.

"Not now."

Someone was slow-clapping. Xaphan had leaned back into the threadbare cushions and was watching them with an amused look on his face.

"Well, well. Dissent in the ranks, Mallory?"

"Shut up."

"No, really. I mean, you honestly think you can win? You can't even control your own underlings."

"Shut up, Xaphan."

"If it wasn't so funny, it would be tragic. You know that, don't you?"

"I... said... shut... up." Mallory strode back to the sofa with his gun, pointing it at Xaphan's nose. Xaphan snorted, and leaned forward so that his forehead was resting against the end of the barrel.

"Well? What are you waiting for?"

Alice could see everything that Mallory was thinking. It was all over his face; etched into the lines around his eyes.

She could stop him.

She *should* stop him.

But.

In the end, it was Castor who placed his hand over Mallory's and turned the gun away. "In my professional opinion," he said softly, "everyone needs to take a moment." He turned to Xaphan. "And you, my friend, need to give some thought to the predicament in which you find yourself. Because you're in a room with a Descended, an Earthbound and a half-born who all want to kill you. Keep pushing. I'll let them take turns, and I will personally see to it that you stay alive long enough for all of them to get a go." He slid Mallory's gun out of his grip and stood there, turning it over in his hands. "Nice. Nice heft, you know? I've been thinking about getting one of these." Before anyone could move, he had slipped his finger across the trigger and shot Xaphan in his injured leg. The gunshot echoed in the tiny room, making Florence clap her hands over her ears. None of the others moved, with the exception of Xaphan, who roared with pain and clutched his leg. Castor blinked at him. "Sorry about that." He handed the Colt back to Mallory. "You want to watch the safety on that, mate,"

"Thanks for the tip." Mallory was smirking. As Castor came back to stand next to Alice, she could have sworn she saw him wink. Xaphan, meanwhile, was whimpering in a most uncharacteristic way, and Florence was clearly wishing she was invisible. Or dead. Or both.

Out of the corner of her eye, Alice saw a spark float up from her hand, and she realised she hadn't been concentrating. Castor's little display had distracted her just enough for her guard to slip. With a sigh, she elbowed her way past Mallory and Vin and stood in front of Florence, arms folded, waiting.

Florence looked up into eyes which were spinning discs of fire, and realised she had no choice but to talk.

THE LAST PLACE anyone had seen Jester was in Hong Kong. He had been with Vin, staying at his apartment with Sari, who knew nothing of the Fallen locked in a crate in the building's basement... not then, at any rate. Jester had been uneasy, had said something to Vin about needing some time, and had gone for a walk. That was the last anyone had heard from him.

Until Florence got word that he had been seen in Mont Saint-Michel. No Man's Land. Which could only mean that he had been taken there, and that he was Michael's prisoner.

"But what the hell would Michael want from Jester? He let us all go." Alice didn't add that she was the only one he said he'd be coming for.

"And why do you care? You picked your side." Vin glared at Florence.

"Because he's still my brother."

"Is he?"

Florence's voice cracked. "I can't just leave him..."

"You already did."

"IT'S NOT MICHAEL." Mallory had listened to everything Florence said, and to Alice and Vin, and he shook his head. "If it was Michael, we'd know. Believe me, we'd know."

"Then why would he be taken?" Florence sniffed.

"Who's to say he has been?"

"No," said Vin. "He's got no reason to be in No Man's Land."

"None except Zadkiel. And don't call it that."

"Whatever. Because knowing Zadkiel's around makes it so much better, doesn't it?"

"Well..." Mallory shrugged.

As usual, Alice felt like she was only hearing half the conversation. "No Man's Land?"

Mallory barely glanced up, so deep was he in thought. "Michael's fortress: it's what some of the... less bright among us call it. It's where he took Lucifer's body. He's holed up there along with half his choir, and Zadkiel."

Alice's mind flashed back to the Archangel from the riot. "And Jester's Zadkiel's choir..."

Mallory nodded. "But I don't know why he'd take him." He paused. "Actually, that's a lie. I know exactly why he'd take him..."

"No." Castor's voice came from the back of the room. Alice glanced round at him and saw his mouth set in a firm line. "Zadkiel wouldn't do that. He's not the type."

"You sure?" Mallory didn't exactly sound convinced, but Vin nodded, and Alice's eyes dropped to his forearm. She'd forgotten he was one of Zadkiel's choir.

"I'm sure. If Zadkiel has him, it's on Michael's orders."

"And Michael...?"

Every eye in the room turned to Alice. She shuffled her feet, uncomfortable at being the focus of their attention. "What?"

"You're the only one here who can tell us anything about Michael. Why would he take Jester?"

"How do I know? Maybe he's pissed off. Maybe he's going to try and make an example of him. Maybe he found out you caught Purson and he wants to give him a medal." She tugged at her hair. It was all too much, and it was too hard not throwing herself at Florence, at Xaphan, and taking out everything she was feeling on them. Her fingers burned, her skin itched and there was a ringing in her ears which threatened to drown out everything else. Realising they were all still watching her, she shrugged. "You want to know my experience of Michael? He's a psychopath. And you want to know what he's capable of? *Anything*."

"Well, that's certainly set my mind at ease," muttered Xaphan, who had recovered himself enough to start being sarcastic. Florence let out a whimper.

Mallory looked at each of them in turn, stony-faced. Eventually, his gaze came to rest on Vin. "Well?"

"Well what?"

"He's one of yours."

"He is."

"You're going to say something stupid, aren't you?"

"You don't know that."

"I know you. You and stupid go hand in hand."

"Like you said, Mallory..."

"Yeah. I know. Stupid." Mallory tipped his head back and stared at the ceiling for a moment, then growled in frustration. "How could you lose him, Vhnori?"

Alice butted in. "How could you get him involved in that in the first place? I thought you were..."

"Better than that?" Vin snapped back. "Well, maybe you were wrong." He turned back to Mallory. "I'll go. I'll go alone."

"You will not. Not after last time. Might I remind you that Michael also took Gabriel with him, and Earthbound or not, he'd still love a chance to take a swing at you – never mind what he might have said to Michael between then and now."

"I can't ask you to get involved."

"And you never have to. But this is on you. You understand?"

Vin nodded back at Mallory, who seemed satisfied – and he rounded on Florence and Xaphan. "And you. I should kill you. Right now, both of you. But I've got a better idea." He leaned closer to them, spreading his wings so that they all but filled the tiny room. "You're going to come with us. This time? I'm going to hand you over to Michael myself. You for Jester. Seems like a fair trade."

"Hardly," Xaphan spat, but Mallory simply laughed.

"You don't get a choice. Your girlfriend there wants our help? She's got it. But it comes at a price, and you're both going to pay."

"Do I NEED to tell you I have a bad feeling about this?" asked Alice.

"No, but I doubt that's going to stop you." Mallory's voice was flat.

"You're not taking this particularly seriously, are you?"

"Well, perhaps you'd care to tell me how I *should* be taking it?" He slid the spring he was cleaning back into the body of his gun and set the whole thing down on the table, wiping his hands with a cloth. "I think it's insanity, but I'm not doing it for me, am I?" He lowered his voice, and looked over his shoulder towards the door. Vin had stepped out 'for some air' a little while before, and Castor and Pollux had between them removed Florence and Xaphan. So it was just Alice and Mallory, sitting side by side on the moth-eaten sofa.

"It doesn't sound like it's his fault…"

"And it's not. But that isn't the point. Vin feels responsible. He's convinced that this is something to do with Jester helping him with Purson. I think there's more to it than that, but he's stubborn, and a miserable git when he's moping about something. He's bad enough over Sari."

"What happened?"

"Shouldn't have said that, should I?" He screwed up his nose. Alice ignored him.

"She left him?"

"You could say that." He picked up another piece of the gun, and began slotting it back together, talking as he worked. "Sari's a bit of an odd one. They've been dancing around each other as long as anyone can remember, but after hell, I think she finally thought she'd give him a shot."

"Which he blew by torturing a Fallen in the basement."

"Pretty much."

"She's got a point. I can't say I'd be keen on my boyfriend going in for torture."

"Right. Who'd do something like that, anyway?"

Alice hit him with a cushion, a little harder than was probably necessary. It was all she had.

For a while, the only sounds were the *clicks* of Mallory reassembling his Colt. Eventually, he sat back, the gun resting on the table in one piece, and rolled his neck. "I like what you've done with the place."

"Cleaned it, you mean?"

"That too."

"Do you miss it?"

"Sometimes. But I was trying to give you a chance to get on with your life. Remember what that's like?"

"Not really."

"I mean it. You don't want to get any more tangled up with us than you need to be. It doesn't usually end well, in case you hadn't noticed..."

"I noticed."

"Exactly. I wanted to give you at least a shot at being... normal. As normal as you get, anyway," he said, nudging her in the ribs. She smiled, but he carried on. "I felt I owed it to you. And what do you do with that chance? You get into fights with the Fallen, and go and work for the Angel of Death. Only you, Alice. Only you."

"Is that why you came back?"

"Something like that." The corners of his eyes creased with the beginnings of a smile.

"And what about you? Are you going to tell me about the magic grey hair? Don't think I forgot."

"Subtle, aren't you? It's not good, put it that way. We're ageing."

"And you shouldn't be, right?"

"Yes and no. Everything ages. We just do it very, very slowly. Or *should* do."

"It's the Fallen, isn't it? Something changed."

"They're winning. That's what. They're in control. In spite of everything we've done – or maybe *because* of it – they're in control."

"So what does that mean?"

"It means all bets are off."

CHAPTER THIRTEEN

Served Cold

Forfax snapped his fingers and Kim the waitress jumped to attention. He didn't bother to speak, simply jabbed at a stack of glasses and a bottle, and she scrabbled to get them onto the tray and to follow him. He spun on his heel and strode off through the bar, his shiny black shoes clicking on the floor and the end of his cane tapping alongside him as he walked. The boss had been in a foul mood all night, and she didn't want to be the one to get on his bad side – not after yesterday, when he'd broken one of the dancers' jaws with the pommel of his cane. She'd been 'out of time,' he'd said as he straightened his sleeves afterwards, leaving her in a whimpering heap on the floor.

The bar was busy – more so than usual – and rowdy, *much* more than usual. Everyone in there seemed louder, drunker, less steady on their feet then they should have been, and the air was thick with the smell of spilled beer and stale sweat. It wasn't a glamorous place to work at the best of times, with its sticky floor and stickier bathroom tiles, but it paid the rent. Just about.

Kim scurried after her employer, weaving between bodies and trying to keep the back of Forfax's head in sight. His oiled hair gleamed under the spotlights as they passed the dancers, heading for a narrow black door to the side of the stage marked 'EMPLOYEES ONLY – STRICTLY NO ADMITTANCE.' He punched a code into the numerical lock and kicked the door open, not bothering to check whether she was behind him. She lunged for the opening, just managing to get the toe of her shoe into the gap before the door swung shut. Something in her foot went *crunch*, but there wasn't time to worry about it. Forfax was walking; and when Forfax walked, you followed.

Behind the door lay a warren of passageways and storage areas, most of them hardly used. Back here, everything smelt damp and green, and stains crawled along the walls. The wiring had corroded in more places than it hadn't, and rats scuttled along the corridor alongside her as she fought to keep the tray steady. The sound of their claws on the floor made her shudder.

The footsteps ahead of her had stopped, and Kim almost dropped the tray as Forfax's face loomed out of the darkness at her. "Is there a problem?" he asked, his pointed nose and pale skin making him look almost vampiric in the gloom.

"No," she said, her voice sounding small.

"Good. I don't want to keep him waiting." And with that, he turned again and was off, whistling as he walked, his cane tap-tap-tapping on the bare concrete.

Kim decided to hand in her notice tomorrow.

Many twists, turns and rats later, the corridor came to an end at a doorway hung with a plastic strip curtain. The broad strips slapped at her bare shoulders as she pushed through them after him. She had never been this far behind the bar: the furthest she'd ever had to go, the furthest she'd ever been *allowed* to go, was to the storeroom where they kept the bottles. She hadn't even known all this was back here, and the slightly sick feeling in the pit of her stomach suggested that might not have been such a bad thing.

Striding ahead, Forfax was making his way through some sort of warehouse. Wooden crates and pallets were stacked ten feet high, towering above her head, and soon she had lost sight of her boss and could do little more than blindly follow the sound of his whistle through the maze.

She emerged from the walls of crates to a scene which could only be described as 'unexpected.' The space opened up, the ceiling disappearing into the dark, and from somewhere high above came the sound of shuffling feathers and cooing pigeons. Directly in front of her were two high-backed leather armchairs, placed with their backs to her, and between them a small wooden table. There was also a standard lamp with an old-fashioned tasselled shade, which was lit, although she could quite clearly see the plug lying loose on the concrete.

Seeing that Kim had stopped, Forfax snapped his fingers again and she hurried forward, carrying the tray as steadily as she could; picking her way between pigeon droppings and what looked like puddles of oil, seeping from the crates dotted around the floor.

There was another man standing beside Forfax, his arms folded in front of him: he was dressed entirely in black, nowhere near as expensively as Forfax in his tuxedo, but there was something very deliberate about the way he was dressed, with the sleeves of his coat bunched up about his elbows, leaving his forearms bare and a bright white band visible around the skin of his wrist. At first, she thought it odd that anyone would be wearing a coat like that so late in the spring, but as the gap between them narrowed, she felt the chill in the air around her and saw her breath misting in front of her.

The man in the black coat was watching her. He said nothing, his face all but expressionless as she drew closer. And then suddenly, he leaned forward to speak to someone in one of the chairs. From her position she couldn't see them; the back of the chair was too high. The man in the black coat's eyes flicked back up to her, and he nodded once, then straightened. Forfax simply pointed to the table.

She set the tray down and every fibre of her being told her not to look at the occupant of the chair. So she didn't. She lined up the three glasses, side by side, and opened the bottle with trembling hands, pouring the contents as carefully as she could. She could feel their eyes on her the whole time: all of them. Forfax nodded towards the chair, and she glanced up to see a hand extended towards her. She stared at it. It stayed there. Waiting. Around the wrist there was the same white band that she had seen on the man with the coat. It reminded her of something... horses, perhaps. Her uncle had bred horses, years ago. He had marked them, hadn't he? With a brand.

Forfax sighed loudly and snapped his fingers again, and Kim realised that she was supposed to be putting a glass into the hand. So she did. Her own hand shook so violently that she almost spilled the drink, but she took a deep breath and steadied her grip, passing the glass safely to the occupant of the chair.

The hand's fingers curled around the glass, removing it from her grasp. And as they did, she was startled to see the surface of the glass frost over, feathers of ice creeping out from beneath each of the fingers.

"Thank you," said a silky voice from the chair; one which was used to being obeyed. "That will be all."

This was not directed at her, she realised, but at the man with the coat, who nodded to Forfax.

Forfax, in turn, handed the other man his cane before beckoning her to come closer. She backed away from the table and the chairs and the odd lamp and the *voice*, and turned towards her employer, who was impatiently tapping his cane against the side of his foot.

"Is there anything else?" Kim asked, hoping more and more that she could get out of the warehouse and back to the relative comfort of the bar.

That's if she could find her way back...

Forfax looked her up and down.

"I have no further need of you," he muttered, and before she had completely registered what he said, he had clamped his hand down on her shoulder and was pulling her alongside him. She lost her balance, but it didn't seem to matter: he wound his hand into her hair and pulled. The pain brought tears to her eyes and she threw her hands up to grab hold of his wrist. The man in the coat smirked as she was dragged kicking past him, past the chair, whose occupant leaned forward and smiled at her with bright red eyes that glowed... dragged screaming and uncomprehending across the floor.

She was still trying to process the face of the man in the chair with the eyes like hot coals, but then she was falling. Falling, and landing hard. The world went bright white, then red, then grey... slowly fading out.

LUCIFER DRAINED HIS glass as Forfax settled in the chair beside him.

"I shouldn't have to come to you, Forfax."

"I understand. It won't happen again."

"When I ask you to keep me updated, remember, *I'm not asking*." He held out his hand for another drink, and Rimmon refilled his glass. Apparently satisfied, he sat back in the chair. "Make the move. And this time, keep – me – updated," he said, and turned his attention to the crumpled form of the semi-conscious woman on the floor of the pit below. Something moved in the shadows at the base of the walls.

Something growled.

"Fifty says she doesn't last five minutes," he said, holding a folded note out to Forfax.

And as the growling grew louder, he smiled.

CHAPTER FOURTEEN

Sub Rosa

"FRANCE?" ALICE WAS well aware that her voice sounded an octave higher than usual. She thought it was pretty justified, given the circumstances.

"France," said Mallory, tapping his finger on the map.

"You have *got* to be kidding me."

"Do I look like I'm kidding?"

He very much didn't. Not even slightly. Blowing out a deep breath, she looked from Mallory to the map, and back to Mallory. "But France? *Really*?"

"Can't you just picture Michael in a nice little beret?"

"Stop it."

"Sorry." Mallory was still tapping his finger on the map, slightly absentmindedly. Alice kept on staring at it.

When they had said Michael had a fortress, she believed them. When they had said it wasn't exactly discreet, she had raised an eyebrow. When they had said that actually, Michael was hiding in plain sight of several million people who passed by each year, she had laughed.

Until Mallory had finally lost his temper and slapped a crumpled map on the table, jabbing at a spot on the coastline of northern France. "There. Believe me now?"

He was pointing at Mont Saint-Michel.

"That's ridiculous."

"Not ridiculous. *Clever*." He squinted at the map some more. "It's Michael all over."

"So, what, he's just hanging out there? Getting photos with the tourists?"

"Not exactly. Well. The photos part, maybe. You know what he's like..." The twinkle in Mallory's eyes suggested he might not be entirely serious.

It was just as well: Alice had had about as much serious as she could take. Castor had left Pollux in charge of Xaphan and Florence and had taken up a sentry post by the door, while Vin had sloped back into the sacristy and perched on the narrow cupboard beside the sink, with a face like thunder. He was angry: she could feel it. Angry with himself, angry with Florence. Angry with just about everybody. But there was more than anger there: there was guilt, too. So much of it. She was about to go over to him, but Mallory's eyes grew serious again and he shook his head.

"Leave him."

"Why?"

"Because he needs time."

"Is he alright?"

"No. But he will be. He's been through worse. He just needs to get his head straight."

"He looks..."

"He looks like he's trying to work out what he did wrong. And rightly so."

"What?"

"You know how this works, Alice. It's Vin's choices which have put him – *us* – here."

"And it's my choice not to leave him to deal with this alone."

"And that's a good choice. A kind choice. But it's not the right one." He met her gaze and held it, and he looked sad. Sadder than she'd seen him.

"You know something, don't you? Something's going to happen..."

"I have my suspicions. That's all they are, though: suspicions. I think Michael's planning on doing something with Lucifer –

something monumentally stupid – but I don't know for sure. I don't know, and I don't like it."

"So what do we do?"

"Well, the first thing we should do is nothing. We've got more important things to worry about than a half-born – no offence, but you see what I mean."

"I suppose."

"Do you know what's happening? Out there?" Mallory sat forward.

"War."

"Wh... Yes, actually." Mallory looked taken aback. "That's exactly what's happening. We've got riots... *everywhere*. And I do *mean* everywhere. The things I've seen, Alice. Cults to the Fallen, cults to angels. *Angels*! Riots, murder... There are people walling themselves into their houses. They'd rather starve to death than face... this." He waved a hand at the door. "And it's only going to get worse. They're in control now. It's their game board."

"Only the beginning..." Alice whispered, and Mallory frowned at her. She cleared her head. "Xaphan. He said that to me. In the street."

"Oh, he knows something. Which is why he's coming with us to see Michael."

"But what if he *does* something?"

"He wouldn't be Xaph if he didn't try." He lowered his voice, keeping one eye on Vin across the room. "If there's anyone we need to watch right now, it's Florence. The Fallen have lost hell: there's nowhere for them to run to. They're stranded, and they die a lot more easily than they'd like. But Florence... she's not branded. That tricky little gift of hers is still active and she's used it against us before. *All* of us," he added, seeing Alice's discomfort.

She didn't like the way he was talking. Everything sounded far too serious again, far too bleak. Far too dark. Even Vin, who was normally the most light-hearted of them all, seemed like someone else. "Things really have changed, haven't they?" she asked Mallory.

He half-smiled at her. "Only on the outside. Vin's still Vin. He's just learning that everything has consequences."

"Like you did?"

"Me? Oh, you know me. The consequences are always the best part." He spun his gun around the palm of his hand.

Standing up, he stretched and raised his voice again. "What we need to do now is work out how we're going to get to Mont Saint-Michel without Michael handing our arses to us on a plate first. I can't imagine he'll be pleased to see us; particularly not if he's planning what I think he is. And if he's got his pit-bull with him..."

"Zadkiel?"

"Zadkiel. I doubt we're among his favourites, either, and that's doubly true of Vin and Florence."

"He didn't seem that bad to me..." Alice began, but tailed off. He had made a street full of people forget what they had seen. He had hidden an army of angels using nothing more than his will. He might not have seemed *bad*, exactly, but she didn't want to see him when he lost his temper.

"Zadkiel won't be a problem," said Castor from the doorway. "Leave him to me."

"Are you sure?" asked Mallory, fixing Castor with a steely gaze.

Castor cracked a cryptic smile. "I know where he'll be looking."

"Then that's settled. We go, we hope Michael's in a mood to listen, we cross our fingers and pray we come back out in the same number of pieces we went in."

"And if Michael's not in a mood to listen...?" asked Alice. She knew what was coming.

"Then you have to convince him, Alice. You're the only one who'll stand a chance. The last thing we need right now is him thinking we're part of the problem."

For a moment, Alice felt like she was looking down on them from somewhere above herself. She could see herself on the sofa, Mallory standing beside her, Vin still sitting glumly beside the sink and Castor leaning in the doorway. Her stomach felt heavy, as though she had swallowed a handful of stones, and everything was wrong.

"Are they going to be trouble?" Mallory meant Xaphan and Florence, and although he sounded calm enough, there was an edge to his voice that Alice didn't like.

"Relax," said Castor. "They're waiting in the confessionals. I thought it might be an idea to separate them while we secured them properly. Pollux is handling it."

"It might help with her, but the only thing that's going to help with Xaph is if we separate his head from his neck."

"I'm surprised you haven't."

"So am I." Mallory sighed. "But, you know. Big picture. Besides, I don't think it's me he's got to worry about." He jerked his thumb towards Alice, who did her best to look offended. "I think I should probably go and give Pollux a hand. Not that I have any idea why I'm going along with this..."

"I want to speak to Florence before we go. Alone." Alice said. She saw both Vin and Mallory tense, and held up her hands. "I'll be nice. I promise."

"You'd better be. And Alice? That temper of yours. Put a lid on it, you hear me?"

"Is that an order, Mallory?"

"You bet your life it is. If we're going to get into this insanity, we're going to do it right."

ACROSS THE CHURCH from the sacristy, a row of wooden booths stood against the wall. Built from dark, stained wood, they resembled glorified cupboards with ornate patterns cut into the doors and brass grilles fitted in their sides. Each booth was divided in two by a screen, with a small seat built into each side.

Xaphan was sitting in the first booth, where Pollux was locking what looked alarmingly like a collar around his neck – and attached to it was a chain. The chain trailed along the ground outside the booth before finally tracking back up to Pollux's hand, where it finished; wrapped around his fist. At regular intervals, the links of the chain were punctuated by what looked like large metal beads.

Xaphan must have heard her; as she passed, he tipped his head forward and looked at her, holding up his wrists to Pollux.

"Don't look so sour, Alice. Haven't you always wanted to see me in chains?" he said, licking his lips. Alice stopped, trying to think of a smart answer – and he lunged forward, trying to loop his chain around her neck. She darted back as Xaphan was jerked back into his seat: yet another chain fastened the collar to the back of the booth.

"No you don't. Not again." Her throat throbbed at the sudden movement, but it was worth it. She could see the frustration in his eyes, and that was all she *could* see. No Lucifer. Not this time.

He raised his chained hands and slid a finger underneath the collar, rubbing at the skin of his neck.

"Oh, did that hurt?" asked Alice. He glared at her, but said nothing. "Good." She turned and walked away, leaving him with his guard.

There were two other booths in the row, their backs to the wall of the church. The middle one was empty, but Florence had been restrained in the furthest. Pollux had secured her first, presumably thinking she was less likely to misbehave... particularly once she was separated from Xaphan. From this angle, the screen dividing the two halves of the confessional hid everything but her feet.

Alice took a deep breath. The air tasted of dust, of incense and ever so slightly of damp. And then she stepped into the other side of the booth and sat down.

Through the screen, she saw Florence twitch.

"Why d'you do it?" Alice asked.

"Alice..."

"It's a simple question. And don't pretend you weren't expecting it."

"Because."

"Because what, exactly?"

"Because I love him." There was more than a hint of defiance in Florence's voice.

"He's one of the Fallen, Florence. The only person he loves is himself."

"And that means I can't love him?"

That stumped Alice. She opened her mouth and closed it before she could come up with anything at all. And even then, all she could manage was: "But he's a bad man. As in: really bad. As in: he's in league with the devil. Literally."

"I can't help that."

"He won't change."

"You don't know that."

"Seriously?"

Florence shifted in her seat. "We're not so different, you and me."

"Yeah, we are. And this isn't about me, is it?" The memory of a man – or someone she'd thought was a man – and how he had died flashed through Alice's mind, but she brushed it aside. "I made a mistake. Maybe you have, too, but the difference is that I didn't know any better. You did. You knew what Xaphan was. *Is*."

"I do, Alice. And I can't help that."

"You think he'll change? You're going to sit there and tell me you honestly think he'll wake up one morning and decide to be someone else?" Alice waited, but there was no answer from the other side of the screen. She could just about make out the outline of Florence's face, silhouetted against the divider. Finally, the answer came.

"I don't want him to be someone else. I just want *him*."

"I'm sorry, Florence. But if that's the truth, then you're as damned as he is." Alice swung herself up from the seat and around the outside of the booth to face Florence, who met her gaze with cool green eyes.

"What would you know, Alice? What do you know about me, or about him? What do you know about *any* of it? You think the angels are on your side? You think they care? What are you to them? You're a pet. A tool. Nothing more. Things could have gone so differently, and you know it. An inch either way and you could be sitting here instead of me. Don't tell me you haven't thought it." she said, lowering her gaze and glancing up at Alice from beneath her lashes. "Enjoy it, Alice. Enjoy it while it lasts, because things are changing."

Alice had heard enough. She looked Florence up and down once more, and without another word, she walked away. Florence's voice, raised now, followed her. She was shouting.

"At least I made my choice!"

MALLORY WAS BESIDE Xaphan's makeshift cell, talking to Castor and Pollux. He had lowered his voice and his back was to her, but Alice could still hear snatches of their conversation.

"I mean it. I'm not happy about this. Not with your history," he was saying to Castor.

"You want to go without me? Fine. I'll keep an ear out for what Michael does to you. Someone's bound to hear the story."

"Michael isn't my primary concern."

"Maybe he should be, Mallory. Being around all those other Descendeds must have scrambled your brain, or you'd remember that Michael's adopted a fairly strict 'kill first, ask questions later, if at all' policy recently."

"Thank you, I'm aware of Michael's tactics. What I'm more concerned about is what happens when we put you, your brother and Zadkiel in the same room. When was the last time that happened?"

"You know the answer to that."

"Yes, I bloody do. When you were Earthbound. So you'll forgive my reluctance to put my life – Vin's life, Alice's life – in your hands, all on your say-so."

"Oh, piss off, Mallory. You're one to talk."

Alice had heard enough. She cleared her throat and their heads snapped round, the conversation stopping dead as soon as they realised she was listening. "Oh, come on. You're going to tell me it's fine to have your little chat in front of him" – she pointed at Xaphan, who was apparently snoozing – "and not me?"

"Because," said Xaphan, not bothering to open his eyes, "everyone already knows this story. The brothers and the Archangel. The star-crossed lovers. The tragedy of their separation... oh." He opened his eyes and smirked. "Everyone except *you*, I suppose." He let out a short, cold laugh and shut his eyes again. "Oh, well."

Mallory's mouth set in a hard line, and he glared first at Xaphan, then at Castor. "Get them in the van."

Castor nodded – but as he headed for Florence's booth, Pollux muttered something under his breath and Castor rounded on him.

"You know what, Pol? Fuck you. Fuck you and every single Descended like you, you fucking prick."

Pollux raised an eyebrow at his brother in response. None of this seemed to bother Mallory.

"Problem, gentlemen?" He was flipping a single bullet between his fingers, spinning it up and over and round again, but his eyes were fixed on Pollux. He tossed the bullet into the air, caught it and dropped it into his pocket. "I asked if we're going to have a problem here. Because solving problems is something I'm very good at."

"We're fine." Pollux hauled Xaphan out of his seat and pushed him towards the front of the church.

Once he'd gone, Mallory let out a long sigh. "Those two are a pain in the arse."

"There's a story there, isn't there?" Alice asked, following him back around to the sacristy.

Mallory laughed. "Story? There's an eight volume Russian fucking novel in there. And no. Not with a barge-pole," he added. "We're leaving. Now."

CHAPTER FIFTEEN

Brothers in Arms

"YOUR CARRIAGE, MY lady," said Mallory as they walked to the front of the church and Alice spotted the van parked outside. It was black, and the words 'Private ambulance' were stencilled in big white letters on the back doors. Her heart sank. She'd seen that van before: it was one of Adriel's.

And that was how they were getting to Michael. All of them.

In a coroner's van.

IT WAS NOT a thought Alice relished, but she climbed in, put her head down and wrapped her arms around her chest, tucking herself into the corner, as far as possible from Xaphan and Florence. Castor immediately took it upon himself to act as their driver, complete with his police uniform and Zadkiel-given ability to mess with people's heads. Mallory rode with him, and that left Alice, Vin, Pollux, Xaphan and Florence – still wearing their chains, which rattled at every bump in the road – in the darkened back of the van. For *hours*.

She had no idea how long they'd been in there, jostled and bruised and growing increasingly bad-tempered, when she finally started to doze. She was tired; more than tired, she was exhausted. As the world dropped away into darkness, she felt someone slide something soft behind her head. It smelled of beer and stale smoke, and – faintly – something else. Vin's jacket.

*   *   *

In the front of the van, Mallory had sunk as far into his seat as was possible and had his feet up on the dashboard in front of him, ignoring Castor's protests. He had also retuned the radio – again, ignoring Castor's protests.

"Usually, driver picks the music," said Castor pointedly.

"Usually, driver doesn't have a Descended with a pistol riding shotgun," Mallory growled back at him.

"Point made."

There was no noise from the back of the van, which both of them could only assume was a good thing, and it wasn't long before Mallory retreated into his thoughts.

They drove. Through the night and into the dawn, they drove.

"Mallory."

Nothing.

"Mallory."

"Hmm?"

"Mallory, *now*."

"What?"

"Something's..." Castor's fingers tightened around the steering wheel.

"I feel it." Mallory sat up, sliding one of his guns out from beneath his seat as he stared through the windscreen. "There's one of them out there. Pull over..."

He didn't get a chance to finish his sentence.

There was someone standing in the road.

"Don't..." said Mallory – but it was already too late, and Castor wrenched the wheel to the left.

Alice had been asleep, of that much she was sure. She had been asleep, and now she was being tipped and tilted and shaken around... Her head cracked against the metal of the wall of the van – or maybe it was the floor. Or the roof. They were rolling. The world turned over and over and over, and they were all thrown about, smashing into the unforgiving metal, into each other, in darkness.

And then it stopped, and there was only the sound of groaning steel and of the van's engine.

"Alice?" Vin's voice was shaky.

"I'm fine. I think." Hers sounded just as bad.

There was a creak, and the sound of glass breaking from the front of the van... or possibly the back. She couldn't tell any more.

"YOU ALRIGHT?" MALLORY peered at Castor, who had a streak of blood running down the side of his face. His hands were still wrapped around the steering wheel, and his eyes were closed, but he nodded in reply.

"Go," was all he said.

Mallory's door had taken the worst of the impact, and was bent in on itself... but it had held. It had held so well that it was never going to open again – but the window had cracked clean across, and it only took one sharp jab from his elbow to shatter it altogether. Broken glass scattered as Mallory hauled himself out through the frame and dropped down onto the grass verge. The figure was still standing in the middle of the road, holding something by its side. A rod, with a chain attached to it – and as Mallory straightened up, it let the chain drop. At the end, swinging like a malevolent pendulum, was a large, spiked metal ball.

It had been a while since Mallory had seen Phenex.

He could have done with it being a little longer.

ALICE FELT A hand on her sleeve in the darkness.

"That your arm?" asked Vin.

"Believe me," she said, pulling herself into a sitting position, "if it wasn't, you'd be the first to know."

There was the sound of someone moving around, then a thud… then another thud, and the van filled with daylight. Alice blinked as her eyes tried to adjust to the sudden glare and her head pounded. Once she could focus, she realised that the thuds had been Pollux kicking the back door of the van open, and that he was now standing outside, looking back in at them. Florence had huddled as close to Xaphan as she could: both of them were pale and battered and Xaphan had a fresh cut above his eye… but there was something about the look on his face that Alice did not like. It was more than self-satisfied; it was almost triumphant.

And that was when she understood. This wasn't an accident. This was an attack.

MALLORY ROLLED HIS head first to one side, then the other. Phenex just stood and watched him, the lethal-looking spiked ball swinging gently back and forth beside his knee.

"So, do you want to make the morningstar joke, or shall I?" Mallory shouted at him, waving his gun at the Fallen's weapon. Phenex sneered. He'd never had much of a sense of humour.

"Flail. It's a flail. Not that it'll make much difference what it's called once I've caved in your head with it, will it?" The voice that answered him was gravelly.

Mallory rolled his eyes. "I thought it was funny," he muttered, sizing up his opponent.

ALICE GROANED AS she straightened up, and – looking past Pollux and seeing Mallory facing down the figure in the road – moved to step around the open door.

"No, you don't," Pollux said, never taking his eyes off his prisoners. "That's Phenex. And however happily you might have dealt with Murmur, Phenex is out of your league."

"Out of my league?" She made sure every single word conveyed her displeasure.

"Leave this to us." Pollux nodded towards the front of the van, where Castor had finally clambered out. He took one look at Mallory and then walked around the van to them, his baton already in his hand. Blood was smeared across his face like war-paint. He peered around the side of the door and into the van, then glanced up again – first at Mallory, then at Pollux. "Go. I've got them."

Pollux didn't hesitate. He shook out his wings and, opening them wide, swooped over to land behind Mallory on the road.

Castor rubbed at the blood on his face, then peered into his hand and grimaced. "Ouch."

"Are you okay?" Alice stared at him, feeling her fingers prickle.

"That depends."

"On what?"

"On this."

Alice turned towards the figures on the road. She could see Mallory, and Pollux a step behind him – and the others. There were three Fallen there now, squaring up to the angels: the one Pollux had called Phenex, and two more behind him. All three were dressed in the same dark clothing and heavy boots – although only Phenex was built like a tank.

"Twelve, right?" she asked Vin, who wrinkled his nose in the direction of the Fallen.

"Phenex is. He's... not very nice."

"*Out of my league.* I got that, thanks."

"No, really. Don't take that the wrong way: Pollux isn't just being a dick – not this time, anyway. Phenex is... yeah." He blinked at the figure with the ball and chain. "You see that thing in his hand? It's a flail. A big, heavy metal ball covered in big, sharp metal spikes and attached to a big, heavy metal chain..."

"I'm seeing a pattern."

"Right. I've seen him take Descendeds' heads off with that thing. Whole heads, clean off. Well. Not *clean*, exactly..."

"You do have a point, don't you Vin?"

"My point? My point is you stay out of Phenex's way."

"And the other two?"

"Them?" He squinted at the two Fallen standing behind Phenex. "I couldn't tell you from here. But if they're hanging around with Phenex, that tells you something about how much they like hitting people with things. Oh, look." He pointed to the Fallen on the left. "A baton. What a surprise."

"Problem?" hissed Castor – spinning his own baton around his wrist, glaring at Vin.

"No problem."

"Good."

"I'm just going to..." Vin ticked his head towards Mallory and Pollux and stuffed his hands into his pockets, looking for all the world like he was going for an afternoon stroll as he stepped out from behind the shelter of the van and took his place beside the other angels.

"You have something of ours." Phenex eyed Vin, Pollux and Mallory as they formed a line between him and the van. "We've come to collect."

"The only thing you're going to collect is a kicking, mate," Vin shouted back.

Mallory raised an eyebrow at him. "Really, Vin? I mean, *really*? Nice of you to finally join us, by the way. Not like we've been waiting or anything."

"I'm touched. Didn't fancy taking them on without me?"

"Whatever gave you that idea?" A grin flickered across his face. "Let's get this over with."

The angels' warnings to stay away from Phenex had stung Alice. After all, she could take care of herself, couldn't she? But there had been an undertone to Vin's voice; one which made her take him more seriously than she would usually have done – particularly given the worried expression on Castor's usually calm face.

She saw Mallory raise his arm. She heard the gunshot, and another, and another.

Phenex dodged every one of them.

It wasn't that he was fast – it was more than that. It was simply that by the time the bullet reached him, he already knew where it was going to be and had moved out of its way. A step to the right, a lean to the left and he might as well have been a ghost for all the good the bullets did. Mallory stopped shooting, and for a moment, Alice thought he was giving up... but then she saw that Vin had rolled up his sleeves; saw that one of his hands was open, saw the familiar grey mist that was his favourite weapon against the Fallen, powerful enough to turn the gates of hell itself into stone. If she hadn't known better, she might almost have felt sorry for Phenex and his sidekicks.

But she *did* know better.

The mist tumbled from Vin's palms. It had covered most of the distance between the two factions, creeping along the ground towards the Fallen – and they had not noticed it.

Mallory's gun was a distraction. And it was working.

They were all so busy watching Mallory miss that not even Phenex spotted the grey cloud reaching out for him until it was almost too late. Caught off-guard, he spun back – still holding his flail – and with his free hand threw the closest of the other two Fallen in front of him, straight into the clutches of the fog.

"So much for leading by example," Alice said to Castor, who either didn't hear or wasn't listening. He was watching the unfortunate Fallen as he tried to drag himself out of the cloud, even as it wrapped itself tightly around him; even as first his feet and then his legs became heavier and heavier as they turned to stone.

Phenex stood behind him, just out of reach: his chest and shoulders heaving up and down. The roar that he let out made the hairs on the back of Alice's neck stand up. As Vin closed his hand and the mist receded, the Fallen hefted his flail up to his shoulder – and even at that distance, Alice heard the links of the chain clank against one another. She got the point Pollux had been trying to make. If that thing hit any of *them*, it would wipe them out. If it hit *her*...

Pollux took advantage of the distraction; with a single step he was in the air, swooping towards Phenex's remaining companion, snatching him up and beating his wings as they soared into the sky.

"Wait for it," said Mallory, tipping his head on one side and raising a finger to his ear.

Alice forced herself to turn away from watching them, towards Castor. "Is he going to do what I think he's going to do?"

"Depends." Castor was busy examining his fingernails. He glanced up when the Fallen screamed as Pollux released him. "Was it that?"

The scream went on and on as the second of the Fallen tumbled back towards the ground, cutting off abruptly as he reached it.

Phenex had had enough of waiting. Raising his flail above his head, he started to swing it round and around and around, whirling it faster and faster overhead as Mallory reloaded.

"Vin. Back. Now."

Vin nodded, sprinting back towards the van: apparently even the Earthbounds weren't crazy enough to take on Phenex.

Mallory, however...

This time, Phenex didn't even try to dodge the bullets: he swatted them away with the flail. Every shot pinged harmlessly off it except for the last one, which ricocheted straight back at Mallory, catching his shoulder and knocking him backwards. Behind the twirling chain, Phenex laughed.

"Is that all you've got, angel?"

Mallory didn't reply. He threw down his gun and he charged, head down, wings tucked close to his back. He ducked beneath the flail and threw his arms around the Fallen's waist in a tackle, lifting him off his feet and sending them both sprawling on the ground.

Out of the corner of her eye, Alice saw Vin tense; flexing his fingers. He wanted to be over there, she could feel it. But Phenex was still thrashing against Mallory, and still somehow managing to swing that flail even as fists rained down upon him, forcing Mallory to sway back... but never to release him, and never to stop. High above, Pollux folded his wings back and hurtled down towards the brawling pair, pulling out of the dive a hair's breadth from them and snatching the flail from Phenex's hand as he blew past in a barrel-roll.

Phenex twisted suddenly beneath Mallory, almost pulling himself free and sliding both his arms around Mallory's back to wrestle him sideways. Locked together, they rolled over and over on the ground, and Alice felt a stab of pain at the top of her spine. "He's trying to break his neck!" she said to Vin. He ignored her, keeping his attention on the brawl in front of them. The pain was replaced by a dull, heavy pressure: Phenex had his hands firmly wrapped around the sides of Mallory's head and was twisting. The Fallen had now managed to completely reverse their positions and was pinning Mallory down... and Alice was afraid to watch as Pollux turned in mid-air and sped back towards them again...

It happened so fast that she almost couldn't follow it: Pollux was there, moving towards Mallory and Phenex, and then he had one hand on the Fallen's shoulder, half-lifting, half-dragging him up and away from Mallory... and tossing the flail down to Mallory, who snatched it from the air even as he scrambled to his feet. Phenex dangled with his feet just above the ground: an easy target for the spiked ball of the flail as, with a yell, Mallory brought it smashing into the middle of his chest.

The airborne angel let go of Phenex, who dropped to his knees; he stared up at Mallory standing over him, and then slumped sideways. Pollux landed gently beside them.

"We should go," he said, resting a hand on Mallory's shoulder.

"One more thing." Mallory tossed the flail aside. It landed in the grass with a loud clatter, and he bent to scoop up his gun before turning to stand over Phenex.

Alice blew out the breath she'd been holding and sagged back against the van's open door. Two shots from Mallory's gun rang out.

"Hope you've got your good shoes on," he said, appearing from behind the van. "It looks like we're on foot from here. It's only about twenty miles, give or take."

"Twenty miles? You're kidding."

"If you'd rather, I'll go the easy way and you can hoof it with this lot..." He fluttered his wings at her, then laughed as she pulled a face. His Colt vanished into his jacket – and Alice could just make out the bullet hole in the leather at his shoulder. He followed her gaze and shrugged. "Don't worry about it."

"Are you...?"

"Yes. I am." He grinned at her. "Enjoy the show?"

"Not exactly."

Behind her, Pollux and Castor were dragging Xaphan and Florence out of the back of the van, still in their chains. Xaphan looked a little less smug than he had before; his face fell as he spotted Phenex's body lying in the road.

"Are you just going to leave him there?" Alice was suddenly struck by the thought of someone finding him. Mallory shook his head.

"I don't imagine he'll stay there very long. I know Phenex: there won't have been only two of them with him."

"Lucky for you they didn't turn up here."

"Lucky for them, you mean." He turned away from her, to Castor. "Shall we?"

"There's not much point hanging around waiting for them to show up, is there?" Castor wrapped the end of the prisoners' chains around his hand. "Shame about the van, though. Adriel's going to be pissed off."

"If I'm right," said Mallory grimly, leaning back through the window to retrieve his other gun from the wreckage, "Adriel's going to be pissed off about a *lot* of things. The van will be the least of his worries."

CHAPTER SIXTEEN
Medea

"THERE IT IS," said Mallory, pointing at something ahead of them. All Alice could see was a bunch of trees.

"That's No Man's Land?" she asked. The sun was setting already; they had spent most of the day walking. No wonder her feet were sore. The light seemed to… shimmer. They had reached the sea at the last moment before the sun sank into the water ahead of her, staining the sky a deep pink, fading to orange, then to a shade of blue she didn't think she had ever seen. She turned away to see Mallory standing with his wings outstretched, the light turning his feathers all the colours of the sunset.

"Not bad, is it?" he asked.

"Not bad," she said.

"You do know you're looking the wrong way, right?" He arched an eyebrow at her, and seeing her frown, he placed a hand on each of her shoulders, turning her almost ninety degrees.

Straight at Mont Saint-Michel.

The island rose steeply out of the sea and up from its causeway; its lower slopes were surrounded by tall stone walls. The windows were tiny pinpricks of light, reflected in the water. And soaring over the walls, dwarfing them, was the cathedral-like structure of Michael's fortress, its spotlit walls rising in a riot of ornate buttresses and turrets. In the evening light, the roofs looked like they were on fire. At the very highest point, gleaming in the last of the sunlight, was a golden statue, its wings outspread.

"Subtle."

"Michael."

"Michael." Alice stared out over the water at the towers. No wonder the tourists loved it: it wasn't exactly a discreet place to hide, but it really was Michael all over. Who else would top his castle with a bloody great statue of himself, she wondered... and then it dawned on her that there was only one other name that came to mind. Lucifer. It was the kind of thing she would expect from him. The idea made her uncomfortable, and without her really meaning to, her fingers found their way to the sigil on her arm. Michael's sigil.

He had warned her, hadn't he? He was an Archangel, the head of her choir. The head of all the angelic choirs. He could see inside her head if he wanted. Was he watching her now? Did he know they were there? And if they did, would he come for them? For her?

"That's what Pollux is here for." It was as though Mallory had read her mind.

"I thought Castor..."

"Castor's going to be busy enough keeping Zadkiel off our trail. Pollux is a Descended, remember, and while he's not a match for Michael if he really wants to find you, he's enough for now."

"But Castor's an Earthbound. And Zadkiel's an Archangel. So how does that work?"

"They have... how do I put this? History? I'd say Castor knows how Zadkiel's mind works. And that's good enough for me."

"This. All this. It's ridiculous."

"I know."

"I don't even understand why we're here. Not really."

"Oh, you do. It's wearing sunglasses and standing about five feet behind you." Mallory jerked his thumb back over his shoulder towards Vin. "This business with Florence has hit him harder than he's letting on. Jester, too. Jester *particularly*."

"And here we are."

"Here we are." He clapped his hands together. "Come on."

"Where?"

"Pub. Obviously."

"Obviously."

THE PUB WAS tiny, and it didn't look promising from the outside – but its sign was encouraging. There was no picture; only curling, swirling script, reading 'The Angel & Pistol.' Alice raised an eyebrow at Mallory. "I thought you said you'd never even met one of Michael's choir. How come I get the feeling you've been here before?"

"I hadn't. And I haven't."

"You want to explain that, then?" She pointed up at the sign.

"Just because I don't know this place doesn't mean they don't know me," he said, pushing his way through the door.

It was like walking into a tomb. Everything was completely still on the other side, and a thick silence filled the air. Mallory's hand immediately moved inside his jacket, pulling out one of his guns. The sound of the safety clicking off was altogether too loud.

"Vin? By the door," he hissed, and Vin nodded, dropping back to the entrance.

"Where is everyone?" whispered Alice. Neither Mallory nor Vin answered. Instead, Vin half-opened the door and peered back into the street to where they'd left Castor, Pollux and the others. "They're still by the road back there. No problems," he said. Mallory leaned over the bar in the far corner of the room and looked at the rickety door that led further into the building. "Stay here," he whispered at Alice, and without another word he slid over the little counter, dropping out of sight.

"Alice? Alice!" It was Vin hissing at her. "Get out the way, yeah?"

"Oh. Good point." Alice scurried across to the wall, where she stood and waited for... anything. Vin had his foot wedged in the door, keeping it open, and was looking back at the van. "Something's not right," he said quietly, his nose wrinkling. "Can you feel it?"

"Feel what, exactly?"

"Not sure. Just something. Something... off." He shivered. "You're really telling me you can't feel it?"

"I don't know." There *was* something in the air. A heaviness. She had just thought it was the silence, but it was more than that. There was an oppressiveness that hung over the whole place... something Alice realised she had begun to feel as soon as they got into town, but which she'd dismissed as a side-effect of all the walking. But it was more than that, and she had felt it before.

"Vin? I think we need to go."

"Go where?"

"Anywhere."

"You *can* feel it..."

"Yeah. And I remember where I've felt it before. Right before the riot."

"Like a storm coming in. It's them."

"The Fallen? Is this a trap?"

"I don't know." He slid his foot out from the door and let it close, peering towards the back of the room. "We need to get Mallory."

"I don't know where he went..."

"Bloody typical. Stay here, alright? I'll be right..."

"No you don't. Either you stay with me or we're both going."

"What?"

"I'm not being left here like some useless... *girl.*" She fumbled for the right word, flapping her hands as she said it. Vin pulled a face.

"You're weird."

"Fine. Are we going?"

He jerked his head sideways, then darted across the room and slid across the bar like Mallory had. Alice followed, but chose to go *around* the bar.

The faint niggling headache she'd had since getting out of the van was getting worse. It was a chilly pressure on the inside of her skull; it crept into the top of her neck and rolled around in her head and showed no sign of abating. And then there was the faint, but insistent, prickling of her palms. There was pain here. A lot of pain.

As she followed Vin through the door to the back of the bar, Alice found herself hoping they had a fire extinguisher somewhere.

THEY FOUND MALLORY in the back, surrounded by barrels and standing in a puddle on the uneven flagstones. Judging by the smell, the puddle was largely beer. It foamed slightly at the edges. Alice ducked through the low doorway after Vin, stopped and rolled her eyes. "Is now really the time?"

Mallory cut her off with a hiss, waving his gun. They stood like statues, listening. Waiting.

Nothing.

And then Mallory pointed to his ear. "Hear it?" he whispered.

And Alice did. At first, there was nothing other than the thick, silky silence. Not counting the overwhelming urge to set fire to... *everything*. But she listened, and she saw something like recognition flicker across Vin's face, and finally, she heard it too.

A low, steady buzz, like flies trapped in a bottle.

"What *is* that?"

"Something happened here," Mallory was stock-still in the middle of the room. "Something bad."

"No shit," muttered Vin. He was watching Mallory, waiting for a word or a sign, but still Mallory did nothing.

The buzzing sound grew louder and louder until there was no mistaking it and no ignoring it. It was everywhere.

She had no idea how long they had been standing there when they first heard the footsteps. Mallory held a finger to his lips and closed his eyes, trying to work out where they were coming from.

They were slow and light. Too light to be either Castor or Pollux, and unlikely to be Xaphan or Florence. "Not angel," Vin whispered across to her, shaking his head. "Not Fallen, either."

"Human?" she whispered back.

"I sure hope so..."

She was about to ask what the alternative might be, when Mallory suddenly spun around and darted out of the room. With barely a second thought, both Alice and Vin took off after him, back through the main bar and out into the street. Mallory had gone through the front door so fast that he had nearly torn it from its hinges; it swung furiously back and forth. All the while, Alice wondered how exactly her life had got so ridiculous. And then she was in the street, and Mallory and Vin had stopped dead in their tracks.

Alice stopped too.

Walking away from them, down the middle of the street, was a woman. She was wearing a plain, grey dress which did nothing to hide how thin she was, and she had bare feet. Long dark hair, streaked with grey, fell loosely to her waist. Her walk was uneven, as though each step caused her pain. No wonder, thought Alice, with her bare feet. She must have heard them rush out of the bar, but she gave no sign of it. She just kept walking.

Alice saw the others exchange looks, and in silence they followed.

The woman walked down the centre of the road, straight as an arrow, and it was only then that Alice noticed there were no cars. There weren't even any pedestrians. Other than themselves and the woman, there didn't seem to be another living soul here. Which seemed odd, given that right across the bay was one of the most obvious tourist destinations for miles around (something she still couldn't quite process, if she was entirely honest). It was – just about – early summer. There should be tourists. There should be... people.

Instead, there was only the stillness and that infuriating buzz and a lone woman walking towards the sea.

Something bad, Mallory had said.

The road took them through the middle of the little town, past deserted junctions and restaurants as the streetlamps flickered on, past traffic lights which phased through their colours for an empty street; past alleys and cafes and houses... and not a soul in sight.

Except.

The first time she saw it, Alice thought it was a trick of the light. A shadow. The wind moving a cafe awning. A sheet of newspaper blowing across the road.

And then she saw it again.

At the end of every street they crossed, there was movement. It was small, and whenever she looked, there was nothing to see. Just more of the same empty streets. She thought about calling out to Mallory or Vin, but instead, she simply stopped and folded her arms and stared up the street crossing her own. And she waited.

One moment, he wasn't there... and the next, he was, looking back at her through the dusk. She could see his armour catching the glow from a nearby streetlight; see the shadow of his wings.

The streetlight behind her suddenly flared, the bulb blowing in a shower of sparks and startling her, and when she looked back towards the end of the street, the angel had vanished.

Mallory and Vin, oblivious to the fact they were being watched, had stayed with the woman. They had reached the far end of the street, where the road ended abruptly in an area of sandy scrub, separated from the beach by a rough, low wall.

Alice could just make out the woman's outline on top of the wall. She was heading for the sea.

Fire flared up in Alice's footsteps as she broke into a run. Sparks fell from the ends of her hair, from the tips of her fingers as flames shimmered up and down her arms. The soles of her trainers made a slapping sound as she ran; every breath caught in her throat, burning as it came. She blazed past Vin, past Mallory, and leapt the wall, not knowing or caring how far the drop down to the beach might be on the other side...

The woman was sitting on a rickety bench. Once, it had been painted green, but the paint had flaked from the half-rotten wood, and little more than rust held it together. Her head was turned towards the island. Alice picked her way over the sand and the rough shingle, through pockets of seaweed and mounds of old shells.

"We knew about the angels, of course." Her voice was quiet, soft, and she spoke in English. Alice froze on the spot. "We thought of them as our guardians. It was a joke, you would say. Local legend. The island of the angels. We thought they would protect us. Protect us from *them*." She looked at Alice. Her eyes were the palest shade of grey. "We trusted them. We were mistaken.

"*They* came in the night. Twenty of them; maybe more. They ran through the streets and howled like animals until the whole village was awake. And then they began. They came to our doors and they threw them open, and they dragged the children from their beds. Such strength. Such rage." She blinked, and played with the fabric of her dress. "The school. They took them to the school, and..." She stopped, and held her hands out in front of her, turning them over and staring first at the palms, then at the backs, flexing her fingers as though she didn't quite believe that they were a part of her. "We had no choice. You must understand. No choice. Even then, we thought the angels would come; that they would save... Even as they closed the doors..." She dropped her hands again and smoothed down the fabric of her dress. "They watched. They stood on their walls and they watched. They saw, and they did nothing. *Nothing*."

"What happened here?" Alice could barely bring herself to ask.

"The school. The school." A single tear ran down the woman's cheek. "And then, after.... *Then* the angels came. The Archangel, he came and he made them forget. All of them. All of them but me." She stood, slowly, unsteady on her feet, and Alice wondered whether she should help her, but then she had found her balance and she drew herself upright and sighed. "They sit inside and they wait to die alone. They have nothing left: not even their memories. And I? I have too many." She reached out, and brushed her fingers down Alice's cheek. "Beware the angels, child, and think: what will you do when they come for *you*?"

"They already did." Alice heard the words as though they were someone else's. The woman looked at her sadly and shook her head.

"Then it is too late."

She pressed something into Alice's hand, closing her palm around it, and then she began to move away, picking her way through the stones and onto the sand. Alice watched her. There was something about the way she moved... as though...

Alice looked at the object in her hand. It was a pebble. Smooth and round, it felt cool against her skin.

Something about the way she moved...

"Stop!" Alice screamed after the woman who was now almost at the edge of the water. She started forward, but found herself held by a pair of strong hands. "Stop!" she screamed again, pulling with all her strength against Mallory. It wasn't enough, and if the woman heard her, she didn't respond.

The woman kept walking. Her head held high as the hem of her dress floated up to her shins, to her knees, and then the stones in her pockets weighed it down.

Weighed *her* down.

Still she walked.

Alice was burning, and Mallory's hands were holding her back.

The waves closed over the woman's head.

The fire died, and Alice felt Mallory relax his grip.

"Sometimes, you just have to let them go," said Mallory. He sat on the sand, wincing as the blisters on his skin faded. It was a good job he healed fast. His jacket was not so lucky; he had dropped it in a sticky, bubbling heap on the beach.

"She said they were waiting for the angels."

"I know."

"And no-one came."

"I know."

"He took their memories."

"Alice, I *know*."

"How could he be so cruel?"

"Cruel? You could call it that. And maybe we seem that way to you. But real cruelty would be letting them remember that the angels did nothing to stop it."

"Like her?"

"Like her. There always has to be someone, Alice. Someone always has to be the witness. And the cruellest thing of all would have been stopping her from walking into that water."

CHAPTER SEVENTEEN

At the Green Chapel

"YEAH, YOU'RE NOT going to want to go in the school." Castor's face was grim. "I stuck my head in, and to be honest I really wish I hadn't. Everything bad about this place is coming from there."

"You know what happened?" Mallory was eyeing Xaphan.

"It doesn't take a huge leap of the imagination." Castor shook his head sadly and gestured to their prisoners, now tied to one another. "Where do you think we got the rope?"

ALICE HAD SAT for a while, staring at the sea, and then allowed Mallory and Vin to lead her to a small lane leading out and away from the coast, into the woods by the little town, the same direction the others had gone. It was just as quiet there, although the silence had none of the oppressiveness of the town: instead, it was calm and peaceful. The trees formed a thick green canopy overhead, shutting out the rapidly darkening sky, but just as Alice was beginning to wonder how they would find their way through the forest in the dark, they turned a corner and she stopped.

The lane they had been following turned into a rough track, which petered out at a low wall ahead. Behind the wall was a chapel, lit by flaming torches fixed to posts in the ground and surrounding it with a ring of fire. It was a strange, squat little building with a lopsided tiled roof, and its stone walls almost completely hidden by green leaves. Ferns, moss and creepers smothered the surface, making the walls look alive with shadows shifting in the flickering light. Tiny white flowers twined through the green, like stars. Even from where she stood, Alice could smell them: a sweet, slightly earthy scent that carried on the air. Tall stems of purple verbena waved gently along the wall, rooted between the stones. "Pretty," she said, running her fingers down one of the stems. Mallory pinched the top off one nearby and handed it to her.

"Look familiar?"

"We used to have it in the garden. I remember my mother planting great big drifts of it against the fence."

"Devil's bane," he said, plucking another of the flowerheads and crushing it between his fingers before rapping on the door of the little chapel. The wood was old and cracked, worn almost grey over the years, studded with rusted iron nails. There were footsteps on the other side, and it creaked open to reveal Castor, backlit by a hundred candles or more. Inside, it smelled of the sea, of moss and the forest; of green and of blue and of safety. The air was cool, but the stone walls felt warm when she touched them. Beside the door was a tiny figure carved into the wall: it had outspread wings and wild, curling hair, and even though the carving was rough and old and half worn away, Alice knew who it was at once. She glanced over her shoulder at Mallory, who nodded. "Raphael. There used to be an abbey here, known for its healing. This was his chapel." He ran his fingers down the face of the carving. "It fell into disrepair when the priory over on Mont Saint-Michel grew. That's Michael for you…" He made a disapproving sound. "This is all that's left now."

"That makes you sad."

"Not… sad. It's better like this, I think, but like I say, that's Michael. Always wanting more." He shrugged, then turned towards Pollux, who was sitting in one of the pews, close to the door.

Vin followed them in, and Castor closed the door behind him, shutting them in. As soon as it closed, Alice felt a weight lift from her. Everything about this place was Raphael, and she was glad the others had found it. What she was less glad about was the two figures sitting side by side in a pew at the far end of the chapel. After her earlier conversation on the beach, the last thing she wanted was to be stuck in another box with any of the Fallen. The van had been bad enough, but that was before…

Before anyone could stop her, she leapt at Xaphan; slapping him hard across the face with a burning hand. Her fingers left a livid red mark where the skin had scorched. He looked up at her from beneath lowered eyelids, daring her to try again, to push a little harder. She stopped, her hand still raised, then took the little flower Mallory had handed her and tucked it into the pocket of Xaphan's jacket. He scowled at it and gagged.

Interesting, thought Alice.

And all the time, Florence just stared at the floor. She refused to meet Alice's eyes or to even acknowledge that Xaphan was in pain.

"She's given up. Just as well." Vin was sitting in the pew in front of them, turned sideways to keep an eye on Florence, his arm draped along the back of the bench. "She knows it's over. Isn't that right, Florence?" She simply turned her head away. "Having second thoughts about your boyfriend, are you? Bit late for that."

"Vin, stop it," Alice said.

"You're right. She's not worth it. Not now." He turned his back on Florence.

Across the chapel, Mallory looked up from his conversation with Pollux. Edging past Vin, he stepped into the pew beside Florence.

"Have you got something you want to say?" Mallory loomed over her, opening his wings and looking every inch a Descended angel. Florence shook her head, her eyes still fixed on the floor.

"Florence. You may not get another chance. Michael isn't known for his listening skills. Or his mercy."

She shook her head again, but shifted in her seat.

"I'm going to ask you one more –"

"Blade!" Vin knocked Mallory sideways. There was a flash of silver, and Alice's view was suddenly full of feathers. Florence screamed from somewhere beneath them, and the next thing Alice knew, she was watching her being dragged from the pew by a furious Mallory. Half dropping her, half throwing her to the floor, he launched himself back into the pew, landing on Xaphan with a roar. The knife skidded across the floor, stopping at Alice's feet, and seeing Florence's eyes searching for it, she snatched it up. Tiny sparks danced along the blade.

Vin was now hauling Mallory off Xaphan, trying to avoid getting hit in the face by the angel's frantic wings. "A little help?" he shouted through a mouthful of feathers. Castor waded in and punched Xaphan once in the face. The Fallen crumpled sideways, smacking his head into the back of the pew, while Castor shook his fist, wincing. As one, Vin, Mallory and Castor turned to Florence; lying on the floor. They didn't get a chance to move before Pollux had stepped between them, hand held out in warning.

"No," was all he said. The others just stared at him, Mallory's chest heaving.

"No?" he asked, his voice controlled, but angry.

"No." Pollux repeated. "Michael knows Alice is here. And he's not pleased. We need them."

"How can he *possibly* know she's here? I thought that was the whole point of bringing…"

"Not us. Someone else." He looked thoughtful.

Castor groaned. "He's right. Someone saw her. I can feel it."

Alice was aware of four pairs of eyes settling on her. "What?"

"Alice," Mallory's voice was almost weary now. "Do you have something you want to tell me?"

"I didn't... I wasn't..." She gave up. There was no point in arguing. "There was someone. An angel. In the town."

"Oh, fantastic. And you didn't bother to mention this?" He held his hand out for the knife and she passed it to him, watching as he snapped the blade in two and tossed the pieces aside.

"I got a little distracted. You know, watching a complete stranger drown herself? And not being allowed to help her?"

"We *were* helping her, Alice."

"Could we," Vin said, "maybe talk about this later? *Talk* being the operative word?"

"I'm not the problem here," Mallory snapped.

Castor had had enough. He grabbed Xaphan by the scruff of his neck and dragged him, unconscious, as far away from the rest of them as he could within the limits of the chapel. He dumped him unceremoniously in the corner behind the altar. Brushing his hands off, he looked first at Mallory, then at Alice, and finally at Vin. "Tell me something. I don't mean to pry, and it's none of my business, but do you lot usually fight this much?"

"What's that supposed to mean?" Mallory snapped back. Castor held up his hands as though Mallory had just proved his point.

"It's just that... I do know *you*, Mallory. And this doesn't strike me as being particularly in character. Has it occurred to you that having *him* hanging around might be..."

"A bit of a downer?" Alice chipped in. Castor pulled a face.

"Not the most elegant way of putting it, but that'll do, yes."

"I was thinking the same thing. Earlier. Ever since they showed up, things haven't been right. And the only time I felt better..."

"...Was in the town. Not that that lasted long." Mallory finished her sentence. "Alright, Castor. You might have a point. Maybe." He rubbed his face. "We've just got to hang on until we can hand them over to Michael. Speaking of whom..." He raised an eyebrow at Pollux, who shrugged.

"It was Zadkiel watching you. I'm sure of it."

"Which would make sense. From what we can gather, he's been the one at work in the town."

"Yes. And he saw you and followed."

"Well that's just marvellous, isn't it? *Marvellous*. So Michael's expecting us, then?"

"Most certainly."

"Great. As if I wasn't already looking forward to tomorrow enough." He stared at the ceiling for a moment, then shook his head. "Fine. Alice: I'm sorry. Are we good?"

"We're good."

"Good. And next time, tell me if we're being stalked by an Archangel, would you?" He scowled at Florence. "I don't want to see her or hear her... not a sound. As far as I'm concerned, she's a bargaining chip and nothing more. I have absolutely no further interest in her. Not making that mistake again. Get her out of my sight." He waved at her dismissively, then turned his attention to Xaphan, who was still unconscious. "Make yourself useful, Vin," he said, tossing him a piece of rope.

"I thought you'd never ask," Vin said, cracking his knuckles. He crouched in front of Xaphan, picked up the rope, and wrapped it around Xaphan's wrists. He rested his fingertips on the coils, and as Alice watched, the rope began to stiffen and grey, hardening as it turned to stone. Vin stood up and stepped back, rolling his shoulders. "Let's see the smarmy little bastard weasel his way out of that one, shall we?"

"You should get some sleep." Mallory slid his back down the wall to the floor alongside her. They had done what they could with Xaphan, and with Florence, who had, at least, seemed to take Mallory's warning seriously and was now as docile as she was ever likely to get. Calm had returned to the chapel.

"After all that? I'm not exactly nodding off here," she said.

He shrugged. "It's likely to be a hard day tomorrow. Everything's a mess; I don't like it."

"So you keep saying."

"Doesn't make it any less true, does it?" He flicked some grit out from under his fingernail, took the cap off his hipflask and took a long, long swig. He held it out to Alice, but she waved it away.

"You know I don't. Besides, I'm sure you were supposed to be giving up."

"People keep saying that to me. Vin threw my last flask into the river in the middle of hell. It wasn't exactly a choice on my part."

"What about the whole being-Descended-again thing? I thought you only drank because you were Earthbound, and... stuff." Alice tailed off, seeing the look on his face.

"You really do think the best of me, don't you?"

"Not always."

"Sure you do. One of us has to." And he raised his flask and took another swig.

CHAPTER EIGHTEEN

Strange Pilgrims

IT RAINED IN the night, and the sound of the raindrops on the roof was surprisingly soothing as Alice sat in the dark. Most of the candles had burned out hours before: only the little stand of votives near the door remained lit. They flickered from time to time, the flames rising and falling in their coloured glass holders. Mallory was asleep on the floor; one gun in his hand, one tucked into the back of his belt. She felt a pang of guilt about what had happened to his jacket. Mallory without his jacket was like... well, like Mallory without his jacket. Vin had propped himself in the end of a pew, leaning his head back against the wall, and was snoring loudly. Even while he was asleep, he still had his sunglasses on. He had taken the whole business with Jester, and with Florence, harder than any of them.

Alice thought about it for a moment, and decided she'd feel a lot calmer once they handed Xaphan and Florence over to Michael. Not all that long ago, she wouldn't have considered handing even her worst enemy over to Michael. She still wasn't sure she would. But Xaphan, and Florence with him?

No problem.

She closed her eyes and drifted off, just as the first pale green light started to creep through the vine-covered windows.

* * *

"OI! ALICE."

There was something nudging her shoulder.

"Fnnghff." She swatted at it. It nudged again. It really was quite insistent.

"Alice. Alice. Alice." A pause. Maybe if she ignored it, it would go away?

"*Alice*!"

"Alice isn't here right now, but if you'd like to leave a message..." she mumbled from behind her hair.

"Fine. Well, when Alice shows up, would you tell her that she needs to get her arse in gear?" Mallory laughed. "You've got two minutes, and then I'm dragging you out by your heels and dropping you in the sea. That'll wake you up." Alice peeled her eyes open. Knowing him, he meant it.

Her skin felt sticky from sleeping in her clothes, and her shoulders ached from the damp stone floor, but other than that she felt surprisingly rested. The chapel was peaceful and calm, and Alice had absolutely no desire to leave it. Not that staying was an option.

Mallory was standing in the doorway, watching Castor and Pollux haul Florence and Xaphan out, stumbling over the step and tripping over their own feet. They had used the spare ropes to tie them together again, like ponies being led along a cliff. Mallory eyed them as they edged past him, turning to Pollux. "Keep them away from me, you understand?"

Pollux nodded and yanked on the rope, dragging them forward. Xaphan sneered at Mallory. Mallory sneered back, but Alice still saw his hand creep down to his guns.

"Good morning. I see you've decided to join the rest of us," he said as she came to the door. "Sleep well?"

"Not really. But I'm getting used to that," she muttered. Mallory shrugged.

"You can sleep when you're dead."

"Thanks. That's immensely reassuring."

"All part of the service." He ducked out through the door.

"Mallory?" Alice followed him out into the dappled light.

"Mmm?" He had opened his wings and was stretching them out as far as they would reach, the feathers catching the light and shining as they moved. This time, the sight stopped her in her tracks. She was so used to seeing angels covered in dust and dirt and blood, had grown so used to them always being in motion and in darkness, that it almost never occurred to her how beautiful they would look to someone else. Someone seeing them for the first time.

Someone who didn't know what they really were; what they really meant.

Someone who would see the man with his wings shining in the sun and not see a soldier, tired and scarred and half-dead on his feet and staring down the barrel of complete and total defeat, and carrying on regardless.

Alice watched him as he folded his wings away and crouched down, pulled both Colts from the back of his belt and ejected the magazines, checking them over. He patted his pockets, checking for more ammunition.

"Mallory?"

"Yup."

"Something's been bothering me. About yesterday."

"Why am I not surprised?"

"Apart from the obvious."

"Right..."

"The woman. The woman on the beach."

"Taken as read, yes." He didn't look up from his guns.

"How did she know I spoke English?"

"She didn't."

"But she's... she was... French, right?"

"Is there a point to this, Alice?"

"She spoke to me in English. How..."

"She didn't. She was speaking in French. I would've thought that was obvious."

"She wasn't."

"She was. Believe me." He stood up again, tucking one gun into his belt. The other disappeared into the pocket of his hoodie, which despite the scorch marks had still fared better than his jacket. "Do you think all angels only speak English? Really?"

"I hadn't given it much thought."

"That's a little narrow-minded of you, isn't it?"

"No. Yes. Pass."

"The sign. The Angel and Pistol. You commented on it. You didn't think it was odd that it was in English?"

"I kind of assumed... tourist pub, you know?"

"You should know better than to assume, Alice." He shook his head, but he was smiling nonetheless.

"Oh, god. This is another one of those..." She flapped her hands, looking for the right word. She gave up. "*Angel* things, isn't it?"

"You're the only person I know who can make the word 'angel' sound like an insult. And I've met a lot of people. Some of them would be happy about being able to understand other languages."

"And I might be, if I'd been warned about it."

"Oh, stop whining."

"Shan't." She stuck her tongue out at him. "Besides, if I'm magically able to understand all these languages, how come I was always so rubbish at Spanish in school?" Another thought occurred to her. "And, how come I couldn't understand Vin when he was speaking Cantonese when I met him?"

"Well, in both those cases, your gift hadn't manifested, had it? Unless you're going to tell me you used to regularly set fire to your school books?" He shrugged and turned away from her, sauntering towards the path back to the town and the sea, and the island. His voice drifted back over his shoulder. "Besides, how d'you know Vin isn't still speaking in Cantonese?"

Alice's mouth dropped open.

* * *

"SERIOUSLY. WHAT LANGUAGE?"

"Alice, give it a rest, yeah?" Vin rolled his eyes at her, but it was obvious that he was enjoying her frustration more than he should. "Have you been sniffing old incense or something?"

"No! I just... it's..."

"It's driving you nuts? I can tell." He stuffed his hands in his pockets. "But here's the thing: does it actually matter?"

"I..."

"Does it?"

"No, but..."

"There you go. Besides," he said, "doesn't matter what language I say it in, you still don't listen to a bloody word, do you?" He ducked, laughing, as she took a half-hearted swing at him.

"Alright, children. Am I going to have to separate you again?" said Mallory, stopping to wait for them. They had almost reached the edge of the town everyone was referring to as Medea – although that was certainly not the name on the signposts – and ahead of them the sea gleamed blue and silver at the foot of Mont Saint-Michel, and the statue of Michael was already catching the sun. The causeway was deserted: too early in the day for tour buses or cars full of holidaymakers, it stood empty, stretching ahead of them through the boggy marshland and the water.

Or almost empty, at least. At the near end, a man was leaning against the low wall that ran along its edge. He could have been anyone, his hooded jacket unzipped over a red t-shirt, basking in the warmth. As they drew nearer, Alice could make out large splatters of what looked like cement on his boots and on his jeans. If she hadn't known better, she might have said he was a builder waiting for a lift. But she *did* know better, and she knew perfectly well that the man waiting for them was the Archangel Zadkiel.

He didn't move as they came closer. He just watched them. His eyes skated over Mallory and Alice and Vin, and even past the Fallen and Florence. His gaze passed over them all, eventually fixing on Pollux, and finally on Castor. It was Castor he watched as they reached the edge of the causeway. And it was Castor's pain that Alice felt surge beneath her ribs. Surprised, she turned to look at him, but he wouldn't meet her eye. He looked straight at Zadkiel. And Pollux, bringing up the rear of their odd little troupe, was looking at *him*.

"D'you maybe want to fill me in on this?" she whispered to Mallory, jerking her head back towards the others. He glanced over his shoulder then shook his head.

"Right now, it's probably better you don't know. Later."

"Later. Like you were going to explain the hair thing, right?"

"Exactly. And I did. So *later*."

He snapped his attention away from Alice and back to Zadkiel. They had stopped at the edge of the causeway, where the clear tarmac of the road gave way to dusty-looking concrete scattered with pockets of sand left by the high tides. Zadkiel's face was stern and unmoving.

"If I'd known, I would have got you something, too." He gestured to Xaphan.

"He's for Michael," said Mallory, drawing himself up to his full height.

"Of course he is," Zadkiel said, and snapped his fingers.

They were suddenly surrounded by angels. Angels in full armour, their breastplates shining so brightly that Alice screwed up her eyes against the light, peering at them as they formed a loose guard around the four at the back, leaving only Alice, Vin and Mallory outside. They didn't look especially friendly: the one nearest to Alice scowled at her as she peered at his arm, looking for a sigil. She just caught sight of the angular lines of Michael's sigil when Zadkiel barked an order and, as one, the angels stood to attention.

And then, with a 'whoomp,' they burst into flames.

The heat that suddenly rolled off them forced both Mallory and Vin back. Even Zadkiel took a step away, but not Alice. Only Alice stood her ground and stared at the angels; stared at the flames boiling across their armour, at the tiny pockets of sand on the causeway which began to bubble and melt. She couldn't imagine quite how hot it must be in the middle of it all, and for a moment she worried about Castor and Pollux; at least, she did until she heard a whistle somewhere above her head and looked up. There they were, Pollux wheeling overhead and Castor beating his wings lazily, keeping a close eye on everything below. So it was just Xaphan and Florence in there, was it? Alice sniffed. She didn't feel an overabundance of sympathy for them. After all, she'd made it through hell, and she wasn't likely to forget the cold there in a hurry. It might do them good to feel a little heat.

The angel at the front of the guard was still scowling at her, but now it looked more like a challenge than anything else. She hadn't jumped back like the others, and he didn't know why. Apparently, half of Michael's choir had toasted their brains and were a tad on the slow side.

Never one to be outdone, Alice closed her eyes, and reached for the dull ache inside her, the one that came from Castor. Flames skipped around her wrists, easily, lightly, and she held them out for the new arrival to see, trying not to look too smug about it. He just carried on scowling, so she shrugged and turned her back on him. "No sense of humour," she said as she wandered across to Mallory. He raised an eyebrow at her.

"What have I told you about playing nice with the other children, Alice?"

"Sorry..."

"What is it with you two? You and Vin. You make me feel like I'm stuck with two bickering kids all the time. If it's not one of you, it's the other."

"Are we done here?" Zadkiel was clearly anxious to move. Not surprising, given there was a phalanx of angels *on fire* standing in the middle of the road.

"You're the boss," Mallory muttered, scuffing his boots in the sand while Vin stared out to sea saying nothing, his eyes hidden, as always, behind his sunglasses. Zadkiel looked them up and down with something approaching bemusement.

"Alright, then."

And with that, the burning angels simply vanished, as did Castor and Pollux and the prisoners. Suddenly, there were only the four of them, alone on the causeway and with the salt wind ruffling their hair.

"Nice trick," said Alice. Zadkiel stepped around Mallory and folded his arms, looking her up and down.

"A trick, is it? How can you be sure?"

"Because I can still feel them."

And she could. She could still feel the heat of the flames on her skin. Besides, Zadkiel had pulled this one on her before, and she wasn't falling for it again. He tipped his head on one side and gave her an oddly approving look. "I can see I'm going to have to keep an eye on you." And then he smiled and turned towards the island at the far end of the causeway. "Shall we?"

Obediently, they fell into step behind him, and even though she couldn't see them or hear them, Alice felt the heat of Michael's choir, *her* choir, following her every step of the way.

Whatever Mallory and Zadkiel were discussing, ahead of her on the causeway, it was serious. Neither of them looked happy. Mallory, in fact, looked deeply uncomfortable. It wasn't surprising. After all, he and Michael didn't exactly see eye-to-eye, and there was still the matter of Gabriel.

From what Alice could gather, Mallory and Gabriel had history: something that went much further back than her arrival on the scene, or even Mallory's doomed attempts to help her mother. There was more to it than Mallory had let on, even before Gabriel blamed the three of them for having lost his favourite, Gwyn, to the Fallen, and his own Archangel status. Gabriel had gone from Archangel to Earthbound in one fell swoop, and whether that was their fault or not, Alice couldn't imagine a version of events where he'd be happy to see them. The comfort she took in knowing that Michael was there too was... limited. She shot another glance at Zadkiel. So far, he seemed slightly less unbalanced than most of the other angels; perhaps there was hope yet.

The moment she thought of his name, Zadkiel paused, the rhythm of his stride breaking as he cocked his head to one side, almost as though he was listening.

Which he was.

Alice mentally kicked herself.

Zadkiel was the Archangel with power over the mind, wasn't he? Of *course* he could hear what was going on inside her head. Just like Michael could, if he wanted to.

Still kicking herself, Alice decided that from now on, she was going to think about kittens and flowers and very little else while they were on Michael's turf.

Pretty. Fluffy. Sparkly. Yes.

There was a snort from up ahead, and Zadkiel shook his head, turning his attention back to Mallory.

"Alright?" Vin fell into step alongside her, his hands in his pockets. He was kicking a stone ahead of him as he walked, watching it bounce along the road.

"Ask me later."

"I know the feeling."

"What about you?" It felt like ever since Vin had turned up at Adriel's desk, he had been holding back, not quite himself. Alice had largely put this down to their uncomfortable proximity to Florence. But there was something more.

Vin sighed. "You want the honest answer or the cheery one?"

"Depends which is the real one, doesn't it?"

"Oh, don't start with your... *words* and that." He laughed, but it wasn't a particularly happy laugh. He kicked the stone again. "Thing is, I'm tired. And I don't just mean... tired. I mean *tired*. Like deep-down, no amount of sleep's going to fix it, bone-cold, dirt-tired."

"'Dirt tired'? That's a thing?"

"Yes, it's a thing. Shut up. I'm talking here." Another kick. "Things are harder now. Not that they've ever exactly been what you'd call *easy*, but lately" – he tipped his head back and stared at the sky – "lately, I've been wondering what it's all for, you know? I mean, we kick the shit out of each other, and half the time I don't even know why. Does it achieve anything? All this time, I feel like we've been running just to stand still. Keeping the balance... what good has that done? We're still fucking losing, however you look at it." He booted the stone so hard that it smacked into the back of Mallory's leg, just below his knee. Mallory immediately spread his wings and leapt into the air, twisting as he jumped and pulling out both of his guns. Zadkiel stopped walking and stared at him as, realising it was nothing to worry about, he sank back to the ground.

"Not that that was an overreaction..." the Archangel muttered. Alice and Vin both simply shrugged. "You get used to it," she said, while Vin looked for another stone to kick.

The Archangel was now staring at all three of them. "You're all completely insane."

"You should know," Mallory said as he tucked his guns away. "Are we waiting for something?" He gestured along the causeway and started walking again.

Alice looked past him, and past Zadkiel (who was trying not to look flustered, and not entirely pulling it off) to the buildings ahead. Even from the causeway, the sheer scale of them seemed impossible.

"It's something, isn't it?" said Vin, following her gaze.

"Have you ever been here before?"

"Me? Are you kidding? Michael's been known to rip the heads off unexpected visitors."

"Doesn't surprise me."

"What d'you think he would have done to us?"

"I'm not even going to consider it." She thought for a moment. "Besides, I'm not sure whether I'd have got off easier or not.

Which is twice the reason not to ever think about it. Anyway. You were saying."

"I was?"

"You were apparently in the midst of some kind of existential crisis."

"What? You don't believe angels can have those?"

"Not at all. I don't believe you know what 'existential' means."

Vin turned towards her, and Alice found herself staring at her distorted reflection in his sunglasses. She could see the glare of the sea, and small white clouds scudding behind her head, but however hard she looked for them, she couldn't see his eyes behind the dark lenses. "Are you going to take those off at any point, Vin?"

"What? And damage my image? Nah," he said, and turned away. Whatever it was he wanted to talk about, he obviously felt he had said enough.

The buildings on the island loomed over them as they drew closer: huge stone walls punctuated by tiny windows and topped with solid-looking ramparts; behind them, smaller buildings – houses, mostly, their lower floors converted to restaurants or shops selling tourist tat – were jammed side by side and almost on top of one another along the steep winding streets. And above it all, the priory: the thing the tourists came to see. Now she was closer to it, it really did look like someone had balanced a hulking great cathedral on top of the little island, or like an enormous ship had somehow washed up there. A ship made of rock, and surmounted by a bloody great statue of Michael swinging his sword about.

As she stared up at it, it occurred to Alice that she may not be viewing it with *quite* the same level of reverence as everyone else who came to the island.

She was kind of okay with that.

Reverent or not, she got the point. It was imposing. And those walls towering over her were definitely sturdy. As was the huge wooden gate. And the big iron studs holding it together. And that was without mentioning the extremely large cannon sitting beside the gate – even if it looked a little on the rusty side.

"It's alright," Zadkiel called back to her, waving a hand at it, "we don't use it anymore. Well. Hardly ever."

"Get out of my head," she growled.

"Sorry. Force of habit." Zadkiel shrugged. He didn't sound sorry in the slightest.

High above them, the sunlight was turning the slate roofs to silver. Vin had finally had enough of kicking his stone along and scooped it up, throwing it overarm into the water to their left. On the right, there was a slightly boggy-looking car park: nothing but scrubland and mud, and one or two metal signs warning of high tide times. Beyond that, there was nothing but water and, at the base of the walls, thick, wet sand.

"Quicksand," said Mallory as Alice and Vin drew level with him. "A lot of people have died out there over the years on pilgrimage. Getting across here before the causeway was built… it was seen as a test of faith."

"Why does that not surprise me?" sighed Alice.

Mallory's face became stern. "Careful, Alice."

"Oh, *come* on."

The only response she got was a steady, steely look.

Zadkiel peeled away from them, heading towards the mud on the left and a set of wooden steps down.

"Into the mud? In these shoes?" Alice pointed at the canvas of her trainers. "Not bloody likely."

"Don't worry. You won't get your feet wet. Our door's up there…" He pointed up. Alice followed his finger. High up in the walls winding around the rock was a door. A wide wooden door which opened out into mid-air. Although she didn't exactly have the best view of it from where she stood, Alice was willing to bet that it was just wide enough for an angel's wings.

CHAPTER NINETEEN

Make the Call

RIMMON WAS FLIPPING channels. He jabbed at the remote control with exasperated impatience, skipping from news channel to news channel, pausing only briefly on what might have been a daytime soap set in a hospital. It failed to hold his attention, and he was off again.

The grainy black and white picture told him what he had been expecting: more riots, more demonstrations, more... everything. Large pockets of the city had become no-go areas, with police drafted in from all over the country to keep the peace. There was even talk of bringing in the army. Meanwhile, with police resources focused on protecting the great and good of the capital, other cities burned unchecked. *Everywhere* burned. The politicians had made one mistake; they assumed the riots had purpose. They assumed there was a reason, a cause. Something that the mob wanted to achieve. Something that could be fixed, or at the very least, protected against.

They were wrong.

They were wrong, and that was the best part.

There was no cause: no cause other than people. And how can you fix *them*?

"Man's inhumanity to man..." said Forfax. They were in the broom cupboard that counted as his office. It was no more than five feet square, but he had somehow managed to shoehorn a desk and two rickety wooden chairs in there, as well as the stool on which the tiny television was balanced. The stool was missing a leg, and there were teeth-marks in two of the remaining three. There wasn't room for both the Fallen to sit down at the same time, so Rimmon sat in the least-splintered of the chairs while Forfax hovered behind him, anxiously peering over his shoulder at the little screen. From somewhere nearby came the sound of barking. A lot of barking.

"Hadn't you better go and see to that?" Rimmon asked, not bothering to look up from his channel-hopping.

"They're fine. It's feeding time: they're just excited."

"Excited? I'd hate to hear them when they're pissed off."

"It's... not pleasant." Forfax looked pained. "But that's what he wanted, isn't it?"

"If that's what he said."

"But you..."

"Look." Rimmon poked at the power button on the television and the stool wobbled dangerously. "I don't interpret the message. I just pass it on. You want to try second-guessing him? Be my guest. But if I were you, I'd just get on with my job, and be grateful."

"Like I have been, you mean?" Forfax's tone was snide. He somehow managed to take a step further into the office. His cane clicked against the floor as he set it down. "Now you listen to me, you little..." He cut himself off as Rimmon folded his arms and looked at him expectantly. Forfax took a deep breath and started again. "You don't scare me, Rimmon. You may be his favourite, but favourites never last long, in my experience. You weren't there at the beginning, and you won't be there at the end."

"That sounds awfully like a threat, old man."

"Old man? Old man?" Forfax rolled back his shoulders and opened what was left of his ruined wings. The remnants of the burned feathers had blackened and matted to the bones, and they made an awful cracking sound as they jerked open. "I could crush you, boy."

"Crush me?" Rimmon darted forward, and before Forfax could respond, had snatched the cane and driven it into the back of the other Fallen's knees, dropping him to the floor. Rimmon pressed the cane across Forfax's throat as he knelt. "Like this?" Rimmon leaned over his shoulder and breathed the words into Forfax's ear. The temperature of the room dropped several degrees, enough for their breath to mist in front of them, and Forfax nodded his defeat. Satisfied, Rimmon shoved him forwards. "The Twelve," he said, sneering. "The best he has. Look at you – it's no wonder he spent all that time losing the war. You, Azazel, Purson, Murmur... all as bad as each other. I'd have left you all in hell to die."

"While I hate to correct you, in Azazel's case, you did."

"Maybe we should have left you there too. You might have been more useful."

Outside the broom cupboard, in the warehouse, the barking reached fever pitch. There was a single scream, abruptly cut off, and then silence.

Except for the footsteps; the sound of hard-soled shoes on concrete.

Rimmon and Forfax glanced at each other, frozen.

The footsteps came closer. Careful, measured steps; never hurrying, never stumbling.

And around the corner walked Lucifer, red eyes blazing.

"What's this? Fighting? Come, come. We can't have that, can we? Not now. Not now we're so close." He gestured to the cane and held his hand out to Rimmon, who passed it to him. Lucifer took it and turned it round in his hands, running his fingers over the ornate pommel: a clear crystal roughly the size of a man's fist, cut with hundreds of facets that sparkled in the light. He held it up as though considering it – and then brought it smashing down into the side of Forfax's face.

The force of the blow knocked the Fallen sideways, throwing him into the side of the desk with a meaty *thunk*. Before he had even hit the floor, Lucifer was already swinging again – this time at Rimmon, who took a blow to his solar plexus. He doubled over, his arms wrapped around his torso.

Lucifer stood in the doorway, surveying the damage, then dropped the cane, letting it clatter to the ground. He straightened the jacket of his suit, smoothing the sleeves and picking off an imaginary speck of fluff, and sighed. "This squabbling. This bickering. This petty, petty behaviour." He ran a hand through his blond hair. "It is simply... *unacceptable*!" He bellowed the last word, his voice echoing around the building and making both Forfax and Rimmon flinch. Somewhere in the warehouse, they heard pigeons taking off, startled by the noise.

"Now, if it's not too much trouble... we're ready." He adjusted his cuffs. "Make the call." And with that, he turned on his heel and was gone, leaving only a chill in the air and the echo of calm footsteps in his wake.

CHAPTER TWENTY

No Man's Land

"Well, that happened," said Alice, peering down out of the doorway. The muddy sand really was a long way down from where she stood. She'd had no say in the matter, either: Zadkiel had simply marched up to her and grabbed her... and then the ground had dropped away beneath her feet, and then she was in the little room beyond the door. It was wide, with a low ceiling; she could see Mallory ducking his head slightly to avoid banging into the arches. There was no furniture: nothing but stone walls and a cobbled floor. The only light came in through the open doorway; the one through which they had just flown. Even thinking about it made Alice's stomach churn.

"You ever touch me again without asking, you're going to lose something." She shook a warning finger at him, but Zadkiel merely blinked at her.

"You *do* know who I am, don't you?"

"Seriously? You think the 'don't you know who I am?' speech works on me?"

"You're angry."

"Like I said: touch me again..."

Mallory interrupted her. "Alice? Let's be nice, shall we?" He raised a hand to guide her away from Zadkiel.

"Touching. No touching!" she snapped. Mallory backed off, holding up his hands.

Vin leaned a little closer towards Zadkiel. "She has some... boundary issues."

"Boundary. Issues." Zadkiel's voice was like a steel door slamming shut.

"Mostly, she's worried about setting us on fire and plummeting to her death. It's best not to startle her. What with the fire, and the burning, and everything."

"I see." Zadkiel glanced over at Alice, shook his head, and muttered something under his breath, before turning back to Vin. "Is she always this difficult?"

Alice watched Vin open his mouth, and pointed at him. "Don't you dare answer that."

As if this was more than response enough, Vin gave Zadkiel a shrug, holding his hands out helplessly.

Zadkiel nodded. "I stand by my earlier statement. Utterly insane." He opened another wooden door on the far side of the room – a smaller and more regularly-proportioned version of the one they had come in by – and sunlight streamed across the floor. "You'll fit right in."

ALICE BLINKED AS they emerged into the bright light again. They were in a narrow street, overlooking a small garden filled with trees, and the scent of sun-warmed pine filled the air. But it was the view which took Alice's breath away.

In front of her, past the trees and the stone walls draped in roses and herbs, the island dropped away. They were, at a rough guess, halfway up the side of the island, and she was looking clear over the roofs of the houses that crowded the base. There was nothing ahead of her but the sea and the sand. Birds wheeled overhead, tiny black specks against the blue of the sky.

"Think again," whispered Zadkiel, pointing up. Alice looked from him to the sky and back to him.

"You're kidding."

"Look."

She did – and as she did, one of the little winged shapes banked sharply into the sun and there was a flash; the glint of bright light on metal.

Angels.

"And no-one can see them? I mean, they're not... you're not hiding them?" she asked, still craning her neck back. Zadkiel glanced up.

"If I did that all the time, I'd never be able to do anything else. Besides, you'd be surprised. I think humans... people... think they're gannets."

"Gannets."

"I did say you'd be surprised."

"What if someone did see? And realised. What then?"

"Well, firstly there's context. You're standing in a place of miracles. Stranger things have happened here."

"And secondly?"

"Secondly, who's going to believe some tourist on a coach trip when he comes back from a leisurely lunch and says he saw an angel?"

"Point taken." Although, Alice thought, here of all places would be the place she'd believe it. "But why?" The question fell out before she could stop it, and Zadkiel, who had been about to lead them away, stopped in his tracks.

"Why do we hide? You know that. We're not here to be seen. We're not here to be acknowledged. We're here to make sure you – *they* – get a fair chance at doing the right thing. The chance they deserve."

"The Fallen don't hide."

"And why should they? People don't need any help to see their own cruelty. They know it's there, and the Fallen play that to their advantage. They are all about forcing the issue; forcing the hand. We are something *more*." He paused, his back still to them, and Alice caught Mallory's eye. He winked at her, and tapped his chest – directly over his heart. *Have faith*, he mouthed. At least he was consistent.

"This way," said the Archangel, turning left out of the garden and leading them along the little street. It was narrow, and the cobbles were rough and uneven, scattered with sand. Alice eyed a dark stain that looked suspiciously like blood.

"Leave it," Mallory hissed into her ear. "If you poke, you're going to find something, and then what do we do?"

"I'm just not entirely sure I'm comfortable with all this."

"Good. You're not totally soft in the head then, are you?"

They followed Zadkiel down the street – which was seeming more and more like an afterthought, wedged between two sets of buildings and getting narrower by the step – and then turned abruptly left, bounding up three stone steps into a cemetery.

"You know," Alice sighed, "Some girls, they try and stay out of graveyards. I seem to spend most of my life in them. Can someone tell me how that happened?"

Vin snorted as he passed her. "Says the one who's been working in the Angel of Death's funeral parlour."

"Did I ask for your input?"

"Well, when you ask for 'someone' to..."

"Alright. You can hush now."

"You *did* ask..." Vin shrugged, turning to find both Mallory and Zadkiel watching him. "What? She did!"

Zadkiel looked at Mallory. "You weren't kidding, were you?"

"I most certainly was not," Mallory said through gritted teeth.

Somewhat unexpectedly for a graveyard halfway up the side of an island fortress – but perhaps less so for one which attracted quite so much attention – the graves were rather pretty. Arranged in neat rows and separated by sandy paths, flowers and herbs had been planted on most of them, making a riot of colour against the weather-beaten stone and dark slate of the roofs. The far wall of the graveyard was smothered in greenery, with pink flowers erupting out of the shade. The whole space was surrounded by an intricate wrought-iron railing.

It was the most peaceful place Alice had ever been. She closed her eyes, not caring for a moment what any of the others thought.

The sound of more footsteps on the path made her open an eye. A broad-shouldered man with close-cropped hair and a long black habit was walking towards them, his hands folded together in front of him. Out of the corner of her eye, Alice saw Mallory tense and reach for his guns, only relaxing when Zadkiel's face broke into a smile. The monk bowed his head towards him, and then did the same in turn to each of the rest of them.

"Welcome." He spoke softly, clasping his hands around one of Zadkiel's, who gestured to him with his free hand.

"This is Brother Phillip, our Quartermaster. He belongs to the Order in the priory here, but we borrow him from time to time." He clapped a hand on the monk's back. "Our... other guests?"

"...will be made comfortable. And *secure*."

"Of course they will. Thank you, Phillip."

"You're most welcome, as always." He was still smiling at them. He was waiting for something.

Mallory's grip on his guns tightened, and he suddenly shook his head. "Oh, no. Not on your life."

"Mallory..." Zadkiel frowned.

"Nope."

"Mallory, hand over your weapons. Phillip will see to it that they are serviced. Surely they could do with it by now?"

"No-one services these but me." Mallory scowled back at the Archangel.

So much for peaceful, thought Alice.

"If I might?" Phillip took a step forward and held out his hand, palm up, towards Mallory. Reluctantly, Mallory handed him one of the Colts.

Suddenly, Phillip's hands were a blur, moving over the gun; pulling, twisting, pushing....

He handed it back to Mallory. "The slider. Smoother?"

Looking like he'd been handed a scorpion, Mallory took it back and drew the slider of the gun back. He blinked twice, then looked from it to Phillip. "Yes. It is."

"I had a life before I joined the brothers here."

"And that was... what, exactly?"

"It was... less than legal." Phillip smiled.

"A monk who's also a gunsmith. If only I'd known, I'd have come sooner," Mallory laughed. But he still hadn't handed over the guns.

"I promise you, you can trust Phillip as you would us," Zadkiel said, noticing his reluctance.

"I was afraid you'd say that," Mallory muttered out of the side of his mouth.

"I can order you to, if you'd prefer...?"

"That won't be necessary." Mallory drew out the other gun from the back of his belt, safetied both and placed them in Phillip's hands. "You take care of those, you hear me?"

"Of course." The guns vanished into the shadows of Phillip's sleeves. "We'll have them back to you by dusk."

"No. No 'we.' Only you. Nobody else touches them. Not a soul."

"I understand." He nodded. "It will be my privilege." And with that, the monk turned towards Zadkiel, leaving Mallory looking slightly bereft. "Will there be anything else? I can have one of the brothers..."

"That won't be necessary, Phillip. I'll take care of them. And I'll ask for the guard on the chapel to be doubled, if you want?"

"That would be most appreciated, I think. Given the circumstances." He smiled, and Alice realised he was much younger than she had taken him for at first: thirty at most. Apparently, hanging out with the angels aged you prematurely. Which reminded her: she'd spent last night on the floor of an abandoned chapel, and most of the day before that walking. She couldn't even *imagine* what she looked like at that particular moment...

The monk retreated, leaving them alone in the little graveyard, the crunch of his footsteps fading into the distance. There was a small chapel at the far end of the cemetery, tucked away in the shadiest corner. A flight of steps led up from the path to its door – Alice got the feeling steps were going to feature largely in her visit here... much as they had in hell, oddly enough. "Balance," she said to herself, right before she saw the shadow beside the chapel move. Blinking, she stared at the patch of darkness. It didn't move again, but there was something odd about it. It looked darker than the rest of the shadow. More *solid*.

"Adriel?"

There was no reply.

"Alice? Is everything alright?" Mallory's voice cut through her thoughts.

"What? No, I'm fine. Just... you know. Thin air."

"If you say so." Mallory peered towards the chapel, following the line of her gaze, but was distracted by Vin slapping his arm.

"And you took the piss out of me being worried about my shades. You're even worse."

"Yes, Vhnori. That's because I'm handing over my weapons. The things which keep me alive. Not my accessories."

"Keep telling yourself that, mate. You might believe it if you say it enough times."

When Alice looked back to the corner of the wall, the shadows were flat and still, and whatever she thought she'd seen, it wasn't there.

After another long stare, she frowned and turned her back on the shadows.

As expected, there were more steps. A lot more steps. And they kept on climbing: sweeping stairways which wound around the sides of buildings, narrow stairs cut into the bare rock between walls... and one heart-stopping rickety wooden staircase which clung to the bare rock, with nothing below it but the sea and a rather unpleasant death. Even Zadkiel hesitated before setting foot on that one, but after a brief pause, he shrugged and ploughed on. "I don't usually come this way," he called back over his shoulder.

"It's very quiet," Alice said, trying to keep her mind, and eyes, off everything below her. Definitely not looking down. Not *thinking* about looking down, either. "I thought there'd be more people about by now."

"What, you mean the people who are busy rioting and watching the world crumble around them? Everything's falling apart. The balance has tipped, even if they don't know it. They can feel it all the same. You really think they're going to put 'holiday' on the top of their to-do list? And if they did, do you think they're going to be queueing up to visit the town where the inhabitants all up and took to the streets and hanged their children in the school hall?"

"You always have an answer, don't you?"

"Archangel. It's my job."

THE STAIRWAY OF near-death brought them up and out again into a cloister, enclosed by an open-sided corridor. It wasn't exactly large, but it was big enough. There was a well to one side, and a wooden bench where two monks dressed in the same black habits as Phillip sat in silence in the sun. But the most striking thing about the square was that it was filled with angels. They weren't just standing around, chatting, either. They weren't walking in loose groups, or sitting, or doing any of the things Alice had got used to seeing them do.

They were in organised lines; blocks. They stood to attention. They *shone*: breastplates strapped over glittering mail, swords in their hands and wings outstretched and scudding with flames. They looked, not to put too fine a point on it, like an army.

Michael's choir were *drilling*, but all Alice could see was the fire. It was everywhere: in their hair, running down their arms. Sparks rose into the air from their swords; danced at the ends of their wings. She could feel it, could smell it: the faint scent of woodsmoke carrying on the breeze, mixing with the smell of the sea.

Home. It smelled like home. Even though she had never been here before, it smelled like *home*.

There was a bark of command and the rows of angels spun to face Zadkiel and raised their swords in salute. He waved them away, looking embarrassed. "I hate that," he said, and then a very complicated expression crossed his face: something between happiness and relief and disappointment... and nudging against despair. And there was that aching pain behind her ribs again, just like the one she'd felt earlier, but stronger now. So much stronger.

There, on the far side of the square and half-hidden by the wings of Michael's angels, was Castor, leaning back against the wall and watching the drill.

"Oh," said Alice. She remembered Xaphan's sneer, back in the church.

Mallory was right behind her. "You don't want to get in the middle of that."

"Castor. And..."

"Castor and Zadkiel. Messy. *Painful*."

"Oh," she said again.

"Want to know the best bit?"

"I thought you said I should stay out of it..."

"No, no. Let me finish."

"Fine."

"The best bit? Is that of all the angels you shouldn't put in a room together, we've come here with three. And the fourth is inside this very fortress. And hates us."

"Gabriel?"

"Gabriel."

"Oh."

"Yeah." Mallory unscrewed his hip flask, and took a long swig before holding it out to Alice. "You sure you don't want any?"

"ALICE!" A FAMILIAR voice boomed across the square, and Alice saw a figure weaving between the others, trailing sparks behind him. He was smiling. And waving enthusiastically.

A'albiel.

Apart from Mallory and Vin, he was one of the few angels who Alice both liked and trusted. It was entirely possible he was the *only* one besides Mallory and Vin. It was A'albiel who had rescued her from Xaphan's first attack, when she was alone and vulnerable and had less than zero control over her gift. It was A'albiel who had helped uncover Gwyn's betrayal in hell; who had made Michael see sense.

And he was here.

He marched over to them, the flames streaming across his wings dying down, the feathers folding in on themselves and away.

"I heard rumours," he said. "I heard rumours, but I did not believe they could be true."

"Were they good rumours?" Alice asked, smiling at him. This appeared to puzzle him, and he frowned. She shook her head. "Never mind."

"Is it true?"

Mallory tucked his flask away again and straightened up. "You're going to have to tell us what the rumours are if you want us to answer that one, Al."

"Indeed." Al nodded. "They say you come to see Michael..."

"No shit."

"If I might? They say you come to see Michael, and to bring him a prisoner. One of the Twelve."

"And his girlfriend," Mallory snorted. A'albiel looked blank again, so Alice stepped in.

"Xaphan, Al. It's Xaphan. And Florence."

"The half-born?"

"Try not to make it sound like a dirty word, would you?"

"My apologies. I meant no disrespect, Alice."

"None taken."

"But you have Xaph?" He glanced from Alice to Mallory and back again. "This seems..."

"Unlikely. Thanks for the vote of confidence," Mallory shrugged. "I know, alright? But apparently, Michael has something they want."

"What can Michael have that the Fallen would want?"

"Oh, I don't know. Power? An army of angels? A great big fuck-off castle?" Mallory kicked at the wall. "It's the brother. The girl's brother. She's a trade."

"She handed herself in?"

"Something like that. Our... paths crossed back in Camden."

"The riots."

"The riots. And as you can imagine, Xaphan was having a fine time dressing up as a copper and beating the shit out of people."

"It wouldn't be the first time."

"No. But it'll certainly be the last."

"Curious."

"How so?"

"That Xaphan would allow himself to be captured – whatever the reason. Now, of all times."

"You're going to have to fill in the backstory, Al. We've been a little busy..."

"Michael believes he has found a way to bind Lucifer together, body and soul. And if he can bind him..."

"He can destroy him."

Alice interrupted. "Destroy Lucifer? Is that even possible?"

"Michael appears to believe it is," said A'albiel. "But only if he is the sum of his parts. Otherwise, you can destroy the body..." He shrugged.

Mallory rubbed his chin. "I was afraid he'd try something like that. It's unheard of. I mean... restoration. It would change everything. *Everything*. Do they know?"

"The Fallen? I can only imagine that they do."

"It would explain a lot, wouldn't it?" Mallory looked thoughtful. "And Michael's sure? How?"

"The library here. He believes there is a text that holds the key. Gabriel is redeeming himself by searching for it."

"I almost feel sorry for him..." Mallory muttered, then turned to Alice. "I don't suppose it's too much to hope that you missed the mention of the word 'library' there, is it?"

"Yes. And now you've said it again, you have my full attention." She batted her eyelashes at him.

"Bloody librarians. You're all the same."

"Thank you. Continue?"

"Michael's library holds... everything. Everything we've ever learned about the Fallen."

"Wait... so, if there's a book that tells you how to destroy Lucifer, why hasn't Michael just done it already?"

"Because of the risk." Zadkiel's voice made Alice jump: she had had no idea he had joined them. "To destroy Lucifer, you must first restore him."

"Put him back together, you mean?"

"No. I mean *restore* him. He can only be destroyed as an Archangel."

"Ah."

"You see. We've never had to consider it before: the war... all this, has always been about the balance. As long as we could always keep the balance, Lucifer was irrelevant."

"Irrelevant? That's one word for it."

"What would you understand? What are you? Human. Human with angel blood running in your veins, perhaps, but human nonetheless."

"Your boss seems to think differently," Alice said, surprised at how smug it sounded when she said it aloud. One of Zadkiel's eyebrows shot up, as did Mallory's.

"Michael has never been as" – Zadkiel paused, considering his choice of word – "desperate as I've seen him lately."

"Desperate?" Mallory stepped in. There was a strange emphasis on the word. Zadkiel shook his head.

"He doesn't like losing."

"You mean he's not *willing* to lose."

"Whatever the cost. In his mind, the end justifies the means – whatever those might be."

Mallory didn't appear to have an answer to that. Instead, he closed his eyes as though in pain, and hung his head. Vin, too, stared at the paving beneath his feet, and even Al looked dejected.

When Mallory spoke again, his voice was hoarse, like he was trying to hold something back. "I'm sorry, Alice. I shouldn't have brought you here. It was a mistake."

"Bollocks. You didn't bring me. I came."

"You don't understand. What Michael's planning – if he succeeds... Archangel against Archangel. It's unthinkable."

"It's a death sentence," Vin said quietly, but Mallory made an impatient 'hush' sound.

"There's a reason no attempt has ever been made to completely destroy him, Alice," Mallory continued. "It's simple: it's because it could destroy everything. All of us. All of *you*, even. Lucifer has always been allowed to remain because he was imprisoned, both by us and by the balance. Everything that spun out from that was... manageable." He smiled sadly. "And Lucifer always knew, I think, that we would never risk trying to destroy him completely. He knew what could happen."

"Mad," said Alice.

"Perhaps..."

"No. Not 'mad.' Mutually assured destruction. Equilibrium strategy. The *balance*."

"This time you've lost me, Alice."

"It's game theory, right? All that stuff?"

"Strategy? You're lecturing me on strategy?" Mallory stepped back and looked her up and down. "What happened to 'I'm a librarian'?"

"Spend long enough around books and some of it sort of sinks in," Alice said with a shrug. She was aware that Zadkiel had cocked his head on one side and was looking at her with a thoughtful expression. "What?" she asked, suddenly embarrassed. She felt like a five-year-old crashing their parents' dinner-party.

"Perhaps Michael's right about you after all," said Zadkiel.

"What's that supposed to mean?"

"It means you've given me an idea." He nodded to A'albiel, who nodded back and walked away. He grew faster and faster as he went, until he was almost running. Zadkiel watched as he disappeared through a door at the base of a tower. "We've always played by the rules of engagement. It's time to change the game."

CHAPTER TWENTY-ONE

Zero-Sum

TO SAY THE stairway was unevenly-lit would have been an understatement, thought Alice. There was the occasional candle stuck to the wall here and there, and the odd little window along the way, but it really wasn't much to work with. Thankfully, there was a thick, braided rope running around the outer wall in soft swags by way of a handrail, so she clung to that and followed the sound of footsteps ahead of her. It wasn't like she could get lost, after all; it was just a case of climbing until they ran out of steps.

If she never saw another staircase – up down or sideways, it didn't matter where it went – it would be too soon, as far as she was concerned. And then she remembered that she was being taken to see Michael, and all of a sudden, the idea of walking up stairs for the rest of her natural life seemed quite appealing.

At last, there were no more stairs. Her heart was hammering against her ribs, and her legs felt like someone had taken hold of her ankles and shaken her. Hard. It was with no small satisfaction that she heard Vin panting behind her. If even Earthbounds found that climb hard going, she wasn't in as bad a state as she'd thought. Mallory and Zadkiel – naturally – looked as if they'd gone for a twilight stroll. Alice shot them both a dirty look, but neither noticed.

The stairs opened onto a small landing, and a door. There was a slightly larger window than the ones which had almost-lit the stairs – an archway cut straight into the stone – and looking out of it, Alice felt dizzy. The sea was so far below now, even the streets on the island looked distant and small. The staircase they had just followed, according to Zadkiel, had been built by some of the first monks there, expressly at Michael's command.

"His command?" asked Alice.

"He appeared to them in a vision," said Zadkiel. "At least that's the story they told."

"And the real story?"

"He sauntered into the refectory one day, sat down and put his feet up on the table and asked when he could expect his room to be ready."

"Bullshit."

"I was there, remember," Zadkiel said with a smile. "And here we are. Secret staircase, secret room. Not even the current monks know where this one is – not that it's stopped them from looking."

"But there was a door. It was kind of… oh." Alice suddenly remembered who she was talking to. "You."

"Me."

"Have you ever said no to him?"

"To Michael? Why would I? He's my commanding officer. More than that: he's my friend."

"You need to pick your friends better," said Alice as the door opened.

"And you still need to learn some respect, child," said Michael from the other side of the doorway.

He was standing in the middle of the room, his hands on his hips and his wings open, watching her.

And she had absolutely nothing to say. All she could do was stand and look at him… at the face which had followed her through her dreams and her nightmares for months. A face which had haunted her in every crowd and made her look for eyes filled with fire. Eyes which peeled back everything she was and saw beneath it all.

Michael was watching her and she was afraid.

And he knew it.

"That's it, is it? You won't respect me, but you fear me?" He laughed, and his laughter bounced off the walls, filling the room with sound. "Well, it's a start." He beckoned her into the room, and her feet obeyed, stopping in front of him. He walked around her in a circle, slowly surveying her, and she could feel his mind crawling over the surface of her own, weighing and measuring and examining everything he found.

"I've been following your progress, Alice. And what progress it's been," he said. "You've been busy. I heard about Murmur. I was impressed. Not as impressed as I might have been if it were say, Purson, but I hear someone else took care of that." His gaze flitted to Vin, just inside the doorway, who gulped audibly. Michael gave up on orbiting Alice, heading instead for Vin. "You again. You think I haven't been watching you, too?"

Vin held his head up and met Michael's gaze, but said nothing. The Archangel narrowed his eyes. "Hmm. Still have spirit, I see. I remember why I liked you. Yes. You can stay. And you..." He spun back to Alice. "What am I to do with you? I take it that you've considered my warning? I told you to think about your priorities. Your place in the world. Have you?"

"You tell me." Alice's voice shook a little more than she would have liked, but she still sounded confident enough. Sort of.

Michael threw back his head and laughed. "You hear that, Gabriel? Isn't she infuriating?"

It was only then that Alice realised there was someone else in the room. Another angel, this one leaning against the far wall, close to a table heaped high with papers and scrolls which spilled onto the floor around it. His wings were clipped, shortened, and the feathers were not the same shining white as Michael's, but the scruffy grey of Vin's. And his eyes, when he locked them on her, were full of fury.

"Hello again, Alice," said Gabriel. His voice could have cut glass. Alice shivered. Even more than Michael, this was what she had been dreading.

After all, it wasn't every day that you got an Archangel demoted. Especially not one as vengeful as Gabriel.

A sudden crack of lightning outside the windows lit the room as Gabriel glowered, but Alice didn't move. She didn't know what else to do. If she flinched, Gabriel would see just how afraid of him she was. And that was *not* going to happen.

"Good girl," said Michael, straightening his shirt sleeves. "Alice, you never fail to impress me. Infuriating you may be, but impressive." He made a sound that might have been another laugh, or perhaps not. "Gabriel, behave, or you'll go back to the dungeon. And I don't think any of us want *that* now, do we?" He waved Zadkiel and Mallory into the room. "Mallory."

"Michael." Mallory's voice was flat.

"You've brought me Xaphan, I hear?"

"It's complicated."

"So I gather. You understand it's a trap?"

"I had a feeling it might be." Mallory nodded.

Alice twitched. "A trap?"

"What would I want with the girl's brother?" Michael asked. "Have you ever known me to be *that* petty?"

"So you don't have him?"

"Oh, no. He's here. But as my guest, not my prisoner."

Hearing this, Vin brightened. "Where is he?"

"In his rooms, I imagine. As I say, he's not a prisoner and he is free to come and go as he pleases. Zadkiel brought him in. He was helping me with something."

"With what?" Alice asked with a sinking feeling.

"With you, obviously." Michael replied, looking straight at her. "He was helping me find a way to convince you to come here. Which, apparently, he's done. And which begs the question of what *exactly* Xaphan is up to. Tricky, tricky Xaph." He glanced at Zadkiel. "They're secure?"

"Brother Phillip has them."

"Good. I don't like the timing, but in that case I don't think there's too much to worry about. You doubled the guard?"

"Twice."

"Mmmm."

"I had a suggestion." For the first time since she had met him, Alice thought Zadkiel sounded unsure of himself.

"I know what you're going to say, Zak. The answer's no."

"But if you reinstate the Earthbounds..."

"I said no."

"Tactically, it gives us the numbers."

"Enough! I said *no*!" Fire erupted from the floor between Michael and Zadkiel, and everyone jumped back, apart from Zadkiel, who simply rolled his eyes.

"Why do you have to be so pigheaded, Michael? Always."

"Because I make the rules. Not you." Michael spat back. "And they've always served well enough before."

"This isn't like before though, is it? And you *know* it." Zadkiel was shouting now, jabbing his finger angrily at Michael. "This isn't like *anything* that's come before."

"And, given that it's like nothing that's come before, you're basing your theory that sheer weight of numbers will save us on... *what*, exactly?" Michael snapped

"On nothing! On hope, alright? Is that what you want to hear?" Zadkiel snapped back, kicking out at the air in frustration.

The flames on the floor died down, and Michael sighed. "I understand, Zak. I do. But this is my responsibility."

There was a long, heavy silence. Finally, Zadkiel said, "Don't mistake responsibility for martyrdom, Michael," and turned on his heel, leaving them. They heard his boots echoing down the stairs.

"I'm sorry," Michael said to no-one in particular. "As you can see, things are a little... tense. Zak's – Zadkiel's – instincts are good, but he's overlooking the most basic fact. Lucifer knows exactly how we think. He knows every move we will make before we make it. He knows that if I reinstate the Earthbounds, our numbers will outweigh his; why do you think he's been so busy with the world? A nudge here, a whisper there... and he has the humans rushing towards their baser nature, tipping the balance in his favour." He opened his arms as if to illustrate his point. "Everything I do, he can predict. But it cuts both ways. He knows us, but I know him. *We* know *them*. If he has set a trap, with the balance against us, it's almost inevitable that sooner or later, it will work. Which is why we're doing it the short way."

"You wanted to see how it pans out." Alice couldn't quite believe what she was hearing. It almost made sense, but not quite. But then, it *was* Michael saying it.

"Exactly. You bringing Xaphan here: it happened because Lucifer wanted it to happen. What I want to know is *why*." He shrugged. "And the quickest way to find out is to let things follow their natural course."

"What then?" asked Mallory. His face had settled into an expression Alice could only describe as 'stony.' "What if things don't play out how you expected they would? What if you're wrong?"

"Then I'm wrong. But tell me, Mallory: what choice do I have?" Michael paced the floor. "I have Lucifer's body, but his mind is adrift. Any prison I build for him, he turns to his advantage: I locked him in hell, he made it a sanctuary; I lock him up here, he mocks me from the shoreline. He turns humanity against itself and gains power from the chaos while my army fights in vain. He openly walks in the world while we remain hidden, and he takes and he takes and he takes, and I... will... not... lose."

"There's always choices, Michael. You don't need me to tell you that. Are you sure you're making the right ones?"

"Ever the philosopher, Mallory." Michael stared out of the window and took a deep breath, letting it out slowly. "I can see why she listens to you."

"I thought that was the point."

"Mmm. We'll see." He brightened. "But all this is irrelevant. We think we've found it. The way to bind him."

"And then what?"

"Then we destroy Lucifer... and every single one of the Fallen with him." Michael turned away from the window and back to face them, and his eyes were white-hot with fire. "Lucifer wants absolute war. I'm only too happy to oblige."

CHAPTER TWENTY-TWO

Run, Brother

THE FIRST THE Quartermaster heard of it was the bell. Not the bells of the priory or the smaller church lower on the island, but a hand-bell, rung hard and fast, and then dropped with a clatter. Phillip looked up from his workbench and muttered something under his breath. That was the alarm bell. And it could mean only one thing.

He ran to the door of his workshop, tucked beneath the little chapel in the cemetery, and wrenched it open. The graveyard was as tranquil as ever; there was no sign of life. But he could hear running footsteps, shouting. Screams. Without thinking, he ducked back into his workshop and snatched up Mallory's guns. He threw them into the middle of a cloth on the table and hastily wrapped them up, before throwing them into a green holdall, along with several boxes of bullets. Slinging the holdall onto his shoulder, he leaned over the table and took hold of one of the stones of the wall. Mortar crumbled under his fingernails as he tugged and worked at the edges of the stone. Something lay in the gloomy space behind: something slender, wrapped in a dirty rag. He hesitated, and then added it to his haul. Without another look back, he slammed the door behind him and raced through the graveyard; his feet crunched on the gravel, and he ran as though the devil was behind him.

As far as Phillip was concerned, he was.

* * *

THERE WAS SHOUTING, and the sound of more running feet; the howl of a wind that had sprung from nowhere, screaming through the streets and slamming into the ancient walls. Phillip wound his way through the buildings of Mont Saint-Michel, the first plumes of oily black smoke curling up from the island beneath him. And still he ran.

He had reached the bottom of a broad flight of steps, overarched by enormous granite buttresses, when he saw the first of the guards. Three of them lay strewn across the steps, their bodies broken, their wings torn and lifeless. Blood seeped out from beneath them, trickling into a pool almost at his feet. Phillip stared at them. "Forgive me," he whispered, looking into the dead eyes below him, then stepped over them, lifting his habit clear of their blood. He clutched his bag and ran up the steps two at a time.

The steps climbed sharply, crowded between high walls, and then levelled out into a long, straight passageway. At the end of the passage was smoke. Smoke and fire. Scorch marks stained the granite blocks on either side, and deep sword cuts in the rock.

Bodies littered the ground ahead of him, and with mounting horror, he realised that he was going to have to go through them to reach the priory. Slowly, he picked his way between them: wings torn apart, littering the ground with feathers, and empty faces, their eyes open and unseeing. Something brushed against his ankle and he recoiled with a gasp: a hand. An angel he didn't recognise, but the sigil on his wrist was Michael's. His fingers were still clasped around the hilt of his sword.

The passageway rang with the sounds of fighting now, screams and howls bouncing off the high stone walls, and Phillip felt cold. So cold. It occurred to him that he could turn back; he could run. And the more he thought about it, the more appealing it seemed. There was nothing to stop him – he knew the island better than anyone. He was sure he could make his way out without being seen, and he certainly knew his way across the sands to the mainland. All he had to do was wait until dark, and he could make a run for it. No-one would think any less of him. After all, he was only *human*.

Phillip's head snapped up. The voice in his mind, the voice telling him to run... *it wasn't his*. He looked down at his feet. He had, without quite realising, turned and taken several steps back the way he came. "I am myself," he said to no-one. "And I choose my own end in peace." The air around him cooled again, the wind swallowing his words. There was no-one there to hear them. It didn't matter. Head held high, Phillip started forwards again.

The thick white smoke now spanned the end of the passageway, hiding everything behind it. There were shapes moving, and flashes of light – of fire – but everything was obscured. He stretched out his hand to touch it, watching it coil around his fingers... then snatched them back, suddenly feeling foolish. Someone on the other side of the veil screamed, and something heavy fell to the ground.

Phillip stepped through the smoke.

PHILLIP HAD NEVER considered hell. He had never claimed to be perfect, and had led a less sheltered life by far than most of the brothers in Michael's service, but the chaos at the end of the passageway was like nothing he had ever seen, either waking or dreaming.

Five angels, fully armoured, surrounded the prisoners, their backs turned inwards. Florence and Xaphan, wrists still bound and tied to one another, cowered in the middle of the circle, while the Descendeds lunged outwards at a half-dozen Fallen. They hurled themselves at the angels in a fury, tearing, clawing, gouging, biting. And despite the fire the Descendeds threw at them, they kept coming. A heap of blackened bodies past the knot of angels suggested there had been more. Far more, judging by the number of dead angels Phillip had passed. He didn't stop to wonder where they had come from; didn't wait to ask. Instead, spotting a glint of silver beneath a pile of scorched feathers, he hurried towards it.

The sword was heavier than he had expected; while the angels swung theirs with one hand, it took both of his and all his strength just to lift it. The point shook wildly as he held it up, with fear and exertion.

He could see the doorway. The one he needed. Less than fifty yards ahead and the wrong side of the pitched battle going on in front of him. If he could get to that, he could get to Zadkiel and Michael.

One of the Descendeds looked up and saw him, frozen in the midst of the chaos. Phillip recognised A'albiel, one of Michael's favourites. He was already wounded: one shoulder hung lower than the other and his face was covered in blood and ash. Flames blazed around him as his chest heaved in and out with the effort of breathing; his breastplate shone under a layer of battle-grime. He would know what to do.

Phillip met his gaze, and A'albiel seemed to understand. He nodded, and shouted something Phillip could not make out. The others must have understood it; they raised their swords as one and whirled – and in a blur of fire and feathers, they had spun around pinning the attacking Fallen back against one of the walls and leaving a narrow gap behind them. They had given up their defensive position, had laid themselves wide open, but they had given him a pathway to the door.

"Go!" A'albiel shouted at him. Phillip dropped the sword and ran for the door.

As he passed them, still running, he thought he saw Xaphan wink at him...

And then he was in the doorway, scrabbling for the handle and tumbling through, slamming the door shut behind him.

* * *

Outside, A'albiel heard the door bang, heard the key turn in the lock. The Quartermaster was safe. He ducked as one of the Fallen threw... *something* at him. It passed by too quickly to see what it was, and Al didn't really care. It had almost hit him, and he lunged forward with a flaming sword; smiling in satisfaction as his assailant took the blade in the face and dropped where he stood.

He was still smiling when the knife slipped into his back, finding its way between the links of the chainmail and down into the root of his wings. Stars bloomed in his eyes and the ground beneath him softened as the blade slid home. His sword dropped from his hand.

He twisted as he fell. He hit the ground, seeing Xaphan casually shaking off his restraints, smiling at him. As the remains of the guard, too, fell around him, Xaphan stepped over a heap that had once been an angel and dropped into a crouch, running his finger down A'albiel's cheek. "Wrong place, wrong time," he whispered. "Everywhere and anywhere. The world is ours." He smiled again, and wiped the blood from his knife on A'albiel's shoulder, before slipping the blade back into his pocket and holding his hand out to Florence. She took his hand, and they turned their backs on A'albiel, the three remaining Fallen following them, vanishing into the drifting smoke.

A'albiel rolled onto his back, feeling the chill spreading out from beneath his wings. His vision clouded, and he turned his eyes to the perfectly empty blue sky.

And inside the abbey, Phillip ran.

CHAPTER TWENTY-THREE

Fire with Fire

THE PIECE OF paper Michael had been holding slipped from his fingers and dropped to the floor. He strode towards the window, frowning. "Smoke," he said, looking out over the roofs.

Alice looked out of the nearest window. He was right. A cloud of smoke hung over the island below them; it was thick and black, greasy. She had seen it before.

"Mallory..."

"I see it. Michael?"

"Hmm." Michael looked thoughtful. "Not the approach I would have taken, but still..."

"Michael!"

"What?" Michael's head snapped around to face Mallory.

"What do you want us to do?"

"To do?" Michael looked puzzled, his eyes moving from Mallory to the window and back again. "We fight, of course."

"With *what*?" Mallory said pointedly. "I hate to point this out, but your Quartermaster relieved me of my guns."

Michael raised a finger and cocked his head. Someone was coming up the stairs.

The door was thrown open as Zadkiel burst into the room. He was carrying a small roll of cloth, which he threw to Mallory. "Brother Phillip sends his regards, and his apologies. Almost got himself killed getting here."

Mallory caught it and unwrapped his guns, dropping the cloth and checking the magazines on both Colts before stuffing them into his pockets. "He's got good timing," he muttered as Zadkiel dropped a green holdall on the floor with a brusque, "Ammo." The Archangel then raced across the room, and whispered something into his commander's ear. Michael's frown deepened.

"Escaped? How did they manage that?"

"I don't know." Zadkiel raised his voice a little, enough for Alice to hear, at least. She pointed out of the window.

"Uhh… that tour bus. Down there. On the causeway. I don't suppose that has anything to do with what you're all panicking about, does it?"

"Tour bus?" Michael's frown finally tipped over into a scowl. "What?"

"There. In the car park. There's a bus. It wasn't there earlier…"

"They came on a *coach*?" Michael's voice was a mixture of bemusement and contempt, while Zadkiel shook his head.

"You're not serious?"

"Look." Alice pointed again. There it was, sitting in the car park at the end of the causeway. A bright red coach, the kind that took tourists on week-long holidays. Exactly the kind of coach Alice would have expected to see here. Which is why, apparently, no-one had noticed it. Until now.

"The sentries?" Michael snapped at Zadkiel.

"Gone."

"Gone where?"

"If I knew, I'd tell you." He ran a hand back through his hair, pacing. "They've yet to breach the priory itself. Phillip made it in through the gate, but they were right behind him. I say we concentrate on the most vulnerable points. Move to defend the scriptorium and the south corridor. If they get through there, we're in trouble."

"Agreed." Michael was still staring out of the window. "Take the corridor. I'll take the scriptorium."

Zadkiel thought for a moment, then glanced at Mallory. "You're with me. Think you can handle it?"

"Can I handle it..." Mallory snorted. Beside the door, Vin was already rolling his shoulders and flexing his fingers. Alice knew what that meant.

"What about me?" she asked. No-one answered.

The voice which finally came from the corner of the room was chilly. It was Gabriel. "And the prisoners?" he asked, almost offhand.

"Gone too." Zadkiel answered.

"Time to find out what Lucifer's up to," said Michael, fire flaring up around him. "Kill them all." And with that, he vanished.

Only after he had gone did Alice notice that Gabriel had disappeared with him. Now, it was her, Mallory, Vin and Zadkiel. They seemed to know what they were doing and had already started towards the door.

"What about me?" she asked again. All three of them stopped and stared at her.

"You're with us, of course," said Zadkiel.

"With you. But you're going to the... the south corridor."

"That's right. Are you always this slow?"

"I don't follow."

"Today, you do." He ran through the doorway, down the stairs.

Mallory drew out one of his guns, turning it over in his hands. "Time to let off a little steam, Alice."

"What's that supposed to mean?"

"You remember how when Florence pitched up, you wanted to kill her?"

"Yes." Alice gritted her teeth.

"Now's your chance." There was a loud 'click' from his gun as he flicked the safety off. "How fast can you run?"

* * *

As it happened, Alice could run faster than she thought. She ran down the stairs... all of them. She ran through the little cloister they had seen earlier – now deserted – and in through another door. Her feet hammered on the floor, almost in step with Mallory's as they ran towards the south corridor of the priory. Wherever that might be. She assumed Mallory and Vin knew better than she did where they were going.

"And we're running why?" she shouted at Mallory as he edged ahead of her. Vin was way ahead of them both, trailing just behind Zadkiel.

"We've been given an order, Alice. This is what we do." Mallory shot a look back at her over his shoulder. "You wanted to run with the angels, right?"

"I didn't think it would be quite so literal..." she muttered, starting to feel out of breath. Mallory didn't seem to be having the same problem.

They rounded a corner, where the others had stopped. Alice forced herself to a halt – almost losing her balance in an attempt not to slam into Zadkiel's back as he stood in the middle of the corridor. It wasn't a dignified stop, but at least it *was* a stop.

"The south corridor," said Zadkiel.

To the right was a narrow doorway, an archway cut directly through the stone of the wall and edged with carvings of fruit. Through it was, as promised, another corridor, and he stepped through into it, gesturing for them to follow him. The passage was windowless and perhaps thirty yards end to end; the ceiling towered above them, tapering to a pointed vault high above their heads. Iron struts spanned the space, bracing the old walls against each other. There were candles in sconces bolted to the walls, and three large iron candelabra dangling from the ceiling on chains.

"That's a *lot* of candles. Who the hell lights all these?" Alice asked, a little too flippantly.

Zadkiel simply said: "You did."

"I what?"

"You did. When you came around the corner." He tapped the sigil on his arm, and she glanced down at her own. "Michael's choir," he said, "are rarely without light when they want it."

"But I didn't..."

"Let it go, Alice. There's no time." He peered past her, down the corridor, and she turned around. There were two angels coming towards them, the corridor barely wide enough for them to walk side by side: Castor and Pollux. Pollux was limping; a long, jagged cut crossed Castor's face, from one side of his jaw to the eyebrow on the other side. Both of them looked like they had been beaten to within an inch of their lives.

"I've got this," said Mallory, handing his guns to Vin, who took them without a word. Mallory went first to Castor, taking his hands gently in his, closing his eyes and tipping his head back. The slash across Castor's face began to knit together and the skin across Mallory's cheek tore itself apart with surprising violence, lengthening across his nose and down to his jaw. He sagged, but shook his head as though he was trying to shake the pain off...

The candles on the walls flared higher.

Mallory stepped back from Castor and turned to Pollux. He held out his hand to the other Descended, and although his back was to Alice and she could no longer see his face, his hand shook. One of the fingers was twisted; the palm slashed almost to the bone in several places.

"Mallory..." she said, about to go to him, but Vin put his arm out to stop her.

"Leave him. It's what he does."

"But both of them? It's too much..."

"No." Mallory's voice was hoarse, but determined. "Pollux needs help. And we need Pollux." He was about to say something else, but he bit off his own words as he took Pollux's hand and a shudder ran through his whole body. With a loud snapping sound, a handful of the long feathers on his wings bent and tore – and that was enough for Mallory, who let out a howl of pain. He dropped Pollux's hand, and slumped sideways against the wall.

Alice strained forward again – still held back by Vin. "You really think that's a good idea? Remember what happened last time..." He pointed at her blazing hands as echoes of Mallory's pain coursed through her, burning away so fast that she barely even felt it. She was grateful; she remembered the last time she had been there when Mallory healed someone. It had been Vin, left for dead by Purson; and she had felt every broken bone, every cut and every tear. Now... now it poured through her like oil and was gone: burned away almost before she knew it had reached her.

But the fire was still there. The fire was always there.

"Mallory?"

He was still slumped against the wall, his head carefully turned away from her and lowered towards his chest.

"Mallory!"

His head rose a little, and he raised one of his hands. It was slow, and his movements were clumsy, but growing more sure with every second that passed. He pulled out his hip flask, and with shaking hands, he unscrewed the cap and emptied the whole thing down his throat. When he turned around, he was himself again, with only the faintest suggestion of a new scar on the edge of his jaw. He spotted Alice staring at him. "They don't go as easily as they used to. Makes me look rugged, right?" he whispered, patting her arm as he reached past and took his guns back from Vin.

"Alright. So that was fun." He turned back to face the far end of the corridor, a gun in each hand. "Now, let's find me something to shoot."

"So, what exactly is the plan here?" Alice asked. "We're supposed to be stopping them coming in, right?"

"Not exactly," said Zadkiel. "We want them in."

"We *what*?"

"Anyone coming into the priory from this side has to pass through this corridor."

"Which is why you want to stop them getting into it."

"No. It's why we want them in here. It's a natural bottle-neck. The trick is..."

"...to stop them getting out again." It made sense. In the corridor, it would only take a few of them to hold it against however many Fallen tried to force their way through. Just as well, because there were six of them. Only six. And they were fish in a barrel.

"So are they, Alice. So are they."

Alice considered telling Zadkiel that this was not nearly as reassuring as he seemed to think – and to stay out of her head – but she thought better of it. Mostly because the others all looked like they had a plan. And she didn't.

Behind her, Castor and Pollux had taken up a position on either side of the doorway, barring the exit. Each was holding a long metal pole as tall as he was, taken from a pile of spare roof struts in the corner. "Well, you two look utterly terrifying."

"And I thought you liked me in uniform," Castor shot back, making her laugh. "Are you ready?"

"No. Yes. Maybe. Ask me later."

"It's no different, you know. No different from the warehouse. No different from any other time."

"Yes, Castor. It is." She turned to face forward again.

Mallory was in front of her, cricking his neck from side to side. Just ahead of him was Vin, sleeves rolled up, his weight on his back foot. They were ready. Zadkiel paced across the doorway at the far end, calling back to them.

"Pollux, you two are our last line. Do not let anyone past you. Whatever you have to do, do it."

"Not a problem." Pollux shuffled his feet, widening his stance. Alice didn't think it *was* going to be a problem: between them, there might as well not have been a doorway at that end.

"Mallory, Vin – I'm going to let as many through as we can get. And then I'm going to shut the door behind them."

"What door?" Vin piped up.

"This door." Zadkiel held up his sword.

"Gotcha."

"Alice?" Zadkiel's voice was softer, but no less determined. "You take out what you can."

"That's it?"

"That's it. That and not getting killed. I don't think Michael would thank me."

"Screw Michael. Worry about how *I'd* feel."

"You can do this, Alice."

"I know," she said, and held up her hands. Flames streamed from the wall sconces closest to her into her open palms; fire wound through her hair. "You didn't say his name," she whispered, seeing Zadkiel start at the flames.

"*What* did you say?" His voice was too low for anyone else to hear, but he was looking over her shoulder at Castor.

"You heard me, Zadkiel. Castor. You didn't say his name."

"Now you listen to me..." His hand was on her arm, and he was gripping it tightly. She glared at it, and flames skipped across his fingers. He let go. "Stay out of things you don't understand."

"Things I don't understand? You know what I understand? *Pain.*" The flames flared brighter, hotter, forcing the Archangel back another step.

"This conversation's over." He turned his head away from the heat of the fire, but she could still hear him muttering, "Just like Michael," under his breath.

He reached the doorway, and his hand went up in warning. "Here they come."

Zadkiel flattened himself back against the wall beside the doorway, and Alice watched as, in spite of the blazing candles and the fire, the shadows around him softened and thickened, wrapping themselves around him, and he was gone.

Except he wasn't. She could still feel him standing there.

There were footsteps coming from the other end of the corridor. Just one set; slow and cautious. A moment later, a head poked around the doorway. One of the Fallen.

He stepped into the opening, peering ahead of him, and Alice realised that he couldn't see them – not clearly, at any rate. He kept screwing his eyes closed and twisting his head this way and that... as though he was sure there was someone waiting for him, someone he couldn't quite make out. Whatever Zadkiel had done to hide himself, it appeared to have covered all of them... at least a little.

The Fallen stopped and sniffed the air, baring his teeth. Like all the Fallen Alice had met, he looked like he had too many, and they were just that little bit too sharp. She watched him sniffing – still turning his head from side to side – and realised she was holding her breath. She let it out... just as the Fallen's wings snapped open. The blackened spines rattled against one another as he moved, stepping carefully, one slow step at a time, into the corridor.

"Smells like angel..." he hissed, and there was suddenly a crowd of them behind him. Watching. Waiting.

He had almost reached Vin, crouched low.

"They're close." The Fallen turned and beckoned to the others behind him, just as Vin exploded up from the floor, grabbing him around the neck and flipping him over, throwing him to the ground.

"You've got no idea, mate," he said, stepping over the dropped Fallen, who was screaming as grey mist wound around his throat, turning his flesh to stone.

Vin shifted from foot to foot, staring down the other Fallen, who had frozen where they stood. "You going to stand there all day, are you?" he jeered, and as one, they took the bait.

The threw themselves into the narrow space with such force that several of them tripped and were almost trampled underfoot, and with a stab of panic Alice saw just how many of them were out there. They streamed through the doorway; charging straight for Vin, who ducked and wove and spun with such speed that Alice could barely follow him. Very few of the first Fallen through got past him; they dropped to the floor with cries and stony *thuds*.

And the ones who managed to get past – the lucky ones – ran head-first into Mallory, who strode out of nowhere, both guns in his hands and a smile on his face. “Hello, boys,” he said, and then he started shooting.

The sound of the gunshots reverberated along the corridor, deafening Alice. She clamped her hands over her ears and squealed, before remembering that she was supposed to be doing something. The corridor, which had felt so empty only heartbeats before, was suddenly crowded; rammed with bodies in motion. And cold. *That* cold. They brought it with them, wherever they went, leaching hope and warmth from the air.

The warmth she could do something about, at least.

One of them had got past Mallory. He hadn’t seen her yet, and she understood what Zadkiel had done. They would stay hidden until the Fallen reached them. It was layer upon layer of ambush. There was no mercy, and no retreat.

The Fallen who had made it past Mallory had now turned and was throwing himself at Mallory’s exposed back, tearing at his wings. The corridor was too narrow for him to open them completely, meaning he couldn’t shake him off, and he was too busy with his guns, picking off the Fallen as they fought for space.

Alice stepped out of the shadows, and the corridor was ablaze with light. She grabbed the Fallen in front of her, pulling him away from Mallory, dodging the sharp sweep of his spiny wings and wrestling him down to the floor. She might have caught him by surprise, but it didn’t last long, and he fought back, hard.

Until he burned.

She was pulled off him, hauled to her feet by a dozen hands. A glance told her that Mallory and Vin had their hands more than full, and Castor and Pollux were just getting warmed up – spinning their makeshift quarterstaffs with ease, jabbing, sweeping, lunging. Zadkiel, too, had emerged from his shadows and was mercilessly cutting down anyone who tried to head back the way they had come. A Fallen lunged at him, aiming his fist at the Archangel's face, but he dodged and responded with a punch of his own.

Faces crowded around her, backing her into the wall. A hand lashed out, and she ducked, springing back up and retaliating with a kick aimed squarely at the knee of the Fallen closest to her. He screamed as her foot connected, his knee popping back on itself. The others recoiled – not much, but enough.

Why weren't they attacking?

They had her against the wall. Literally, against the wall. She had nowhere to go, but apart from that one lunge at her, they did nothing.

There was a sudden flash of red in the eyes around her; a laugh that sounded a little too familiar... and Alice decided not to wait to find out.

She closed her eyes, and let the fire out.

It raged across the stone, pouring onto the floor and wrapping around the legs of the Fallen; streaming from her fingers and sparking from her hair.

And still the Fallen stood, simply looking at her.

One of them took a step towards her and she froze. His clothes were alight, and the stench of burning hair and flesh made her gag. He stretched a hand towards her and she saw his lips move even as they blistered.

"Thank you."

Behind her barricade of fire, Alice's mouth dropped open.

He swayed, the flames taking hold, and at last, he dropped to his knees. Alice couldn't take her eyes off him.

The kneeling Fallen suddenly jerked sideways, his body falling forwards. Startled, Alice looked into the gap the Fallen had left behind, and there was Mallory, one of his Colts still smoking in his hand. "Thank me later," he shouted over the noise.

There was another shout, from the far end of the corridor.

"I need a weapon!" Zadkiel shouted. He had his sword in one hand, and what looked like a slender silver rod, about as long as his palm, in the other. He held it at arm's length, and with a sharp twist of his wrist jerked it up and sideways. It snapped open, flipping over itself, and suddenly he was holding a knife. But he didn't have the space to swing the sword any longer, and his reach with the knife was not long enough for comfort. Not that it stopped him. As Alice looked from him to Mallory, she saw the Fallen closest to him drop with a knife-wound to his neck.

Mallory stopped shooting. "Up!" was all he said.

And with that, both his guns were back in his belt, and he had spun on the spot, jumping and wrapping his hands around one of the struts just above his head and pulling himself up. He paused on the way up to kick another one of the Fallen smartly in the face, then crouched on the bar, his boots balancing on the metal rod. Opening his wings as far as he could in the narrow space and throwing out his hands, he glanced back down at Alice. She nodded at him, and watched as slowly, carefully, he drew himself upright. He wobbled, and for a second it looked as though he might topple back, but then he had his balance, and his guns were out again and he began to half-hop, half-run from one metal bar to the next, shooting down into the crowd of Fallen below, all the while drawing closer to Zadkiel, who was still holding his corner.

"Weapon!" shouted Mallory, and Zadkiel's head snapped up to see one of Mallory's guns spinning towards him. The Archangel reached up and snatched it out of the air; bringing it down and firing without pause.

The air smelled of dust and smoke and cordite, and the Fallen were... falling. Castor and Pollux held their ground behind a tangled pile of bodies, their eyes wide and their poles held at arm's length. Vin's hair was streaked with dust and he was slowing now, moving more deliberately through the Fallen who remained. There weren't many. The angels had seen to that.

Mallory was still up on his perch, surveying everything below. He had dropped into a crouch on the metal bar, balancing on the balls of his feet as he scanned the floor for movement. Satisfied, he tucked his gun into the back of his belt and jumped down, landing in a neat crouch on the floor. "Are you hurt?" He straightened and crossed the floor towards Alice, stepping over an outstretched hand. It was still twitching.

"No, I'm not hurt." Alice frowned, watching the hand on the floor behind him.

"You're something, though. What's wrong?"

"Nothing... I... what?" Alice was still staring at the dead Fallen's fingers tick-ticking against one another. Mallory followed her gaze. He cocked his head on one side, blinked, whipped out his gun, and shot the hand through the middle of the palm. What was left of it stopped twitching.

"You were saying?" He turned back to Alice.

"I'm not sure that was strictly necessary."

"Oh, I'm sorry. I didn't realise you were going to be the voice of my conscience today."

"Someone has to be!"

"Really? Because funnily enough, I seem to remember having to shoot one of them for you."

"You didn't *have* to."

"No. You're right. I didn't."

"Wanker."

"Ingrate."

"Are we done here?" Zadkiel was leaning against the wall, watching them. "And while we're on the subject, have you two considered some kind of joint therapy?"

"We're done." Mallory gave Alice a look, and she pulled a face at him as he turned his back.

"Anyone injured? No?" Zadkiel waited, then shrugged. "Good work. Corridor's secure. Pollux? You stay here and keep it that way. Just you." He shot a glance at Alice. "Castor? Vhnori, Mallory. With me. Alice – you too."

"Where are we going?"

"To Michael."

"And what about this?" She gestured back at the bodies on the floor. There were too many of them. Far too many. And one of them had thanked her as he died.

"You're right. I don't suppose you could..."

"Take care of it?"

"I could, of course, always tell Michael that you refused..." Zadkiel shrugged.

"Because Michael knows how much I enjoy being told what to do, is that it? It's funny: you all like reminding me that I'm not one of you, until it suits you to say otherwise. And then you expect me to follow orders."

"Now you listen to me." Zadkiel dropped his voice to a low hiss. "This is a war. *The* war. There is no stopping; no getting out. You're in this – just like the rest of us – to the end. So, frankly, I don't give a shit if you do it because you're following orders, or because you want to make it through the day alive, or because you like the look of my fucking haircut. Just get it done."

Alice stared at him, and felt a flush creeping up her cheeks, but was determined to stand her ground.

"You didn't say please."

"Excuse me?"

"You didn't say please."

"I didn't say please?"

"No."

"Fine. Alice: would you *please* take care of this?"

"Seeing as you asked nicely..." She shrugged; out of the corner of her eye, she spotted Castor giving her a thumbs-up and Vin trying to hide a smile behind his hand. Even Mallory seemed to have succumbed to a mysterious coughing fit.

"Pollux? You might not want to be in the middle of the corridor. But, you know, up to you..." She waited for him to move back to the doorway with the others, and knelt down on the floor, placing her hands on the stone.

The paving was sticky, stained; scuffed and scraped by boots and smeared with blood. Closer to it, she could smell the Fallen

– a thick, oily, greasy scent, mixed with burning feathers. It turned her stomach.

She was used to the Fallen. She'd faced them often enough: on the streets and in hell. She knew how they worked. And yet, there was something that felt wrong here. Something about the way they had come at her… then stopped. Something about the eyes of the man who had burned. Something didn't add up.

But apparently it wasn't her job to ask questions. She rolled her eyes, knowing Zadkiel couldn't see her… and was alarmed when he cleared his throat loudly behind her.

"Don't think that because I can't see you, I don't know what's going on in your head. Just to make that clear. Now, can we…?"

"Angels." Alice sighed, and she set the floor alight.

Fire snaked along the stone; the candles flared as their flames clung to the walls, spreading up and out and along until the whole of the corridor was an inferno.

The angels stepped back from the arched doorway, forced back by the heat. Even Mallory was driven back, although not for one second did he take his eyes off the flames.

When Alice walked out of the corridor, the fire closing like a curtain behind her, the first thing she saw was the look of relief on Mallory's face.

CHAPTER TWENTY-FOUR

This Aspect of Iron

IF ALICE THOUGHT the corridor was bad, the place Michael had called the 'scriptorium' was worse. And it was hot. *Unbearably* hot. Turning the corner into it was like walking straight into a hot metal wall. Vin felt it first, spinning back on his heel. "What the fuck…?"

The stone all around them was steaming. Clouds of vapour poured out of the round stone columns which ran in parallel rows down the centre of the room, supporting the vaulted roof. Sunlight streamed through broad arched windows tucked beneath the ceiling, and a huge stone fireplace dominated one end of the room, more than tall enough for an angel to stand in with his wings outstretched. Alice could be fairly confident of that, because she could see one doing just that. He was bringing his sword down onto something furry, something dark; something that writhed beneath him and then went limp as the blade struck home.

Fire clung to the stone ribs of the ceiling, making them glow a deep red. And beneath them, Michael's choir moved between the columns, their breastplates shining white in the heat. In the midst of it all stood Michael: armoured, his sword raised and his eyes blazing. Flames curled from the tips of his wings and the ends of his hair and his eyes were white-hot with fire, and Alice wondered if that was how *she* looked. Surely not. She was just Alice, while he was an Archangel, and he moved this way and that – never stopping – his sword slicing through the air like silk. Behind him was another fireplace, the same size, but this one heaped with… piles of fur. They were charred. Alice looked away, but found her eyes drawn back to Michael.

One of the Fallen knelt before him, chin tilted up towards the roof, and Michael's face as he looked down was completely calm. There was nothing there – no rage, no triumph. Nothing. Just Michael towering over the Fallen with his sword raised. Alice couldn't move, couldn't think: all she could do was watch as he whirled around the kneeling figure, a column of flame, stopping behind him and driving his sword, point-down and shining in the heat, into the spine of the defeated Fallen.

There was a sharp cracking sound from somewhere across the room and she whipped around. Mallory was right behind her, beads of sweat glistening on his forehead. "When we met, I told you that Gabriel would be the last of us. Do you see why?" He pointed to the far corner of the hall, which was alive with white light. Lightning arced from pillar to pillar and bounced back into the steam. There was a yelp, and then silence… and Gabriel strode out of the steam, wreathed in flickering sparks. Everything that was absent from Michael's face was there, in his: rage, fury, pure loathing. And madness.

There were only angels left now: angels and what was left of the invaders, crumpled on the floor.

"Michael. The dogs. We need to discuss…" one of Michael's choir, a Descended with burning wings, shouted.

Michael tossed his sword to another angel, who caught it, although it almost took his head off.

"I don't see anything to discuss. They brought dogs. Why would that be unexpected?"

"But…"

"It means nothing. Forfax's little pets. Nothing more than that."

"Dogs?" asked Alice, raising an eyebrow at Mallory.

"Dogs." He replied. "Forfax: one of the Twelve. He breeds them; feeds them on human flesh." He paused as she shuddered. "I know, I know. We thought they had all burned with hell. Obviously we were wrong."

"And that's..." She waved in the direction of the fireplace and the furry thing. It now looked a little less furry and a little more gooey.

"Yep."

"You know, just when I think I've got a handle on... all this, you somehow manage to raise the bar. Every time."

"They're just dogs, Alice. Bastard dogs with big fucking teeth..."

"...which eat people..."

"Which eat people, yes, but they're still just dogs." He rubbed his temple with the barrel of his gun, and pulled a face. "Although. Maybe you *do* have a point," he conceded, as Michael came through the steam toward them.

Zadkiel stepped forward to meet him. "South corridor's secure."

"You contained them?"

"We did."

"And you killed them?"

"Every last one." Zadkiel leaned closer to Michael and murmured something to him, making him laugh. He raised an eyebrow, and moved around Zadkiel to Alice.

"So. I hear you can follow orders after all."

"He asked me nicely."

"Did he? Must be losing his touch." Michael rubbed his hands together, pulled a small red cloth from beneath a wrist guard and wiped his fingers with it before tucking it back into his armour. "Gabriel!"

"Here," he answered. Alice took an instinctive step backwards – although not as large a step as Vin.

Michael held his hand out towards the other angel, who took it and knelt. "I think it's time."

"Thank you."

"You've earned it. And I'm told we need the numbers." With his free hand, Michael traced a shape in the air above Gabriel's head, twisting and looping his fingers around each other and leaving faint trails of fire in the clearing steam.

"You may want to take another step back," said Zadkiel, who was suddenly about five paces behind them. Alice frowned.

"Wh..." She didn't get to finish the sentence.

There was a deafening *crack* – and another, and another – and a wind howled through the hall, rushing between the columns and whistling as it went. But it was the lightning that sent Alice scrambling backwards, as two bolts smacked into the stone an inch in front of her feet.

"I did warn you," said Zadkiel, his arms folded.

Lightning filled the hall; slamming into the walls and floor and curling around the columns. It lit the whole space up with bright, clear light, and the smell of ozone filled the air. Gabriel and Michael were lost in the glare... then, as soon as it had come, it was gone: the light fading to a dim point on Gabriel's chest, and then to nothing.

Slowly, Gabriel stood. He stretched out his wings, and Alice bit her lip. They were restored: bright white and crackling with electricity, and sweeping the floor behind him as he stretched.

Gabriel was an Archangel again.

"Oh, shit," said Vin, speaking for all of them. Gabriel heard him; his head snapped round, blinking at them. A cold smile flashed across his face, but was gone in an instant.

"Just what we need," Mallory said out of the side of his mouth. If Gabriel heard the barb, he didn't rise to it. Instead, he straightened up and looked Michael in the eye, nodding once. Michael nodded back, his eyes searching Gabriel's face, then he turned abruptly and went to inspect one of the fireplaces, where two members of his choir were standing to attention. The others might as well have melted into the stone or blown away on the wind; there was no sign of them. The lump in the fireplace smouldered gently.

"Well, Mallory," Gabriel said, the smile spreading back across his face. "Perhaps, seeing as you and your little friends are still here, you might like to make yourselves useful by finding out exactly what happened to those prisoners you seem to have lost..."

"*I* lost?" Mallory's jaw tensed.

"Your prisoners, your problem." Gabriel arched an eyebrow at them.

"Just like old times, I see."

"Just like old times." Gabriel locked his fingers together and cracked his knuckles. "Find them. That's an order."

"BUT WE ALREADY know what's happened here: even Alice can work this one out, right?"

"Oi!"

"I didn't mean it like *that*."

"Yeah, right."

Alice and Vin were slouching down yet another corridor behind Mallory, 'following orders.' Vin had taken to making little quote marks in the air with his fingers every time the phrase came up. Mallory had taken to kicking him every time he did it.

Zadkiel said something about needing to check the remaining corridors. "The priory is secure, but I need to be sure there's no more surprises."

"That wasn't a surprise. That was a diversion, and you know it." Mallory didn't bother to hide the frustration in his voice – Archangel or not. Zadkiel's shoulders dropped a little.

"I know. The question is: what didn't they want us to see?"

"A big show of force and Xaphan and Florence disappearing... you don't think those two might be *slightly* connected?"

"If you think that's all there is to this, Mallory, you're as big a fool as Gabriel seems to take you for."

Zadkiel flicked his fingers up in a gesture which could have been a salute and smiled sadly, handing Mallory's second gun back to him.

"Thank you for the weapon. Castor! With me." He shot Alice a look, and strode off down the corridor with Castor, leaving the three of them alone.

"The guy's a master of the backhanded compliment, I'll give him that," Mallory sighed. "I'm still not sure how to take that one."

"I guess it depends on what you make of Gabriel," said Alice.

Mallory snorted. "Mmm. Speaking of whom, seeing as Senor Sparky is back in Michael's good graces, we'd better trot along on our little errand, hadn't we?" He checked the gun's magazine, ejected it and slotted in a fresh one from his pocket. "And after that little performance, I don't care what Xaph's got to say for himself. If he so much as sniffs at me, I'm going to give him an exciting new hole to breathe out of."

THEY AMBLED THROUGH the corridors without any real urgency, and Alice wondered if they were as tired as she was. Neither Mallory nor Vin showed any sign of flagging, but both of them were dusty and covered in battle scars. There was no way they could still be feeling fresh. She caught herself... and then relaxed. There was no Zadkiel here, peering into her thoughts. Knowing that felt like a huge weight lifting from her shoulders: she hadn't realised how hard she found it, always feeling that someone might be listening. Strangely, she didn't care if Michael could see what was going on in her head: he wouldn't like what he found, and if she was honest, it served him right. Zadkiel, though... Zadkiel was different. Unlike Michael, it appeared that he really did *listen*. And he remembered.

A rattling sound pulled her back to the corridor. Mallory was shaking the handle of a door, a little louder than was strictly necessary. "I think it's locked," Alice said pointedly.

"The question is whether it's locked from the outside, or the inside. And if it's locked from the *inside*, who locked it?"

"I also think you're taking this a bit personally."

"You bet I'm taking it personally." Mallory gave up rattling the handle and kicked the door. It sprang free of its hinges with a popping sound and dropped through the frame, leaving Mallory tumbling after it.

Into thin air.

Mallory swore as he hurtled down the sheer stone wall and toward the rocks far below, snapping his wings open and beating them once, twice to bring him back up to the level of the doorway. He floated outside, peering back in.

"Well, that was unexpected." He folded his wings as he stepped back onto firm ground, and leaned out into empty space again, looking down at the rocks.

"I should have known it was you lot from the noise," said a new voice, and Alice spun round.

There, framed in a doorway across the corridor – one which did not appear to lead to a messy death – was a solidly-built man with green eyes and black hair slashed across with white. The shadows of old bruises were visible across one of his cheeks, but he looked well enough, and he was watching them with barely-disguised amusement.

Jester.

Alice was almost knocked off her feet as Vin barged past her, charging Jester and flinging an arm around his shoulders, slapping him on the back... then apparently changing his mind and standing back with his arms folded.

"Do you have any idea how worried we were? How worried I was?"

"No, Mum."

"Piss off." Vin scowled – particularly when he heard Mallory snigger.

He turned back to Jester. "You do realise the mess you've made, right?"

"Mess? What mess?" Jester looked puzzled, glancing from Vin to Mallory and Alice. He closed his eyes slowly. Sadly. "It's her, isn't it?"

"Florence? Yes."

"What's my sister done this time?"

"Where do I start?"

"Probably after I tell you that whatever you think, it's not true."

"I had a horrible feeling you were about to say that..."

What Jester told them made Alice's stomach knot. Mallory nodded, his face sober. Vin turned an increasingly queasy shade of grey beneath his sunglasses.

Jester had said he needed some time, and had gone for a walk on the streets of Hong Kong; not going anywhere particular, just walking. Hands in his pockets, he had wandered through Sai Wan and as far as Fung Mat Road – almost as far as the market and the water. He'd lost track of time, been waiting to cross the road... and that was when he thought he had seen her. Just a glimpse of her, through a crowd. Florence. He froze, and then he had started to edge through the people around him, shouldering them aside until he had a clear view of her. It *was* her. Standing on the opposite side. Alone.

Something had made him turn around. He didn't know what it was, even as he told Alice and the others about it. But *something* had, and as he turned, he saw her *standing behind him*. With Xaphan.

And Jester had done the only thing he could. Run.

He had been running back to the apartment, hoping he could keep them off his back long enough to reach Vin and Sari. Hoping that he could lose them in the streets... and then he had realised that he was leading *them* straight to Vin, too. That was enough to stop him right where he was.

Out of the corner of his eye, he could see people being jostled, shoved, pushed aside as the Fallen came for him. They had surrounded him, and he hadn't even known it. He had taken a deep breath... and then there had been a soft *thud* and the sound of feathers behind him, and he had looked over his shoulder to see an angel he immediately knew to be Zadkiel, and who had simply told him to close his eyes. So he had.

"And then, I'm here." Jester held out his hands to illustrate his point.

"Let me get this straight." Mallory said. "They came for you. In Hong Kong."

"Yes."

"And Zak brought you here. He rescued you."

"Yes."

"Fuck."

"Is that a bad thing?"

"It's you. They want you." Mallory's eyes opened, and both his guns were in his hands. "They want you, and we've brought them straight in. *Fuck*!" He kicked the wall.

"They want me? What for?"

"I don't know, and right now, I don't care. All I care about is getting you back to the nearest Archangel. So let's do that."

The temperature suddenly dropped. Alice, who was watching Jester, saw him tense.

The voice came from the other end of the corridor.

"Or – here's an idea – let's not."

Xaphan.

Mallory's first bullet went wide, smashing into the stone to the right of Xaphan's head as he limped towards them – and there wasn't a chance for another shot, as Xaph pulled Florence out from behind him, using her as a shield.

"Don't think I won't shoot her, Xaph," said Mallory from behind his gun.

"Oh, I know you would. But I doubt he'll let you." Xaphan's grin was wider than it should have been as he nodded towards Vin. The scar tissue covering one side of his face crinkled as he smiled.

"Get them out of here, Mallory." Vin's voice was barely louder than a whisper. He was rolling up his sleeves again, curling and uncurling his fingers.

Mallory shook his head. "Not likely."

"Get them both out. The Fallen want him? They can't have him."

"We're not leaving you."

Xaphan was watching them with amusement. Another three Fallen had appeared from the depths of the corridor and had arranged themselves into a loose line, blocking the way back.

Vin stepped in front of Mallory. It was almost casual, the way he moved, and somehow, he had got between them and the Fallen. "I'll buy you as much time as I can."

"Vhnori..."

"My mess. My fault. I said *go*."

MALLORY STARED AT Vin's back as he calmly walked towards Xaphan. Jester shouted something Alice didn't quite catch. The Fallen behind Xaphan and Florence lunged forward, only to be driven back as Mallory fired into them... and Vin walked on, with the bullets screaming past his head.

"Go!" Mallory shouted, and she felt him pull on her sleeve as she started to run.

They were leaving him.

Or perhaps it was the other way around...

CHAPTER TWENTY-FIVE

Thirty Bullets

VIN LISTENED TO their footsteps fading. He was alone with the Fallen.

A voice danced on the edge of his memory: a voice and a shadow, which asked him if he knew what he was getting into.

There was one way to find out.

He balled his hands into fists, squeezing them until his knuckles turned white and his nails bit into his palms. Blood seeped from between his fingers, dripping onto the floor – and still the Fallen waited. They were smiling. They thought this was going to be easy.

Like hell it was.

Vin snapped his fingers open, and braced himself as they charged him.

THE CORRIDOR SLOPED down, curving in a long spiral. Alice had no idea where they were. She couldn't hear anything from behind them, and it frightened her. What had happened to Vin? Flames sprang to life around her wrists, glowing gently as she ran. Mallory was just ahead of her, but spent more time checking back over his shoulder than he did looking where he was going. Jester ran alongside him, his face frozen.

Alice could tell what Mallory was thinking, even before he slammed into the wall and stopped running.

"I'm going back."

"But..."

"Don't argue with me, Alice. He's not following, and they aren't screaming, which means Vin's in trouble. Get Jester to one of the Archangels: Zadkiel, if you can. Take this." He thrust one of his guns at her, and she took it like it might bite her, holding it as far away from her body as possible. "You really do have a strange attitude to guns."

"Just because you like them doesn't mean I have to."

"You will when they save your life." He held her gaze. "Go."

He turned to run back up the corridor, just as the first of the gas grenades landed at their feet.

VIN SNAPPED HIS fingers open, and braced himself as they charged.

The air in front of him shook; everything went grey.

Through the mist, he saw Xaphan haul Florence off her feet, spinning back into a doorway... and nothing else. There was nothing else there. Just the empty corridor, filled with dust that swirled around him, settling on the floor, on his shoulders. The air tasted oily, somehow...

He lifted his hands; stared at them. "Wh –?"

He was so busy staring at his fingers in shock that he didn't hear the footsteps behind him in time, and didn't stand a chance of avoiding the metal bar that smashed into the back of his head.

As he crumpled to the floor, Xaphan dropped the bar with a clatter. "That's quite enough of *that*," he said, dusting off his hands.

GAS AND SMOKE filled the corridor: thick, greenish-white. Alice's eyes streamed and she stumbled forward into Mallory, who caught her and set her back on her feet. "Change of plan," he shouted into her ear over the hiss of the smoke, taking back the gun he had handed her. "Where's Jester?"

There was no sign of him; not that they could have made him out amid the smoke clogging the passageway.

"Jester?" Mallory called his name, but there was no answer. "Jester!"

Still no response.

Alice could barely breathe, and she clung to Mallory, gasping for air. The gas scorched her throat, her eyes, her lungs.

"We have to get out of here..." Even Mallory was choking, his eyes red. "Stay with me."

They staggered away from the wall. A soft *thwomp* from somewhere in the smoke was followed by the clatter and hiss of another grenade, and the gas drowning them thickened. Alice felt the world spin and leaned into Mallory's side, hoping he wouldn't let her fall.

The haze thinned, further ahead. It was still hard to see, was still hard to breathe, but it was better, and Alice could at least make out the point where the walls ended and the floor began.

A red door stood out in the murky air and Mallory threw himself at it. It gave with little resistance, opening not onto a sheer cliff, but into a small, mostly empty room. A room filled with clean air. They lay on their backs on the floor, gulping air into their aching lungs, and Alice thought that was it: they had made it. But Mallory was already pulling himself to his feet, shaking his head to clear it as the wall of smoke and gas headed their way. "Come on. We've got to go, Alice. Get up. Get up!"

"I can't..."

"You have to! Get up!" He looked around the room. There was very little of any use here: just a small wooden table and a long bench with a high back. A tapestry hung on one wall.

"Shit," he muttered... and then he saw the tapestry move.

He was across the room before Alice could even register what he was doing, wrapping a hand around the tapestry and pulling. The fabric came away from the wall, bringing the rod that held it up.

Behind it was a staircase.

It wasn't much: a tiny spiral stairway that looked like it had been cut out of the wall rather than built, and it only led up, but it was something.

"Alice!" Mallory pointed to the stairs, one eye on the door.

"I *can't*."

"Yes, you can."

"No more. No more running. Unless you're coming with me, I'm done."

"You're not done. You're not done because I say you're not. Now get up."

"No." Even the word was an effort. She closed her eyes.

The faint clicking sound made her open them again.

She was looking straight into the barrel of Mallory's gun. Behind it, his face was dark, his mouth grim.

"I'm not leaving you. We left Vin: I won't leave you."

"Yes, Alice, you will. Now *get up*."

Alice got up, pressing herself back against the wall, edging around it towards the staircase as the barrel of Mallory's Colt followed her. She knew he wouldn't shoot – at least, she *thought* he wouldn't – and she hesitated.

All he said was: "Go."

She ducked into the stairway, her foot on the first stair, and froze. Mallory had turned away and was standing in the middle of the room, his back to her. His arms hung by his sides, a gun in each hand; his wings opened wide and shining as he watched the door.

Alice took one last look back at him, and she started running up the stairs.

THE SMOKE HUNG in the doorway, not moving one way or the other. Just sitting there, sullen. Mallory didn't move. He was watching the door. And he had a horrible feeling he knew who was about to come through it.

It was a vague shadow at first, gradually taking shape inside the cloud, as shoes clicked closer and closer on the stone floor.

There was a rapid crunching, grating noise and then the *ping* of something small hitting the floor and rolling. A shotgun cartridge rolled to a halt at Mallory's feet. An extremely *large* shotgun cartridge. He glanced down at it, and raised his eyes just as the cloud of smoke cleared around the man striding into the room, the shotgun clasped to his chest and his red eyes shining.

Mallory had been expecting Lucifer. And given that Lucifer's body was, at that moment, locked up several hundred feet below them both, Mallory had been expecting him to be ensconced in a Fallen angel's body, but the sight still shocked him.

Blond hair and a smart suit, and what should have been cool blue eyes staring out of a narrow face.

Gwyn.

Mallory started shooting.

Not a single bullet found its mark: Lucifer simply waved them away like summer flies – annoying, but harmless. His eyes glittered as Mallory took a step back, still firing, and Lucifer took a step forward.

"Now, now, brother. Still using your fists and not your head, I see."

Mallory had run out of bullets. He fumbled with the guns, dropping the empty magazines on the floor and groping for fresh ammunition from his pockets.

"It's different, this time, isn't it?" Lucifer said. "Now you don't have the upper hand. Tell me: how does it *feel*, hmm?"

"How does it feel?" Mallory felt the click of the second magazine sliding into place. "It feels a little like this." He brought his arm up, pulling the trigger as it came. The bullet spun out of the barrel, towards Lucifer… who caught it.

He held it up to his eye, peering at it. "How very metaphorical of you." Without lowering his hand, he dropped the bullet. The *ting* of the metal bouncing on the stone echoed around the room. "Head, Mallory." He tapped the side of his head, Gwyn's head, and all Mallory could do was stare in horror.

Alice's face flashed through his mind, and he hoped she could make it to Michael. Michael was her only chance. Not Zak, and not Gabriel. Only Michael stood a chance against Lucifer now.

"Oh, one more thing!" Lucifer held up a finger. "I just want you to know, before I go, that *this is all him*." He smiled, his grin splitting Gwyn's face open, and then the red glow faded from his eyes, leaving Mallory alone with Gywn for the first time since hell.

"Gwyn."

"Hello, Mallory." Gwyn raised the barrel of the shotgun. "Goodbye, Mallory." He pulled the trigger.

THE STAIRS SPIRALLED up and up and up, with barely room for Alice to turn along with them. The treads were so narrow that her heels hung off the edge of each step, her toes jammed up against the riser of the next. The only sound was that of her struggling for breath... and then gunfire. Mallory's guns. Even with what must have been several storeys between them, the noise filled the stairwell. Then, as suddenly as it had begun, it stopped, followed by a single shot... and then a blast from something which sounded much, much bigger. Alice clamped her hands over her ears, her eyes wide.

Another blast, and another, and another.

Should she turn back?

What if Mallory...

Vin. Mallory. Jester. Castor. Pollux. Zadkiel. What had happened to them? Should she go back for them...?

MALLORY DUCKED, THE shot from Gwyn's gun rattling overhead. There was that awful *clunk* again – the sound of a new cartridge entering the chamber – and another deafening blast. Mallory threw himself down and rolled.

The third blast hit him full in the chest, the buckshot ripping through him. He cried out as the metal bit into his flesh.

Gwyn was reloading.

Forcing himself to roll over, ignoring the pain in his chest, Mallory swung his arm around and opened fire – so desperate to make the most of the time that he didn't even bother looking. He knew his target: all he could do was shoot and hope. There was a grunt as a bullet hit – the shoulder, Mallory thought.

He didn't get another shot. There was another roar from the shotgun, and this time the blast hit him across his shoulders. A thousand needles jabbed into his spine as the shot tore through his wings. The next blast followed almost immediately behind it.

Mallory crawled along the floor; the world was blurring, fading out at the edges. There was another shot, but he could barely feel it this time; there was too much pain coursing through him already, and he had no hope of healing his wounds. He was too far gone.

A pair of black shoes, polished to a mirror shine, came into view, stopping an inch in front of his nose. It took all of his strength to roll himself onto his back and his broken wings. He looked up to see Gwyn leaning over him, his face upside-down and twisted into a cold smile. He blinked once or twice at Mallory, lying blood-spattered at his feet, then reached down, peeling Mallory's fingers from around the grip of the gun clutched to his chest and kicking the other away. And then he smashed the butt of the gun down into Mallory's face.

The world went dark.

THE SHOOTING HAD stopped. There had been a sound... a sound Alice knew could only have been Mallory. Barely able to breathe, she felt for him – felt for whatever it was he felt – and the wave of pain she found was so strong that it threatened to swallow her. She shut it out, knowing it would drown her. Even as she did so the fire burning at her wrists brightened. It was enough to light her way.

There were footsteps. Someone was coming after her. And it wasn't Mallory.

Yet again, she ran.

The staircase turned and turned and turned, up and up and up, and suddenly, she was out in the open. She was on a small roof, surrounded by a low wall. A gust of wind threatened to sweep her feet out from under her as she looked for somewhere to go.

Other than the staircase she had just come up, there was nowhere.

The wind tore at her hair, blowing it in front of her face; into her eyes and her mouth… and the footsteps were getting louder. There were voices too: someone was most definitely coming up the stairs. They were chasing her.

Jester. Vin. Mallory.

Alice brushed her hair away from her face, holding it back against the wind. She took a deep breath, and fixed her eyes on the wall.

"One," she whispered, "two…"

The footsteps were right behind her now. Another few turns of the spiral and they would be out on the roof.

"Three." She let her hand drop and ran for the edge, her hair streaming behind her in the wind.

She heard them burst out of the staircase, heard them shout… but it was too late. She already had one foot on the wall.

Throwing her arms out wide, Alice jumped.

CHAPTER TWENTY-SIX

Leap of Faith

THE RUSH OF air tore at her skin, at her hair, at her clothing. The rocks below raced to meet her with unbelievable speed, and however hard she tried, she could not close her eyes; they were pinned open by the wind, giving her no choice but to look at the ground as it came up to meet her.

Still, she thought, *at least this way I get a good look at my landing spot…*

The air shimmered around her as she fell. More than shimmered; for an instant, she could have sworn it *glowed*.

An instant was all she had. No sooner had she thought it than the rocks were there, and everything went black.

ALICE GROANED.

Everything hurt.

Everything.

She wondered if that meant she was dead.

Should being dead hurt this much? Really?

She was lying down, she knew that much. Her head hurt – a lot – and her whole body was shaking. One of her shoulders throbbed hotly.

Wherever she was lying, it was cold. Cold and smooth.

So… not the rocks. She'd had plenty of time to get a good look at those and they had been big and jagged and spiky. Definitely spiky.

She tried to roll over onto her back. Something jangled, like pieces of metal moving over one another.

It sounded rather like...

She opened one eye.

Chains.

There were chains piled on the floor in front of her.

She was on a floor.

Definitely not on the rocks.

As she forced her eyes to look beyond the heap of links, she saw movement. A boot. Two boots. And legs above them.

Everything else was blurry, but there were definitely boots there.

A person.

Great.

But that didn't explain the chains.

And then, behind the boots-and-legs, she caught a glimpse of white feathers, sweeping down to the floor.

Angel.

Angel. Floor.

Jumping.

She groaned again – but not, this time, because it hurt.

Angel. Floor. Chains.

There was no way this could be good.

"She's coming round," said a voice. It sounded as though it came both from somewhere a long way off and somewhere very close, and the words took longer than they should have to unscramble themselves in her head.

"I should think so," said another voice. This one was crystal clear. It could only be Michael.

She groaned again, and peeled both eyes open, lifting her head and trying to clear it. The world was fuzzy, and sparkled around the edges. "Well, that was fun," she croaked as she tried to pull herself into a sitting position. A hand gripped her arm, helping her, and the scent of cut grass and the sun on concrete overwhelmed her.

"Easy..." said Zadkiel. "You alright?"

"Probably." She nodded, her eyes beginning to clear. There were three Archangels watching her. One looked concerned, one looked indifferent, and Alice could only describe the look on the other's face as 'spectacularly pissed off.' She held up her wrists and rattled the chains around weakly. "Who do I have to thank for the jewellery?"

"It's a reminder. And a precaution." Michael's voice was chilly, despite the heat which rolled off him.

'Pissed off' apparently didn't quite cover it.

"A precaution against what, exactly?"

"Forgive me for pointing out the obvious, but one of the most dangerous of the Fallen and his whore are loose in my fortress; a half-born we brought here to protect is gone, along with an Earthbound and one of the best soldiers I have in my army. Not to mention all the members of my choir who have been slaughtered in the process. And yet here you are, Alice, sitting in front of me. You, who brought them in. The chains are a precaution against *you*, and a reminder of who and what you are."

"A precaution against me. Seriously?"

"You."

"Yeah, right." Alice rolled her eyes.

The blow to her face caught her by surprise. Michael had darted forward and slapped her cheek, hard, while Gabriel and Zadkiel stood by, impassive apart from the twitch at the side of Gabriel's mouth, which could have been a smirk. It stayed there as he looked her up and down, then strode out of the room.

The fire around Alice's wrists flared into life, coiling under and through and around the chains, making the metal shine as it grew hotter and hotter... but it did not melt. Michael stood back, watching her as she clambered to her feet; the weight of the chains dragged against her, but she resisted their pull and managed to keep upright. Michael scowled at her, and she scowled back at him.

Alice flinched as the flame rushed towards her, wrapping itself around the two of them and locking them inside a sphere of fire. There was nothing beyond it; the world outside simply disappeared. All that was left was Michael, searching her mind inside the inferno. She could feel him crawling over the surface of her thoughts, riffling through her memories. Everything he touched blazed, scorching her from the inside out... but still she held his gaze. Even as her knees began to buckle, she held his gaze. Even as he pulled at the memories she had tried to forget – memories of hell, memories of the cold, of the pain, of her mother – and dragged them out into the light and made them dance before her. Even as he did all this, she held his gaze and would not look away.

Michael pulled away from her and let the fire die. "Mallory and Vin are missing," he said.

"Missing?"

"Gone. As is Jester. And, apparently, Xaphan and Florence. And all I have to show for it are a lot of dead angels."

"And Fallen."

"Those I don't care about. They're dead."

"I thought this place was supposed to be all high-security. What happened?"

"That's what I'd like to know." Michael snarled. "Well?" He raised an eyebrow at Alice.

"You were in my head. You know already."

"Remind me."

So she did. She told him how they had run into Jester in the corridor. How they had been ambushed by Xaphan; how Vin had stayed behind to buy them more time. How the smoke had come from nowhere, choking them and separating them from Jester. How Mallory had...

Mallory. Mallory was missing.

How could he be missing? How could Vin?

"Michael? Don't you think that's enough? You've made your point." Zadkiel's voice was quiet, but firm. Michael waved him away, but Zadkiel simply said Michael's name again.

"Fine." He waved a hand and the chains around Alice's wrists clattered back to the floor; Alice stepped over the pile, rubbing her wrists. Her cheek still stung, but not as much as knowing that Michael had thought she might actually be a part of all this. But that was just one among many hurts she felt, so she decided to simply throw it on the heap. She rubbed at her shoulder, which felt like someone had swung her around by it.

"What about the part I don't know?" she asked. "What happened to me?"

"You," said Michael, the anger on his face fading into amusement, "took a swan-dive off the roof."

"I remember."

"I only just caught you in time."

"You caught me?"

"You'd rather I hadn't?"

"Thank you."

"What's this?" He sounded surprised. "Gratitude? From you?"

"You'd rather I didn't thank you?" He narrowed his eyes as she spoke. A heat-haze shimmered in the air above him... and Alice remembered how the air had, just for a second, glowed as she fell. Michael had caught her. By her arm, she was willing to bet. Her hand went to her shoulder.

"Next time," he said, "if you're planning to jump off the top off my priory, you might like to pick a better spot. Or at least give me a little warning."

"I didn't have much of a choice. They were behind me."

"*They*?"

"I don't know who. Someone. Mallory tried to stall them, but they followed me all the way up the stairs. There was nowhere else to go."

"So you chose to jump, rather than to be taken."

"It seemed like a good idea at the time."

"You'll stay here until we can discover where they're being held."

"As a guest? Or a prisoner?"

"I still think 'guest' sounds better, don't you?"

"Nice to know we're on the same page," she muttered.

Michael turned away, and stepped lightly onto the dais beside the wooden throne, skirting around it. "I wouldn't be so glib, if I were you. Mallory. Vhnori. Jester. They all have one thing in common. What do you suppose that might be, Alice? And has it occurred to you that *you* might be next?"

"Guest it is. One thing, though?"

"You aren't exactly in a position to be asking for favours."

"I don't think you'll have a problem with this one."

"Oh?"

"When we find them, Vin and Mallory – and we will – and we find who's responsible for this? I go with you."

"Done." But as he said it, Michael's back was turned to Alice, and she did not see the slow smile that spread across his face...

CHAPTER TWENTY-SEVEN

Only a Soldier

IT WAS THE dripping that woke him. Something dripping onto his face. Something regular and insistent.

It was cold.

It was annoying.

Mallory raised a hand to his cheek to wipe the drip away, and was surprised to discover, firstly, that his whole face was wet, and secondly, that there was something around his left wrist. A band of some kind. It felt like metal.

He opened his eyes and blinked at the darkness, and heard someone or something scuttle away.

That was enough to get his eyes completely open, and he sat bolt upright, pulling himself into a defensive crouch and feeling for his guns.

They had gone. Frantically, he felt along the line of his belt. Nothing. In his pockets: no guns. No bullets. Worse: no hip flask.

He groaned.

There was another scuttling sound. And, unless he was mistaken, someone *breathing*.

"Who's there?" he called into the darkness.

"... THE FUCK." VIN moaned as he rolled over. He was somewhere cold and dark and wet. And he had an appalling headache.

Almost like he'd been hit over the head. He blinked. It didn't appear to make any difference. It was still dark. He tried to remove his sunglasses, hoping that might help. They weren't there.

"Well, that's not a good start, is it?" he said to no-one in particular. Only the echoes of his voice answered him.

The throbbing pain in his head radiated from a point at the back of his skull; he felt for it and yelped as he found a large lump. Red and white pain spiked through his head, blooming in front of his eyes. Someone *had* hit him over the head. "Bastards," he muttered through his teeth. The pain was subsiding – a little. Not that it improved the situation much: as his eyes grew accustomed to the dark, he started to pick out walls, and a concrete floor. And very little else.

"Mallory?"

Silence.

"Alice?"

Silence.

"Anyone?"

Somewhere, not too far away, something barked.

"Bollocks," said Vin.

"WHO'S THERE? I can hear you, so there's not much bloody point in pretending, is there?"

The breathing on the other side of the room was a little calmer now; a little less afraid. Mallory closed his eyes, trying to pinpoint where it came from.

"I know you're there," Mallory said, softer this time. Whoever it might be, he certainly wasn't in the mood, nor the condition, for a fight. His chest ached where the buckshot had torn holes in his flesh; the feel of his feathers rubbing against each other was like razors sliding down his back… but he was healing. He *knew* he was healing, because if he wasn't, he'd be dead. What he didn't know was how long it would take.

"Look, I'm sure you have your reasons for pretending you can't hear me, but I've had a difficult day. Days. I don't know. Either way, my patience is wearing pretty thin, and I've got fuck-all to drink, so you can either come out and talk to me, or you can hide in the shadows and wait for me to come find you. And if I have to come find you, I can promise you I'll be even more pissed off than I am now. Your choice." He hunkered back on his heels.

There was a sound which could have been someone clearing their throat, somewhere in the gloom.

"He said..." said an unfamiliar voice, rough from disuse, "he said to tell you that it was to stop you from pulling a vanishing act. To keep you here. He said the walls wouldn't be enough." The voice stopped, then cleared its throat again, as though speaking had been an effort.

"It?"

"He said you'd know what that meant."

"Oh, this." Mallory tapped the manacle – because that, he had realised soon enough, was what was wrapped around his wrist – with his fingernail. It *tinged* dully. "Figured." He peered back into the gloom. "I don't suppose you could tell me who 'he' is, do you?"

"The man."

"Yes..."

"I don't know his name. He's the only one I've seen."

"The only one of *who*?"

"Them."

"Right." Mallory sighed. "How about you stop me when I start going wrong?" He paused. The voice didn't answer. Mallory took this as an invitation. "'They' brought you here, am I right? Just like 'they' brought me here."

"You were bleeding."

"No shit." It was all he could do not to laugh, but he pulled back. "They brought me here, and one of... *them*... put something round my wrist and gave you that message for me. He didn't tell you his name, but I'll bet he seemed like he knew me."

"Yes."

"He had blond hair."

"No. Dark."

"Oh?" This took Mallory by surprise, but not for long. "And kind of a pointy face. Nose too long; cheekbones too sharp. Smile like a piranha."

"I only saw him smile once."

"Once?"

"As he closed the door. After they brought you."

"That sounds about right." Mallory blew out a long breath. He knew exactly who had brought him here.

It was Rimmon – and somewhere, in the back of Mallory's head, one cog clicked into another, and gears started to turn.

He squinted into the darkness; his eyes just about adjusted enough to make out a hunched shape at the far end of the space. Not so much a room as a cell, and longer than it was wide. But whoever was at the other end was no angel – no Fallen either – and clearly meant him no harm. After all, he'd been wiping Mallory's face with a damp cloth: cleaning the blood and the dirt away, and you didn't do that to someone you wanted to hurt. Unless Rimmon had come up with a particularly new and interesting way to test his patience, of course, but Mallory doubted it. After all, why break the habit of a lifetime?

He did his best to sound friendly. He suspected he missed by a mile, but hoped he at least made it close to 'non-threatening.' "What about you? How long have they kept you here?"

"I don't know. It's always dark."

"Why?"

"Because there's no..."

"No – I mean, why are you here?"

"I don't know. It's hard to remember. I saw something. Something I don't think I was supposed to see. I didn't think it was real – not to begin with. But I've been thinking about it, and I can't... I don't know. Maybe I did something..." The voice tailed off, although Mallory was sure he could still hear it whispering. He thought he caught the words 'deserve it.'

"Well, it looks like we're going to be in each other's company for a while." Mallory slid his feet out from under him, easing himself into a sitting position on the floor. "Might as well introduce ourselves properly." He held up a hand in greeting, not knowing if the other man could see it. "I'm Mallory."

"Toby," came the reply.

"Nice to meet you, Toby." And even as he said it, his heart sank. Because when it came to the Fallen, there were no coincidences.

THE BARKING CONTINUED for quite some time. It wasn't helping Vin's headache, but at least he knew where he was. His gut told him that Lucifer would only entrust one of the Twelve with holding prisoners right now. And, assuming Mallory was also somewhere nearby, it would have to be one of the older ones; not someone who'd been promoted after the angels had taken hell. He mentally ticked off a few names. The dogs really were the giveaway: it had to be Forfax. And that meant he was either somewhere near Forfax's sleazy bar, or the Fallen had branched out into kennels. A mental image of Forfax – with his tuxedo and that ridiculous cane of his – hanging onto the leads of a dozen miniature dogs popped into Vin's head, and despite himself he sniggered.

"Something amusing, Vhnori?" An unpleasantly familiar voice echoed around the cell and, startled, Vin looked around to see where it had come from. A small grille had opened in what he assumed was a door, and a pair of eyes were watching him from the other side. The light filtering in past them was dim, and somehow grubby, but it hurt his eyes all the same.

"Hello, *you*," he said, as brightly as he could. "I was just thinking about you. Speak of the devil, right?"

"Don't get cute with me."

"Oh." Vin sighed. "And I thought you liked me. I mean, you bring me to this lovely dungeon, and..."

"Vhnori..." The voice had changed. It was still the same, and yet, somehow, it was different. Vin didn't need to see the red eyes blinking back at him from the far side of the door to know why.

"Been a while, Lucifer."

"Has it? I couldn't say. You see, you never were very memorable – even before they clipped your wings."

"Open the door. I'll give you something to remember me by."

"Oh, really?" Lucifer threw back his head and laughed. It made Vin's skin crawl. "You're a brave little thing, aren't you? Tell me, why do you insist on staying on the wrong side?"

"Like I said: open the door."

"You could do great things working for me. You know that, don't you? I could find use for someone with your spirit."

"Funny – Michael said exactly the same thing to me. Almost word for word. Right after we kicked your arse the last time."

"That's just it. 'Last time.' What's past is past, little Earthbound. And mark my words, that will be the *last* time. I'm offering you the chance to be more. More than just a foot soldier. More than a pawn. Better to reign..."

"Yeah, yeah. I've heard it before." Vin yawned loudly, stretching his arms and his wings out to illustrate his point.

Lucifer snarled. But he did stop talking, and that was all Vin needed. He wove his fingers together and cracked his knuckles. "Was there something you actually wanted, Lucifer? It's just... well, we kicked seven shades of shit out of your boys back at Michael's place, and I'm kind of beat. Need my beauty sleep, you know?"

"They have abandoned you. Know that. The Archangels, the Descendeds... even that little half-breed. Where is your rescue? Where are they? Tell me that."

"Okay, firstly: if you'd been listening, you'd have heard me say I'm trying to take a nap and you're just out there, giving it all this..." Vin made a flapping-mouth gesture with his hand. "Secondly?" He sprang up and leapt at the door, wrapping his hands around the bars of the grille and pulling himself right up to the metal so he was eye-to-eye with Lucifer. "Secondly, who said anything about me needing a rescue?"

Lucifer's eyes locked on to his, and he must have seen something he didn't like, because he took a step back.

"You'll regret this, Vhnori. I promise you that. You will regret this." What started as another snarl became a high-pitched giggle... and the red of his eyes vanished, leaving just Forfax staring in through the bars. Vin uncurled his fingers and turned back to the corner he'd been sitting in.

Forfax's voice followed him back across his cell. "He's right: you'll regret it. The tide's turned and soon he'll be back. And then what will you do?"

"Maybe then I'll be able to get some *fucking sleep*!" Vin roared, his back still to the door.

He heard Forfax slam the hatch over the grille shut, heard his footsteps click-clacking away. Only when he was sure the Fallen had gone, when the sound of his shoes had faded into absolute silence, did Vin allow himself to sink back down into his corner, rocking quietly in the darkness.

CHAPTER TWENTY-EIGHT

Mea Culpa

"THERE'S NO SIGN." Zadkiel sounded tired, and didn't look any better than he sounded. His armour had gone, and he was back in the hooded top – the one Alice was coming to think of as his 'civilian clothes.' Michael, however, remained in his armour, blood spatters and all. He was pacing again. He'd been doing a lot of that. She could only assume it was preferable to him setting the ceiling on fire again. He'd done that, too.

"No sign of the Fallen, no sign of Xaphan, no sign of Mallory..."

"And no sign of how they got in or out," Michael snapped. "That's what I'm most interested in, Zak."

"Alice already told you that. The bus, remember?"

"No." Michael shook his head. "That's how they got here, not how they got in."

"There's a thousand ways..."

"Believe me, Zak, there aren't. I know every stone of this fortress, and I'm telling you that I can count the ways into it on the fingers of one hand. So I want to know how they got in, and I want to know *now*!" The room shook as he raised his voice, but Zak merely blinked at him.

"I'll do my best, Michael, but I think you already know what happened."

"No. That's not it."

"Yes, it is. Whether you want to admit it or not."

"Who, then? Who would you have me blame?"

"Whoever let them in." Zadkiel shrugged and stared out of the window.

Alice looked at the two of them. "What about Mallory? And Vin? And Jester?"

"What about them?" Michael asked.

"Don't you care what's happened to them?"

"Not especially, no," he snapped back at her, making her widen her eyes in shock. "Mallory and Vin are soldiers. They are soldiers who were foolish enough to be captured, and they understand the consequences of this. My priority is to keep the priory secure."

"But..."

"No. No, Alice. You do not get to have an opinion, you do not get to criticise my actions, and above all, you do *not presume to give me orders!*"

"Wow. You're a fruitcake. You know that?"

"I'm sorry... what?" Michael's temper evaporated and Alice suddenly had his full attention. She wasn't sure that this was necessarily a good thing.

"You know. Nuts. Mad. Bonkers. Psycho. Crazy. Two biscuits short of a packet. Not quite the full shilling..."

"You're trying my patience, Alice. If you have a point, now is the time to make it. And make sure it's valid."

"You're threatening me."

"I don't make threats..."

"Because that sounds like a threat."

"No. My telling you that if you don't have a reason for all... *that*, I could kill you; that's not a threat. My telling you that I would kill you without a second thought, and then find and kill Mallory, Vhnori and anyone you've ever called a friend... not a threat." He leaned forward. "It would be a promise." He glared at her, and his eyes were liquid fire.

It crossed Alice's mind that this might have been slightly the wrong approach. But it was too late to do anything other than carry on.

"My point is that you're apparently happy to leave Mallory and Vin to rot while you go on some kind of witch-hunt."

"And?"

"They could help. If you..."

"You need to stop talking, Alice."

"I just..."

"Now, Alice."

"You..."

"*Alice*!" Michael's voice had risen to a roar again, and Alice flinched. Michael, however, was determined to make his point – and slowly, deliberately, he walked towards her, sparks hissing across his open wings and scattering across the floor. "Before you extol the virtues of two of my angels to me any further, I should remind you that Vhnori is an Earthbound, serving out punishment for his crimes. Moreover, he and his half-born have mostly been taken by the Fallen in retaliation for the unsanctioned torture of one of Lucifer's preferred generals."

"*Unsanctioned...*?"

"And while I hate to be the bearer of bad news..."

"Michael!" Zadkiel interrupted, suddenly at Alice's side. Alice frowned as Zadkiel held out a hand towards the other Archangel. "Don't."

"Why? She should know, shouldn't she? After all, this is the man she holds up as a shining beacon of all that angels should be."

"Should know... what?" asked Alice, with a familiar sinking feeling.

Michael smiled coldly at her. "About Mallory."

"Is he... Did he...?" She couldn't bring herself to say it.

"Dead?" Michael laughed. "No. Not dead."

Alice sagged with sudden relief, which was replaced almost immediately by a chill. "Wait... You think *he* did this?"

Zadkiel turned from Michael to Alice. "You have to admit, it doesn't look good. Not given the circumstances..."

"The circumstances? I was there, with him. The whole time. You *know* that!" She could hear her voice getting higher, louder.

"It's not that..." Zadkiel tailed off, refusing to meet her eye.

Michael laughed again. Laughed *at* her, this time: laughed at her confusion, laughed at her obvious fear.

"The circumstances, Alice, are that someone has betrayed us. And when it comes to betrayal, Mallory is the first one among us I would suspect."

"Mallory? No! I don't understand! Why..." Alice saw Zadkiel step back, his eyes still fixed on the floor. Michael smiled straight at her.

"Because he's done it before."

A LOUD RINGING filled Alice's ears. Across the room, she could see Zadkiel's mouth moving; could see him gesturing angrily at Michael, but all she heard was white noise.

Mallory. Betrayal?

The buzz in her ears receded, and she could just about make out Zadkiel shouting the word "dramatic" at Michael – who was still watching her. Watching, no doubt, to see what she would do next. He had wanted to subdue her, hadn't he? It had worked; she had nothing to say.

"...now really the time?" Zadkiel finished. Michael continued to ignore him. Eventually, he rubbed his hand across his eyes and sighed. "Zak?"

"Michael."

"You're dismissed."

"What?"

"Dismissed." He didn't even look at Zadkiel – who opened and closed his mouth once or twice, then gave up. With one last backward glance at Alice, he stormed out of the room, leaving just the two of them.

"You were warned about Mallory," Michael said, circling her; his hands were in his pockets, his tone almost casual. "I know you were: I've seen it in your memories. That Fallen, the one you knew."

"Rob."

"Abbadona. *That* was his name. Use it. He warned you about Mallory; told you that Lucifer was afraid of him. That they all were."

"He told me... he said that you would have to be mad not to be afraid of him."

"A slight exaggeration, perhaps, but sound in theory. Mallory is wild, uncontrollable. Unpredictable."

"I didn't see you complaining about that earlier. You know, before you accused him of being a traitor."

"Unpredictability has its uses. Particularly when your enemy is like ours." Michael waved her comment away. "But tell me – seeing as you know so very much about him – why is Lucifer so afraid of Mallory? Why has he made it his personal mission to destroy not me... but Mallory? And you with him? He could have killed you in hell, and you could not have stopped him, if that's what he wanted; gift or no gift. You walked out of hell because *he let you*. I know him better than anyone else. Me, he just wants to defeat. You, however, he wants to *destroy*. You and Mallory both."

Alice blinked back tears, determined not to show the Archangel how much his words hurt. Because hurt they did. Even if it had crossed her mind more than once that Lucifer could have killed her. Even if Rob's warning about the angels not telling her everything had rung in her head for months. It had been at the back of her mind every time she had gone out, looking for the Fallen; every time she had found one. Every time she had fought them. What if Lucifer had simply let her go? What did that mean?

Something more than fear wound its way around her heart, into her throat, threading itself through her. Doubt.

"You were a librarian, were you not?" Michael suddenly asked. Alice simply stared back at him, dazed.

"Am. Not was. Am." It was an automatic answer, and technically, it wasn't true. What she was, currently, was the Angel of Death's receptionist. And even then, she was on what was best described as a sabbatical.

"I have something to show you. Come with me."

"Where?"

"My library, of course. Where else?"

THERE WAS NO door. Of course there wasn't. Because that was something normal people had: doors, and stairs. And bookshelves. Alice had always considered bookshelves to be an integral part of the library experience.

Not here.

Michael hadn't given her a chance to respond; had simply snatched up her hand. The world had spun, lost in a blur of scarlet and woodsmoke. Up became down became up became down... and that was it. She was standing in the middle of the strangest library she had ever seen.

It was circular, the walls curving up to a dome above her head. The floor was made of wooden boards that followed the line of the walls; sweeping past and beneath her and polished to such a shine that she could see herself reflected in them. There were no windows – and, strangely for this place, no candles. The light seemed to seep out from the walls themselves: soft and white and everywhere at once. The room *glowed*.

About halfway between the floor and the curve of the dome, a narrow gallery ran the entire circumference of the walls, jutting out from them with no visible support as though it had just grown there. And everywhere, there were books and papers, piled high on the floor, on tables, on chairs. Hanging from the walls between carvings and what looked like reliefs of faces, draped across stools... everywhere. The air smelled of paper and ink and dust... and Alice just stared.

"How do you like it?" Michael asked, standing beside her and watching her take in her surroundings.

"It's extraordinary," she whispered. And then, she saw it. Half-hidden among the other carvings on the wall ahead of her; a small, square relief of three angels. One was clearly Michael: a crown of blazing fire upon his head and his sword in his hand. One was fairly obviously Lucifer, bound in chains, a cloud emerging from his mouth. And between them, his face solemn, even in stone, was Mallory.

Alice lifted her fingers to the stone, hesitating an inch or so before they touched it. It was him, clearly him. Mallory. Between Michael and Lucifer… watching as Lucifer Fell.

She urged her fingers forward and they grazed the carven Mallory's face. He looked so serious, and so sad. It was so lifelike that she half-expected the stone to give under the pressure of her touch, to see him flinch. To see him blink.

"What is this?" she asked Michael, hearing the floor creak behind her.

"The truth," he said. "The reason Lucifer fears Mallory. Fears him and hates him. Because he trusted him, and Mallory betrayed him. To me."

"To you? But…"

"There was no-one Lucifer trusted more than Mallory. When he planned his little coup, who do you think he turned to first?"

"Mallory…" The name came out as a whisper.

"Mallory. And Mallory, being the creature that he is, came to me."

"He turned him in." She saw it flash by in her mind's eye: Lucifer walking into a room much like the one she was in; finding Mallory waiting for him. A question hanging in the air. "*Mallory, why are you armed?*" And Mallory, clad in his armour and with his hand on the sword she had never seen him use, turning his back on his oldest friend.

"He turned him in. Everything that has come since…"

"You mean Mallory started the war?"

"*Lucifer* started the war. Mallory, well, Mallory was trying to prevent it." Michael sighed. "Much good that it did us." He drew away from her, back into the middle of the room. "Look at the banner," he said, pointing to a wide stripe that ran around the walls, just above head height. It was covered with symbols Alice didn't recognise. She tore her eyes away from the carving of the angels and looked, but could make no sense of them. They were familiar, somehow, and yet alien. There were thousands of them; hundreds of thousands, running on forever around Michael's library.

"Names," he said.

"Names?" She stretched up, running her fingers across one of the symbols. "These are letters?"

"No. These are names. Each one an angel lost to the war."

Alice's hand snapped back. "But there are…"

"Countless names. Not quite. *I* count them. I know the tally."

"Who put them here?"

"Adriel, of course." Michael brushed his hair back from his forehead. "We remember. The Fallen had their river of blood. I have this." He waved at the wall. "Mallory has his books."

"His books…" A memory scraped at the edge of Alice's mind. Notebooks. Notebooks filled with scrawled letters and shapes, utterly indecipherable. Pages spilling across a dirty floor…

"That's your handwriting? I've never seen anything like it before. It's not shorthand; what kind of language is it?"

"Mine."

"He keeps track? Of all of them?"

"He feels he must."

"Oh, Mallory." It was all she could say, even though he wasn't there to hear it.

Suddenly, she understood. She understood him. She understood it all, and she turned to face Michael. "We have to find him."

"Why? Because this changes anything? How? Simply because you now know something, does it make what went before any less true? Mallory is still a soldier. Still a prisoner. Still a loose cannon, and I still can't trust him. So he stays where he is."

"I trust him."

"And I don't trust you." His tone was flat. Hard. "Everything I have done for you, and I still can't trust you." He folded his arms, his eyes raking over her. "Some would ask why I give so much to a traitor's brat, who consorts with traitors. How can you be anything more than the sum of your parts? Human. Traitor. Fool. Weak."

"By 'some,' you mean Gabriel." It was almost funny. "He's not exactly perfect, either."

"Perhaps not. But who is?"

"I am *more*. More than that."

"Are you? I wonder." It wasn't a threat this time. It wasn't even a question. More than anything, Michael seemed to be thinking aloud. There was silence then: the kind of silence that settles in libraries and places where old books are kept. A silence which was thick and soft and knowing and full of the names of the dead. He walked away from her, his footsteps heavy on the shining boards, and his back was still to her as he started to speak, louder now and clearer. A challenge. "Prove it."

"What?"

"Prove it to me. Prove that you are more than the things that make you. Give me your life, Alice. That's how this works. Give your life to me. Give your life *for* me. Bleed for me, burn for me – and in return, I would die for you. Kill for you. I will tear down the stars if only you ask. Prove them wrong. Prove Gabriel wrong. Prove *me* wrong." He spun on his heel and his eyes locked on to hers, and there was no fire behind them. For once, Michael's eyes did not burn. "Prove you are all that you can be. All that you could be. Prove that you are more than you *should* be."

He finished speaking, and the silence wrapped itself around them both again, because Alice had no answer.

* * *

Zadkiel stood on the top of the outer wall, looking out at the sea. Something wasn't right; he could feel it, deep down in his bones. Something felt wrong, felt off. It felt like betrayal – Michael was right, of that much Zak *was* sure. He sighed, and opened his mind to No Man's Land. A thought, a flicker, a memory... anything; but there was only darkness beneath the touch of his mind. Darkness and the sound of the waves.

"The castle is beset, within and without," said Castor, leaning on the stone beside him. Zak hadn't noticed him come out onto the wall, and didn't acknowledge him. Not that it bothered Castor. He rested his elbows back against the wall, propping himself up with his back to the sea. "That's what you're thinking."

"One of us has to be at least a little poetic."

"I'm a policeman, mate. What do I know about poetry?"

"Don't." Zadkiel turned his head towards Castor and gave him a hard stare. "With anyone else, fine. But not with me." He turned back to the sea again, but repeated himself. "Not with me."

"I forgave you, you know," said Castor, almost conversational. "You never thought I could, did you? But I did. I forgave you the second they cut me loose. Well. As soon as my wings stopped aching, at least."

"Forgave me? For what?"

"I know what you did. You protected me, didn't you? It was either you or Gabriel, and you volunteered. You were the one who banished me. You were the one who cut my wings. Because you knew that Gabriel would take them forever."

"And I knew that you would hate me for it." Zadkiel was still staring at the sea, but his voice strained as he spoke. "Better that than to see you Fall."

"I could never hate you, Zak." Castor smiled, straightening up. "You're supposed to be able to read minds, you dickhead: couldn't you see?"

"I didn't look. I couldn't bring myself to." Despite himself, Zadkiel's face cracked into a smile. "And you watch your mouth. I'm still your Archangel."

"Still." Castor watched as Zadkiel sighed; turned away from the sea to face him. He saw the smile reach his eyes – then saw it rapidly fade, flashing through first horror, then determination. He moved fast, but it seemed so slow: Zak's hand reaching out to Castor, his fingers closing on his shoulder, pushing him down to the floor, hard and fast and with little regard for anything as Zadkiel stood over him.

And Castor rolled over just in time to see the first lightning bolt smash into Zadkiel's unarmoured chest.

CHAPTER TWENTY-NINE

Lux Aeterna

To Castor, Zadkiel appeared frozen. Unblinking, unmoving. Unwavering, even as the lightning crawled across his skin and one bolt after another slammed into his body with a force that would have knocked a lesser man off his feet. But Zadkiel wasn't a man. He was an Archangel, and even as white sparks swarmed around his eyes, burrowing into his skin, he stood firm.

As Zadkiel died, he stood firm and he opened his wings.

And all Castor could do was watch.

Watch as the final blast of white lightning drove into Zak's chest.

Watch as his strength finally gave out and he fell to his knees.

Watch as he blinked once, just once, at Castor – lying useless on the stone walkway – before the life went out of his eyes and he slumped to the floor.

And now it was Castor who was frozen; frozen as Gabriel strode along the top of the wall towards them, white sparks still flying from his fingers and a smile on his face. He dropped into a crouch beside Zadkiel's hollow body, his hands skimming his clothing... and then stopped.

His eyes travelled along Zak's limbs, where he had fallen, and over Castor, who could do little except tremble in fear and in rage and in utter disbelief.

"Tell him, Earthbound. Tell him who did this, and why. And tell him that he will be next."

Gabriel slid his hand into one of Zadkiel's pockets and – with a look of triumph –pulled out a small bundle of dirty cloth. He closed his fingers tightly around it.

"Tell him, Castor. Tell Michael. I want him to know. I want him to know that finally, the war is over. The war is over, and he… has… lost."

Gabriel straightened, slowly, as if he had all the time in the world. The sun glinted off the feathers of his wings as he opened them, stretched them wide.

He stepped onto the parapet, and with a single beat of his wings, he was gone… leaving Castor cowed and weeping as he cradled the body of the dead Archangel on the walls of Mont Saint-Michel.

CHAPTER THIRTY

The Price We Pay

MALLORY RUBBED AT the sore patch on his wrist where the manacle dug into his flesh. He was getting desperate. The boy was fading. And he *was* little more than a boy, Mallory had come to realise. Maybe twenty, thirty at most, and he had no idea what had happened to him, no idea what he had got involved in. None. Which begged the question of what the Fallen actually *wanted* with him. As far as Mallory had been able to work out, he hadn't even done anything particularly interesting – certainly nothing that would catch their attention.

At least it gave him something to think about. Mallory was bored. Worried and bored. It wasn't a pleasant combination. There was no way of measuring the time here: it was always dark, always damp. There was food, from time to time, shoved through a slot in the base of the door, but it seemed to arrive whenever their captors remembered (or could be bothered) rather than at regular intervals.

Toby slept much of the time. Mallory – who had never needed much by way of sleep – listened to the rise and fall of his breath as he slept, wondering whether Alice was safe. Hoping that Alice was safe. And wondering how the hell he was going to get out of this.

He had healed. He knew that much. His wings were sore – and would be for some time, he thought grimly – but more than anything, they ached to be stretched. They ached from the damp and the dark. *He* ached from the damp and the dark, and the simple fact that he was a prisoner. The manacle, he had discovered, was attached to a length of chain and, in turn, to a bolt on the floor. Testing it had occupied his mind for a little while, but it was pointless. Neither was going to give in a hurry, and it was a waste of strength fighting them. As an extra bonus, the manacle felt as though it had letters carved or cast into it – and while the light wasn't quite enough to make them out, Mallory would gladly put money on them being Enochian, and on their being put there to keep him in his place. So he could heal, but he certainly hadn't been able to leave. And that meant there was someone smarter than Rimmon behind this. It had to be Xaphan. And if it was Xaphan, then it absolutely confirmed everything he had feared. The whole of the trip to Mont Saint-Michel had been a set-up. But for what? Too many questions... and none of the possible answers were comforting.

Mallory rested his head back against the wall, closing his eyes and listening to Toby's breathing from across the cell. He was sleeping again. *Just as well*, though Mallory. *Whatever he's dreaming about, it has to be better than being awake.*

Toby did not get to sleep for long.

A quiet buzzing sound made Mallory open an eye. Not that it made much difference in the dark. But the buzz... it sounded like...

Bright light exploded across Mallory's field of vision, making him wince and turn his head away. The sound dimmed, faded... and so did the flare of light.

A single lightbulb hung from the ceiling in the middle of their little cell. It swung gently back and forth, throwing rapidly shifting shadows on the dingy walls. Mallory's eyes, accustomed to the dark, protested as he took in the room.

It was longer than he had imagined, and there was a steel door: patched and welded, but solid enough. Toby was curled into a small ball on a trestle bed at the end of the room. The walls were concrete, chipped and scuffed and generally the worse for wear. Something was smeared along one of them, dark fingermarks distinct on the grubby surface. There were bolts set into the walls at several points, and more in the floor, but only the bolt closest to Mallory was being used. It certainly explained how Toby was able to come across the room to him: he wasn't restrained. What would be the point, looking at him? It wasn't like he was going to give them any trouble. *Had* he, Mallory wondered, before he had given up and turned in on himself? He doubted it. He didn't look like a fighter.

There was a scrape outside the door, followed by the sound of bolts being drawn back, and the rattle of a key in a lock. The hinges squealed as the door opened inwards, grating against the concrete floor.

And who should walk through the door with a smile on his face but Rimmon?

Mallory was on his feet and lunging for him in a heartbeat... but the chain was too short, and abruptly wrenched him back by his wrist. Rimmon beamed at him.

"How's life on a leash, Mallory?"

"How about you come a little closer and I'll fucking show you?"

"Temper, temper." Rimmon's smile stretched a little wider and he disappeared back through the door, leaving it open. He reappeared a moment later, carrying a chair; the wooden seat and back splintered, and one of the metal legs so thoroughly rusted through that it very nearly fell off when Rimmon banged it down on the floor, his eyes never leaving Mallory. "I thought you boys could do with a little company."

"Brilliant. When do they get here?"

"Why does it always have to be like this with you, Mal?"

"Oh, I don't know. Maybe because after all this time, you're still a little shit?"

"You're going to regret that." Rimmon wagged his finger at him, and spun the chair so that it faced Mallory, before sitting down on it – still just out of reach. He rested his elbows on his knees and examined his fingernails.

Mallory sighed. "The only thing I regret is not having killed you when I had the chance."

"Well, you won't get another one," Rimmon said, not looking up from his nails. "Not now. I tried to help you, remember. I gave you a chance."

"And I gave you an answer."

"You tied me to a fucking tree, Mallory. You tied me to a tree, and you shot me. And then you had that little bitch burn me."

"And yet you still don't seem to get the message..." Mallory's eyes narrowed.

"Oh, don't you worry. I got the message alright. You've chosen your side, and now you can rot there. I just wanted to say... you know, no hard feelings."

"Are you kidding me?" Mallory laughed. It was not a happy laugh. Rimmon sat back in his seat and pulled out a thin-bladed folding knife from inside his coat, and slid the point of the blade underneath his nails to clean them, wiping the knife on his knee after each one.

"If I were the vindictive type," he began, the knife scraping at his nails, "I might use this opportunity to level the scores. To repay some of the kindnesses you've shown me." He snapped the knife shut, and with one hand pulled up his shirt, exposing the side of his ribs and his abdomen. Scars rippled across his flesh; some long and jagged, some like a starburst.

Like a bullet hole.

He lowered his shirt and smiled at Mallory. "But I'm not the vindictive type. You made me what I am, after all."

"You made *yourself* what you are. You made your own choices." Mallory held his gaze. He had enough scars of his own.

"Well, that's where we're going to have to agree to disagree, I'm afraid. Still, this has been fun!" Rimmon tapped his hands on his knees and winked at Mallory, standing up and laying his hand on the back of the chair. Seeing Mallory frown, he made a show of looking surprised. "Oh, wait... you thought I was here for you?" He lifted a hand to his chest. "Mallory. That *ego*!" Another grin. "I'm here for *him*."

He pointed to the crumpled heap of Toby at the far end of the room, and his smile twisted into something much uglier. His fingers closed around the back of the chair, and he tipped it onto its front legs and dragged it across the concrete. The noise was awful, driving into Mallory's skull like a spike... and again, Mallory was straining against the chain, pulling at it – tearing at it now – because he knew exactly what Rimmon was about to do.

"WAKEY-WAKEY!"

A wave of freezing cold water hit Toby in the face, snapping him back to consciousness.

"There you go. Can't have you sleeping through and missing the best part of the day, now can we?"

Toby realised he was sitting in a chair. His hands were tied behind his back.

"Well. I say 'best part of the day.' Best part of my day, I mean. Yours? Not so much."

A hood was pulled roughly over Toby's face, plunging him into darkness, and he heard Mallory shouting. Even through the hood, Toby could hear the anger...

And all Toby could do was wonder what it was he had done to make anyone hate him so very much.

MALLORY DID NOT stop wrenching at the chain that held him back – even though he knew it was pointless; even though the manacle bit into his flesh, scoring it almost to the bone. He would heal. He got it. He would heal, whatever they did to him, and Rimmon would make him watch as he worked on the boy. He couldn't reach him, couldn't help him.

Rimmon had finally been able to do what the rest of the Fallen never could. He'd found the perfect torture for Mallory.

RIMMON STOOD BACK and admired his handiwork. He was sweating, pale in the light of the single bulb that still swung back and forth above them. Careless, he clipped the rim of the bucket he had dropped with the edge of his foot and it rolled away from him across the floor, its handle flopping over and over. It didn't matter. It was empty now.

He picked up the rope at his feet and wound it around his shoulder. The heavy knot at one end hung down to his waist, brushing against Toby's arm as he leaned forward to rip the soaked hood up and away. Toby flinched at the touch and whimpered. His eyes were screwed shut, and as soon as the hood came off he turned his head away; down… anywhere except towards Rimmon. He was shaking so hard that the chair rocked on the floor. The legs juddering against the concrete made a sound like teeth chattering.

Rimmon took in the boy's terror; the bruises rising on his cheeks, the water dripping from his chin and his hair… and he smiled.

He turned around, and walked straight into the bucket Mallory had flung at him. It smashed into his nose, breaking it. Blood dripped into his mouth, but he was still smiling.

They stood there: Rimmon laughing, his teeth painted red and a coil of stained rope hanging from his shoulder… Mallory, his arm almost pulled from its socket, his weight on his back foot and pure rage in his eyes.

"Is that the best you've got?" Rimmon rubbed the swelling bridge of his nose. "We can restore Lucifer, and we will. Soon. He'll wipe the floor with the lot of you: angels, half-borns, humans. It won't matter. He's like a tidal wave. Like a storm. Unstoppable. We *will* bring hell to this world you fought so hard to protect, Mallory, and there will be no end to the suffering we create." Rimmon wiped the end of his nose with the back of his hand. "But you could stop it. All you have to do is agree to join us. Things could go back to the way they were."

"We've already had this conversation. And my answer's still the same. Go fuck yourself. Lucifer too."

"There's that ego again. Still, it's all very well when it's just you at stake, but what about when it's someone else who has to take the fall – so to speak?" He looked pointedly at Toby, still tied to his chair and shivering. "I've got some things to do. You know how it is: people to see... busy, busy, busy. But I'll be back. And then we'll see if I can interest you in changing your mind."

Rimmon winked at Mallory, laughing as he went through the door. It slammed behind him, and a moment later, the light snapped off.

Mallory sank to the floor, his head pounding and his heart breaking in the darkness.

VIN HEARD THE footsteps pass his door, and pressed himself back against the wall. Like it would do any good. But the footsteps did not stop: they carried on – almost jauntily – down the corridor outside.

He wasn't sure whether that was a relief or not.

Never one to look a gift horse in the mouth, he turned his attention back to the hinges of the cell door.

At first, he hadn't been sure it would work: after all, other than the gate the Fallen had built across the mouth of hell – which was its own special case, all things considered – he hadn't exactly tried to use his gift on much beyond the Fallen themselves. But if it had worked on the Bone-Built Gate... and considering the way the last Fallen he faced had not just turned to stone, but imploded in a shower of dust, he liked the odds.

The first hinge had taken what felt like months. It could only have been hours, but with no way to gauge the passing of time, he couldn't be sure. It was rusted and half-seized, and that gave him hope. If he couldn't destroy the hinges, perhaps he could still damage them.

One way or another, he was getting out.

CHAPTER THIRTY-ONE
The Mercy Seat

Alice was still searching for an answer when Michael's head snapped up, eyes alight once more, as though he had heard a sudden sound.

"Something's wrong."

"Really."

"Stay here..." And just like that, he was gone in a swirl of flame.

"So I'll just wait then, yeah?" Alice shouted at the empty air. There wasn't a door: the only way in or out seemed to be by angel-express. "Bloody angels," she sighed. It was something she was saying far too often, and she was getting tired of it. Michael's little speech had caught her off-guard, and she still wasn't sure what it had meant. It was either a profession of undying love – doubtful, admittedly – or a confession he needed her help. He wasn't ordering her; he was asking her. Which was new.

Without the Archangel, the library was even quieter. He obviously had a thing about giving her lectures in libraries, she thought, remembering the first time they had met. Perhaps he thought it lent him some kind of gravitas. Like he needed that. But there *was* something special about the place... and surrounded by the books and the scrolls and the piles of paper, she was aware of the sound of her breathing, of the sound of her heart. Above her and around her, the scroll of names wheeled and the war went on... and something was very, very wrong in Michael's fortress.

She could feel it now: it wasn't an ache, exactly. More like a dull pressure behind her eyes. It was like nothing she had ever felt before – either before or after she had realised she could feel the pain of others. It didn't stab, didn't scratch. It was a fist, clad in iron and steel and pressing up against the inside of her skull, pushing to be let out. She frowned and rubbed at her temple, and stared up at the list of names on the wall.

Each symbol was a name. There had to be tens, hundreds of thousands. Each one an angel. A death.

A death for which Mallory still blamed himself.

"You always have to make it about you, don't you?" she muttered, and would have said more if she hadn't been distracted by a small trickle of dust falling from the ceiling high above...

"What..." said Alice, holding her hand out. Tiny white flecks began to collect in the curve of her palm, and she looked up. As she looked, squinting against the ache in her head, there was a grinding sound, and the whole room shook. It was almost enough to knock her off her feet, and she threw out an arm to catch herself, knocking a pile of books off a table as she did. The shower of dust became a torrent, white, sparkling flecks pouring down around her, and the names carved into the wall above her began to burn. One by one, the symbols flared into life, the lines carved into the stone filling with fire and glowing a hot orange; each symbol shining in turn until the circle was complete. A band of fire with no end and no beginning. The shaking stopped, and Alice pulled herself up, away from the table she'd been clinging to, and stepped into the middle of the library.

No wonder the room had shaken: running across the dome, from one side to another, was a huge crack. The shadows cast by the flames on the walls danced across it like clouds, transforming it into a break in the sky.

"Michael?" Her voice bounced back to her. "Michael!"

The fire in the walls blazed higher, and her head throbbed harder and harder.

"Michael..."

There was a sound somewhere behind her: a sound like whispering voices, and Alice knew who was there before she turned and saw the black wings.

"Come with me," said Adriel, and the world pitched and spun and went dark.

WHATEVER ADRIEL DID to get her out of the library, it did not help Alice's head. In fact, not only did it *not* help, it made her want to throw up, which wasn't exactly a step in the right direction. Closing her eyes, she breathed deeply, slowly, driving out each breath like she meant it. When she was *relatively* confident she wasn't going to be sick on anyone's shoes, she opened her eyes.

She was in the room at the top of Mont Saint-Michel again – the room with the throne. And through the windows, the mount was burning. Flames raged across the roofs, along the walls, through the streets below; they bounced from building to building. Somewhere, a bell was ringing wildly, and Michael sat on the dais at the foot of the throne, his head in his hands, as he wept.

Alice glanced at Adriel, who shook his head. "Zadkiel is dead," he said gently.

"Zadkiel." Alice thought she must have misheard, but Adriel nodded. "Oh," she said, and stared at the floor.

"Zadkiel is dead, and we are betrayed," murmured Michael, wiping his hand across his face as he gathered himself together.

"You knew that, though. The betrayed bit, at least."

"But now I know by whom."

"And that would be...?"

"Gabriel."

"You're kidding me." Alice gaped at him. *Gabriel*?

"Gabriel murdered Zak, and has betrayed us all." Michael turned his back on Alice and Adriel and stared out of the window, down over the roofs where his grief burned out of control.

"You must act, Michael. You know you must." Adriel stepped forward.

"There's still time."

"There is *not.*" Adriel gazed sternly at Michael, who looked over his shoulder at him.

"Time for what, exactly?" asked Alice. The pain in her head made sense now: it was Michael. Michael *hurt.* And the only way she was going to make it stop was to help him.

Neither angel responded to her question.

"Has he taken Lucifer's body?" Adriel asked, now sounding anxious.

"What do you think?"

"Then there is no time at all."

"Hmm." Michael looked thoughtful.

"Michael?" Adriel had started rubbing his wrist. It was an odd gesture, and not one Alice had ever seen him make before.

Michael wheeled back to face them. "They have his body. They have the Morningstar and they have the key to his prison. All they need is blood. And that, they'll have soon enough." He strode past Alice and towards the door.

"Where are you going?" Adriel shouted after him.

Michael's voice floated back up the stairs to them. "To finish what has been started."

"ALICE. THERE ARE things you need to know."

"You *think*?"

"Alice..." Adriel had slipped into his 'remember who you're talking to' tone.

"How long do we have?"

"'We'?" He raised an eyebrow at her.

"Oh, come on. Just for once, can you forget all the mystery and tell me?"

Adriel frowned, and fiddled with his wrist. "It isn't as simple as that. There are things which..."

"...which I won't understand? Fine. Make it easy, or skip them. Tell me what I need to know."

"What you need to know? In simple terms, Gabriel has betrayed Michael. He has taken Lucifer's body and has run to the Fallen. They have, we believe, the means to restore him."

"And when you say 'restore,' you mean 'stuff his mind back in his body.'"

"More than that. It won't simply reunite him. It will restore him. He will become an Archangel again..."

"...with everything that entails." Alice finished the sentence for him, and shook her head. "Well, who thought up the plan that lets that happen? It's pretty bloody stupid, isn't it?"

"There is always a reason, Alice. In this case, it was a failsafe: if the time ever came when Lucifer had to be destroyed, this was the only way it could be done. But perhaps we should keep to the more relevant points."

"Whatever." Alice waved a hand dismissively. She was fairly sure she could guess what he was going to tell her next: Lucifer was levelling back up to Archangel, and with Gabriel's defection, the sides had gone from 'angels versus Fallen' to 'angels versus Fallen-plus-two-Archangels'.

"Lucifer once had a choir, Alice. If he's restored..."

"His choir have to answer to him. This just gets better and better."

"His choir will have to answer to him..."

"Oh, now you really *are* taking the piss. *You*? *Seriously*?"

"Wheels are in motion which I cannot stop. Lucifer will rise, and he will call and I will have no choice but to answer."

"Wait." Alice held up her hand and Adriel blinked at her with his black eyes. She was almost afraid to ask, but she was going to do it anyway. "Lucifer had a choir. What did he control?"

"You already know." Adriel hung his head.

"I do." Alice felt as though someone had pulled the floor sideways from beneath her.

Lucifer had been the Archangel of Death.

"It's his throne. The mercy seat, they call it." Adriel nodded at the chair on the dais. "Michael took it, as a reminder."

"What about you? How did you..."

"I did not follow Lucifer."

"That's pretty obvious."

"I seconded Mallory."

"You what?"

"When Mallory told Michael of Lucifer's plans, I was his second. As Mallory betrayed him, so did I. And in many ways, my betrayal was worse: I rebelled against my commander." He scratched at his wrist again, and pulled back his sleeve. There on his arm was a sigil – but unlike the others Alice had seen, which looped and swirled, Adriel's was nothing more than a circle, clear against the pale skin of his arm. "Endless, you see. No beginning and no ending. Eternal." He rubbed it thoughtfully. "Lucifer liked it so much, he kept on using it."

"The brands!" The white brands worn by all the Fallen around their wrists, like shackles. The brands which bound their minds to Lucifer's, just as the sigils bound the choirs.

"He took what was good, and he corrupted it," Adriel said. "It is in his nature, perhaps. He is the darker side of death: rot and decay and fear and despair. He is the cold. He is destruction, and he is oblivion."

"And now he has an electric psychopath as his wingman..." Alice chipped in – and was surprised to see Adriel almost smile. Not *quite*, but close enough.

"Michael needs you. After Seket... after your mother... there were no more Travelers. No more angels bridging the divide between human and angel. It was seen as too much of a risk.

And so they forget, little by little. The angels forget. They forget what it is to have mercy, to have hope. They forget that there is more to the world than their war."

"I don't think they forgot." Alice was surprised by how bitter she sounded. "I don't think they ever cared."

"They did. They do still. They just need to be reminded what it is they're really fighting for. It isn't to win, and it isn't to defeat the Fallen. It's for them. For *you.*" He pointed at the window – or rather, the world beyond it.

"Well, that's all gone to shit, hasn't it?"

"Because they don't remember what it's all for, Alice. *Remind* them."

"Me?"

"You. You, the half-born who fights against the Fallen. The child who walked into hell with a smile on her face..."

"I think that's a slight exaggeration..."

"I have seen you, Alice. I have seen who you are. I *know* who you are, even if you don't. The half-born who wants so much to be one thing or another that she forgets she is the best of both." He smiled this time, but his smile was distant – as though he was listening to a voice Alice couldn't hear. "Help them. Help Michael. Help Mallory. Help them all. They'll need it, though they may not thank you for it." He drew away from her. "It has been my honour to serve as the Angel of Death. Not always painless, but a privilege. I was bound to serve only my purpose, answering to no-one, but I fear I was impartial when I should have been otherwise, and now I must be partial when I would be not." He paused, and half-smiled again. "Tell Michael the apprentice is ready."

"What the hell does that mean?"

"It means he will rise and I must Fall. Not that it matters: with Gabriel gone, we are all as good as Fallen. I wonder, though, with Zak dead... who will remember us?"

"I will," said Alice, and she looked straight into his black eyes.

"I hope so," he said, sadly. And he nodded once, and then he was gone, leaving Alice alone and baffled in the throne room.

"Well, that's all just marvellous, isn't it?" she said, and sat down on the floor, trying to work out exactly what had just happened.

CHAPTER THIRTY-TWO

Making Monsters

TOBY HAD BEEN slumped in the chair, as far as Mallory could make out, ever since Rimmon left. Certainly, he hadn't heard any movement from the other side of the room. Not that he had a lot of choice – the Fallen had, ever thoughtful, apparently left him tied there.

"Toby?"

Nothing.

"Hey, Toby. Are you in there?"

Nothing.

"It's just, well, I'll be honest. This floor's starting to get uncomfortable, and you're not being very fair. I think, seeing as I'm basically your guest, that the least you could do is stop bogarting the chair..."

There was a soft hiccuping sound. It might have been sobbing, it might not.

"So, what do you say? You want to let me have a turn?"

"I would," came the answer, in a voice that was far too thick for comfort, "but my hands, so to speak, are tied." The hiccuping sound again, and with a sigh of relief, Mallory realised it was laughter. Or something like it. Maybe he was a fighter after all.

"How are you doing?" he asked, more serious now.

"How do you think?" There was no sarcasm there. It was a simple question.

"I think... not so good."

"You'd be right." There was a groan from across the room, and the sound of the chair creaking, of the rope straining, as Toby sat up. "Mallory, right?"

"That's right."

"You know this guy, don't you? The way you talk..."

"I know him. We go back a long way."

"What did I do?"

"I'm not sure I follow." Mallory was glad it was dark: it meant Toby couldn't see the look on his face.

"To deserve this. What did I do?"

"Take my advice: questions like that are rarely helpful." Mallory chewed on the edge of one of his fingernails. "Particularly not when you're dealing with Rimmon."

"How do you know him? You're not friends, are you." It wasn't a question, and Toby's voice cracked as he spoke. At that moment, Mallory wished more than anything that he could reach him. But he could not. He'd tried, and he'd failed. Repeatedly.

"You don't want to know."

"If I didn't want to know, I wouldn't ask, would I? Besides, it's not like I've got anything better to do." He coughed, and there was a wet sound as though he had spat on the floor – although Mallory suspected it was something far less pleasant than that.

"It's a long story..."

"I've got time."

Mallory stifled a cold laugh. He had a feeling Toby had far less time than he imagined. "I'll tell you a story instead, how about that? A long time ago, there was a village. Out in the middle of nowhere, a real backwater. They grew their crops, they kept their animals, they occasionally went crazy and sold some surplus at the market in the nearby town. But pretty much, they kept to themselves. That was how it went there: how it had gone, and always would go – until a baby was born beneath the comet.

"They weren't exactly what you'd call 'enlightened,' so the boy was regarded with deep suspicion. Any day, as he grew, they expected him to sprout horns or hooves or something equally stupid, but he never did, so their suspicions began to fade. After all, portents came and went and there was no saying that a sign in the night sky over one village wasn't meant for the people of the next. The kid had the right number of fingers, the right number of toes and when – by his twelfth year – a tail or a forked tongue were both still conspicuously absent, they decided that he was in the clear. Which was, as it happened, a year too soon.

"It was a spring morning, early, and one of the farmers went out to check on his animals in the field. He found every single one of them dead: their skins scorched, their eyes burned out, the grass where they had fallen yellowed and dried. Like they'd been hit by lightning. But the strangest thing about it was that they'd all fallen facing the same way: towards the house where the comet-child, as he was known, lived. So the farmer decided to pay him and his mother a little visit...

"They ducked her. Tied her to a chair and ducked her in the river. They made her son stand on the riverbank and watch while she drowned. Of course, that proved that she wasn't a witch, so all eyes turned to him. And then he did the most extraordinary thing: he fell to his knees and begged their forgiveness, and when he held up his hands, they were full of lightning. All round his head, and in his hands and in his eyes and his mouth... everywhere. They ran, afraid for their lives. All of them ran – all but one.

"He was a stranger to the boy, and still he did not run. Instead, he took him away and taught him that what he had was a gift, and that he could learn to control it. The boy tried, but he was frightened. *Too* frightened, perhaps. And the man was a terrible teacher, which didn't help. They fled to the woods, and there they hid: living off whatever came their way, and every once in a while, the man would go off poaching to supplement their larder, or gambling – and thieving – to keep their purse filled.

"It was a day like that, a day in the winter when there was frost in the trees and smoke in the air, that the boy met a devil. A devil who mixed just enough truth with his lies to make the boy believe. To make him doubt everything that the man had told him, to make him afraid: afraid of his past, afraid of his future, afraid of himself – and more than anything, afraid of the man who had tried to save him.

"And so he left with the devil, and when the man returned from the market, he found he was alone. The boy was lost."

There was silence.

Then: "That was a weird story."

"Was a bit," Mallory said with a shrug. "Sorry about that. Probably a bit bleak, now I think about it."

"A bit bleak? You could say that."

"You didn't specify cheerful, did you?"

"I'd have thought it was obvious!" Toby sounded indignant, and despite himself, Mallory smiled. It was working.

"Fine. You want cheerful, then you're going to have to do the talking, I'm afraid."

"Fat lot of good you are, mate."

"I'm all ears."

VIN GROANED AS he sat back, finally dropping his hands. The hinges were, as far as he could see, done. Just as well, because he was so tired he could barely move. Turning metal to stone – even old, rusty and generally knackered metal – was clearly more energy-intensive than he had imagined. On the plus side, old, rusty and generally knackered metal made for uneven stone, riddled with fault lines. It made it *weak*.

And that could only be a good thing.

All he had to do now was wait.

* * *

"So, this girl. How did you meet her?" Mallory asked. Toby's definition of 'cheerful' seemed to focus almost entirely on the description of a woman. He was quite clearly besotted, and listening to *that* wasn't exactly Mallory's definition of fun. He missed his flask. More than he missed his flask, he missed his guns – because if nothing else, he could at least shoot himself in the head if he sensed another description of Little Miss Perfect heading his way. More troubling, however, was the fact Toby had stumbled over several words. Words which shouldn't have caused a five year-old any problems.

"Work. She works in the office."

"And that would be where?"

"The undertaker's. I work out back. I'm training, you know? Learning to run funerals and that."

"Undertaker." Mallory felt a twinge in the pit of his stomach as everything he'd feared was confirmed. *Just this once, why couldn't it be a coincidence?* he thought.

"It's a good job. People think it's..." Toby tailed off again and Mallory's attention snapped back to the cell, but then Toby carried on. "Are you alright? You just sounded a bit... off."

"Your boss. He wouldn't happen to be called Andrew, would he?"

"Mr Langham? You know him?"

"In a manner of speaking," Mallory groaned inwardly. "And god help me, because I can't quite believe I'm saying this... but that... *girlfriend* of yours. Alice, yes?"

"You know Alice?" Toby's voice perked up considerably.

"Oh, yes," Mallory mumbled. No such thing as a coincidence, was there; not here, not now. Not ever. Click-click-click went the cogs in his head.

Toby was talking again – animated now. He was telling Mallory how accident-prone Alice was; how twitchy. How sad she seemed. How alone. How he knew that all she needed was someone to take care of her...

"You ever think she might be able to take care of herself?"

Toby snorted, which immediately set him off into a coughing fit. "I thought you said you knew Alice. She couldn't take care of a stick insect, let alone herself!" He coughed again – a damp, unpleasantly sticky sound – and moaned. They were done talking for the time being, by the sound of it, and Mallory rested his head back against the wall. How could Toby have Alice so very wrong? Thinking that she needed taking care of? She was more than capable of taking care of herself; he'd seen her.

But the Alice that Toby had described was so different – so very different – she might as well have been someone else. How could that be? People were who they were, weren't they? They didn't flip a switch and change from one thing to another...

Not unless someone tried to make them.

Not unless someone told them they were two things and then left them hanging midway between the two.

That was the kind of thing that could break someone, make them take the wrong turnings; make the wrong choices. He knew it better than anyone: Rimmon had taught him that, all those years ago.

Mallory thumped his head back against the wall so hard that he saw stars, and he hoped that Alice – *his* Alice – was stronger than Toby believed her to be.

She would have to be.

VIN LISTENED FOR footsteps, a sound... anything. Anything at all that might suggest someone was coming.

Naturally, there was only silence – if you discounted the dogs. There was always noise from the dogs. But given what Forfax actually fed his pets, Vin wasn't sure he didn't prefer the racket they made when they were hungry. At least then he knew they weren't eating someone...

He had no idea what he was going to do when he actually managed to get out of this cell. None. He'd tried to come up with a plan, but it hadn't exactly worked out – so instead, he was working on the basis that he was going to find Mallory and ask him what *his* plan was. Mallory was bound to have a plan.

All Vin had to do was get to him.

He had no idea how long he waited but, finally, there were footsteps. No cane, by the sound of it, which meant it wasn't Forfax. Maybe that was a good thing. The more he listened, the more footsteps he heard: it was at least six or seven people, he decided, walking quickly and quietly. One of them sounded like they were dragging their feet.

He held his breath as the footsteps passed the door and started to fade, and then – as hard as he could – he slapped the door with the flat of his hand. The metal made a loud *bong*, ringing in his ears and making his eyes water. A noise like that must have got someone's attention...

The grille in the door slid back with a rattle, and Vin dropped into a crouch below it, sliding as close to the door as he could. He could hear the Fallen on the other side breathing as they peered in... but couldn't see him. A key turned in the lock; a bolt was slid back.

He crossed his fingers and hoped it was one of the stupider ones, and then he moved.

Quick as a flash, he was on his feet. He darted back a couple of paces from the door – and before the unfortunate creature on the other side had time to move, Vin had thrown himself feet-first straight at the metal.

He didn't have time to consider what might happen if the hinges did not give, which was just as well. Give they did, shattering in puffs of dust. The door ripped free from the wall, twisting under its own weight and the force of Vin's attack, and spun into the corridor. The Fallen who had been foolish enough to be on the other side of it was pinned beneath it as it fell. He screamed once, then fell silent. Vin didn't much care. All he cared about was getting away: the metal door had sung like a cathedral bell as it fell, and someone would have heard it.

Looking first up, then down the corridor, Vin weighed his options. The footsteps had passed from left to right, hadn't they? They had sounded like someone was being taken somewhere – someone reluctant. A prisoner. So were they being taken to or from a cell? He thought about it a moment more, then spun abruptly to the left and set off along the corridor at a cautious jog.

CHAPTER THIRTY-THREE

Thicker Than Water, Stronger Than Death

THERE WERE MANY things Jester wished he could change. He would have told Vin to stop being an idiot. He would have done his physics homework in the fourth year of secondary school. He would have asked Alice how it felt, being a half-born, just to see if it was the same for both of them, even though he doubted it could be. Not with Alice being Alice.

But of all the things he would change if he could; of all the glittering possibilities, he would have listened to his sister.

If he had listened to his sister, things might have been different.

If he had listened to his sister, he would have heard her telling him that she had met someone. He would have known when she began to withdraw, to change. He would have noticed the bags under her eyes, the fading light behind them. He would have *known*.

At least, this was what he told himself when the door shut behind them and the two of them were alone in the room.

It wasn't much for a family reunion: a rectangular concrete box with a table in the middle, bolted to the floor. A mirror ran the length of one of the longer walls, but Jester knew what that *really* was. A small, round speaker jutted out of the opposite wall, and a tiny CCTV camera blinked at them from the corner. There was nothing else in there except for the knife on the table. And Florence.

The problem was that Jester recognised the knife – or at least, he thought he did. He didn't know how, exactly, but it tugged at some part of him he couldn't quite find. It rattled around in the back of his mind like a half-forgotten promise. It made him think of summer, of learning to ride his bike. Of the smell of poster paint…

It made him *remember*.

Zadkiel. It was Zadkiel's.

And it was here.

He looked at Florence across the table.

The room filled with white noise as the loudspeaker crackled into life.

"The door can only be opened from the outside, so don't try to be clever." The voice that piped through the speaker was strained; echoey. And unpleasant. "It's a very simple principle here: two half-borns enter the room. We only need one of you. Actually, I'll rephrase that. We only need one of you dead, which means one of you is free to leave. Which one that is… that's up to you."

The speaker cut out, leaving Jester and Florence staring at each other across the table, and then it spoke again. It was the same voice, but easier now: less cold, somehow. "Florence? I'd prefer it if it was you…" This time, when it cut out, it stayed silent.

OF ALL THE things Jester wished he could change, he wished he had listened to his sister.

"WE CAN'T," HE said, holding her gaze. Her eyes were flat, lifeless; her hands hung by her sides.

"We have to. He said."

"Who?"

"Him. Lucifer. You have to do what he says."

"Why?"

This seemed to stump Florence, and she blinked in surprise. "Because."

"No, really, Flo. Why?"

"Because you have to do what he says."

"I don't. And neither do you."

"He'll hurt Xaph."

"Fuck Xaph. What's he *done* to you?"

"Don't talk about him like that. You mustn't." She glanced over her shoulder at the camera, its red light blinking on and off. Jester sighed and waved at the window.

"They can see us, you know. They're watching. They're standing right there. Right on the other side of the glass."

"I know." Her hand crept forward, Jester's heart sank.

"And you know that if I took it... if I took the knife, he wouldn't lift a finger to save you?"

"I'm past saving."

"No, you're not." He reached out and closed his fingers over hers, around the handle of Zadkiel's butterfly knife. "Don't help them. Leave him."

"I love him..."

"He doesn't love you."

"He does, in his own way."

"I don't think he can." Jester kept his voice low. She looked so broken, so fragile. If only he could get her to see... But her eyes suddenly hardened and she pulled her hand away from his.

Jester knew it was hopeless. "Fine. You won't listen to me. I never listened to you, so that's fair. But you can't help them, Flo. Look what they're doing."

"Taking back what's theirs. That's all."

"If you believe that..."

"I love him."

"You're wrong. I'm not going to fight you over this. I'm not going to make it easy."

"It isn't."

"There's a reason they're doing this. You know there is. What if we both refuse?"

"Then Lucifer will kill us both without a thought." Florence took a step around the table; a step closer to Jester. He took a deep breath.

"Then you do what you have to do."

"OH, COME ON. I thought you liked this sort of thing!" Rimmon was grinning at Mallory, while Toby whimpered in his chair. There was a small puddle of blood around his feet, which was steadily growing. "Maybe," Rimmon said with a laugh, "maybe it's just that you don't like to watch. You want to be involved... a little more hands-on. Is that it?" He had his back to Mallory, who was on the floor, his back against the wall and his face turned away from what was happening. Rimmon's attack on Toby was remorseless, pitiless and merciless. He cut and he slashed and he hacked and he twisted... over and over again. And when he was bored with that, on went the hood and out came the bucket.

Three times, he had come and gone – and each time he had left, it was harder and harder to reach Toby. Mallory had tried. But the second time, the words that came back to him from the far end of the cell were slurred; the pauses between them longer than they should have been. The third... there was barely anything more than a moan. Rimmon had almost broken him, and he knew it.

"You see, Mallory, you did me a favour. Purson left a gap in the chain of command when he died. And it turns out that torture's one of my talents."

There was another wail from Toby and Rimmon chuckled.

"Let him go," Mallory said.

"I'm sorry?"

"Let him go."

"And why would I do that?"

"Because it's not him you want. It's me. You have me. Let him go."

"Oh, no." Rimmon turned away from the chair and towards Mallory, wiping his hands on a cloth he'd pulled from his pocket. It was stained unpleasantly red. "And you know why? Because it's killing you to watch, isn't it? Tell me: how does it feel to be helpless?" He dropped into a crouch in front of him, hands resting on his knees. "So you know what I'm going to do? I'm going to keep you here, like a pet. You'll stay here, chained to this floor, and every day, I'll bring you a new friend, and every day, you will watch them die, slowly, painfully, begging for you to save them. And every day, I will ask you again."

"Ask me what?"

"To join us." Rimmon stood up and stretched. "And sooner or later, you *will* say yes."

"I won't."

"Then you're going to have to get used to this..." Suddenly, Rimmon had a jagged metal spike in his hand, and almost gracefully, he rammed it deep into Toby's thigh. Toby screamed, and Rimmon smiled. "You could save him: all you have to do is say yes. How much blood are you willing to have on your hands, Mallory?"

"As much as it takes."

For the first time, Rimmon frowned. "Make your peace with this one," he said, ruffling Toby's hair. "I don't think he's going to last much longer." He patted Toby's cheek, and winked at Mallory. "I'll leave the light on this time, petal. Just so you can get a really good look at what you've done." He was humming a tune as he walked out, leaving his instruments strewn across the floor.

Mallory couldn't look at Toby. He tried; he did. But he couldn't bring himself to. The problem was that he knew Rimmon meant what he said. Toby would die, and after him there would be another and another and another. An endless procession of bodies, just to break him. And that was the worst of it: hadn't Toby asked what he had done to deserve this? Nothing. He had done nothing.

Mallory, on the other hand...

THERE WAS A scratching sound from the other side of the door. It was too soon for Rimmon to be back: based on his other disappearances, he'd be gone for some time yet – and if there was one thing Mallory could be sure of, it was that no-one else was going to be allowed to play in his sandpit. He'd staked his claim to Mallory, and that was the way it was going to be. So who was at the door? And why didn't they just walk in, instead of lurking out there, trying to be quiet–

"Vin?" Mallory was careful not to raise his voice.

"How'd you know it was me?"

Mallory's heart leapt with relief. Not only was Vin alive, he might be able to get them out. Or at least help *Mallory* to get them out...

"I've never met anyone who makes as much noise trying to be quiet as you do. It couldn't have been anybody else. Where are we?"

There was muffled swearing on the other side of the door. "Forfax's place."

"You're kidding me."

"Don't suppose you know how we got here, do you?"

"You expect me to know that?"

"Call it blind optimism."

"Well, can you blindly and optimistically open the door, Vin?"

"Hang on." There was some scuffling, and a scraping sound. More swearing... and the door creaked open.

"Tadaa!" said Vin brightly, sticking his head inside.

His smile faded as he took in first Mallory – dirty, ragged, his clothing full of buckshot holes – and the mess on the floor... and finally the chair, complete with Toby, slumped like a rag doll beneath his bonds.

"They've really stepped up their game, haven't they?" He let out a whistle.

"Well, you made it easy. You left a spot on the team open when you took Purson out."

"Who?"

"You can have three guesses. You won't need them."

"Rimmon?"

"Rimmon."

"Look who's all grown up..." Vin said under his breath. Mallory scowled.

"I heard that. I don't know how long we've got. Can you get us out?" He lifted the chain in his hand, and Vin took it, weighing it in his palm. He frowned, closed his eyes and frowned some more.

"Nothing."

"Nothing?"

"Nothing. I don't know what it's made from, but I can't even dent it." He grabbed Mallory's wrist and rubbed at the manacle. "Same with this." He leaned in closer, peering at the band. "Is that Enochian?"

"If it is, it's not like any I've ever seen." Mallory pulled his arm away. "But it's effective. I can't leave, I can barely heal. And I can't help *him*." He nodded to Toby, but Vin was already there. He picked his way through the detritus Rimmon had left, and through the spatters of blood on the floor, his face creased into a scowl. As he reached Toby, and finally saw his face clearly, he sucked in a sharp breath and glanced back at Mallory. Without a word, he checked over the ropes that tied Toby, and the chair... and then he picked his way carefully back.

"I can't help him."

"He's only tied with rope, Vin. Even you can deal with that."

"You're asking for my help, and you're still insulting me? Charming." Vin shook his head. "But no. It's not just rope. There's some kind of metal thread in there."

"Don't tell me: same metal as this." Mallory waved his wrist, and his chain jangled.

"I'd put good money on it."

"Looks like they managed to get some of their helliron out of Xaph's lab, doesn't it?" Mallory flicked at the manacle round his wrist. "Bloody stuff."

"Given we tied him up with rosary chains, you've got to laugh at the irony, right?" Vin shrugged and looked at Mallory. Mallory glared back at him with a face like a thunderstorm.

"Oddly, I don't."

"No. Right." Vin stared at the floor.

THEY STOOD IN silence: Vin listening, and Mallory turning over every possible option in his mind. None of them were great. A couple of them were *terrible*. Only one made any sense – and even then, it was about as far from ideal as it was possible to be.

"Vin..." he said, looking up, "I don't think I'm going to get out of this one."

"Don't even start."

"I think you're..."

"Would you shut up already?" Vin snapped at him, but Mallory smiled grimly.

"You know what I'm asking."

"Yeah, and you can go fuck yourself. I'm serious."

"No you're not. You'll do this because I'm asking you to and because it's a mercy."

"No way.

"Vin..."

"Nope."

"Vin..."

"I'm not listening."

"Kill me. Kill me and leave – before we all lose the chance to make the choice."

CHAPTER THIRTY-FOUR

Gambit

"You're out of your fucking *mind*!" Vin spluttered. "It's absolutely out of the question. You're insane – and even if you weren't, it's still not going to happen."

"I wish I was." Mallory sighed, but it felt better, having said it. "This isn't about him." He gestured towards Toby. "It's about me. It's about me and it's about Rimmon, and it always has been and it always will be."

"That's it, isn't it? You've finally lost it."

"I've not lost it, Vin. I'm collateral damage."

"Round the twist, that's what you are."

"He told me, alright? He told me. That kid, over there, is going to die. Because of me. And then they're going to throw him out like so much garbage… and they're going to find themselves another one. And another one after that. And I can't help them, and I can't stop it!" His voice trembled with rage, and Vin took half a step back. He'd never seen Mallory like this.

"It won't end. Not until I give them what they want."

"And what is it they want?" Vin already knew, but he still had to ask.

"Me. They want me." Mallory hung his head.

"Why? You're bolshy, bad-tempered, you drink like a fish and you've got an itchy trigger-finger. And, by the way, you owe me money."

"I always owe you money, Vin."

"Exactly my point."

"Stop. Please." Mallory was too serious for Vin to carry on pretending.

"Alright. But I'm still not doing it."

"There's no other way."

"There's always another way."

"Not this time." Mallory shook his head. "I won't stand by and let them torture and kill and say it was all because of me."

"Coward." Vin looked Mallory in the eye as he said it. And meant it.

"Coward? Really? You think that's what I am?"

"You're running away. You're giving up. That's cowardice, isn't it? Where's your faith? Where's your fight, for that matter?"

"Look at him." Mallory held Vin's gaze, unblinking, but raised his hand and pointed at Toby's broken form. "Look at him. You want that on your conscience? Because I don't. I *can't*."

"You know that anyone else would let him die. *Everyone* else. I'm not so sure *I* wouldn't."

"Not him."

"Why? What's so special about him?"

"Nothing. That's the point," replied Mallory.

"I DON'T THINK I've ever heard anything so messed up. And I've heard a lot of messed-up shit." Vin was still shaking his head in disbelief. "This isn't about Rimmon, or the kid. It never has been. It's about you. You think Rimmon's doing this as some kind of taunt, don't you? You seriously think he's smart enough to come up with this all by himself? He's a flunkey: you've said it yourself a thousand times. This? This is Lucifer. It's *always* Lucifer. It's why he goes after you, it's why Rimmon went after Alice" – Vin watched Mallory's face darken – "and which I now remember Raphael told me to make sure you never found out about. Yes. Moving on.

"How is it possible that you – the smartest guy I know – can be so thick? I mean, tactically you're the best of us. Better than…"

He paused and lowered his voice. "Better than Michael, even. But sometimes, talking to you's like talking to a rock. A *stupid* one."

"You know, I'm beginning to wish Rimmon would come back. Then I could suggest that maybe he'd like to kill me instead. Or you. Either would work."

"I'm trying to help you."

"I don't think you can. Unless..."

"Just listen. You're not seeing it all, are you? You're still not seeing it. It's all Lucifer. All along. He knew you'd talk: it's why he picked you. He wanted to send a message to everyone that he wasn't to be messed with, and he knew you wouldn't be able to help yourself. And so it goes – right up to now. Lucifer picked this kid because he knew you'd feel responsible for him, just like you'd feel responsible for the next one."

"Then he's right."

"You're impossible." Vin kicked out at the wall.

"It doesn't matter why it's happening, Vin. It doesn't matter what the reasoning is behind it, and it doesn't matter who did it, or why. What matters is that they will kill him, right there" – Mallory pointed at the chair – "and they will do it, ultimately, to get at me. Maybe because it's part of a bigger 'torment Mallory' plan just for shits and giggles; maybe because I won't do what they want. End result is the same."

"There must be another way..."

"And if you can come up with it, then I'm all ears. But I don't think there is one. I *will* not Fall, and I *will* not let this stand."

"There *has* to be another way." But Vin was starting to sound doubtful.

"Then find it. But find it fast."

Vin sighed, and stared at the floor. "Jester?"

Mallory shook his head. "I think we both know what that means."

"This whole thing. It's..."

"Yes, Vin. Yes, it is."

* * *

DOWN THE CORRIDOR, across the warehouse floor with its stacked crates and its pit, through an opening draped with plastic sheeting and down a flight of dark stairs, stood a door; and beside it, a window. It looked not out, but in: behind it, there was a room with nothing in it but a table, bolted to the floor. A small group of men gathered on the outside, looking through the glass. One was tall and blond, and wore a suit: his red eyes reflected in the silver of the glass. One had dark hair and carried a cane. One would have been handsome, but for the scars which covered half of his face and smeared his features into one another, drawing his lips back in a too-wide smile. The last of them had wings which shone with white sparks, crackling as the feathers rubbed against one another. They looked through the window, and they waited.

At a nod from Lucifer, Xaphan unlocked the door and opened it wide, grinning as Florence stepped unsteadily out. She held out a red-smeared hand, pressing the sticky knife into his outstretched palm, and slumped against him.

"Did I do alright?" she asked, her voice pleading.

"You were perfect." He draped his arm around her and drew her close. "It could have been a little quicker, perhaps, but other than that..."

"Oh." She hung her head.

"But not to worry. I'm sure next time will be better." He ruffled her hair and shot a glance over the top of her head towards the others. Handing the knife to Gabriel, he nodded. "And that should be it," he said.

Lucifer blinked at the window and then – quietly at first, but with increasing energy – he began to laugh.

"MALLORY, WHEN ARE you going to get it through that thick head of yours that it doesn't matter to Rimmon? It won't make a blind bit of difference to him. How do you know he doesn't already realise who he's got in that chair?"

"I don't doubt he already knows."

"Then what's the point?"

"Because I couldn't save Rimmon from them... but I might be able to save *him*." Mallory cleared his throat, rolled his shoulders and his neck. "You wait. You find a way, and you get him out of here."

"You think he's going to be able to walk out? Seriously? I'd be shocked if he's got a single bone that's not broken. Have you *seen* him?" Vin hissed.

"I don't need to see him."

"But you'll die for him. That's veering dangerously close to heroic. And you know how I feel about that kind of thing."

"What happened to my being a coward?"

"Isn't it the same thing?" Vin shrugged. He was so matter-of-fact about it that Mallory laughed.

"I think they're supposed to be the opposite. It's being brave. Doing the things that are necessary. Like you will, because you know that it needs to be done."

"Wait... did you just call *me* heroic?"

"Maybe. Don't get used to it."

It wasn't in anything that Mallory said, or did. It wasn't in the tone of his voice or the look on his face. It wasn't even in the fact he might possibly have said something that counted as nice to Vin... but he knew that Mallory had made up his mind. There would be no convincing him otherwise; no talking him down.

Mallory was right. As things stood, there was no other way out of this. Not for him. Watching Rimmon torture and kill his way through a busload of people – just because he could? That would kill Mallory too. But it would be slow, and it would be painful, and it would be his spirit that died first. All that would be left was a shell.

However much he hated the idea on every level, Vin was starting to wonder whether Mallory might be right.

He bit his lip, and hoped that Alice would come.

CHAPTER THIRTY-FIVE

Transition

ALICE WAS ON the stairs. Again. She was on the stairs, turning over everything Adriel had just told her in her mind, and trying to separate out the useful bits from the typically Adriel-ish mysticism. "I think I preferred him when he was just a slightly creepy undertaker," she muttered as she stomped down the stairs in search of... anyone.

The roofs were still burning, but the fire showed no sign of spreading, and she wondered if there was more to it than just normal flames. It was Michael's, after all. What did it look like from the mainland? Was there even anyone to see, and if there was, did they care? If the world really was falling apart around them, would anyone notice the death of a single angel?

The news that Zadkiel was dead, that Gabriel was with the Fallen... she had heard it, and she had understood it – but she couldn't make herself *feel* it. Michael's anger had gone beyond mere rage: it was grief, she knew... and something else.

Fear.

She had felt that, alright. A stab of it, deep inside her, as he had left the room. Right after he had mentioned Lucifer.

They were going to restore Lucifer. The Fallen wouldn't just be the Fallen any longer. They would be an army, led by two Archangels and reinforced by an entire choir, and the current Angel of Death.

And they had Mallory and Vin.

The day was just getting better and better.

She hurried down the stairs fast enough to make herself dizzy. The stone walls no longer felt cold to the touch: now, they were warm, even on the inside, thanks to the flames outside. Michael had a temper... not that that was news to Alice. A temper, combined with grief, was about the most mindlessly destructive force there was. Alice didn't need anyone to tell her that: she'd been there. She just hoped that in this case, there was someone around to pick up the pieces.

She turned the corner at the bottom of the stairs and stepped out of the doorway into the cloister. There, angels were lining up – as she had expected. What she'd seen earlier was a drill. This was the real thing. This was, as Michael had already said, absolute war. Their armour caught the light of the fire above them, glowing deep red in the fading light. Alice glanced up: she hadn't noticed, but it was almost dusk, and the deepening blue sky was slashed across with red and pink.

She thought back to her first sight of the priory, from the shore of the village they called Medea. The sunset had made the roofs look like they were burning then... now, they were.

A dark figure at the far side of the cloister caught her eye; not in armour, like the others. An Earthbound, with sandy hair, ruffled and streaked with dirt. He was dressed in black – including what looked to Alice like a stab-proof vest. A police vest. Castor.

He barely acknowledged her as she crossed the cloister to him, weaving between angels and ducking beneath outstretched wings as they opened. His face was empty, his eyes dull and red-rimmed.

"Castor...?"

There was no reaction.

"Castor, I'm sorry." Alice put a hand on his arm and he flinched, but then his eyes seemed to come into focus and he looked at her, recognising her at last.

"He's dead. Zadkiel is dead," was all he said, and his voice was little more than a rasp.

"I know. I'm sorry."

"He's gone. I lost him, Alice. I lost him." It almost looked as though he was going to say something else, but he changed his mind and covered his eyes with his fingers. Alice rested her hand on his arm, wishing there was more she could say, but there was nothing. Behind them, the angels clattered to attention – all swords and plate and feather – and none of them thought to look in the corner. Not one of them saw Castor weep for his Archangel.

A bell rang somewhere nearby, tolling across the cloisters, and the angels fell silent. Alice looked round just as Michael swept into the cloister, his wings folded behind his back. He cocked his head on one side, listening as the last echoes of the bell died away, and then he folded his arms across his chest, armour blazing not with the light of the sunset, but with flame.

"Tonight, the Angelus has rung without Gabriel. You will know by now that he has betrayed us. He has abandoned us; he has turned on us. He has murdered our brother and opened our gates to the damned."

There was a quiet murmur from the crowd of assembled angels.

"He has broken our trust, and taken what was not his to take. Tonight, we take it back."

A cheer.

Alice could have sworn she saw the corner of Michael's mouth twitch... and at that moment, she realised there was suddenly nothing under her hand. Castor had moved. In fact, Castor was now out in the middle of the cloister, striding towards Michael. "Oh, bollocks," muttered Alice, scrambling after him.

"What about Zak, Michael?" he shouted. "What about vengeance?"

"Vengeance?" Michael asked, raising his voice. Every single pair of eyes was now very definitely on Castor, and Michael's face broke into a broad smile. "Vengeance was always what Gabriel did best, wasn't it? I think it's time we showed him what vengeance really means."

Another cheer, and this time the angels began to step out of their lines. They were forming a crowd, with Castor and Michael as the centre.

"We take them. We take them now!" Michael shouted, raising his sword towards the sky. The angels roared in response and Alice stared open-mouthed at them as they bayed not for Lucifer's blood, not for the Fallen, but for *Gabriel's*. Gabriel, who until hours before had been one of their own.

"Not your bad guy anymore," she whispered, remembering what Mallory had told her the first time he'd mentioned Gabriel.

"Alice, when the lights go out and the world stops, at the end of time, and there's nothing left but dust and ash and embers... Gabriel will still be standing there with blood on his hands."

"He sounds like a piece of work. You're sure he's one of the good guys?"

"He is. He's just a bad one."

"Can't say I've ever seen much of a difference between the bad good guys and the good bad ones."

"Oh, there is one. Namely that he's ours."

The memory didn't exactly make her comfortable.

THE SOUND OF wings filled the cloister; the rustle of feathers as angels took flight. It was either an extraordinary thing to see, or a ridiculous one. Alice was too tired to be sure. She felt like she had stumbled into the middle of something; something too big for her. Finally, she was ready to call it quits and to go home – because this... this, she knew, would break her.

"Doubt? You?" The voice was an inch from her right ear. She froze.

The air smelled of woodsmoke, and she could hear his wings.

"Not doubt."

"I should hope not. What, then?"

"I don't know."

"Adriel gave you a message for me."

"Yes. Now can you stop breathing in my ear?" Alice snapped, glaring at Michael and taking a step away from him. He straightened up, raising an eyebrow at her.

"Message, Alice."

"He said to tell you the apprentice was ready. What does that even mean?"

"It means that Adriel has done the right thing."

"Which is...?"

"The Angel of Death cannot be partial: he cannot be 'ours' or 'theirs.' Not at a time like this. He simply... is."

"Which is why Lucifer isn't any more."

"Quite. You can imagine how that would have gone, can't you?" Michael scowled, but continued. "Adriel was chosen from those of Lucifer's choir who remained. He was the most... level-headed. The most balanced."

"Looks good in a suit, too."

"Yes, I'm sure that was one of our main considerations." He sighed. "Everything will change, Alice. If Lucifer is restored. Everything. Do you understand?"

"Not even slightly."

"Perhaps it's best that you don't. And do you still want to come with us?"

"Do they still have Vin and Mallory?"

"They do."

"Then what do you think?"

"I think I would have immense trouble keeping you here. But don't for a moment make the mistake of thinking that I couldn't. Or wouldn't. And you would not enjoy that at all."

"I'm not going to blithely shut up and do what I'm told, so let's not even waste time on that conversation."

Michael made a sound which might have been a growl, but she pretended not to notice. After a moment, he sighed. "It doesn't matter what I say to you, what I order you to do, does it?"

"No."

"You realise that they are there, in part, because of you?"

"No. They're there because they made choices. Just like I'm here."

"Mallory chose to give you time to get away."

"That's why he's my friend."

"Tell me, Alice: why would you risk so much to save him? To save them?"

"Because he… *they're* worth saving."

"Would you do the same for me? Am I… *worth saving*?"

"I'm not sure."

Michael laughed, but there was very little joy behind it. "One thing you will obey me in, Alice, and this I do mean. The Fallen will have other prisoners. Mallory is being held with a human. You cannot save them both."

"Why?"

"Because. Human or angel. Make your choice."

Alice stared at him. "You're telling me – you, Michael, all-powerful angel and all that – you can only save one of two people in a room."

"No, Alice. I'm saying *you* can only save one of them."

"What's the catch?"

"That's for you to decide. Now choose. Choose, or stay behind – and remember, if I take you, it's nothing more than as a show of faith. Stay out of my way. I have work to do, and there's more at stake than the lives of a couple of angels."

"You're a caring type, aren't you?" She was getting used to Michael's utter disregard for anyone else, but even so… "Of course I'm going to pick Mallory. Why wouldn't I want to help him?"

"And therein lies the bane of my daily existence." He opened his wings. "Remember your choice, Alice."

"You're not going even going to try another 'do as you're told or I'll muzzle you' speech? Frankly, I'm disappointed."

"Do not provoke me, Alice." He stood in front of her with his wings wide open and his eyes burning, holding out a hand. "Besides, by your choices, you muzzle yourself."

His fingers closed around hers and the world filled with flame.

* * *

"I HATE THAT," she said, opening her eyes. Wherever they were, it was dark. It was dark and it was damp and it smelled like oil and, quite possibly, vomit. Old vomit, at that. "I really hate that."

"You would rather have walked?" Michael sounded even more sarcastic than usual.

"No, I'd rather have…" Alice started to look around, and tailed off. "Where the hell are we, anyway?"

"Where they are." Michael nodded to a warehouse just ahead of them. "The Fallen. Gabriel. Lucifer." The last name came out in a hiss.

Behind them, Alice could just see the outlines of Michael's choir: they were trying to blend in, trying to be subtle. Trying, not succeeding. And she realised that this was where they were going to miss Zadkiel: not just because he hid them, made them forgettable when they needed to be… but because he was merciful.

What had driven Gabriel to Lucifer? Vengeance, she was willing to bet. Vengeance on… everyone – on Michael, most of all. And what would Michael do without Zadkiel behind him? Adriel had told her to help him, to help Michael. To help the angels to remember.

Human or angel. Make your choice.

There it was. What Adriel, more than anyone, had been trying to make her see. That there *was* no choice. She was both. That was the point of it all. She was both and always would be, and that was where she stood – between the two. More than that, it was where she belonged. And Adriel – impartial Adriel – had not only seen it, but he had tried to tell her so, before all hell had broken loose.

He'd seen it all coming.

So what was this 'apprentice' business, and what did it mean?

The angels were restless, shifting their weight from foot to foot; ruffling their feathers and muttering amongst themselves.

Alice looked at them all, and she knew they would not be merciful.

Betrayed not once, but twice, by their brothers. Betrayed by one of their generals. Besieged and attacked in their own safe haven, and forced to watch as the world they had been protecting tipped away from them.

No. There was no way they were going to be merciful.

ALICE HAD THE strangest sense of deja vu. The warehouse, she knew, would have a green neon sign on the front: the entrance to a sleazy-looking club. Around the corner was an alley full of rubbish, and just along from that was another warehouse. Or what was left of one.

She'd been here before.

She'd been here the night she had caught up with Murmur.

"Michael?"

"Alice."

"You said this is where they're hiding. Since when?"

"Since we burned them out of hell."

"And you knew that?"

"Of course I did. But I had no reason..."

"You knew they were here, and you did nothing?"

"Would you have had me do, Alice?"

"Stop them! Kill them! Anything!"

"And then what?"

"Excuse me?"

"Then what? I could have taken Forfax at any time. Xaphan too, and any number of the others. But Lucifer would still be dust in the wind, and it's him I want. Him, and now Gabriel."

"But you could have stopped this. If you'd taken them... Zadkiel... Medea... those kids. You could have saved them!"

"And what good would it have done me? Would it have brought me any closer to Lucifer? No."

"But his generals. The Twelve..."

"Would have been replaced. They always are." He adjusted the edge of his breastplate. "For all this time, I have fought a war of attrition. I have tried to wear them down faster than they wear us down. I have followed the rules: rules which, by the way, Lucifer is more than content to break. I have been patient. No more."

"I just think you don't like the idea of losing."

Alice was prepared for Michael to be angry, but the violence of his reaction still took her by surprise. One second she was standing on dark, damp, vomit-spattered tarmac, the next she was... somewhere else.

It was a box, mirrored on all sides. The floor, the roof, each wall... all reflected her own frightened face. Not quite a cube, it was tall enough for her to stand, and wide and long enough for her to reach out her arms. She couldn't see how it was lit, but it was certainly light enough for her to make out her surroundings. With mounting panic, she realised that was part of the point.

"What are you doing, Michael?" she asked, her voice bouncing back to her with tinny resonance. The only other sound was her breathing, and it crossed her mind that she had no idea how much air she had...

"Michael?" She called his name, louder. There was no answer.

Not unless she counted the tiny red spark which appeared in front of her nose. It hung in the air, dancing... and then slowly, slowly, it fell. It landed at her feet.

The floor caught fire.

Flames shot up from the glass, burning nothing and everything all at once. And it hurt.

It *hurt*.

Alice was so shocked that she almost didn't feel the pain. Almost. But as the flames swallowed her feet, wrapped around her shins, stretching – *reaching* – for her, she started to scream.

It hurt.

It shouldn't hurt. It couldn't.

It's not real, she told herself. *It's not real. It's in my mind. Michael's in my head.*

But it felt real – and that was the last clear thought she had. Everything else was screaming and heat and blinding, blistering pain.

It hurt.

She tried to bang on the glass, but it was too hot to touch and she was appalled to see that where her fingertips brushed it, there were smeared red-black marks.

She could smell burning hair.

And it hurt…

…And with a jolt she was back on the concrete. Michael was in front of her, watching her with narrowed eyes, while behind her a troop of angels waited for his command.

She held her hands up in front of her, turning them over to check first the backs and then her palms. She was fine. There wasn't even a speck of ash on her. She'd been right: it wasn't real. It was all in her mind.

"Do not provoke me, Alice," he said again.

He didn't wait for her to answer: perhaps he knew that she was far too shaken to speak. Perhaps he didn't care if she did or not. All he did was turn on his heel and walk away… towards the warehouse.

"Wasn't real. Wasn't real. It wasn't real…" she told herself – without pausing to wonder why, if it wasn't real, her mouth felt so dry, and why she could taste burning hair at the back of her throat…

There was movement in the shadows beside the warehouse, and Alice watched a figure detach itself from the dark and approach Michael. Castor, and beside him, carrying a long staff, was Pollux. They were speaking to the Archangel, and Alice could see Michael nodding as he listened, following Castor's gestures as he pointed to various sections of the building. They were almost ready.

Mallory and Vin were in there. That was all that mattered to her: she didn't care about the rest of it – not really. She didn't care about the Fallen. She didn't care about Gabriel. She didn't care about Lucifer. She didn't care about Rimmon or Xaphan. She didn't even care about finally getting her hands on Florence, she realised. She didn't care about their battles; their war. She didn't care about the world and whether it kept on turning.

She cared about *them*.

Castor and Pollux broke away from Michael, moving to the side of the building, and Michael squared up to the warehouse. His wings unfurled, feathers trembling as they opened wide and orange sparks jumped across the surface. She heard wings behind her, and she turned to see every angel there, lined up on the empty tarmac, with their wings open. Waiting. Still waiting.

Michael looked like a statue. His sword raised, his head tipped back. His wings wide open...

Alice's heart raced in her chest.

There was a sudden shout – a battle cry – and every angel's wings burst into life: the fire was so bright that Alice threw an arm up in front of her face to shield her eyes. All she saw was fire. Metal glittered deep within it, but the fire...

Another shout, and Michael jabbed at the dark sky with his sword. There was a cheer from the angels – loud enough to make Alice's ears ring – and they began to move.

It was no stampede, no rush. No disorganised charge. They marched. One foot, then the other. Even, steady. Holding the lines, burning like suns. And Michael led them: lost at the heart of the flames, only his sword visible behind his blazing wings, he walked calmly towards Lucifer's hiding place.

Alice watched as they passed; column after column, row after row. Their eyes forward, their swords ready. They didn't question, didn't hesitate. They would follow Michael wherever he led... How many of them, she wondered, had had the shiny-box treatment?

Michael had given her no orders. Not really. He knew what she would do.

She would find them, whatever it took. Whatever it cost.

She was the only one who would try.

The last of the lines moved past her, and she squinted towards the warehouse, sitting squat and dark on the far side of the fire. The Fallen knew they were coming. It's what Michael wanted. There was no attempt to hide – not from Lucifer, and not from the rest of the world. Anyone could have seen them... but perhaps that was the point. There had been something about staying hidden, hadn't there? Perhaps the time had come for them to move out of the shadows. Perhaps it was their only chance.

"Far too philosophical, Alice," she said to herself, and closing her eyes she reached out to the warehouse. If that was where the Fallen had been hiding all this time, there would be more than enough pain there. More than enough fuel for the fire.

It washed over her, around her; crowding her and crushing her and shutting out the world. Closing her off to everything but someone else's pain. It ate through her, pushing its way into her fingers, her lungs, her bones... it wove and threaded itself through her, and deep in her eyes, when she opened them, were spinning circles of fire.

Alice looked at thc warehouse, and her mind cleared.

One foot, then the other. Even. steady. And Alice followed the angels into hell on earth.

CHAPTER THIRTY-SIX

Pull the Pin

"WAIT... DID YOU just call me heroic?"

"Maybe. Don't get used to it."

Mallory closed his eyes, and Vin shot a glance around the room. Rimmon had left it scattered with... a lot of things Vin didn't like the look of, if he was honest. But they'd do.

"I still..."

"Vin. You know how it goes. Michael won't come for us. You can get out. You have to leave."

"I'm not leaving you here." Vin slid his hand behind his back; his fingers stretched along the floor, reaching...

"You're right. You're not. But you *are* leaving."

"You don't get to give me orders, Descended or not. And you really don't get to do it now."

"I've made up my mind, Vhnori. Do it." Mallory's eyes were still closed – as if he couldn't bring himself to look at Vin.

"Fair enough. Give me your hand." Vin reached forward and took Mallory's hand in his. The chain rattled as the manacle shifted on his wrist, sliding down. There was a ring of blood beneath it, and dark lines trailed up Mallory's arm away from it, beneath his skin. Vin flinched – only slightly, but still enough for Mallory to laugh.

"Helliron. What can you do?" he said with a shrug.

"You ready?" Vin asked, his voice sad.

"I'm ready."

"Good," said Vin – and he jerked Mallory's arm towards him, pulling him closer, at the same moment as he brought up the knotted rope Rimmon had dropped on the floor. He swung it with all the strength he had, and the huge knot connected with the side of Mallory's head, knocking him, unconscious, across the floor.

Vin let out a sigh of relief, and lowered his friend's hand. "All these years, and you've never once managed to piss me off enough to actually *try* to kill you. If you think I'm going to do it now, you're dumber than you look. And that's saying something."

Vin tossed the rope aside and he sat there, legs stretched out, in between Mallory – unconscious on the floor – and Toby – unconscious in the chair. He looked from one to the other.

"I knew I should've stayed in Hong Kong."

THE BOTTLES ON the shelf rattled, gently at first, but with increasing violence. No-one in the bar noticed – they were too absorbed in their own affairs, and the music was loud – but when the first bottle threw itself from its spot and smashed on the floor, its contents bursting into flame as it hit the concrete, they paid attention. A half-dozen men in crumpled suits, collars open and ties tucked in their pockets, glanced round. Paul the barman, a man with bright red hair, stared wide-eyed at the broken glass and the burning puddle before reaching under the counter and pressing a small black button, pulling a metal rod out from beneath the bar and setting it on the top, just in case. The remaining bottles behind him rattled ever-louder, some of them jumping in place and rocking alarmingly, and a phone mounted between the shelves rang.

One eye on the bottles, Paul picked up the receiver – plugging his other ear with his finger to better hear the voice on the other end. He listened, his face expressionless, and then he spoke.

"They're coming," was all he said.

He listened again and nodded, then hung up the phone and disappeared through a black door behind the bar, turning a dial on the music control pad as he left.

No-one saw him leave.

The music grew louder.

When the next bottle fell, nobody noticed.

Michael's choir reached the warehouse, but instead of launching themselves straight at it, as Alice had expected, they stopped.

"Michael's waiting," whispered a voice from the shadows, and Alice twitched. She thought she was the last one there. Peering into the dark, she saw a vague shape… and a pale face in the gloom. Castor. Dressed head to toe in black, he was almost impossible to make out in the shadows.

"Waiting for what?"

"The most effective moment."

"He's giving them warning."

"Of course he is." He folded his arms.

"That's crazy…"

"Not if you're Michael. He wants them to know he's coming. And that he's coming for *them*."

"For *whom*, exactly?"

He didn't answer, so she changed tack. "What about you?" she asked. "I thought you'd be out front, leading the charge…"

"Me? No. I'm an Earthbound, remember? Don't belong." He stepped into the light of Alice's flames, twirling his baton in his hands. "You're going in after Mallory, aren't you?"

"Yes."

"Then you're going to need a little backup. What do you say?"

"What do I say?" She pointed to what looked like a loading-bay door, padlocked shut. "I say… what are we waiting for?"

The door was a corrugated metal shutter, large enough for a van to back through. Castor peered at the hasp of the padlock, attached to a small steel loop set into the ground. "Just to make this clear," he said, smashing his boot down onto it – once, twice, three times until it cracked – "I'm very much *off* duty right now." He kicked the fragments of metal out of the way and heaved on the door, which rattled up and over their heads, leaving a gaping hole ahead of them. Alice shot a look over her shoulder. The angels were still waiting.

She and Castor were not.

The smell was like walking into a wall. Solid, thick, heavy. She couldn't just taste it, she could *feel* it. There was a faint green glow coming from the emergency lighting in the rafters, high above – just enough to make out the stacks of crates that stood around the space. They were going to have to tread carefully.

"What on earth is that smell?" Alice's voice was muffled by her sleeve, clamped over her face in an attempt to shut it out.

Castor didn't seem particularly bothered by it. He pointed at something in the far corner. "That. Come on."

"You want me to get *closer* to it? *Why*?"

"Because." He tugged at her arm and headed towards it. Pulling a face, she followed – only to walk straight into his outstretched arm a moment later.

"What…?"

He was pointing down with his other hand.

She looked.

He had stopped her on the edge of a large pit in the floor, her toes actually sticking out into empty air. It reminded her of the mechanic's pit in the garage her father used to take their car to when she was little. Only that pit had been smaller – much smaller. And less full of…

She peered into the pit, straining her eyes in the faint light.

…Less full of entrails.

"Oh, god."

"Believe me when I say there's absolutely nothing godly about this place."

"What is that?"

"You really want me to tell you?"

"No. I really don't." More than anything, Alice wanted to look away, but she couldn't. Her eyes just kept on staring. They wouldn't close, wouldn't blink, wouldn't move. "I think I can see a finger."

"I think you need to stop looking." Gently, he pushed her back and away from the pit, although he didn't move himself. "This is what they do, Alice. *This*. They were like us, once. All the Fallen. They were just like us."

"What happened to them, do you think?"

"Lucifer happened. Lucifer promised them freedom: he just neglected to tell them what he was freeing them *from*. Hope. This is the work of the hopeless. No-one with any hope in their soul could do this." He stared down into the pit.

"One of them thanked me. As he burned, he thanked me."

"You were killing him. It's probably the first mercy he's seen since he Fell." At last, he stepped back from the pit. "Don't let it bother you."

"Bother me? Compared to what? This?" She waved towards the mess on the floor of the pit. "Because this is taking 'bothering me' to a whole new level."

Somewhere in the darkness, something growled.

"And that was what?" Alice asked, taking an involuntary step closer to Castor.

"Time we weren't here."

"Guard dog?"

"If only. Come on." He skirted around the pit and towards the stacks of crates, with Alice close behind.

They threaded their way through the towers of boxes, and Alice couldn't help but stop once or twice, listening for the growling again. It was still there, but it was faint – and, thankfully, getting fainter.

"You're not going to tell me what that was?" she asked.

"Nope. Certainly not here, in the dark. You'll thank me later."

"If there *is* a later..." she muttered. Funnily enough, running face-first into Lucifer bothered her a whole lot less than unspecified animals growling at her in the dark.

At the end of the maze of boxes, they came to another stretch of concrete, and a door. Beside the door sat a heap of what looked like black binbags. It looked like someone had emptied a skip against the wall, letting the bags fall where they would; some had spilled their contents across the floor and each other.

In front of them, Alice saw what was unmistakably part of an arm, just lying there. Almost casually.

"I need to leave now," she said.

"I don't think this is the worst of it." Castor's grip tightened on his baton, and he tucked it behind him.

"Does it say more about you or about me that I knew you were going to say that?"

He didn't answer. Instead, he crept ahead and pushed the door open with the end of his baton.

He stepped through, fumbling for a light switch on the other side, and Alice felt them. She felt them before she saw them. She felt the pain and the fear and the hate... and it broke her heart.

There were cages lining the corridor. It stretched the full length of the warehouse; cramped, mesh-fronted cages.

And there were people in them.

Men. Women. Children.

Young and old; frightened and filthy and locked in cages in the dark.

They flinched as the lights burst into life overhead – some cowering back into their cages, some merely blinking at the strangers in the light.

"Who are they?" she asked Castor. He was turning from one row of cages to the other, a puzzled expression on his face.

"I don't know." One cage in particular had caught his eye, and he crouched down in front of it. There was a tiny, dirty bundle at the back of it. It didn't appear to be moving. "Hey," he said as softly as he could. "Hey there..."

The bundle moved. Not much, but it definitely moved.

"I've come to help. Will you let me help you?"

The bundle moved again.

"Can you keep a secret?" Castor leaned up to the mesh, hooking his fingers through.

A face appeared above the fabric at the back of the cage. It was a little boy. He couldn't be more than five or six; his hair stuck up in a dozen different directions and his face was streaked with dirt. At first, he gazed blankly at Castor, who smiled in encouragement.

"I said: can you keep a secret?"

The boy nodded.

"Well, alright, then." And in one movement, Castor tightened his fingers on the door and pulled, wrenching it free. He stood up, tossing it aside... and without taking his eyes from the little boy, he opened his wings.

It was slow, and it was deliberate, and all of them saw it. Everyone in the cages. They saw as Castor's wings unfurled, the feathers stretching over one another. Clipped or not, they were the first angel wings these people had ever seen.

He opened his wings, and Alice realised that she could hear someone laughing... or not laughing, exactly, but giggling.

It was the boy.

Doing her best to extinguish the flames that still burned about her, she crouched in front of the now-open cage and held out her hand.

"My name's Alice. What's yours?"

He looked at her, and shook his head.

"That's alright – you don't have to tell me. Are you ready to come out of there?"

He nodded, and slowly began to crawl out. She reached in and helped him as much as she could, but he recoiled at her touch. She couldn't blame him.

"It's okay. I won't hurt you. This is my friend Castor. We're here to get you out."

The boy turned his face towards Castor, and the first thing he did was to reach for his wings.

Castor knelt down in front of him, rolling one of his wings forwards around his shoulder for the little boy to touch. He giggled again as his fingers brushed the feathers, and he smiled at Castor. After a moment, Castor rolled his wing back.

"So, you didn't answer my question. Can you keep a secret?"

"Yes..." he said.

"That's good. Your name. It's Riley, isn't it?"

"Yes."

Alice raised an eyebrow, but Castor simply tapped his wrist. Zadkiel's choir.

"Riley, do you see that door, right there?"

Riley turned his whole body to follow Castor's finger, saw the door, and turned back. He nodded.

"I want you to go through that door, and straight through the warehouse on the other side. I don't want you to look at anything. Can you do that?"

Another nod.

"There's a big hole in the floor in the middle, so be careful you don't fall. On the other side, there's a big door and it's open. As soon as you can see it, I want you to run for it. You run, you hear me? No matter what you hear, no matter what you see. You run for that door and you *do not look back*."

Riley slid his hand into Castor's.

"I'm afraid not. I have to help more people. But I want you to be the first one out, so they know the way to go. They'll follow you." He squeezed the child's hand. "Can you be brave, and show them? Can you do that for me?"

There was a pause, and another nod – solemn this time.

"I thought so." Castor slid his hand away from Riley's and reached behind him. There was a faint snapping sound, and he produced a large, dirty-grey feather which he handed to the boy. "Here. Take this. It'll help you to be brave."

Riley eyed it for a moment, then closed his fist tightly around it – and just like that, he turned and ran for the door. The sound of his footsteps, fast and light, echoed through the warehouse, and Alice and Castor watched him fade into the dark.

"Now," said Castor, rubbing his hands together, "Let's do something about the rest of these people, shall we?"

The doors to the cages had started to rattle. Some were being shaken by the captives behind them; some were... not. Something was shaking them, something else. Something outside. The people locked inside were shouting; screaming. A few stayed silent.

"Let me," said Alice. She had been looking at the cages while Castor talked to the boy. They didn't look as though they had been built to withstand much by way of heat...

"Alice, if you get this wrong..."

"I won't."

"You'll kill them all..."

"I *won't*. I can do this. You'll see."

"Alright..." Castor took a step backwards, and raised his voice over the noise. "Everybody get back! We're getting you out of here, but you need to trust us! Get right back. Cover your faces if you can..." He shot a glance at Alice, who tipped her head back and took a deep breath. She thought about the length of the corridor. The space between the cages. The wire mesh.

"Ready?"

"Ready."

"On three. One... two..."

Alice stretched out her arms on either side of her; slipping her fingers through the mesh on either side.

"Three."

Alice closed her eyes, and the mesh burned. It burned in a moving wave, scorching its way down the corridor, filling the space with blinding red light. There was a scream from somewhere ahead of them, but no other sound but the fire.

And as suddenly as it had flared, it was gone.

The fronts of the cages had simply melted away, leaving their occupants frightened and, in some cases, a little scorched around the edges, but otherwise unharmed. Where the doors had been were jagged-edged holes, and rapidly setting silver puddles on the floor.

Castor didn't wait.

"Everybody out! Out! Out now!" he shouted, and the prisoners leapt into life, scrambling past them and past one another. Several of them slowed as they passed; some stared at Alice with something between disbelief and fear, and more than one gazed open-mouthed at Castor's wings.

As the last of them fled through the darkness of the warehouse, Castor nodded.

"It's time we stopped hiding," he said to Alice, and set off down the corridor.

Sitting on the floor between Mallory and Toby, and still trying to work out what he should do next, Vin heard something rattle. Frowning, he looked around, and after a while he had managed to narrow it down to either Mallory's chain, or one of the fantastically unpleasant bits of metal Rimmon had strewn across the floor.

As the rattling got louder, and louder... and louder, he realised it wasn't either of them.

It was *all* of them.

"Mallory," he hissed, grabbing Mallory's shoulder and shaking it. "Mallory!" There was no response. "Mallory, you jackass. Wake the fuck up! The cavalry's coming...."

CHAPTER THIRTY-SEVEN

Pay the Piper

RIMMON RAN, AS fast as he could. His coat flared out behind him and his shoes slipped on the concrete floor, sending him skidding into a wall, but he didn't let it stop him.

He ran and ran and ran, with only one thought on his mind.

They're here.

He barely managed to stop before he ran into the door ahead of him, and slapped his hand on it three times by way of a knock. He didn't wait for an answer, but threw himself through it.

There, Lucifer stood peering at his own frozen face. The eyes that should have been Gwyn's shone red, reflected in the ice in which his body was locked. He traced a finger down the block, trailing it along the chains and the padlocks, and then – smiling – he lifted his finger to his mouth and licked it.

"Why am I still waiting?" he asked, and although his tone was light and breezy, it was hard to miss the menace in it. "Michael will be here any moment, and I'm nowhere near ready to greet my brother..."

"A few minutes," muttered Gabriel from behind the block, where he was huddled with Xaphan and Forfax.

"Gabe... Gabe?" Lucifer rubbed his hands together. "A moment, if you would?"

Gabriel edged around the block, careful not to so much as brush against its surface. He stood in front of Lucifer, shifting his weight uncomfortably.

"You've only just joined us – and we couldn't be more delighted to have you here – so I'll let that little... *faux pas* slide. But from now on?" He lashed out with his fingers, scoring deep lines across Gabriel's cheeks. "*No-one* tells me to wait. *I* tell *you* what to do. Am I abundantly clear?"

"Yes. You are." Chastened, Gabriel hung his head.

"Good, good. Now, why are you standing around talking to me? You're wasting time..."

Gabriel said nothing, and edged back round the block to where Forfax was raising his cane. The jewel on the top of it glittered in the light as he spun it around his hand, throwing fragments of rainbows onto their faces. The light sparkled and danced, and suddenly it was gone, the gem clouding over and turning black. Forfax held it steady, and all three watched it intently as it cracked across the top, the crack deepening and widening and *opening*... and inside, there was a cube.

Xaphan pulled a pair of tweezers out of his pocket and jabbed them into the decaying bauble, fishing the cube out. It could have been metal, although colours swirled across the surface. Xaphan held it up and they all nodded approvingly at it before he snapped his fingers and held out his hand. Gabriel unwrapped the roll of cloth he had been holding, and took out a slim rod. It had a groove at one end, and a flat disc at the other, and it resembled nothing so much as a key. A broken key.

With a look of triumph, Xaphan held up the two pieces, one in each hand – and pressed the side of the cube into the groove at the end of the rod. There was the faintest of clicks, and the key was whole.

The room shook, and Lucifer leaned around the ice block, raising an eyebrow at them.

"Any time. Any time..."

Gabriel felt the chill of Lucifer's gaze on his back, and he watched Xaphan pull a cloth out of a plastic bag beside his feet. The cloth oozed, dripping something thick and dark onto the floor as he wiped it over the palm of his hand.

"I think it's time to show the angels that the world has changed... don't you?" He grinned, showing too many teeth, and slapped the flat of his hand onto the surface of the ice.

Lucifer's head snapped back, red eyes staring at the ceiling as the hand-print wept blood. All eyes except Lucifer's were on it, watching... watching as the scarlet thickened, darkened and turned to rust – and was sucked into the ice. The mark grew fainter and fainter, fading fast... but behind it, thin red lines began to creep through the solid blue of the prison.

"This is it," said Forfax, discarding his cane. It had served its purpose.

Xaphan wiped his hand clean. "This is it."

THE WHOLE BUILDING was shaking by the time Alice and Castor cleared the corridor; it felt not unlike standing underneath a low-flying helicopter. Or six.

"Why aren't they coming?"

"They already have." Castor's mouth set in a grim line. "They're here."

"So where are they?"

"Following orders."

They pushed through a pair of metal swing doors and found themselves in another long room lit by emergency lighting. There were low counters running down it, splitting it into three... and there was that smell again. Sweeter, though, and mixed with something else. Bleach.

"Castor... where are we?"

"Kitchen."

"Kitchen?"

"Kitchen."

"Promise me you're not going to turn on the lights?"

"Absolutely."

They fumbled their way through in the near-dark, relying on dim green bulbs and flickering flames, and Alice was more grateful than she imagined possible when they reached the far end.

"I hate this," she said to Castor. He stopped, and when she turned to him, all she could see was the shadow of his face.

"I know," he said. "But it's what we do."

"You ever thought about changing career?"

"Sure. I became a copper, didn't I?" There was something close to a laugh in his voice. "World of difference."

"Castor..."

"Mmm?"

"I need to... I just... Look." Alice cleared her throat. "I'm having a hard time being around you. You..."

"He died protecting me, Alice. He died *for* me. I can't exactly put a lid on that... on how it feels."

"I know. It's..."

"Besides, you've not melted the roof. Or the floor. Or my face, so you're doing fine. But point taken. We'll move it along. Carefully. We don't know where they are, or if they're waiting for us."

"They're *always* bloody waiting for us," Alice groaned.

There was an ear-shattering crash from somewhere in the building, and the floor beneath them shook. Alice looked at Castor, and Castor looked back at her.

"Following orders."

"WAKE UP. WAKE up. Wake up." Vin was almost yelling into Mallory's ear. "You great big..."

He froze at a sound in the corridor, pressing himself against the wall behind the door. Footsteps.

Rimmon was coming back.

Vin picked up his rope again, winding it around his fingers and letting the knotted end dangle. When Rimmon came to the doorway, he would swing it up and around the side of the door, and it should hit him in the face. Or the throat. Or possibly go straight over his head: Vin realised he had no idea how tall Rimmon actually was... Still, maybe he'd be lucky. And maybe Rimmon had the keys on him. And if neither of those things worked, he could always improvise... even if he'd have to face Mallory sulking about it afterwards.

The footsteps came closer, hurrying now. There was more than one set. Two, maybe? Three? The echo made it hard to be sure. But they were coming closer, and fast.

They approached the door, and stopped.

Took another step closer and, finding the door open, halted again.

They stepped into the doorframe... and Vin swung into action, throwing out his arm. The rope curled up and around the door, where it met what looked like a baton. It wound itself round the rod, and the knot grazed the door with a harmless *clunk*.

Vin stared at the baton poking around the edge of the door.

The rope started to smoulder, smoke spiralled up and into the air.

Now *that* was something Vin *did* recognise... and he stepped out from behind the door.

Alice and Castor, his baton still raised, stared back at him.

Without a word, Alice threw herself at him, hugging him tight. "You're alive."

"I don't die easy. Not like this one..." Vin jerked his thumb over his shoulder.

"No. He's not..."

"He's not. But it's not for lack of trying." He stood aside before she could push him out of the way, and Alice rushed over to Mallory.

"What happened?" She stared at him.

"We had a slight... disagreement."

"What the hell about?"

"About whether or not his dying was an option."

"*What?*"

"Don't."

"*Seriously?*"

"It wasn't my idea..."

"And you decided to test the sodding hypothesis, Vhnori!" she shouted, slapping her hand on the floor. "You're unbelievable! Why didn't you just get him out?"

"Can't." Vin knelt beside her, and lifted Mallory's wrist. The lines tracking up his arm seemed to be spreading.

"What is that?" Alice peered at them, and Vin shook his head.

"I don't know. There's something about this manacle. It's stopping him being... him. We can't break it, and whatever it's doing, he can't heal it. Raphael could, maybe..."

"Raphael's not here. But Michael is."

"And the others?"

"About that..." She tailed off, unsure how to continue, but Castor cut in.

"Zadkiel is dead. Gabriel betrayed us, and has joined Lucifer. They have the key."

"Restoration?"

"I'd say so."

"Huh. I try and relax for a couple of hours and the whole world goes to shit..."

"Now's not the time to kid around, Vin. Adriel said something about Lucifer calling his choir."

"Yeah... he will. Adriel included." Vin frowned; bit his lip. "So that'll be fun."

"What now?"

"You're the rescue party, you tell me."

There was a soft groan from the other side of the room, making them all jump. Alice looked up from Mallory, and for the first time, she noticed the chair.

"What's that?" she said, her attention suddenly on nothing but the slumped shape there.

"That's... a long story."

"The long story just groaned."

"Rimmon was using him as leverage. To get to Mallory." Vin paused, and made a face. "Guess it wasn't that long a story after all."

"And you're just going to leave him tied to the chair?"

"Same problem I've got with Mallory. I can't untie him."

"What, you never went to boy scouts or something?" Alice was walking across to the chair.

"Don't," Vin called out, but it was already too late.

"Toby?"

His face was swollen almost beyond recognition. Almost. But she knew him. She knew the curve of his jaw; the scar that ran down his cheek and which stood out despite the slick covering of blood and sweat and who knew what else. And she knew his eyes when they opened and looked at her.

"Toby..."

"Alice." He spoke in barely more than a whisper.

"What happened?"

"Am I dead?"

"What?"

"Am I in hell?"

"No. You're not in hell – trust me on that one. Although..." She rocked back on her heels and looked around at the cell. Based on what she'd seen so far, this was nothing like hell. It was far, far worse.

"Come on. We're going to get you out of here," she said, her fingers running up and down the ropes, looking for a knot.

His chest was heaving, and for a moment she was afraid he was too badly hurt: that he was having a seizure, or going into shock – or whatever else people did when they'd been treated like this. He hurt so badly that he could barely even feel the pain: he was numb, and Alice was appalled to realise that she was grateful. He couldn't feel it... so she didn't have to, and she was ashamed of the relief she felt.

The ropes were stiff and tight, and she couldn't move them. She looked up at Vin and Castor, both of whom stood beside Mallory's prone figure on the floor.

"Are you going to help me?"

"Alice..."

"I need you to..."

"Alice."

"If I can just..." Her fingers were digging into the ropes, but still they didn't move.

"Alice!"

"*Help me!*"

"They won't," said a voice from outside the door, one that echoed inside Alice's head; and Michael stepped into the cell. There had been fighting already – that much was clear from the state of his armour... and the look on his face. He stepped into the cell and fixed his gaze on her, and Alice felt very small.

"I need to untie the ropes..."

"You need to step away."

"All I have to do..."

"What you have to do is stop, and step away."

"No."

"I'm telling you to step away."

"No." Alice drew closer to the chair. Toby shifted, confused.

"Alice? What's happening?"

"Nothing. It's alright, Toby. I'm going to get you out of here..."

Michael took another step closer – and too late, Alice saw the warning flash in his eyes.

The mirrored room was there again, pressing on the edges of her mind. She could feel it, the cold of the glass and the heat of the flames. She could smell burning skin... and still she would not move away from Toby.

Michael sighed, and it was more a sigh of pity than of anger, but the expression on his face did not change.

"You made your choice."

"I didn't know...."

"You didn't know? I told you there was a human here. I told you to choose: human or angel. You chose to save the angel."

"It's Mallory..."

"Quite. And you said it yourself: you would always have chosen him."

"But you didn't tell me..."

"You never thought to ask."

Alice hung her head. "I can't."

"You can. And you will – unless you would leave Mallory here to die?"

"No!"

"Then step away." At last, Michael's voice softened. "You see, Alice, making the choice is easy. *Living* with it... that's something altogether different."

Michael turned away from her and towards Mallory, stepping past Vin (who had backed himself as far into the wall and away from Michael as he possibly could) and stooping to examine the chains. He rubbed them between his fingers and looked thoughtful. "Helliron. How quaint." He ran a fingertip over the symbols set in the metal and laughed coldly. "I see Xaphan's grammar hasn't improved... still, this is new for him. Clever. We shall have to remember this." With his other hand, he made a quick gesture, drawing something in the air – and the manacle flared red. It didn't spring open, as Alice had hoped it would, but the writing on it flamed once, then vanished. Michael let the chain drop back to the floor with a clatter. "Still unpleasant, but now he should be able to get himself out of it. And if he can't... well, frankly, he deserves to stay put."

He knelt beside Mallory, and his fingers moved through the air; twisting and spinning and looping around and over themselves, drawing a complex shape which hung over the unconscious angel's head, glowing... then vanished. Michael whispered something into Mallory's ear. He stood, nodded at Castor, and gave Vin a strange look that Alice did not quite understand.

"I've wasted enough of my time. When he wakes, give him these and tell him to report. And bring her." He handed Castor a familiar L-shaped bundle of cloth. "You hear me? Bring her."

"'By your choices, you muzzle yourself'?" Alice repeated his words back to him, and he nodded thoughtfully.

"Now you live with it. As we must."

And just that like, he was gone.

Apparently on cue, Mallory sat bolt upright, squinting at Vin. "You hit me. You bastard! You hit me!"

"You deserved it."

"I was... I was saying something, wasn't I? It was important."

"No idea, mate. I usually tune you out: you're just a string of annoying sounds to me."

"Now..." Mallory fell silent as he spotted Alice, and his face cracked into a smile. "You're alright."

"'Alright' is a relative term."

"You're alright enough." He took in her face, how close she was to the chair; her hands still resting on the rope. "You know."

"What – you were hoping I wouldn't?"

"I'm sorry."

Alice saw Mallory glance at Vin, who shook his head. Mallory's shoulders sagged and his face clouded.

"Michael said to leave him, didn't he?"

"He said it was you or him... but he didn't say it was him, and I don't know what to do."

"Michael offered you a choice."

"But I didn't know!"

"We never do. We never know what our choices will do – either to us or to other people. That's what makes them *choices*. If we knew what would happen, we'd always take the easy outcome: hardly choosing, is it?"

"If..."

"I'm sorry, Alice. That's all I can say." He stood, slowly; wincing as he straightened. Giving his wrist a shake, he peered at the manacle. "Michael couldn't be bothered to actually unlock it, then?" he asked. Vin shrugged, and Mallory sighed. "Of course not. I've got to do that my bloody self, haven't I?"

As he fiddled with the manacle, Castor cleared his throat.

"He said to give you these," he said, holding out Mallory's guns. Mallory brightened.

"Ah. I was wondering where they'd got to." The manacle pinged open. "So much for that," he said, rubbing his wrist. He took the guns from Castor, checking them over and pulling back the slider on one, then on the other. As he went over the second one, he glanced up at Castor.

"You need one?"

"I'm fine."

"Here." Mallory held it out to him. "It's yours."

"I said I'm fine."

"You're lying. You're a long way off fine. I don't know what's happened, but it's not good. Take the gun." He waved it, grip-first, at Castor, who finally took it and nodded his thanks.

"Michael wants us?" Mallory asked Vin, tucking his gun into the back of his belt.

"He does." Vin glanced from Mallory to Toby to Alice… and slipped out into the corridor with Castor.

"Well, then." Mallory looked at Alice, still huddled close to Toby's chair. "I'll give you a minute – no longer. We can't risk it. One minute and then you're coming with us. Even if I have to carry you," he said. He paused beside the door. "I was prepared to die for him, Alice. I want you to know that. Still am…"

"So how come you're walking away?" Her voice was hard, bitter.

"You want the simple answer? Fine. It's Michael. If he says the choice is made and you have to live with it, that's it. So do we. Choice is made."

"And that's it, is it? You're prepared to die for him, until Michael wags a finger at you?"

"It's not like that."

"Then tell me, Mallory. Tell me what the fuck it *is* like. Because I thought you were supposed to be an angel. If you won't help him, what good are you?"

Mallory rubbed his face wearily with a filthy hand. "It's not my choice, Alice. You made the choice. You. You chose."

"But you didn't. So *help him*!"

"I can't. Because it was your choice, I don't have the power to overturn it. Michael has seen to that. I *cannot* help him. I don't have the free will. I have to follow my orders."

"Hypocrite." Alice bit back a tear. "You're a hypocrite, you know that? You talk about *choices*. You talk about how they matter. About how every decision we make matters..."

"It does..."

"And then when it's convenient, you stand there and you shrug and you say that, hey, it's not up to you..."

"It's not! It was up to *you*!" Mallory's voice rose as he lost his temper and banged his hand against the door. "You stupid girl; you still don't understand, do you? I'm not *like* you. I'm not *human*. I don't follow the same rules as you, and sometimes freedom is a luxury I don't have. This is one of those times. Right now, I can't help him. You want to see what happens if I try? *Fine*." He spat the last word at her, and strode towards Toby... and suddenly stopped, halfway there, as though he had hit a wall. His whole body jerked back, and there was the unmistakable smell of burning feathers as the tips of his wings started to smoulder. "Choose, Alice. Choose. We leave him, or you have me die trying to save him... and you lose us both."

Alice stared at him, at the smoke coiling up from the edges of his wings, and she understood. Michael had given him an order – a real order – and he was powerless to disobey. Michael had made sure that it wasn't only Alice shackled by her choice: he'd tied Mallory to it as well. Just to be doubly sure. The woman on the beach had been right: the angels were cruel. She shook her head, and – relieved – Mallory took a step back. He relaxed instantly, ruffling his wings as they healed. "Thank you."

"Don't thank me, Mallory."

"One minute." He watched her for a moment, his face inscrutable, then stepped outside, leaving Alice alone with Toby.

He barely seemed to know what was happening. She wasn't surprised, and she couldn't blame him. He had no idea where he was, why he was there, what he had done (or not done), and none of it made any sense. He must have been there since the riot. She'd tried to push him away. To protect him. She'd done well at that, hadn't she?

She brushed his hair away from his face.

"Alice... what's happening?"

"You got in the middle of something, Toby. You didn't mean to, and it wasn't your fault. But now you're in."

"I don't understand."

"I don't either."

He was looking at her now; straight at her. His eyes locked on to hers. "You're going to leave me here, aren't you?"

"I'm sorry, Toby. I'm so, so sorry."

"You said you were going to get me out..."

"I don't have a choice."

"You're just going to leave me."

"I can't..." Alice found herself drawing back from him. She hadn't meant to – not at all – but still, she had pulled away.

"You're going to leave. With them."

"I have to."

"You don't have to. You can help me!" He strained against the ropes, and the chair rocked from side to side. "Please! You can help me!"

"I can't. I can't untie the ropes, and I have to go. I'm sorry." She dropped a kiss on his forehead, along with her tears. "Someone will come back for you and get you out, I promise... I'll send someone. Just... hold on."

"You can stick your promise, Alice." Toby's voice was heavy, and it hurt Alice more than anything else in that room. She was abandoning him, and he knew it.

"I'm sorry..." she said again, and she meant it. But somehow she was beside the door and he was still tied to the chair. Still tied to the chair and beaten. Still tied to the chair and bleeding.

And she was beside the door where the angels were waiting.

Toby turned his head away from her, and there was nothing else to say.

Mallory's face was grim, but he was still waiting. "It's time to go," he said. Alice nodded.

"I know."

"Alright, then." He glanced up at Castor and Vin. "Let's go."

Toby heard them walk away. By the time the echoes of their voices had faded, the only sound left was his sobbing.

CHAPTER THIRTY-EIGHT

The Garments of Vengeance

ALICE HAD BEEN right about the fighting. While she and Castor were looking for Mallory and Vin, Michael and his choir had torn through the rest of the warehouse. Things were burning everywhere Alice looked. Sheets of paper blew along corridors – some scorched, some still on fire – and pools of fire dotted the floor. Shouts echoed through the building; shouts, and the occasional scream. Alice felt dizzy, unstable. Nothing made sense. She had left Toby. Toby, a prisoner of the Fallen, and she had left him to be tortured, perhaps even to die. Beside her was Mallory, his face blank. But he was angry, and he was hurt. Whatever Michael had done, it hurt – and more than that, it had forced him to obey. Something which never sat well with Mallory...

They rounded a corner and walked almost straight into two of the Fallen, who recoiled and gnashed their teeth at the sight of Mallory. He sidestepped one, dodging neatly and bringing his gun level with the other's heart. He pulled the trigger, and the unfortunate creature took a bullet in the chest, falling back with a shriek. Without breaking his stride, Mallory whirled around and smashed the butt of the gun into the other's face, knocking him to the ground.

"Where is he?" he shouted, leaning over the Fallen, who grinned and spat up into his face.

"He's coming home," he hissed.

"Lucifer? Fuck that. That's not who I meant and you know it," said Mallory, and sharply brought his boot up under the Fallen's chin. His head snapped back and lolled against the floor.

"Coming home, indeed. Load of old bollocks." Mallory muttered.

Castor was staring at him.

"What?" he said, stopping mid-stride.

Castor blinked back. "You're a crazy person. An actual crazy person."

"Me? No. No, right now, I'm angry. You want to see what happens when I get crazy?"

"Is that likely to happen tonight?"

"That depends on how long it takes me to find Rimmon."

"MICHAEL!" ONE OF the angel's wings was broken, and hung down at his side. Michael pulled his sword up and out of the body on the floor and turned to look at him.

"What?"

"Xaphan has been sighted. He's heading..."

"Follow him."

"You don't want us to stop him?"

"Not yet. Xaph's usually the first one to run, and he's usually the one who knows where to go. So watch him, follow him... whatever it takes."

"We could..."

"And if you kill him, what do you think Lucifer will do?"

"I understand."

"Good." Michael wiped his sword clean. "I won't have our plans spoiled – not now we're so close."

"Yes, sir." The angel saluted and hurried off.

"MICHAEL TOLD YOU to report to him." Alice was having trouble keeping up with Mallory, who was now storming ahead of them.

"Yes, he did."

"You're not, are you?"

"Oh, I will. Just not yet."

"Why?"

"Because he made this personal."

"Who? Michael?" Mallory turned abruptly to face her, and she stumbled to a halt.

"Not Michael. Rimmon."

"Oh, not again..."

"Alice?"

"What?"

"Listen to me – just for once. This is personal. More personal than you can imagine. It always has been, and I've had enough. So yes, I will go and report to Michael like the good little soldier I am... but first, I'm going to find Rimmon and I'm going to hurt him. And I'm going to enjoy it." There was an edge to his voice that Alice recognised. "So if you don't want to be there for that, I suggest you go. Now." He steamed ahead again, not waiting for a reply.

Alice frowned. "After all this? You think you can just walk away? You think you can do this without me?" she shouted after him. Behind them, Castor looked at Vin.

"They're always like this, aren't they?" he asked, gesturing to them both.

"Welcome to my life."

MALLORY THREW THE door open and marched through. "Rimmon!" he shouted. Something nearby rattled. "Rimmon!"

"He's going to get away..." Alice mumbled, following him through. It was dark on the other side, but here and there she could make out reflections: light glinting on metal. It was a big room, and it smelled of booze. "Mallory..." she said. "I don't like this."

He paid no attention. Instead, he banged his gun down on something and carried on shouting. "Rimmon! I know you're in here, you little shit!"

"Mallory...."

He was still ignoring her – but Alice had found the light switch... or rather, a bank of them. Switch by switch, she flicked them on, and then wished she hadn't.

The room smelled of booze because it was a bar. They were standing beside the counter: clad in black plastic with gold edging, it wanted to look like marble and failed. There was what seemed to be a dance floor ahead, and coloured lights spun above it, casting weird, shifting shadows. A small, round podium stood in the middle of it all, complete with a golden pole fixed to the ceiling, and Alice felt an overwhelming desire to wash her hands.

Every bottle behind the bar was broken. Some of the remains of the bottles lay on their shelves, spilling a liquid rainbow which pooled on the floor and glittered with broken glass.

But worse than the broken glass, worse than the podium, worse than the knowledge that Rimmon was in here and that Mallory wouldn't leave until he'd found him... worse than all that were the bodies.

Some of them still held shattered glasses, smashed as they fell. Some of them had been trying to run – or at least, to get away. One or two looked as though they had been trying to shield themselves, or possibly each other. Much good had it done them. A man in what had been a black suit lay face-down not three feet from Alice. The back of his head was charred and sticky. He had one arm outstretched; his fingers clasping a wallet. It was still smoking.

The Fallen had not done this.

Michael had done this.

These were not the Fallen. These were people. Michael hadn't come for Lucifer; he had come for *them*. He was sending a message to Lucifer the only way he knew how; the only way he thought Lucifer would understand. With a trail of bodies.

Alice didn't see Rimmon step out of the shadows, she didn't see Mallory grab his gun. The first she knew was the bullet that zipped past her ear, making her dive for cover behind the bar

"You aiming for me, or her, Mal?" asked Rimmon, lurking across the room. "I only ask because from here, it was kind of hard to tell."

"You're going to have to speak up, Rimmon. I can barely hear you all the way back there." Mallory waved his gun at the Fallen. "It's funny, you were so keen to get in my face earlier. Now..." He shrugged.

Rimmon snorted, but he didn't get any closer. "Why should I bother myself with you? We've won... and there's nothing you can do about it."

"I'm not sure the pissed-off Archangel knocking around the building's going to agree with you on that one."

"Michael? Are you kidding? He's the one who let all this happen! He could have stopped us at any point, but he didn't. You know why? Because he's so damn set on getting his hands on Lucifer. He doesn't care about the rest of it. He never has, and he never will. The sooner you wake up to that, the better." Rimmon laughed. "Mind you, you've never been the brightest of the bunch, have you? Look at you, standing there. You're a blunt instrument."

"Really? Want to see how blunt I can be?" Mallory squeezed the trigger of his gun, unloading the entire magazine at Rimmon's chest.

With each impact, Rimmon staggered back... and finally, finally, he fell.

Mallory didn't move. Arm still raised, he stood.

Rimmon lay flat on his back on the dancefloor... and then he started to laugh. Louder and louder he laughed, until the whole place echoed with the sound. He hauled himself to his feet – still laughing – and tugged at the front of his jacket. It fell open.

Underneath was a solid black vest, its front studded with flattened bullets.

"Same old Mallory," he said, tapping the bulletproof vest with a smirk, and pulling a gun of his own from his pocket.

Alice ducked again – wondering where the hell Vin and Castor had gone – and listened to the burst of gunfire. She found herself counting the shots... and hoping Mallory at least had enough sense to duck. Or move. Or do something sensible. The room was swimming in alcohol: one misplaced spark from her and the whole place could go up, taking them all with it. Without knowing where he was, she didn't dare risk trying to help, so instead she hid helplessly behind the bar and counted the shots.

They stopped, and she scrambled to her feet. Rimmon was still holding his arm out, the gun now swinging from his fingers and his mouth open as though he couldn't quite believe what he was seeing.

Mallory was in exactly the same spot. He hadn't moved, and at first, Alice thought that the bullets must have missed. But they hadn't. His clothing was punctuated by neat bullet holes, almost lost amid the buckshot holes, and a trickle of blood ran down the left side of his chest.

"You're going to have to try a lot harder than that, Rimmon," he said, and from where Alice was standing, it almost looked like he smiled. Rimmon turned to run... but Mallory was there first, making it across the room in the blink of an eye.

He had left his gun on the bar.

In his hand, he had a metal rod.

"VHNORI? ARE YOU alright?" Castor caught Vin's arm as he stumbled. Something was wrong. Castor's mind itched as the other Earthbound gasped for breath, and Vin slumped against the wall, his face twisting in pain.

"You need to fetch them. Fetch Alice. Fetch Mallory. There's no more time. Get them out." He stared straight into Castor's eyes... and Castor flinched.

Vin's eyes were completely black.

ONE BY ONE, the chains fell away from the ice. Each made a sound like a funeral bell as it hit the floor.

A single crack split the surface of the block, running from top to bottom... and deep inside the ice, Lucifer's eyes opened.

"MALLORY!" ALICE WAS screaming at him, but he didn't hear her; he *couldn't* hear her. All he could hear was the sound of blood rushing as he brought the rod he'd picked up from the bar down on Rimmon's prone form. The metal was glowing bright red, and it hurt to hold it – Alice's doing – but he held on all the same, the skin of his palm blistering. There was fire nearby – he could feel that too – but nothing else mattered. Only this.

"Mallory!"

TOBY WAS STILL weeping when he heard another set of footsteps.

It was Alice. It had to be. She'd come back for him.

"Afraid not," said a voice he did not know, but it was not kind, and at that moment, he despaired. Whatever hope he had left abandoned him.

"They left you, didn't they? Left you behind. Abandoned you when you needed them the most. Even her. *Especially* her." There was a sigh. "See, that's the thing about angels. Can't trust them. The second you do, that's when they'll always, *always* let you down. Never rely on them. That was your mistake. That's what got you into this mess in the first place." He paused, and Toby could hear him smiling. "Now... you and I. We should have a little chat, don't you think?"

* * *

CASTOR BURST THROUGH the door and saw them through the fire. Alice was burning, shouting Mallory's name as he leaned over the figure on the floor, and Castor knew instantly what was happening. Without thinking, he aimed the gun that Mallory had given him and he pulled the trigger.

The shot caught Mallory's shoulder, punching a hole through muscle and bone... and he dropped the rod. He hesitated, and it was all Alice needed. She slipped in front of Mallory, the fire dying as she moved, and placed herself between him and Rimmon.

"Stop," she said. "Stop now."

"No."

She could see him shaking with anger, and there was something dark in his eyes.

"This is what they want. It's all part of the game to them."

"I don't care."

"But I do." She put a hand on his shoulder. "This isn't you."

"You have no idea who I am, Alice." Mallory's shaking subsided. He was coming back to himself.

"Sure I do," she said gently.

Castor tucked the gun away. "Mallory!" he called. "It's Vin..." He hurried back out through the door, and Mallory charged after him.

Alice stood over Rimmon, who had curled himself into a ball under the ferocity of Mallory's attack.

"You should have let him kill me..." His voice was thick with blood, and it sounded altogether too like Toby's.

"Maybe. I mean, that was a hell of a beating. And you don't heal like he does. I'm not sure you ever really recover from something like that." Alice looked down at him. "Mercy's not something the angels are very good at, is it? I wonder whether they even understand the concept. Humans: they get it. Or at least they did before you came along and started changing everything. They understand mercy. They may not always like it, but they *get* it. So there's humans, and there's angels. And then there's me. It's taken me long enough to figure it out, but I can be both. I'm not one or the other." She leaned close to Rimmon's ear. "Guess which one I'm being right now?"

He made a whimpering sound, and Alice stood up. "I'll leave you to work on that, shall I?" She walked towards the door. "See you round, Rimmon."

The door swung shut behind her, and Rimmon lay on the floor, surrounded by bodies, as the bright disco lights swirled above him.

CHAPTER THIRTY-NINE

Death, Be Not Proud

THE ICE SHATTERED. Diamond shards flew across the room, clattering into the walls and showering Gabriel with chips of ice... and Lucifer stepped out of his prison and extended his wings, laughing as the shackles fell away.

"Call them," he said. Gabriel nodded.

Lucifer stretched his arms out wide, curling his fingers in on his palms and smiling.

"I knew I was always your favourite."

"They'll fight..."

"Of course they will. And I wouldn't enjoy it nearly so much if they didn't."

THERE WAS THE sound of feathers, and something like whispering voices... and Adriel appeared from the shadows. He looked the same as always: neat in his morning suit, with his beard and hair clipped. He didn't flinch when he saw Lucifer, nor when he saw Gabriel behind him. He simply waited.

Lucifer smiled at him, holding out his arms.

"Welcome, brother."

"You called me."

"I did. You aren't pleased to see me?"

"I hardly think you need to ask."

"Clearly it's been too long since you had to answer to anyone... *Kneel.*"

Adriel blinked his black eyes and knelt before Lucifer, smoothing the fabric of his suit as he did.

Lucifer circled him. "Do you serve?"

There was no answer.

"I say again... do you serve?"

Adriel still didn't answer, but simply cocked his head on one side and blinked again.

"Adriel... I won't ask again."

Adriel lowered his head and opened his wings. "I serve."

Lucifer beamed... but then his smile became a frown. Adriel was smiling... and his eyes were bleeding; staining his face not red, but black. His wings, too, were changing. Fading; the colour leaching out of them until they were first grey, then white. And Adriel knelt before Lucifer and laughed at him, shaking out his wings and looking up at him with brown eyes.

"You can force me to serve. You cannot force me to surrender."

"Who is it?" Lucifer grabbed him by the throat, hauling him to his feet. "Who?"

"You cannot take the office by force, Lucifer. You of all people should know that. It must be earned. It can be passed on, but never taken.

"You abdicated, and so have I. You can't have it back."

"*Who*?" Lucifer's angelic face twisted, and for a moment it seemed that he had too many teeth; that his cheeks were too long and too hollow... and that his mouth should not open quite as wide as it did.

"You'll find out soon enough," said Adriel. "And in the meantime, I serve." He pulled free from Lucifer's grasp and swept into a low, mocking bow.

THEY STUMBLED OUT into the street. There were angels flooding out of the warehouse, and smoke curling from its windows.

"We're not going to be popular when Michael catches up with us," Mallory said through gritted teeth. Vin's arm was draped around his shoulder. Something exploded in the building behind them.

"No change there," said Alice, sliding out from beneath Vin's other arm as they set him down on the ground, everything else forgotten. His teeth were chattering. "What's wrong with him?"

Vin suddenly hunched over, clutching his ribs and crying out, and Alice started back. "Can't you help him?" There was fire at her wrists and in her hair; sparks dancing behind her and drifting into the night.

Mallory looked grim. "There's nothing I can do."

"What's..."

But Alice was cut off by another yelp from Vin, and the horror on Mallory and Castor's faces mirrored her own as they watched his wings stretch; saw the darkness seep along them from the tips like ink, creeping further and further up the feathers until his wings were black to the roots... and then there was nothing more. Alice crouched in front of Vin, edging closer. She could see his back heaving with each breath; see the outline of his wings shaking as they folded in on themselves.

"Vin?"

There was no answer.

"Alice..." Mallory was ducking down, holding out his hand. "You should come over here to me."

"No. I... Vin!" she said, and scooted closer to him, wrapping her arm around his shoulders. She could feel him trembling; feel the damp of the sweat that had soaked his clothes.

"I'm okay..." he said. "I just... need a minute." His voice shook almost as badly as the rest of him. "I'm fine..."

"Yeah, right," muttered Mallory, and Alice glared at him before turning back to Vin.

"What..." And she tailed off – because Vin was looking at her. His forehead dripped with sweat, and his short, dark hair was drenched with it… but all Alice could see as he raised his head were eyes of pure black.

"Vhnori…" she whispered, "what did you *do?*"

"Why d'you think I was in Adriel's office?" Vin had finally stopped shaking, and was sitting at least vaguely upright on the tarmac.

"I thought you were waiting. For us."

"Well, there was that…" He wagged his head from side to side. "Adriel knew what was going to happen. All this was planned."

"Planned. Because this looks so beautifully planned." Alice waved sadly at the burning warehouse. There was no sign of the fire brigade, despite the plumes of smoke and the flames spilling from the windows. She imagined they had quite enough on their hands elsewhere. One more fire was nothing.

"Alright… maybe not the details. But Michael knew. He knew Gabriel would turn on him; he has done ever since hell."

"But he told Gabriel that he'd restore him if he found the way to… Oh. Boy, do I feel stupid." Alice's eyes closed in resignation as she realised what had happened.

Michael had set it up. All of it.

All along, he'd wanted Lucifer restored… and the Fallen had done it for him.

"Bingo."

"But… you."

"Yeah. Me."

"You knew."

"Most of it."

"And you didn't say anything?"

"Who do you think I'm more afraid of? You, or Michael?"

"Me. It should definitely be me."

"Funny you should say that… No." He grinned weakly. "Adriel knew Lucifer would summon him."

"He wanted his old job back..." Mallory interrupted. "But he couldn't have it if Adriel had already passed it on."

"Exactly," said Vin, wiping his forehead with the back of his sleeve. "Which is where I come in."

"But why you?" Alice asked.

"Like I'm supposed to know?"

"Well, yes." Alice shook her head. "All this." She glanced at Castor, who was keeping his face absolutely blank. "All this... for what?"

"For victory," said Mallory. "Everything else is just collateral damage."

"*Everything*?"

"Everything. He wants to win. And he wants to stay the winner. Absolute war, remember?"

"He's more of a bastard than I thought." She thought about the library; about everything he'd said. "He almost had me fooled that time."

"Alice..." Mallory cleared his throat, breaking into her train of thought.

"What?"

"It's... it's nothing."

"No, what?"

"Well, it's just... if Vin's taken over from Adriel..."

"Yes?"

"Well..." – Mallory coughed into his hand – "doesn't that... kind of make him... your new boss?"

"I quit."

And as the fire raged behind them and the angels scattered, they sat on the tarmac and Alice buried her head in her hands, and despite themselves and despite everything else they tried to understand, and to work out who had won. *If* anyone had won.

They didn't see Castor slip away into the darkness.

They didn't see Michael narrow his eyes at the sound of their voices, his sword strapped to his side and his breastplate spattered with blood and soot, before turning away and melting back into the shadow, ready for the next fight.

They didn't see the first of the blue and red lights flashing on the far side of the building.

They didn't see Rimmon half-walk and half-crawl out of the door to the loading bay, and they didn't see the shadows which moved across them as something flew high above in the dark sky.

"You know that from now on, it gets harder, don't you?" said Mallory at last.

"This has been easy? Up to now?" Alice said. "Easy? Seriously?" She looked at Vin and blew out an exasperated breath, "And *you* I can't even begin to talk about... You're telling me that was *easy*?" She didn't mention Toby. She couldn't bring herself to; not until she could decide who she blamed more: Mallory, Michael, or herself. The first tear spilled down her cheek, lighting up the darkness. The wound was going to take a long time to heal.

"Easy? Sure it was. Walk in the park. Now the fun really starts: the balance is well and truly in their favour, and I think it's fair to say we're outnumbered and outgunned. Which is just how I like it. Except for that shotgun Gwyn had. Bastard thing. I *hated* that." Mallory rolled his head back, stretching his neck and looking up at the sky.

Alice sniffed, then scrubbed at her face. Adriel had told her to help them; to help them remember that there was more than just their war at stake. That was exactly what she was going to do, whatever it cost her. Because that was what she was needed for.

It was Vin who finally broke the silence.

"Anybody else hungry...?"

"Vin!"

"What? I'm starving!"

"Shut up."

"Look, if you'd had the kind of night I've had.... Can I order Alice to get me a burger or something? That's how this works... Ouch! That *hurt.*" He glared at Mallory, who had smacked him on the back of the head, hard.

"Don't push your luck."

"How about a sandwich?"

"Vin!"

"Hey, I'm asking nicely here..."

"I'm going to kill you. I'm actually going to kill you."

"Angel of Death. Like to see you try."

"Now I *really* need a drink..."

CODA

THEY CAME FROM all over; the Twelve, the Fallen. Earthbounds, Descendeds... Lucifer's choir and many of Gabriel's.

Some rebelled and remained, but many answered their Archangels' calls, and they came.

Some of them brought half-borns. Some came alone.

Some of them brought their followers – there were more than a few bored Fallen who had set themselves up as cult leaders in the chaos of the previous months... and given the short time they'd had, Lucifer was impressed.

Hidden from the unfriendly gaze of the angels, he looked out over the crowd that had assembled before him.

"Michael thinks he can outmanoeuvre me," he said to Gabriel, standing behind him. "Let's see him outmanoeuvre this."

And as he raised his fist, a cheer went up, loud enough to make even Lucifer's ears ring. He turned and smiled at his generals: at Forfax – idly toying with a fob watch, now he had lost his cane – and at Xaphan with his scarred face and with Florence, eyes downcast, on his arm; at Mammon, who had been so busy stirring the riots in the city, and at Rabdos, who brought new meaning to the word 'pandemonium' – at least, he did when he put his mind to it. He beamed at Gwyn, who stood behind Gabriel, and he beamed at Rimmon, whose left hand had yet to recover from his beating, and rested claw-like in a sling.

But most of all, Lucifer beamed at the figure on the far side of Rimmon, whose eyes met his without fear as he bore Lucifer's banner; most of all, Lucifer beamed at Toby, and as another cheer went up, he threw his head back and he laughed.

"It's time to take what's ours."

Acknowledgements

Everyone at Solaris Books, for all their incredible work and support: Jonathan Oliver, David Moore, Ben Smith, Pye Parr and Michael Molcher.

Kim, Bryony, Paul and Lee for the names.

Juliet, for the kwan.

Will and Vinny, for the phone calls, and for the occasional judicious application of beer and / or sanity.

My friends and my family, for their extraordinary patience and encouragement.

James and Oliver. Always. Because.

I am also grateful for the guidance on police equipment and procedures I've received: any inconsistencies or errors are entirely mine, and not those of my generous advisors.

Most of all, I am incredibly grateful to everyone who has supported the first book, and to everyone reading this now. It means the world.

With all my heart, thank you.

LM

About the Author

Born and raised in Wales, Lou Morgan studied medieval literature at UCL, and now lives in the south-west of England with her husband, son and the obligatory cat. Her first novel, *Blood and Feathers*, was published by Solaris Books in 2012, and her short stories have appeared in anthologies by Jurassic London, PS Publishing and Solaris.

She likes cathedrals and pizza (but probably not at the same time) and can be found online at loumorgan.co.uk or wasting time on Twitter as @LouMorgan.

Playlist

Just as I did with *Blood and Feathers*, I wrote and edited *Rebellion* to a playlist. Most of these tracks fit to a specific scene or chapter… but which goes where, I'll leave you to figure out for yourself.

Bleed it Out: Linkin Park
My Songs Know What You Did In The Dark: Fall Out Boy
Iron: Woodkid
In My Remains: Linkin Park
Devil's Choir: Black Veil Brides
Hell Above: Pierce the Veil
Professional Griefers: Deadmau5 feat. Gerard Way
iLL Manors: Plan B
Titanium: David Guetta feat. Sia
Finale (Original Mix): Madeon
Edge of the Earth: 30 Seconds to Mars
Unknown Soldier: Breaking Benjamin
21 Guns: Green Day
Like A Dog Chasing Cars: Hans Zimmer
My Body is a Cage: Peter Gabriel
Skyfall: Adele
Jar of Hearts: Christina Perri
First Responder: Michael Wandmacher
Razors.Out: Chino Moreno
P5hng Me A*wy: Linkin Park

Angelic Sigils

THE ANGELIC SIGILS which appear in *Blood & Feathers* are, technically, "real"... that is to say, these are some of the sigils historically used by alchemists and others as part of rituals to invoke or conjure angels: the most famous (or infamous) practitioner being John Dee.

Along with Edward Kelley, Dee devised (or "received," as he claimed) an angelic language and alphabet which he recorded in his journals, and which later became known as Enochian.

The sigils for the six Choirs in the *Blood & Feathers* world are shown below.

Barakiel

"If I told you Barakiel's very handy round the card table..."

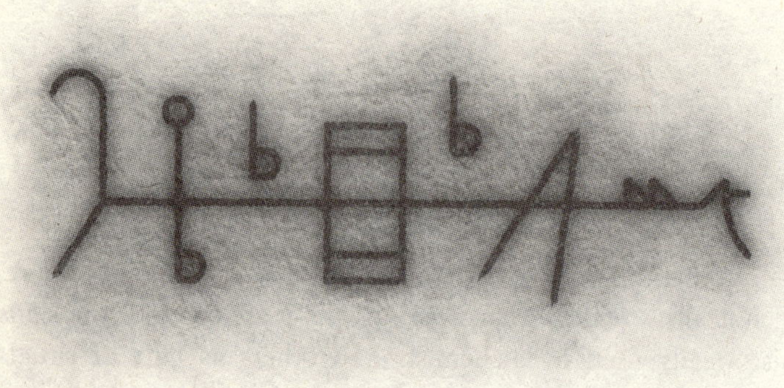

Gabriel

"When there's nothing left but dust and ash and embers
Gabriel will still be standing there with blood on his hands."

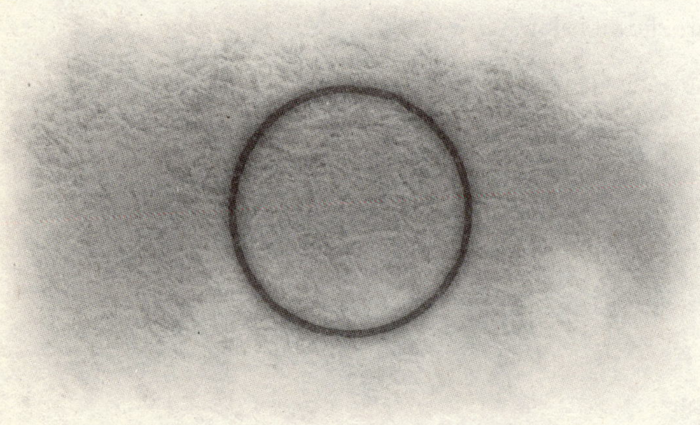

Lucifer

"He is the darker side of death:
rot and decay and fear and despair."

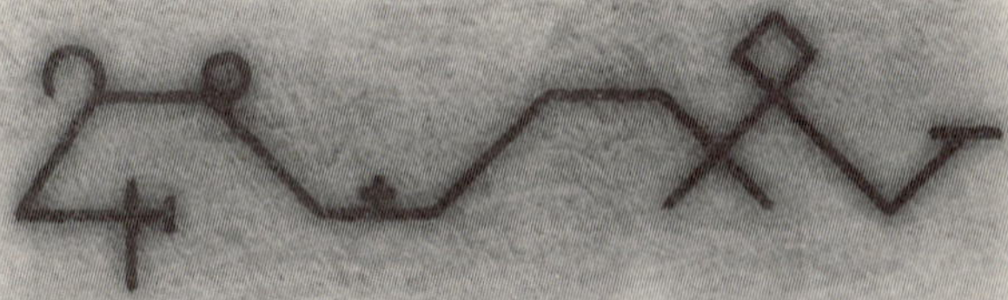

Michael

"You want to know what Michael's capable of?
Anything."

Raphael

"You're a healer, aren't you? That's what you *do*, isn't it, when you're one of Raphael's. That's all you do."

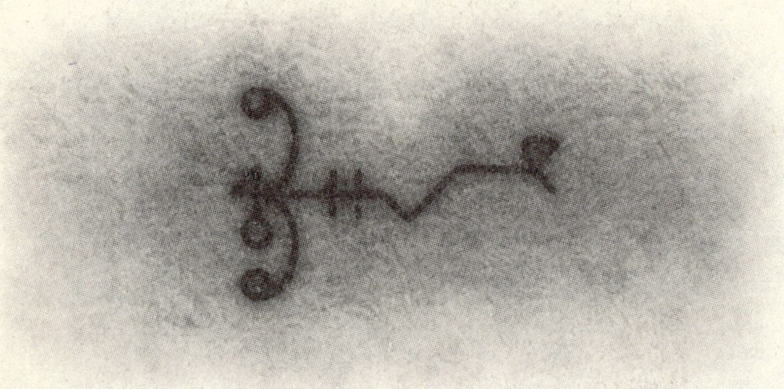

Zadkiel

If Zadkiel could make a hundred, two hundred people all forget what they had seen, what else could he do?

UK ISBN: 978 1 78108 018 4 • US ISBN: 978 1 78108 019 1 • £7.99/$9.99

Alice isn't having the best of days – late for work, missed her bus, and now she's getting rained on – but it's about to get worse.

The war between the angels and the Fallen is escalating and innocent civilians are getting caught in the cross-fire. If the balance is to be restored, the angels must act – or risk the Fallen taking control. Forever. That's where Alice comes in. Hunted by the Fallen and guided by Mallory – a disgraced angel with a drinking problem he doesn't want to fix – Alice will learn the truth about her own history... and why the angels want to send her to hell.

What do the Fallen want from her? How does Mallory know so much about her past? What is it the angels are hiding – and can she trust either side?

WWW.SOLARISBOOKS.COM

Follow us on Twitter! www.twitter.com/solarisbooks

UK ISBN: 978 1 907992 04 9 • US ISBN: 978 1 907992 05 6 • £7.99/$7.99

POLICING THE DAMNED

They live among us, abhorred, marginalised, despised. They are vampires, known politely as the Sunless. The job of policing their community falls to the men and women of SHADE: the Sunless Housing and Disclosure Executive. Captain John Redlaw is London's most feared and respected SHADE officer, a living legend.

But when the vampires start rioting in their ghettos, and angry humans respond with violence of their own, even Redlaw may not be able to keep the peace. Especially when political forces are aligning to introduce a radical answer to the Sunless problem, one that will resolve the situation once and for all...

WWW.SOLARISBOOKS.COM

Follow us on Twitter! www.twitter.com/solarisbooks

Cover TBC

UK ISBN: 978 1 78108 049 8 • US ISBN: 978 1 78108 050 4 • £7.99/$8.99

BLOOD ON THE EASTERN SEABOARD

The east coast of the USA is experiencing the worst winter weather in living memory, and John Redlaw is in the cold white thick of it. He's come to America to investigate a series of vicious attacks on vampire immigrants – targeted kills that can't simply be the work of amateur vigilantes. Dogging his footsteps is Tina "Tick" Checkley, a wannabe TV journalist with an eye on the big time.

The conspiracy Redlaw uncovers could give Tina the career break she's been looking for. It could also spell death for Redlaw.

OCTOBER 2012

WWW.SOLARISBOOKS.COM

Follow us on Twitter! www.twitter.com/solarisbooks

UK ISBN: 978 1 907519 62 8 • US ISBN: 978 1 907519 63 5 • £7.99/$7.99

Jordan helps kids on the run find their way back home. He's good at that. He should be - he's a runaway himself. Sometimes he helps the kids in other, stranger, ways. He looks like a regular teenager, but he's not. He acts like he's not exactly human, but he is. He treads the line between mundane reality and the world of the supernatural. Ben McCallan's urban fantasy debut takes you on a teffifying journey.

WWW.SOLARISBOOKS.COM

Follow us on Twitter! www.twitter.com/solarisbooks

UK ISBN: 978 1 78108 051 1 • US ISBN: 978 1 78108 052 8 • £7.99/$8.99

Desdaemona's done a bad, bad thing.

A thing so, so terrible that she has to run away from the consequences. Again. Where better to look for shelter than with the boy she was running from before?

But trouble follows. And if it's not Jacey's parents who sent the deadly crow-men, the Twa Corbies, in chase of her, then who is it? Deep under London, among the lost and rejected of two worlds, answers begin to emerge from Desi's hidden past. Answers that send her north in a flight that turns to a hunt, with strange companions and stranger prey. Dangers lie ahead and behind; inconvenient passion lays traps for her, just when she needs a clear head; at the last, even Desi has to beg for help. From one who has more cause than most to want her dead...

WWW.SOLARISBOOKS.COM

Follow us on Twitter! www.twitter.com/solarisbooks

UK ISBN: 978 1 907992 37 7 • US ISBN: 978 1 907992 38 4 • £7.99/$8.99

Babylon Steel, ex-sword-for-hire, ex... other things, runs The Red Lantern, the best brothel in the city. She's got elves using sex magic upstairs, S&M in the basement and a large green troll cooking breakfast in the kitchen. She'd love you to visit, except...

She's not having a good week. The Vessels of Purity are protesting against brothels, girls are disappearing, and if she can't pay her taxes, Babylon's going to lose the Lantern. She'd given up the mercenary life, but when the mysterious Darask Fain pays her to find a missing heiress, she has to take the job. And then her past starts to catch up with her in other, more dangerous ways.

Witty and fresh, Sebold delivers the most exciting fantasy debut in years.

WWW.SOLARISBOOKS.COM

Follow us on Twitter! www.twitter.com/solarisbooks

UK ISBN: 978 1 907992 43 8 • US ISBN: 978 1 907992 44 5 • £7.99/$8.99

Imagine there was a supernatural chiller that Hammer Films never made. A grand epic produced at the studio's peak, which played like a cross between the Dracula and Frankenstein films and Dr Terror's House of Horrors...

Four passengers meet on a train journey through Eastern Europe during the First World War, and face a mystery that must be solved if they are to survive. As the Arkangel races through the war-torn countryside, they must find out: What is in the casket that everyone is so afraid of? What is the tragic secret of the veiled Red Countess who travels with them? Why is their fellow passenger, the army brigadier, so feared by his own men? And what exactly is the devilish secret of the Arkangel itself?

Bizarre creatures, Satanic rites, terrified passengers and the romance of travelling by train, all in a classically-styled horror novel.

WWW.SOLARISBOOKS.COM

Follow us on Twitter! www.twitter.com/solarisbooks

www.solarisbooks.com ISBN: 978-1-84416-541-4

Supernatural investigator Quincey Morris and his partner, white witch Libby Chastain, are called in to help free a desperate family from a deadly curse that appears to date back to the Salem Witch Trials. To release the family from danger they must find the root of the curse, a black witch with a terrible grudge that holds the family in her power.

SOLARIS DARK FANTASY

UK ISBN: 978 1 84416 766 1 • US ISBN: 978 1 84416 765 4 • £7.99/$8.99

Supernatural investigator Quincey Morris and his partner, "white witch" Libby Chastain, are each in pursuit of a vicious killer. One is murdering small children for their bodily organs; the other is hunting down white witches – and Libby may be next. Along a trail that leads from Iraq to Turkey, to the US, all clues point to crazed billionaire Walter Grobius, a man obsessed with harnessing the ultimate evil. Morris and Chastain, teamed with the deadly Hannah Widmark, must fight desperately to stop a midnight rendezvous between forces so powerful that the fate of the world may be at stake. And the clock is ticking...

Evil Ways continues the electrifying new series of supernatural thrillers following the exploits of investigators Quincey Morris and Libby Chastain.

WWW.SOLARISBOOKS.COM

Follow us on Twitter! www.twitter.com/solarisbooks

'Menacing and uncanny'
The Guardian on *Mortality*

'Immaculately sinister'
TLS on *Mortality*

'A thoroughly satisfying, thought-provoking and beautifully realised work that will keep you pondering for days and will seep into your dreams'
Infinity Plus on *Antwerp*

WWW.SOLARISBOOKS.COM

Follow us on Twitter! www.twitter.com/solarisbooks